Free and Other Stories

Theodore Dreiser

Free and Other Stories

Copyright © 2020 Bibliotech Press
All rights reserved

The present edition is a reproduction of previous publication of this classic work. Minor typographical errors may have been corrected without note; however, for an authentic reading experience the spelling, punctuation, and capitalization have been retained from the original text.

ISBN: 978-1-63637-044-6

CONTENTS

FREE 1
McEWEN OF THE SHINING SLAVE MAKERS 28
NIGGER JEFF 42
THE LOST PHOEBE 64
THE SECOND CHOICE 78
A STORY OF STORIES 95
OLD ROGAUM AND HIS THERESA 118
WILL YOU WALK INTO MY PARLOR 135
THE CRUISE OF THE "IDLEWILD" 178
MARRIED 192
WHEN THE OLD CENTURY WAS NEW 209

FREE

The large and rather comfortable apartment of Rufus Haymaker, architect, in Central Park West, was very silent. It was scarcely dawn yet, and at the edge of the park, over the way, looking out from the front windows which graced this abode and gave it its charm, a stately line of poplars was still shrouded in a gray morning mist. From his bedroom at one end of the hall, where, also, a glimpse of the park was to be had, came Mr. Haymaker at this early hour to sit by one of these broader windows and contemplate these trees and a small lake beyond. He was very fond of Nature in its manifold art forms—quite poetic, in fact.

He was a tall and spare man of about sixty, not ungraceful, though slightly stoop-shouldered, with heavy overhanging eyebrows and hair, and a short, professionally cut gray mustache and beard, which gave him a severe and yet agreeable presence. For the present he was clad in a light-blue dressing gown with silver cords, which enveloped him completely. He had thin, pale, long-fingered hands, wrinkled at the back and slightly knotted at the joints, which bespoke the artist, in mood at least, and his eyes had a weary and yet restless look in them.

For only yesterday Doctor Storm, the family physician, who was in attendance on his wife, ill now for these three weeks past with a combination of heart lesion, kidney poisoning and neuritis, had taken him aside and said very softly and affectionately, as though he were trying to spare his feelings: "To-morrow, Mr. Haymaker, if your wife is no better I will call in my friend, Doctor Grainger, whom you know, for a consultation. He is more of an expert in these matters of the heart"—the heart, Mr. Haymaker had time to note ironically—"than I am. Together we will make a thorough examination, and then I hope we will be better able to say what the possibilities of her recovery really are. It's been a very trying case, a very stubborn one, I might say. Still, she has a great deal of vitality and is doing as well as could be expected, all things considered. At the same time, though I don't wish to alarm you unnecessarily—and there is no occasion for great alarm yet—still I feel it my duty to warn you that her condition is very serious indeed. Not that I wish you to feel that she is certain to die. I don't think she is. Not at all. Just the contrary. She may get well, and probably will, and live all of twenty years more." (Mentally Mr. Haymaker sighed a purely spiritual sigh.) "She has fine recuperative powers, so far as I can judge, but she has a bad heart, and this kidney trouble has not

1

helped it any. Just now, when her heart should have the least strain, it has the most.

"She is just at that point where, as I may say, things are in the balance. A day or two, or three or four at the most, ought to show which way things will go. But, as I have said before, I do not wish to alarm you unnecessarily. We are not nearly at the end of our tether. We haven't tried blood transfusion yet, and there are several arrows to that bow. Besides, at any moment she may respond more vigorously to medication than she has heretofore—especially in connection with her kidneys. In that case the situation would be greatly relieved at once.

"However, as I say, I feel it my duty to speak to you in this way in order that you may be mentally prepared for any event, because in such an odd combination as this the worst may happen at any time. We never can tell. As an old friend of yours and Mrs. Haymaker's, and knowing how much you two mean to each other"— Mr. Haymaker merely stared at him vacantly—"I feel it my duty to prepare you in this way. We all of us have to face these things. Only last year I lost my dear Matilda, my youngest child, as you know. Just the same, as I say, I have the feeling that Mrs. Haymaker is not really likely to die soon, and that we—Doctor Grainger and myself— will still be able to pull her through. I really do."

Doctor Storm looked at Mr. Haymaker as though he were very sorry for him—an old man long accustomed to his wife's ways and likely to be made very unhappy by her untimely end; whereas Mr. Haymaker, though staring in an almost sculptural way, was really thinking what a farce it all was, what a dull mixture of error and illusion on the part of all. Here he was, sixty years of age, weary of all this, of life really—a man who had never been really happy in all the time that he had been married; and yet here was his wife, who from conventional reasons believed that he was or should be, and who on account of this was serenely happy herself, or nearly so. And this doctor, who imagined that he was old and weak and therefore in need of this loving woman's care and sympathy and understanding! Unconsciously he raised a deprecating hand.

Also his children, who thought him dependent on her and happy with her; his servants and her and his friends thinking the same thing, and yet he really was not. It was all a lie. He was unhappy. Always he had been unhappy, it seemed, ever since he had been married—for over thirty-one years now. Never in all that time, for even so much as a single day, had he ever done anything but long, long, long, in a pale, constrained way—for what, he scarcely dared think—not to be married any more—to be free—to be as he was before ever he saw Mrs. Haymaker.

2

And yet being conventional in mood and training and utterly domesticated by time and conditions over which he seemed not to have much control—nature, custom, public opinion, and the like, coming into play as forces—he had drifted, had not taken any drastic action. No, he had merely drifted, wondering if time, accident or something might not interfere and straighten out his life for him, but it never had. Now weary, old, or rapidly becoming so, he condemned himself for his inaction. Why hadn't he done something about it years before? Why hadn't he broken it up before it was too late, and saved his own soul, his longing for life, color? But no, he had not. Why complain so bitterly now?

All the time the doctor had talked this day before he had wanted to smile a wry, dry, cynical smile, for in reality he did not want Mrs. Haymaker to live—or at least at the moment he thought so. He was too miserably tired of it all. And so now, after nearly twenty-four hours of the same unhappy thought, sitting by this window looking at a not distant building which shone faintly in the haze, he ran his fingers through his hair as he gazed, and sighed.

How often in these weary months, and even years, past—ever since he and his wife had been living here, and before—had he come to these or similar windows while she was still asleep, to sit and dream! For some years now they had not even roomed together, so indifferent had the whole state become; though she did not seem to consider that significant, either. Life had become more or less of a practical problem to her, one of position, place, prestige. And yet how often, viewing his life in retrospect, had he wished that his life had been as sweet as his dreams—that his dreams had come true.

After a time on this early morning, for it was still gray, with the faintest touch of pink in the east, he shook his head solemnly and sadly, then rose and returned along the hall to his wife's bedroom, at the door of which he paused to look where she lay seriously ill, and beside her in an armchair, fast asleep, a trained nurse who was supposedly keeping the night vigil ordered by the doctor, but who no doubt was now very weary. His wife was sleeping also—very pale, very thin now, and very weak. He felt sorry for her at times, in spite of his own weariness; now, for instance. Why need he have made so great a mistake so long ago? Perhaps it was his own fault for not having been wiser in his youth. Then he went quietly on to his own room, to lie down and think.

Always these days, now that she was so very ill and the problem of her living was so very acute, the creeping dawn thus roused him—to think. It seemed as though he could not really sleep soundly any more, so stirred and distrait was he. He was not so much tired or physically worn as mentally bored or disappointed.

3

Life had treated him so badly, he kept thinking to himself over and over. He had never had the woman he really wanted, though he had been married so long, had been faithful, respectable and loved by her, in her way. "In her way," he half quoted to himself as he lay there.

Presently he would get up, dress and go down to his office as usual if his wife were not worse. But—but, he asked himself—would she be? Would that slim and yet so durable organism of hers—quite as old as his own, or nearly so—break under the strain of this really severe illness? That would set him free again, and nicely, without blame or comment on him. He could then go where he chose once more, do as he pleased—think of that—without let or hindrance. For she was ill at last, so very ill, the first and really great illness she had endured since their marriage. For weeks now she had been lying so, hovering, as it were, between life and death, one day better, the next day worse, and yet not dying, and with no certainty that she would, and yet not getting better either. Doctor Storm insisted that it was a leak in her heart which had suddenly manifested itself which was causing all the real trouble. He was apparently greatly troubled as to how to control it.

During all this period Mr. Haymaker had been, as usual, most sympathetic. His manner toward her was always soft, kindly, apparently tender. He had never really begrudged her anything—nothing certainly that he could afford. He was always glad to see her and the children humanly happy—though they, too, largely on account of her, he thought, had proved a disappointment to him—because he had always sympathized with her somewhat unhappy youth, narrow and stinted; and yet he had never been happy himself, either, never in all the time that he had been married. If she had endured much, he kept telling himself when he was most unhappy, so had he, only it was harder perhaps for women to endure things than men—he was always willing to admit that—only also she had had his love, or thought she had, an actual spiritual peace, which he had never had. She knew she had a faithful husband. He felt that he had never really had a wife at all, not one that he could love as he knew a wife should be loved. His dreams as to that!

Going to his office later this same day—it was in one of those tall buildings that face Madison Square—he had looked first, in passing, at the trees that line Central Park West, and then at the bright wall of apartment houses facing it, and meditated sadly, heavily. Here the sidewalks were crowded with nursemaids and children at play, and in between them, of course, the occasional citizen loitering or going about his errands. The day was so fine, so

4

youthful, as spring days will seem at times. As he looked, especially at the children, and the young men bustling office-ward, mostly in new spring suits, he sighed and wished that he were young once more. Think how brisk and hopeful they were! Everything was before them. They could still pick and choose—no age or established conditions to stay them. Were any of them, he asked himself for the thousandth time, it seemed to him, as wearily connected as he had been at their age? Did they each have a charming young wife to love—one of whom they were passionately fond—such a one as he had never had; or did they not?

Wondering, he reached his office on one of the topmost floors of one of those highest buildings commanding a wide view of the city, and surveyed it wearily. Here were visible the two great rivers of the city, its towers and spires and far-flung walls. From these sometimes, even yet, he seemed to gain a patience to live, to hope. How in his youth all this had inspired him—or that other city that was then. Even now he was always at peace here, so much more so than in his own home, pleasant as it was. Here he could look out over this great scene and dream or he could lose the memory in his work that his love-life had been a failure. The great city, the buildings he could plan or supervise, the efficient help that always surrounded him—his help, not hers—aided to take his mind off himself and that deep-seated inner ache or loss.

The care of Mr. Haymaker's apartment during his wife's illness and his present absence throughout the day, devolved upon a middle-aged woman of great seriousness, Mrs. Elfridge by name, whom Mrs. Haymaker had employed years before; and under her a maid of all work, Hester, who waited on table, opened the door, and the like; and also at present two trained nurses, one for night and one for day service, who were in charge of Mrs. Haymaker. The nurses were both bright, healthy, blue-eyed girls, who attracted Mr. Haymaker and suggested all the youth he had never had—without really disturbing his poise. It would seem as though that could never be any more.

In addition, of course, there was the loving interest of his son Wesley and his daughter Ethelberta—whom his wife had named so in spite of him—both of whom had long since married and had children of their own and were living in different parts of the great city. In this crisis both of them came daily to learn how things were, and occasionally to stay for the entire afternoon or evening, or both. Ethelberta had wanted to come and take charge of the apartment entirely during her mother's illness, only Mrs. Haymaker, who was still able to direct, and fond of doing so, would not hear of it. She was not so ill but that she could still speak, and in this way could

5

inquire and direct. Besides, Mrs. Elfridge was as good as Mrs. Haymaker in all things that related to Mr. Haymaker's physical comfort, or so she thought.

If the truth will come out—as it will in so many pathetic cases—it was never his physical so much as his spiritual or affectional comfort that Mr. Haymaker craved. As said before, he had never loved Mrs. Haymaker, or certainly not since that now long-distant period back in Muskegon, Michigan, where both had been born and where they had lived and met at the ages, she of fifteen, he of seventeen. It had been, strange as it might seem now, a love match at first sight with them. She had seemed so sweet, a girl of his own age or a little younger, the daughter of a local chemist. Later, when he had been forced by poverty to go out into the world to make his own way, he had written her much, and imagined her to be all that she had seemed at fifteen, and more—a dream among fair women. But Fortune, slow in coming to his aid and fickle in fulfilling his dreams, had brought it about that for several years more he had been compelled to stay away nearly all of the time, unable to marry her; during which period, unknown to himself really, his own point of view had altered. How it had happened he could never tell really, but so it was. The great city, larger experiences—while she was still enduring the smaller ones—other faces, dreams of larger things, had all combined to destroy it or her, only he had not quite realized it then. He was always so slow in realizing the full import of the immediate thing, he thought.

That was the time, as he had afterward told himself—how often!—that he should have discovered his mistake and stopped. Later it always seemed to become more and more impossible. Then, in spite of some heartache to her and some distress to himself, no doubt, all would be well for him now. But no; he had been too inexperienced, too ignorant, too bound by all the conventions and punctilio of his simple Western world. He thought an engagement, however unsatisfactory it might come to seem afterward, was an engagement, and binding. An honorable man would not break one— or so his country moralists argued.

Yes, at that time he might have written her, he might have told her, then. But he had been too sensitive and kindly to speak of it. Afterward it was too late. He feared to wound her, to undo her, to undo her life. But now—now—look at his! He had gone back on several occasions before marriage, and might have seen and done and been free if he had had but courage and wisdom—but no; duty, order, the beliefs of the region in which he had been reared, and of America—what it expected and what she expected and was entitled to—had done for him completely. He had not spoken. Instead, he had gone on and married her without speaking of the change in himself, without letting her know how worse than ashes it had all become. God, what a fool he had been! how often since he had told himself over and over.

Well, having made a mistake it was his duty perhaps, at least according to current beliefs, to stick by it and make the best of it;—a bargain was a bargain in marriage, if no where else—but still that had never prevented him from being unhappy. He could not prevent that himself. During all these long years, therefore, owing to these same conventions—what people would think and say—he had been compelled to live with her, to cherish her, to pretend to be happy with her—"another perfect union," as he sometimes said to himself. In reality he had been unhappy, horribly so. Even her face wearied him at times, and her presence, her mannerisms. Only this other morning Doctor Storm, by his manner indicating that he thought him lonely, in danger of being left all alone and desperately sad and neglected in case she died had irritated him greatly. Who would take care of him? his eyes had seemed to say—and yet he himself wanted nothing so much as to be alone for a time, at least, in this life, to think for himself, to do for himself, to forget this long, dreary period in which he had pretended to be something that he was not.

Was he never to be rid of the dull round of it, he asked himself now, never before he himself died? And yet shortly afterward he would reproach himself for these very thoughts, as being wrong, hard, unkind—thoughts that would certainly condemn him in the eyes of the general public, that public which made reputations and one's general standing before the world.

During all this time he had never even let her know—no, not once—of the tremendous and soul-crushing sacrifice he had made. Like the Spartan boy, he had concealed the fox gnawing at his vitals. He had not complained. He had been, indeed, the model husband, as such things go in conventional walks. If you doubted it look at his position, or that of his children; or his wife—her mental and physical comfort, even in her illness, her unfailing belief that he was all he should be! Never once apparently, during all these years, had she doubted his love or felt him to be unduly unhappy—or, if not that exactly, if not fully accepting his love as something that was still at a fever heat, the thing it once was—still believing that he found pleasure and happiness in being with her, a part of the home which together they had built up, these children they had reared, comfort in knowing that it would endure to the end! To the end! During all these years she had gone on molding his and her lives—as much as that was possible in his case—and those of their children, to suit

7

herself; and thinking all the time that she was doing what he wanted or at least what was best for him and them.

How she adored convention! What did she not think she knew in regard to how things ought to be—mainly what her old home surroundings had taught her, the American idea of this, that and the other. Her theories in regard to friends, education of the children, and so on, had in the main prevailed, even when he did not quite agree with her; her desires for certain types of pleasure and amusement, of companionship, and so on, were conventional types always and had also prevailed. There had been little quarrels, of course, always had been—what happy home is free of them?—but still he had always given in, or nearly always, and had acted as though he were satisfied in so doing.

But why, therefore, should he complain now, or she ever imagine, or ever have imagined, that he was unhappy? She did not, had not. Like all their relatives and friends of the region from which they sprang, and here also—and she had been most careful to regulate that, courting whom she pleased and ignoring all others—she still believed most firmly, more so than ever, that she knew what was best for him, what he really thought and wanted. It made him smile most wearily at times.

For in her eyes—in regard to him, at least, not always so with others, he had found—marriage was a sacrament, sacrosanct, never to be dissolved. One life, one love. Once a man had accepted the yoke or even asked a girl to marry him it was his duty to abide by it. To break an engagement, to be unfaithful to a wife, even unkind to her—what a crime, in her eyes! Such people ought to be drummed out of the world. They were really not fit to live—dogs, brutes!

And yet, look at himself—what of him? What of one who had made a mistake in regard to all this? Where was his compensation to come from, his peace and happiness? Here on earth or only in some mythical heaven—that odd, angelic heaven that she still believed in? What a farce! And all her friends and his would think he would be so miserable now if she died, or at least ought to be. So far had asinine convention and belief in custom carried the world. Think of it!

But even that was not the worst. No; that was not the worst, either. It had been the gradual realization coming along through the years that he had married an essentially small, narrow woman who could never really grasp his point of view—or, rather, the significance of his dreams or emotions—and yet with whom, nevertheless, because of this original promise or mistake, he was compelled to live. Grant her every quality of goodness, energy, industry, intent—as he did freely—still there was this; and it could

8

never be adjusted, never. Essentially, as he had long since discovered, she was narrow, ultraconventional, whereas he was an artist by nature, brooding and dreaming strange dreams and thinking of far-off things which she did not or could not understand or did not sympathize with, save in a general and very remote way. The nuances of his craft, the wonders and subtleties of forms and angles—had she ever realized how significant these were to him, let alone to herself? No, never. She had not the least true appreciation of them—never had had. Architecture? Art? What could they really mean to her, desire as she might to appreciate them? And he could not now go elsewhere to discover that sympathy. No. He had never really wanted to, since the public and she would object, and he thinking it half evil himself.

Still, how was it, he often asked himself, that Nature could thus allow one conditioned or equipped with emotions and seekings such as his, not of an utterly conventional order, to seek out and pursue one like Ernestine, who was not fitted to understand him or to care what his personal moods might be? Was love truly blind, as the old saw insisted, or did Nature really plan, and cleverly, to torture the artist mind—as it did the pearl-bearing oyster with a grain of sand—with something seemingly inimical, in order that it might produce beauty? Sometimes he thought so. Perhaps the many interesting and beautiful buildings he had planned—the world called them so, at least—had been due to the loving care he lavished on them, being shut out from love and beauty elsewhere. Cruel Nature, that cared so little for the dreams of man—the individual man or woman!

At the time he had married Ernestine he was really too young to know exactly what it was he wanted to do or how it was he was going to feel in the years to come; and yet there was no one to guide him, to stop him. The custom of the time was all in favor of this dread disaster. Nature herself seemed to desire it—mere children being the be-all and the end-all of everything everywhere. Think of that as a theory! Later, when it became so clear to him what he had done, and in spite of all the conventional thoughts and conditions that seemed to bind him to this fixed condition, he had grown restless and weary, but never really irritable. No, he had never become that.

Instead he had concealed it all from her, persistently, in all kindness; only this hankering after beauty of mind and body in ways not represented by her had hurt so—grown finally almost too painful to bear. He had dreamed and dreamed of something different until it had become almost an obsession. Was it never to be, that something different, never, anywhere, in all time? What a

9

tragedy! Soon he would be dead and then it would never be anywhere—anymore! Ernestine was charming, he would admit, or had been at first, though time had proved that she was not charming to him either mentally or physically in any compelling way; but how did that help him now? How could it? He had actually found himself bored by her for more than twenty-seven years now, and this other dream growing, growing, growing—until—

But now he was old, and she was dying, or might be, and it could not make so much difference what happened to him or to her; only it could, too, because he wanted to be free for a little while, just for a little while, before he died.

To be free! free!

One of the things that had always irritated him about Mrs. Haymaker was this, that in spite of his determination never to offend the social code in any way—he had felt for so many reasons, emotional as well as practical, that he could not afford so to do—and also in spite of the fact that he had been tortured by this show of beauty in the eyes and bodies of others, his wife, fearing perhaps in some strange psychic way that he might change, had always tried to make him feel or believe—premeditatedly and of a purpose, he thought—that he was not the kind of man who would be attractive to women; that he lacked some physical fitness, some charm that other men had, which would cause all young and really charming women to turn away from him. Think of it! He to whom so many women had turned with questioning eyes!

Also that she had married him largely because she had felt sorry for him! He chose to let her believe that, because he was sorry for her. Because other women had seemed to draw near to him at times in some appealing or seductive way she had insisted that he was not even a cavalier, let alone a Lothario; that he was ungainly, slow, uninteresting—to all women but her!

Persistently, he thought, and without any real need, she had harped on this, fighting chimeras, a chance danger in the future; though he had never given her any real reason, and had never even planned to sin against her in any way—never. She had thus tried to poison his own mind in regard to himself and his art—and yet—and yet— Ah, those eyes of other women, their haunting beauty, the flitting something they said to him of infinite, inexpressible delight. Why had his life been so very hard?

One of the disturbing things about all this was the iron truth which it had driven home, namely, that Nature, unless it were expressed or represented by some fierce determination within, which drove one to do, be, cared no whit for him or any other man or woman. Unless one acted for oneself, upon some stern conclusion nurtured within, one might rot and die spiritually. Nature did not care. "Blessed be the meek"—yes. Blessed be the strong, rather, for they made their own happiness. All these years in which he had dwelt and worked in this knowledge, hoping for something but not acting, nothing had happened, except to him, and that in an unsatisfactory way. All along he had seen what was happening to him; and yet held by convention he had refused to act always, because somehow he was not hard enough to act. He was not strong enough, that was the real truth—had not been. Almost like a bird in a cage, an animal peeping out from behind bars, he had viewed the world of free thought and freer action. In many a drawing-room, on the street, or in his own home even, had he not looked into an eye, the face of someone who seemed to offer understanding, to know, to sympathize, though she might not have, of course; and yet religiously and moralistically, like an anchorite, because of duty and current belief and what people would say and think, Ernestine's position and faith in him, her comfort, his career and that of the children—he had put them all aside, out of his mind, forgotten them almost, as best he might. It had been hard at times, and sad, but so it had been.

And look at him now, old, not exactly feeble yet—no, not that yet, not quite!—but life weary and almost indifferent All these years he had wanted, wanted—wanted—an understanding mind, a tender heart, the some one woman—she must exist somewhere—who would have sympathized with all the delicate shades and meanings of his own character, his art, his spiritual as well as his material dreams— And yet look at him! Mrs. Haymaker had always been with him, present in the flesh or the spirit, and—so—

Though he could not ever say that she was disagreeable to him in a material way—he could not say that she had ever been that exactly—still she did not correspond to his idea of what he needed, and so— Form had meant so much to him, color; the glorious perfectness of a glorious woman's body, for instance, the color of her thoughts, moods—exquisite they must be, like his own at times; but no, he had never had the opportunity to know one intimately. No, not one, though he had dreamed of her so long. He had never even dared whisper this to any one, scarcely to himself. It was not wise, not socially fit. Thoughts like this would tend to social ostracism in his circle, or rather hers—for had she not made the circle?

And here was the rub with Mr. Haymaker, at least, that he could not make up his mind whether in his restlessness and private mental complaints he were not even now guilty of a great moral crime in so thinking. Was it not true that men and women should be

11

faithful in marriage whether they were happy or not? Was there not some psychic law governing this matter of union—one life, one love—which made the thoughts and the pains and the subsequent sufferings and hardships of the individual, whatever they might be, seem unimportant? The churches said so. Public opinion and the law seemed to accept this. There were so many problems, so much order to be disrupted, so much pain caused, many insoluble problems where children were concerned—if people did not stick. Was it not best, more blessed—socially, morally, and in every other way important—for him to stand by a bad bargain rather than to cause so much disorder and pain, even though he lost his own soul emotionally? He had thought so—or at least he had acted as though he thought so—and yet— How often had he wondered over this!

Take, now, some other phases. Granting first that Mrs. Haymaker had, according to the current code, measured up to the requirements of a wife, good and true, and that at first after marriage there had been just enough of physical and social charm about her to keep his state from becoming intolerable, still there was this old ache; and then newer things which came with the birth of the several children: First Elwell—named after a cousin of hers, not his—who had died only two years after he was born; and then Wesley; and then Ethelberta. How he had always disliked that name!—largely because he had hoped to call her Ottilie, a favorite name of his; or Janet, after his mother.

Curiously the arrival of these children and the death of poor little Elwell at two had somehow, in spite of his unrest, bound him to this matrimonial state and filled him with a sense of duty, and pleasure even—almost entirely apart from her, he was sorry to say— in these young lives; though if there had not been children, as he sometimes told himself, he surely would have broken away from her; he could not have stood it. They were so odd in their infancy, those little ones, so troublesome and yet so amusing—little Elwell, for instance, whose nose used to crinkle with delight when he would pretend to bite his neck, and whose gurgle of pleasure was so sweet and heart-filling that it positively thrilled and lured him. In spite of his thoughts concerning Ernestine—and always in those days they were rigidly put down as unmoral and even evil, a certain unsocial streak in him perhaps which was against law and order and social well-being—he came to have a deep and abiding feeling for Elwell. The latter, in some chemic, almost unconscious way, seemed to have arrived as a balm to his misery, a bandage for his growing wound—sent by whom, by what, how? Elwell had seized upon his imagination, and so his heartstrings—had come, indeed, to make him feel understanding and sympathy there in that little child; to

12

supply, or seem to at least, what he lacked in the way of love and affection from one whom he could truly love. Elwell was never so happy apparently as when snuggling in his arms, not Ernestine's, or lying against his neck. And when he went for a walk or elsewhere there was Elwell always ready, arms up, to cling to his neck. He seemed, strangely enough, inordinately fond of his father, rather than his mother, and never happy without him. On his part, Haymaker came to be wildly fond of him—that queer little lump of a face, suggesting a little of himself and of his own mother, not so much of Ernestine, or so he thought, though he would not have objected to that. Not at all. He was not so small as that. Toward the end of the second year, when Elwell was just beginning to be able to utter a word or two, he had taught him that silly old rhyme which ran "There were three kittens," and when it came to "and they shall have no—" he would stop and say to Elwell, "What now?" and the latter would gurgle "puh!"—meaning, of course, pie.

Ah, those happy days with little Elwell, those walks with him over his shoulder or on his arm, those hours in which of an evening he would rock him to sleep in his arms! Always Ernestine was there, and happy in the thought of his love for little Elwell and her, her more than anything else perhaps; but it was an illusion—that latter part. He did not care for her even then as she thought he did. All his fondness was for Elwell, only she took it as evidence of his growing or enduring affection for her—another evidence of the peculiar working of her mind. Women were like that, he supposed—some women.

And then came that dreadful fever, due to some invading microbe which the doctors could not diagnose or isolate, infantile paralysis perhaps; and little Elwell had finally ceased to be as flesh and was eventually carried forth to the lorn, disagreeable graveyard near Woodlawn. How he had groaned internally, indulged in sad, despondent thoughts concerning the futility of all things human, when this had happened! It seemed for the time being as if all color and beauty had really gone out of his life for good.

"Man born of woman is of few days and full of troubles," the preacher whom Mrs. Haymaker had insisted upon having into the house at the time of the funeral had read. "He fleeth also as a shadow and continueth not."

Yes; so little Elwell had fled, as a shadow, and in his own deep sorrow at the time he had come to feel the first and only sad, deep sympathy for Ernestine that he had ever felt since marriage; and that because she had suffered so much—had lain in his arms after the funeral and cried so bitterly. It was terrible, her sorrow. Terrible—a mother grieving for her first-born! Why was it, he had

13

thought at the time, that he had never been able to think or make her all she ought to be to him? Ernestine at this time had seemed better, softer, kinder, wiser, sweeter than she had ever seemed; more worthy, more interesting than ever he had thought her before. She had slaved so during the child's illness, stayed awake night after night, watched over him with such loving care—done everything, in short, that a loving human heart could do to rescue her young from the depths; and yet even then he had not really been able to love her. No, sad and unkind as it might seem, he had not. He had just pitied her and thought her better, worthier! What cursed stars disordered the minds and moods of people so? Why was it that these virtues of people, their good qualities, did not make you love them, did not really bind them to you, as against the things you could not like? Why? He had resolved to do better in his thoughts, but somehow, in spite of himself, he had never been able so to do.

Nevertheless, at that time he seemed to realize more keenly than ever her order, industry, frugality, a sense of beauty within limits, a certain laudable ambition to do something and be somebody—only, only he could not sympathize with her ambitions, could not see that she had anything but a hopelessly common-place and always unimportant point of view. There was never any flare to her, never any true distinction of mind or soul. She seemed always, in spite of anything he might say or do, hopelessly to identify doing and being with money and current opinion—neighborhood public opinion, almost—and local social position, whereas he knew that distinguished doing might as well be connected with poverty and shame and disgrace as with these other things—wealth and station, for instance; a thing which she could never quite understand apparently, though he often tried to tell her, much against her mood always.

Look at the cases of the great artists! Some of the greatest architects right here in the city, or in history, were of peculiar, almost disagreeable, history. But no, Mrs. Haymaker could not understand anything like that, anything connected with history, indeed—she hardly believed in history, its dark, sad pages, and would never read it, or at least did not care to. And as for art and artists—she would never have believed that wisdom and art understanding and true distinction might take their rise out of things necessarily low and evil—never.

Take now, the case of young Zingara. Zingara was an architect like himself, whom he had met more than thirty years before, here in New York, when he had first arrived, a young man struggling to become an architect of significance, only he was very poor and rather unkempt and disreputable-looking. Haymaker had found him several years before his marriage to Ernestine in the dark offices of Pyne & Starboard, Architects, and had been drawn to him definitely; but because he smoked all the time and was shabby as to his clothes and had no money—why, Mrs. Haymaker, after he had married her, and though he had known Zingara nearly four years, would have none of him. To her he was low, and a failure, one who would never succeed. Once she had seen him in some cheap restaurant that she chanced to be passing, in company with a drabby-looking maid, and that was the end.

"I wish you wouldn't bring him here any more, dear," she had insisted; and to have peace he had complied—only, now look. Zingara had since become a great architect, but now of course, owing to Mrs. Haymaker, he was definitely alienated. He was the man who had since designed the Æsculapian Club; and Symphony Hall with its delicate façade; as well as the tower of the Wells Building, sending its sweet lines so high, like a poetic thought or dream. But Zingara was now a dreamy recluse like himself, very exclusive, as Haymaker had long since come to know, and indifferent as to what people thought or said.

But perhaps it was not just obtuseness to certain of the finer shades and meanings of life, but an irritating aggressiveness at times, backed only by her limited understanding, which caused her to seek and wish to be here, there and the other place; wherever, in her mind, the truly successful—which meant nearly always the materially successful of a second or third rate character—were, which irritated him most of all. How often had he tried to point out the difference between true and shoddy distinction—the former rarely connected with great wealth.

But no. So often she seemed to imagine such queer people to be truly successful, when they were really not—usually people with just money, or a very little more.

And in the matter of rearing and educating and marrying their two children, Wesley and Ethelberta, who had come after Elwell— what peculiar pains and feelings had not been involved in all this for him. In infancy both of these had seemed sweet enough, and so close to him, though never quite so wonderful as Elwell. But, as they grew, it seemed somehow as though Ernestine had come between him and them. First, it was the way she had raised them, the very stiff and formal manner in which they were supposed to move and be, copied from the few new-rich whom she had chanced to meet through him—and admired in spite of his warnings. That was the irony of architecture as a profession—it was always bringing such queer people close to one, and for the sake of one's profession, sometimes, particularly in the case of the young architect, one had

15

to be nice to them. Later, it was the kind of school they should attend. He had half imagined at first that it would be the public school, because they both had begun as simple people; but no, since they were prospering it had to be a private school for each, and not one of his selection, either—or hers, really—but one to which the Barlows and the Westervelts, two families of means with whom Ernestine had become intimate, sent their children and therefore thought excellent!

The Barlows! Wealthy, but, to him, gross and mediocre people who had made a great deal of money in the manufacture of patent medicines out West, and who had then come to New York to splurge, and had been attracted to Ernestine—not him particularly, he imagined—because Haymaker had built a town house for them, and also because he was gaining a fine reputation. They were dreadful really, so gauche, so truly dull; and yet somehow they seemed to suit Ernestine's sense of fitness and worth at the time, because, as she said, they were good and kind—like her Western home folks; only they were not really. She just imagined so. They were worthy enough people in their way, though with no taste. Young Fred Barlow had been sent to the expensive Gaillard School for Boys, near Morristown, where they were taught manners and airs, and little else, as Haymaker always thought, though Ernestine insisted that they were given a religious training as well. And so Wesley had to go there—for a time, anyhow. It was the best school.

And similarly, because Mercedes Westervelt, senseless, vain little thing, was sent to Briarcliff School, near White Plains, Ethelberta had to go there. Think of it! It was all so silly, so pushing. How well he remembered the long, delicate campaign which preceded this, the logic and tactics employed, the importance of it socially to Ethelberta, the tears and cajolery. Mrs. Haymaker could always cry so easily, or seem to be on the verge of it, when she wanted anything; and somehow, in spite of the fact that he knew her tears were unimportant, or timed and for a purpose, he could never stand out against them, and she knew it. Always he felt moved or weakened in spite of himself. He had no weapon wherewith to fight them, though he resented them as a part of the argument. Positively Mrs. Haymaker could be as sly and as ruthless as Machiavelli himself at times, and yet believe all the while that she was tender, loving, self-sacrificing, generous, moral and a dozen other things, all of which led to the final achievement of her own aims. Perhaps this was admirable from one point of view, but it irritated him always. But if one were unable to see him- or herself, their actual disturbing inconsistencies, what were you to do?

And again, he had by then been married so long that it was

almost impossible to think of throwing her over, or so it seemed at the time. They had reached the place then where they had supposedly achieved position together, though in reality it was all his—and not such position as he was entitled to, at that. Ernestine— and he was thinking this in all kindness—could never attract the ideal sort. And anyhow, the mere breath of a scandal between them, separation or unfaithfulness, which he never really contemplated, would have led to endless bickering and social and commercial injury, or so he thought. All her strong friends—and his, in a way— those who had originally been his clients, would have deserted him.

Their wives, their own social fears, would have compelled them to ostracize him! He would have been a scandal-marked architect, a brute for objecting to so kind and faithful and loving a wife. And perhaps he would have been, at that. He could never quite tell, it was all so mixed and tangled.

Take, again, the marriage of his son Wesley into the De Gaud family—George de Gaud père being nothing more than a retired real-estate speculator and promoter who had money, but nothing more; and Irma de Gaud, the daughter, being a gross, coarse, sensuous girl, physically attractive no doubt, and financially reasonably secure, or so she had seemed; but what else? Nothing, literally nothing; and his son had seemed to have at least some spiritual ideals at first. Ernestine had taken up with Mrs. George de Gaud—a miserable, narrow creature, so Haymaker thought—largely for Wesley's sake, he presumed. Anyhow, everything had been done to encourage Wesley in his suit and Irma in her toleration, and now look at them! De Gaud père had since failed and left his daughter practically nothing. Irma had been interested in anything but Wesley's career, had followed what she considered the smart among the new-rich—a smarter, wilder, newer new-rich than ever Ernestine had fancied, or could. To-day she was without a thought for anything besides teas and country clubs and theaters—and what else?

And long since Wesley had begun to realize it himself. He was an engineer now, in the employ of one of the great construction companies, a moderately successful man. But even Ernestine, who had engineered the match and thought it wonderful, was now down on her. She had begun to see through her some years ago, when Irma had begun to ignore her; only before it was always the De Gauds here, and the De Gauds there. Good gracious, what more could any one want than the De Gauds—Irma de Gaud, for instance? Then came the concealed dissension between Irma and Wesley, and now Mrs. Haymaker insisted that Irma had held, and was holding Wesley back. She was not the right woman for him.

17

Almost—against all her prejudices—she was willing that he should leave her. Only, if Haymaker had broached anything like that in connection with himself!

And yet Mrs. Haymaker had been determined, because of what she considered the position of the De Gauds at that time, that Wesley should marry Irma. Wesley now had to slave at mediocre tasks in order to have enough to allow Irma to run in so-called fast society of a second or third rate. And even at that she was not faithful to him—or so Haymaker believed. There were so many strange evidences. And yet Haymaker felt that he did not care to interfere now. How could he? Irma was tired of Wesley, and that was all there was to it. She was looking elsewhere, he was sure.

Take but one more case, that of Ethelberta. What a name! In spite of all Ernestine's determination to make her so successful and thereby reflect some credit on her had she really succeeded in so doing? To be sure, Ethelberta's marriage was somewhat more successful financially than Wesley's had proved to be, but was she any better placed in other ways? John Kelso—"Jack," as she always called him—with his light ways and lighter mind, was he really any one!—anything more than a waster? His parents stood by him no doubt, but that was all; and so much the worse for him. According to Mrs. Haymaker at the time, he, too, was an ideal boy, admirable, just the man for Ethelberta, because the Kelsos, père and mère, had money. Horner Kelso had made a kind of fortune in Chicago in the banknote business, and had settled in New York, about the time that Ethelberta was fifteen, to spend it. Ethelberta had met Grace Kelso at school.

And now see! She was not unattractive, and had some pleasant, albeit highly affected, social ways; she had money, and a comfortable apartment in Park Avenue; but what had it all come to? John Kelso had never done anything really, nothing. His parents' money and indulgence and his early training for a better social state had ruined him if he had ever had a mind that amounted to anything. He was idle, pleasure-loving, mentally indolent, like Irma de Gaud. Those two should have met and married, only they could never have endured each other. But how Mrs. Haymaker had courted the Kelsos in her eager and yet diplomatic way, giving teas and receptions and theater parties; and yet he had never been able to exchange ten significant words with either of them, or the younger Kelsos either. Think of it!

And somehow in the process Ethelberta, for all his early affection and tenderness and his still kindly feeling for her, had been weaned away from him and had proved a limited and conventional girl, somewhat like her mother, and more inclined to listen to her than to him—though he had not minded that really. It had been the same with Wesley before her. Perhaps, however, a child was entitled to its likes and dislikes, regardless.

But why had he stood for it all, he now kept asking himself. Why? What grand results, if any, had been achieved? Were their children so wonderful?—their lives? Would he not have been better off without her—his children better, even, by a different woman?—hers by a different man? Wouldn't it have been better if he had destroyed it all, broken away? There would have been pain, of course, terrible consequences, but even so he would have been free to go, to do, to reorganize his life on another basis. Zingara had avoided marriage entirely—wise man. But no, no; always convention, that long list of reasons and terrors he was always reciting to himself. He had allowed himself to be pulled round by the nose, God only knows why, and that was all there was to it. Weakness, if you will, perhaps; fear of convention; fear of what people would think and say.

Always now he found himself brooding over the dire results to him of all this respect on his part for convention, moral order, the duty of keeping society on an even keel, of not bringing disgrace to his children and himself and her, and yet ruining his own life emotionally by so doing. To be respectable had been so important that it had resulted in spiritual failure for him. But now all that was over with him, and Mrs. Haymaker was ill, near to death, and he was expected to wish her to get well, and be happy with her for a long time yet! Be happy! In spite of anything he might wish or think he ought to do, he couldn't. He couldn't even wish her to get well.

It was too much to ask. There was actually a haunting satisfaction in the thought that she might die now. It wouldn't be much, but it would be something—a few years of freedom. That was something. He was not utterly old yet, and he might have a few years of peace and comfort to himself still—and—and— That dream—that dream—though it might never come true now—it couldn't really—still—still— He wanted to be free to go his own way once more, to do as he pleased, to walk, to think, to brood over what he had not had—to brood over what he had not had! Only, only, whenever he looked into her pale sick face and felt her damp limp hands he could not quite wish that, either; not quite, not even now. It seemed too hard, too brutal—only—only— So he wavered.

No; in spite of her long-past struggle over foolish things and in spite of himself and all he had endured or thought he had, he was still willing that she should live; only he couldn't wish it exactly. Yes, let her live if she could. What matter to him now whether she lived or died? Whenever he looked at her he could not help thinking how helpless she would be without him, what a failure at her age, and so on. And all along, as he wryly repeated to himself, she had been thinking and feeling that she was doing the very best for him and her and the children!—that she was really the ideal wife for him, making every dollar go as far as it would, every enjoyment yield the last drop for them all, every move seeming to have been made to their general advantage! Yes, that was true. There was a pathos about it, wasn't there? But as for the actual results—!

The next morning, the second after his talk with Doctor Storm, found him sitting once more beside his front window in the early dawn, and so much of all this, and much more, was coming back to him, as before. For the thousandth or the ten-thousandth time, as it seemed to him, in all the years that had gone, he was concluding again that his life was a failure. If only he were free for a little while just to be alone and think, perhaps to discover what life might bring him yet; only on this occasion his thoughts were colored by a new turn in the situation. Yesterday afternoon, because Mrs. Haymaker's condition had grown worse, the consultation between Grainger and Storm was held, and to-day sometime transfusion was to be tried, that last grim stand taken by physicians in distress over a case; blood taken from a strong ex-cavalryman out of a position, in this case, and the best to be hoped for, but not assured. In this instance his thoughts were as before wavering. Now supposing she really died, in spite of this? What would he think of himself then? He went back after a time and looked in on her where she was still sleeping. Now she was not so strong as before, or so she seemed; her pulse was not so good, the nurse said. And now as before his mood changed in her favor, but only for a little while. For later, waking, she seemed to look and feel better.

Later he came up to the dining room, where the nurse was taking her breakfast, and seating himself beside her, as was his custom these days, asked: "How do you think she is to-day?"

He and the night nurse had thus had their breakfasts together for days. This nurse, Miss Filson, was such a smooth, pink, graceful creature, with light hair and blue eyes, the kind of eyes and color that of late, and in earlier years, had suggested to him the love time or youth that he had missed.

The latter looked grave, as though she really feared the worst but was concealing it.

"No worse, I think, and possibly a little better," she replied, eying him sympathetically. He could see that she too felt that he was old and in danger of being neglected. "Her pulse is a little stronger, nearly normal now, and she is resting easily. Doctor Storm and Doctor Grainger are coming, though, at ten. Then they'll decide what's to be done. I think if she's worse that they are going to try transfusion. The man has been engaged. Doctor Storm said that when she woke to-day she was to be given strong beef tea. Mrs. Elfridge is making it now. The fact that she is not much worse, though, is a good sign in itself, I think."

Haymaker merely stared at her from under his heavy gray eyebrows. He was so tired and gloomy, not only because he had not slept much of late himself but because of this sawing to and fro between his varying moods. Was he never to be able to decide for himself what he really wished? Was he never to be done with this interminable moral or spiritual problem? Why could he not make up his mind on the side of moral order, sympathy, and be at peace? Miss Filson pattered on about other heart cases, how so many people lived years and years after they were supposed to die of heart lesion; and he meditated as to the grayness and strangeness of it all, the worthlessness of his own life, the variability of his own moods. Why was he so? How queer—how almost evil, sinister—he had become at times; how weak at others. Last night as he had looked at Ernestine lying in bed, and this morning before he had seen her, he had thought if she only would die—if he were only really free once more, even at this late date. But then when he had seen her again this morning and now when Miss Filson spoke of transfusion, he felt sorry again. What good would it do him now? Why should he want to kill her? Could such evil ideas go unpunished either in this world or the next? Supposing his children could guess! Supposing she did die now—and he wished it so fervently only this morning— how would he feel? After all, Ernestine had not been so bad. She had tried, hadn't she?—only she had not been able to make a success of things, as he saw it, and he had not been able to love her, that was all. He reproached himself once more now with the hardness and the cruelty of his thoughts.

The opinion of the two physicians was that Mrs. Haymaker was not much better and that this first form of blood transfusion must be resorted to—injected straight via a pump—which should restore her greatly provided her heart did not bleed it out too freely. Before doing so, however, both men once more spoke to Haymaker, who in an excess of self-condemnation insisted that no expense must be spared. If her life was in danger, save it by any means—all. It was precious to her, to him and to her children. So he spoke. Thus he felt that he was lending every force which could be expected of him, aside from fervently wishing for her recovery, which even now, in spite of himself, he could not do. He was too weary of it all, the conventional round of duties and obligations. But if she recovered, as her physicians seemed to think she might if transfusion were

21

tried, if she gained even, it would mean that he would have to take her away for the summer to some quiet mountain resort—to be with her hourly during the long period in which she would be recovering. Well, he would not complain now. That was all right. He would do it. He would be bored of course, as usual, but it would be too bad to have her die when she could be saved. Yes, that was true. And yet—

He went down to his office again and in the meantime this first form of transfusion was tried, and proved a great success, apparently. She was much better, so the day nurse phoned at three; very much better. At five-thirty Mr. Haymaker returned, no unsatisfactory word having come in the interim, and there she was, resting on a raised pillow, if you please, and looking so cheerful, more like her old self than he had seen her in some time.

At once then his mood changed again. They were amazing, these variations in his own thoughts, almost chemic, not volitional, decidedly peculiar for a man who was supposed to know his own mind—only did one, ever? Now she would not die. Now the whole thing would go on as before. He was sure of it. Well, he might as well resign himself to the old sense of failure. He would never be free now. Everything would go on as before, the next and the next day the same. Terrible! Though he seemed glad—really grateful, in a way, seeing her cheerful and hopeful once more—still the obsession of failure and being once more bound forever returned now. In his own bed at midnight he said to himself: "Now she will really get well. All will be as before. I will never be free. I will never have a day—a day! Never!"

But the next morning, to his surprise and fear or comfort, as his moods varied, she was worse again; and then once more he reproached himself for his black thoughts. Was he not really killing her by what he thought? he asked himself—these constant changes in his mood? Did not his dark wishes have power? Was he not as good as a murderer in his way? Think, if he had always to feel from now on that he had killed her by wishing so! Would not that be dreadful—an awful thing really? Why was he this way? Could he not be human, kind?

When Doctor Storm came at nine-thirty, after a telephone call from the nurse, and looked grave and spoke of horses' blood as being better, thicker than human blood—not so easily bled out of the heart when injected as a serum—Haymaker was beside himself with self-reproaches and sad, disturbing fear. His dark, evil thoughts of last night and all these days had done this, he was sure. Was he really a murderer at heart, a dark criminal, plotting her death?—and for what? Why had he wished last night that she would die? Her case must be very desperate.

22

"You must do your best," he now said to Doctor Storm. "Whatever is needful—she must not die if you can help it."

"No, Mr. Haymaker," returned the latter sympathetically. "All that can be done will be done. You need not fear. I have an idea that we didn't inject enough yesterday, and anyhow human blood is not thick enough in this case. She responded, but not enough. We will see what we can do to-day."

Haymaker, pressed with duties, went away, subdued and sad. Now once more he decided that he must not tolerate these dark ideas any more, must rid himself of these black wishes, whatever he might feel. It was evil. They would eventually come back to him in some dark way, he might be sure. They might be influencing her. She must be allowed to recover if she could without any opposition on his part. He must now make a further sacrifice of his own life, whatever it cost. It was only decent, only human. Why should he complain now, anyhow, after all these years! What difference would a few more years make? He returned at evening, consoled by his own good thoughts and a telephone message at three to the effect that his wife was much better. This second injection had proved much more effective. Horses' blood was plainly better for her. She was stronger, and sitting up again. He entered at five, and found her lying there pale and weak, but still with a better light in her eye, a touch of color in her cheeks—or so he thought—more force, and a very faint smile for him, so marked had been the change. How great and kind Doctor Storm really was! How resourceful! If she would only get well now! If this dread siege would only abate! Doctor Storm was coming again at eight.

"Well, how are you, dear?" she asked, looking at him sweetly and lovingly, and taking his hand in hers.

He bent and kissed her forehead—a Judas kiss, he had thought up to now, but not so to-night. To-night he was kind, generous—anxious, even, for her to live.

"All right, dearest; very good indeed. And how are you? It's such a fine evening out. You ought to get well soon so as to enjoy these spring days."

"I'm going to," she replied softly. "I feel so much better. And how have you been? Has your work gone all right?"

He nodded and smiled and told her bits of news. Ethelberta had phoned that she was coming, bringing violets. Wesley had said he would be here at six, with Irma! Such-and-such people had asked after her. How could he have been so evil, he now asked himself, as to wish her to die? She was not so bad—really quite charming in her way, an ideal wife for some one, if not him. She was as much entitled to live and enjoy her life as he was to enjoy his; and after all

23

she was the mother of his children, had been with him all these years. Besides, the day had been so fine—it was now—a wondrous May evening. The air and sky were simply delicious. A lavender haze was in the air. The telephone bell now ringing brought still another of a long series of inquiries as to her condition. There had been so many of these during the last few days, the maid said, and especially to-day—and she gave Mr. Haymaker a list of names. See, he thought, she had even more friends than he, being so good, faithful, worthy. Why should he wish her ill?

He sat down to dinner with Ethelberta and Wesley when they arrived, and chatted quite gayly—more hopefully than he had in weeks. His own varying thoughts no longer depressing him, for the moment he was happy. How were they? What were the children all doing? At eight-thirty Doctor Storm came again, and announced that he thought Mrs. Haymaker was doing very well indeed, all things considered.

"Her condition is fairly promising, I must say," he said. "If she gets through another night or two comfortably without falling back I think she'll do very well from now on. Her strength seems to be increasing a fraction. However, we must not be too optimistic. Cases of this kind are very treacherous. To-morrow we'll see how she feels, whether she needs any more blood."

He went away, and at ten Ethelberta and Wesley left for the night, asking to be called if she grew worse, thus leaving him alone once more. He sat and meditated. At eleven, after a few moments at his wife's bedside—absolute quiet had been the doctor's instructions these many days—he himself went to bed. He was very tired. His varying thoughts had afflicted him so much that he was always tired, it seemed—his evil conscience, he called it—but to-night he was sure he would sleep. He felt better about himself, about life. He had done better, to-day. He should never have tolerated such dark thoughts. And yet—and yet—and yet—

He lay on his bed near a window which commanded a view of a small angle of the park, and looked out. There were the spring trees, as usual, silvered now by the light, a bit of lake showing at one end. Here in the city a bit of sylvan scenery such as this was so rare and so expensive. In his youth he had been so fond of water, any small lake or stream or pond. In his youth, also, he had loved the moon, and to walk in the dark. It had all, always, been so suggestive of love and happiness, and he had so craved love and happiness and never had it. Once he had designed a yacht club, the base of which suggested waves. Once, years ago, he had thought of designing a lovely cottage or country house for himself and some new love—that wonderful one—if ever she came and he were free. How wonderful it

24

would all have been. Now—now—the thought at such an hour and especially when it was too late, seemed sacrilegious, hard, cold, unmoral, evil. He turned his face away from the moonlight and sighed, deciding to sleep and shut out these older and darker and sweeter thoughts if he could, and did.

Presently he dreamed, and it was as if some lovely spirit of beauty—that wondrous thing he had always been seeking—came and took him by the hand and led him out, out by dimpling streams and clear rippling lakes and a great, noble highway where were temples and towers and figures in white marble. And it seemed as he walked as if something had been, or were, promised him—a lovely fruition to something which he craved—only the world toward which he walked was still dark or shadowy, with something sad and repressing about it, a haunting sense of a still darker distance. He was going toward beauty apparently, but he was still seeking, seeking, and it was dark there when—

"Mr. Haymaker! Mr. Haymaker!" came a voice—soft, almost mystical at first, and then clearer and more disturbing, as a hand was laid on him. "Will you come at once? It's Mrs. Haymaker!"

On the instant he was on his feet seizing the blue silk dressing gown hanging at his bed's head, and adjusting it as he hurried. Mrs. Elfridge and the nurse were behind him, very pale and distrait, wringing their hands. He could tell by that that the worst was at hand. When he reached the bedroom—her bedroom—there she lay as in life—still, peaceful, already limp, as though she were sleeping. Her thin, and as he sometimes thought, cold, lips were now parted in a faint, gracious smile, or trace of one. He had seen her look that way, too, at times; a really gracious smile, and wise, wiser than she was. The long, thin, graceful hands were open, the fingers spread slightly apart as though she were tired, very tired. The eyelids, too, rested wearily on tired eyes. Her form, spare as always, was outlined clearly under the thin coverlets. Miss Filson, the night nurse, was saying something about having fallen asleep for a moment, and waking only to find her so. She was terribly depressed and disturbed, possibly because of Doctor Storm.

Haymaker paused, greatly shocked and moved by the sight— more so than by anything since the death of little Elwell. After all, she had tried, according to her light. But now she was dead—and they had been together so long! He came forward, tears of sympathy springing to his eyes, then sank down beside the bed on his knees so as not to disturb her right hand where it lay.

"Ernie, dear," he said gently, "Ernie—are you really gone?" His voice was full of sorrow; but to himself it sounded false, traitorous.

25

He lifted the hand and put it to his lips sadly, then leaned his head against her, thinking of his long, mixed thoughts these many days, while both Mrs. Elfridge and the nurse began wiping their eyes. They were so sorry for him, he was so old now!

After a while he got up—they came forward to persuade him at last—looking tremendously sad and distrait, and asked Mrs. Elfridge and the nurse not to disturb his children. They could not aid her now. Let them rest until morning. Then he went back to his own room and sat down on the bed for a moment, gazing out on the same silvery scene that had attracted him before. It was dreadful. So then his dark wishing had come true at last? Possibly his black thoughts had killed her after all. Was that possible? Had his voiceless prayers been answered in this grim way? And did she know now what he had really thought? Dark thought. Where was she now? What was she thinking now if she knew? Would she hate him—haunt him? It was not dawn yet, only two or three in the morning, and the moon was still bright. And in the next room she was lying, pale and cool, gone forever now out of his life.

He got up after a time and went forward into that pleasant front room where he had so often loved to sit, then back into her room to view the body again. Now that she was gone, here more than elsewhere, in her dead presence, he seemed better able to collect his scattered thoughts. She might see or she might not— might know or not. It was all over now. Only he could not help but feel a little evil. She had been so faithful, if nothing more, so earnest in behalf of him and of his children. He might have spared her these last dark thoughts of these last few days. His feelings were so jumbled that he could not place them half the time. But at the same time the ethics of the past, of his own irritated feelings and moods in regard to her, had to be adjusted somehow before he could have peace. They must be adjusted, only how—how? He and Mrs. Elfridge had agreed not to disturb Doctor Storm any more to-night. They were all agreed to get what rest they could against the morning.

After a time he came forward once more to the front room to sit and gaze at the park. Here, perhaps, he could solve these mysteries for himself, think them out, find out what he did feel. He was evil for having wished all he had, that he knew and felt. And yet there was his own story, too—his life. The dawn was breaking by now; a faint grayness shaded the east and dimly lightened this room. A tall pier mirror between two windows now revealed him to himself—spare, angular, disheveled, his beard and hair astray and his eyes weary. The figure he made here as against his dreams of a happier life, once he were free, now struck him forcibly. What a farce! What a failure! Why should he, of all people, think of further happiness in love, even if he were free? Look at his reflection here in this mirror. What a picture—old, grizzled, done for! Had he not known that for so long? Was it not too ridiculous? Why should he have tolerated such vain thoughts? What could he of all people hope for now? No thing of beauty would have him now. Of course not. That glorious dream of his youth was gone forever. It was a mirage, an ignis fatuus. His wife might just as well have lived as died, for all the difference it would or could make to him. Only, he was really free just the same, almost as it were in spite of his varying moods. But he was old, weary, done for, a recluse and ungainly.

Now the innate cruelty of life, its blazing ironic indifference to him and so many grew rapidly upon him. What had he had? What all had he not missed? Dismally he stared first at his dark wrinkled skin; the crow's-feet at the sides of his eyes; the wrinkles across his forehead and between the eyes; his long, dark, wrinkled hands—handsome hands they once were, he thought; his angular, stiff body. Once he had been very much of a personage, he thought, striking, forceful, dynamic—but now! He turned and looked out over the park where the young trees were, and the lake, to the pinking dawn—just a trace now—a significant thing in itself at this hour surely—the new dawn, so wondrously new for younger people—then back at himself. What could he wish for now—what hope for?

As he did so his dream came back to him—that strange dream of seeking and being led and promised and yet always being led forward into a dimmer, darker land. What did that mean? Had it any real significance? Was it all to be dimmer, darker still? Was it typical of his life? He pondered.

"Free!" he said after a time. "Free! I know now how that is. I am free now, at last! Free! . . . Free! . . . Yes—free . . . to die!"

So he stood there ruminating and smoothing his hair and his beard.

McEWEN OF THE SHINING SLAVE MAKERS

It was a hot day in August. The parching rays of a summer sun had faded the once sappy green leaves of the trees to a dull and dusty hue. The grass, still good to look upon in shady places, spread sere and dry where the light had fallen unbroken. The roads were hot with thick dust, and wherever a stone path led, it reflected heat to weary body and soul.

Robert McEwen had taken a seat under a fine old beech tree whose broad arms cast a welcome shade. He had come here out of the toil of the busy streets.

For a time he gave himself over to blank contemplation of the broad park and the occasional carriages that jingled by. Presently his meditation was broken by an ant on his trousers, which he flipped away with his finger. This awoke him to the thought that there might be more upon him. He stood up, shaking and brushing himself. Then he noticed an ant running along the walk in front of him. He stamped on it.

"I guess that will do for you," he said, half aloud, and sat down again.

Now only did he really notice the walk. It was wide and hard and hot. Many ants were hurrying about, and now he saw that they were black. At last, one more active than the others fixed his eye. He followed it with his glance for more than a score of feet.

This particular ant was progressing urgently, now to the right, now to the left, stopping here and there, but never for more than a second. Its energy, the zigzag course it pursued, the frequency with which it halted to examine something, enlisted his interest. As he gazed, the path grew in imagination until it assumed immense proportions.

Suddenly he bestirred himself, took a single glance and then jumped, rubbing his eyes. He was in an unknown world, strange in every detail. The branched and many-limbed trees had disappeared. A forest of immense flat swords of green swayed in the air above him. The ground between lacked its carpet of green and was roughly strewn with immense boulders of clay. The air was strong with an odor which seemed strange and yet familiar. Only the hot sun streaming down and a sky of faultless blue betokened a familiar world. In regard to himself McEwen felt peculiar and yet familiar. What was it that made these surroundings and himself seem odd

28

and yet usual? He could not tell. His three pairs of limbs and his vigorous mandibles seemed natural enough. The fact that he sensed rather than saw things was natural and yet odd. Forthwith moved by a sense of duty, necessity, and a kind of tribal obligation which he more felt than understood, he set out in search of food and prey and presently came to a broad plain, so wide that his eye could scarce command more than what seemed an immediate portion of it. He halted and breathed with a feeling of relief. Just then a voice startled him.

"Anything to eat hereabout?" questioned the newcomer in a friendly and yet self-interested tone.

McEwen drew back.

"I do not know," he said, "I have just—"

"Terrible," said the stranger, not waiting to hear his answer. "It looks like famine. You know the Sanguineæ have gone to war."

"No," answered McEwen mechanically.

"Yes," said the other, "they raided the Fuscæ yesterday. They'll be down on us next."

With that the stranger made off. McEwen was about to exclaim at the use of the word us when a ravenous craving for food, brought now forcibly to his mind by the words of the other, made him start in haste after him.

Then came another who bespoke him in passing.

"I haven't found a thing to-day, and I've been all the way to the Pratensis region. I didn't dare go any further without having some others with me. They're hungry, too, up there, though they've just made a raid. You heard the Sanguineæ went to war, didn't you?"

"Yes, he told me," said McEwen, indicating the retreating figure of the stranger.

"Oh, Ermi. Yes, he's been over in their territory. Well, I'll be going now."

McEwen hastened after Ermi at a good pace, and soon overtook him. The latter had stopped and was gathering in his mandibles a jagged crumb, almost as large as himself.

"Oh!" exclaimed McEwen eagerly, "where did you get that?"

"Here," said Ermi.

"Will you give me a little?"

"I will not," said the other, and a light came in his eye that was almost evil.

"All right," said McEwen, made bold by hunger and yet cautious by danger, "which way would you advise me to look?"

"Wherever you please," said Ermi, "why ask me? You are not new at seeking," and strode off.

29

"The forest was better than this," thought McEwen; "there I would not die of the heat, anyhow, and I might find food. Here is nothing," and he turned and glanced about for a sight of the jungle whence he had come.

Far to the left and rear of him he saw it, those great up-standing swords. As he gazed, revolving in his troubled mind whether he should return or not, he saw another like himself hurrying toward him out of the distance.

He eagerly hailed the newcomer, who was yet a long way off.

"What is it?" asked the other, coming up rapidly.

"Do you know where I can get something to eat?"

"Is that why you called me?" he answered, eyeing him angrily. "Do you ask in time of famine? Certainly not. If I had anything for myself, I would not be out here. Go and hunt for it like the rest of us. Why should you be asking?"

"I have been hunting," cried McEwen, his anger rising. "I have searched here until I am almost starved."

"No worse off than any of us, are you?" said the other. "Look at me. Do you suppose I am feasting?"

He went off in high dudgeon, and McEwen gazed after him in astonishment. The indifference and sufficiency were at once surprising and yet familiar. Later he found himself falling rapidly into helpless lassitude from both hunger and heat, when a voice, as of one in pain, hailed him.

"Ho!" it cried.

"Hello!" he answered.

"Come, come!" was the feeble reply.

McEwen started forward at once. When he was still many times his own length away he recognized the voice as that of his testy friend of a little while before, but now sadly changed. He was stretched upon the earth, working his mandibles feebly.

"What is it?" asked McEwen solicitously. "What ails you? How did this happen?"

"I don't know," said the other. "I was passing along here when that struck me," indicating a huge boulder. "I am done for, though. You may as well have this food now, since you are one of us. The tribe can use what you do not eat," he sighed.

"Oh, nothing of the sort," said McEwen solicitously, the while he viewed the crushed limbs and side of the sufferer. "You'll be all right. Why do you speak of death? Just tell me where to take you, or whom to go for."

"No," said the other, "it would be no use. You see how it is. They could do nothing for me. I did not want your aid. I merely wanted you to have this food here. I shall not want it now."

"Don't say that," returned McEwen. "You mustn't talk about dying. There must be something I can do. Tell me. I don't want your food."

"No, there isn't anything you could do. There isn't any cure, you know that. Report, when you return, how I was killed. Just leave me now and take that with you. They need it, if you do not."

McEwen viewed him silently. This reference to a colony or tribe or home seemed to clarify many things for him. He remembered now apparently the long road he had come, the immense galleries of the colony to which he belonged under the earth, the passages by which he had made his way in and out, the powerful and revered ant mother, various larvæ to be fed and eggs to be tended. To be sure. That was it. He was a part of this immense colony or group. The heat must have affected his sensory powers. He must gather food and return there—kill spiders, beetles, grubs, and bring them back to help provision the colony. That was it. Only there were so few to be found here, for some reason.

The sufferer closed his eyes in evident pain, and trembled convulsively. Then he fell back and died.

McEwen gazed upon the now fast stiffening body, with all but indifference, and wondered. The spectacle seemed so familiar as to be all but commonplace. Apparently he had seen so many die that way. Had he not, in times past, reported the deaths of hundreds?

"Is he dead?" asked a voice at his side.

"Yes," said McEwen, scarcely bringing himself out of his meditation sufficiently to observe the newcomer.

"Well, then, he will not need this, I guess," said the other, and he seized upon the huge lump with his mandibles, but McEwen was on the alert and savage into the bargain, on the instant. He, too, gripped his mandibles upon it.

"I was called by him to have this, before he died," he shouted "and I propose to have it. Let go."

"That I will not," said the other with great vigor and energy. "I'll have some of it, at least," and, giving a mighty wrench, which sent both himself and McEwen sprawling, he tore off a goodly portion of it and ran, gaining his feet so quickly that he was a good length off before McEwen arose. The latter was too hungry, however, to linger in useless rage, and now fell to and ate before any other should disturb him. Then, feeling partially satisfied, he stretched himself languorously and continued more at his leisure. After a time he shook himself out of his torpor which had seized on him with his eating, and made off for the distant jungle, in which direction, as he now felt, lay the colony home.

He was in one of the darkest and thickest portions of the route thither when there was borne to him from afar the sound of feet in marching time, and a murmuring as of distant voices. He stopped and listened. Presently the sounds grew louder and more individual. He could now tell that a great company was nearing him. The narrow path which he followed was clear for some distance, and open to observation. Not knowing what creatures he was about to meet, he stepped out of it into a thicket, at one side and took up a position behind a great boulder. The tramp of many feet was now so close as to bode contact and discovery, and he saw, through the interstices of green stalks, a strange column filing along the path he had left. They were no other than a company of red warriors—slave makers like himself, only of a different species, the fierce Sanguineæ that Ermi had spoken of as having gone to war.

To war they certainly had been, and no doubt were going again. Nearly every warrior carried with him some mark of plunder or of death. Many bore in their mandibles dead bodies of the enemy or their larvæ captured from a Fuscan colony. Others bore upon their legs the severed heads of the poor blacks who had been slain in the defense of their home, and whose jaws still clung to their foes, fixed in the rigor of death. Still others dragged the bodies of their victims, and shouted as they went, making the long, lonely path to ring with uncanny sounds as they disappeared in the distance.

McEwen came furtively out after a time and looked after them. He had gotten far to the left of the warriors and somewhat to the front of them, and was just about to leave the shadow of one clump of bushes to hurry to a neighboring stone, when there filed out from the very shelter upon which he had his eye fixed, the figure of one whom he immediately recognized as Ermi. The latter seemed to await a favorable opportunity when he should not be observed, and then started running. McEwen followed. In the distance could be seen a group of the Sanguineæ, who had evidently paused for something, moving about in great excitement, in groups of two or three, gesticulating and talking. Some of those not otherwise engaged displayed a sensibility of danger or a lust of war by working their jaws and sawing at heavy stones with their mandibles. Presently one gazed in the direction of Ermi, and shouted to the others.

Immediately four warriors set out in pursuit. McEwen hastened after Ermi, to see what would become of him. Discreetly hidden himself, he could do this with considerable equanimity. As he approached, he saw Ermi moving backward and forward, endeavoring to close the entrance to a cave in which he had now taken refuge. Apparently that warrior had become aware that no time was to be lost, since he also could see the pursuing Sanguineæ. With a swiftness born of daring and a keen realization of danger, he arranged a large boulder at the very edge of the portal as a key, and then others in such position that when the first should topple in the others would follow. Then he crawled deftly inside the portal, and pulling the keystone, toppled the whole mass in after him.

This was hardly done when the Sanguineæ were upon him. They were four cruel, murderous fighters, deeply scarred. One, called by the others Og, had a black's head at his thigh. One of his temples bore a scar, and the tip of his left antenna was broken. He was a keen old warrior, however, and scented the prey at once.

"Hi, you!" he shouted to the others. "Here's the place."

Just then another drew near to the portal which Ermi had barricaded. He looked at it closely, walked about several times, sounded with his antennæ and then listened. There was no answer.

"Hist!" he exclaimed to the others.

Now they came up. They also looked, but so well had Ermi done his work that they were puzzled.

"I'm not sure," said Og, "it looks to me more like an abandoned cave than an entrance."

"Tear it open, anyway," advocated Ponan, the second of the quartette, speaking for the first time. "There may be no other exit."

"Aha!" cried Og, "Good! We will see anyhow."

"Come on!" yelled Maru, a third, seizing the largest boulder, "Mandibles to!"

"Out with him!" cried Om, jumping eagerly to work. "We will have him out in a jiffy!"

It was not an easy task, as the boulders were heavy and deep, but they tore them out. Later they dragged forth Ermi, who, finding himself captured, seized the head of Maru with his mandibles. Og, on the other hand, seized one of Ermi's legs in his powerful jaws. The others also had taken hold. The antennae of all were thrown back, and the entire mass went pushing and shoving, turning and tumbling in a whirl.

McEwen gazed, excited and sympathetic. At first he thought to avoid it all, having a horror of death, but a moment later decided to come to his friend's rescue, a feeling of tribal relationship which was overwhelming coming over him. Springing forward, he clambered upon the back of Og, at whose neck he began to saw with his powerful teeth. Og, realizing a new adversary, released his hold upon Ermi's limb and endeavored to shake off his new enemy. McEwen held tight, however. The others, however, too excited to observe the newcomer, still struggled to destroy Ermi. The latter

33

had stuck steadily to his labor of killing Maru, and now, when Og's hold was loosened, he gave a powerful crush and Maru breathed his last. This advantaged him little, however, for both Ponan and Om were attacking his sides.

"Take that!" shouted Om, throwing himself violently upon Ermi and turning him over. "Saw off his head, Ponan."

Ponan released his hold and sprang for Ermi's head. There was a kicking and crushing of jaws, and Ponan secured his grip.

"Kill him!" yelled Om. "Come, Og! Come!"

At this very moment Og's severed head fell to the ground, and McEwen leaping from his back, sprang to the aid of Ermi.

"Come!" he shouted at Ponan, who was sawing at Ermi's head. "It's two to two now," and McEwen gave such a wrench to Ponan's side that he writhed in pain, and released his hold on Ermi.

But recovering himself he leaped upon McEwen, and bore him down, sprawling.

The fight was now more desperate than ever. The combatants rolled and tossed. McEwen's right antenna was broken by his fall, and one of his legs was injured. He could seem to get no hold upon his adversary, whom he now felt to be working toward his neck.

"Let go!" he yelled, gnashing at him with his mandibles, but Ponan only tightened his murderous jaws.

Better fortune was now with Ermi, however, who was a more experienced fighter. Getting a grip upon Om's body, he hurled him to the ground and left him stunned and senseless.

Seeing McEwen's predicament, he now sprang to his aid. The latter was being sadly worsted and but for the generous aid of Ermi, would have been killed. The latter struck Ponan a terrific blow with his head and having stunned him, dragged him off. The two, though much injured, now seized upon the unfortunate Sanguinea and tore him in two, and would have done as much for Om, had they not discovered that that bedraggled warrior had recovered sufficiently to crawl away and hide.

McEwen and Ermi now drew near to each other in warm admiration.

"Come with me," said Ermi. "They are all about here now and that coward who escaped will have them upon us. There is a corridor into our home from here, only I was not able to reach it before they caught me. Help me barricade this entrance."

Together they built up the stones more effectually than before, and then entered, toppling the mass in behind them. With considerable labor, they built up another barricade below.

"You watch a moment, now," said Ermi to McEwen, and then hurried down a long passage through which he soon returned bringing with him a sentinel, who took up guard duty at the point where the fight had occurred. "He will stay here and give the alarm in case another attack is made," he commented.

"Come now," he added, touching McEwen affectionately with his antennæ. Leading the way, Ermi took him along a long winding corridor with which, somehow, he seemed to be familiar, and through various secret passages into the colony house.

"You see," he said to McEwen familiarly, as they went, "they could not have gotten in here, even if they had killed me, without knowing the way. Our passageways are too intricate. But it is as well to keep a picket there, now that they are about. Where have you been? You do not belong to our colony, do you?"

McEwen related his experiences since their meeting in the desert, without explaining where he came from.

He knew that he was a member of some other colony of this same tribe without being sure of which one. A strange feeling of wandering confusion possessed him, as though he had been injured in some way, somewhere, and was lost for the moment.

"Well, you might as well stay with us, now," said Ermi. "Are you hungry?"

"Very," said McEwen.

"Then we will eat at once."

McEwen now gazed upon a domed chamber of vast proportions, with which, also, he seemed familiar, an old inhabitant of one such, no less. It had several doors that opened out into galleries, and corridors leading to other chambers and store rooms, a home for thousands.

Many members of this allied family now hurried to meet them, all genially enough.

"You have had an encounter with them?" asked several at once.

"Nothing to speak of," said Ermi, who, fighter that he was, had also a touch of vanity. "Look after my friend here, who has saved my life."

"Not I!" cried McEwen warmly.

They could not explain, however, before they were seized by their admirers and carried into a chamber where none of the din of preparation penetrated, and where was a carpet of soft grass threads upon which they might lie.

Injured though they were, neither could endure lying still for long, and were soon poking about, though unable to do anything. McEwen was privileged to idle and listlessly watch an attack on one portal of the cave which lasted an entire day, resulting in failure for the invaders. It was a rather broken affair, the principal excitement occurring about the barricaded portals and secret exits at the end of the long corridors, where McEwen often found himself in the way. The story of his prowess had been well told by Ermi, and he was a friend and hero whom many served. A sort of ambulance service was established which not only looked to the bringing in of the injured, but also to the removal of the dead. A graveyard was prepared just outside one of the secret entrances, far from the scene of the siege, and here the dead were laid in orderly rows.

The siege having ended temporarily the same day it began, the household resumed its old order. Those who had remained within went forth for forage. The care of the communal young, which had been somewhat interrupted, was now resumed. Larvæ and chrysalis, which had been left almost unattended in the vast nurseries, were moved to and fro between the rooms where the broken sunlight warmed, and the shadow gave them rest.

"There is war ahead," said Ermi to McEwen one day not long after this. "These Sanguineæ will never let us alone until we give them battle. We shall have to stir up the whole race of Shining Slave Makers and fight all the Sanguineæ before we have peace again."

"Good," said McEwen. "I am ready."

"So am I," answered Ermi, "but it is no light matter. They are our ancient enemy and as powerful as we. If we meet again you will see war that is war."

Not long after this McEwen and Ermi, foraging together, encountered a Sanguinea, who fought with them and was slain. Numerous Lucidi, of which tribe he found himself to be a member, left the community of a morning to labor and were never heard of again. Encounters between parties of both camps were frequent, and orderly living ceased.

At last the entire community was in a ferment, and a council was called. It was held in the main saloon of the formicary, a vast chamber whose hollowed dome rose like the open sky above them. The queen of the community was present, and all the chief warriors, including Ermi and McEwen. Loud talking and fierce comment were indulged in to no point, until Yumi, long a light in the councils of the Lucidi, spoke. He was short and sharp of speech.

"We must go to war," he said. "Our old enemies will give us no peace. Send couriers to all the colonies of the Shining Slave Makers. We will meet the Red Slave Makers as we did before."

"Ah," said an old Lucidi, who stood at McEwen's side, "that was a great battle. You don't remember. You were too young. There were thousands and thousands in that. I could not walk for the dead."

"Are we to have another such?" asked McEwen.

"If the rest of us come. We are a great people. The Shining Slave Makers are numberless."

Just then another voice spoke, and Ermi listened.

"Let us send for them to come here. When the Sanguineæ again lay siege let us pour out and destroy them. Let none escape."

"Let us first send couriers and hear what our people say," broke in Ermi loudly. "The Sanguineæ are a vast people also. We must have numbers. It must be a decisive battle."

"Ay, ay," answered many. "Send the couriers!"

Forthwith messengers were dispatched to all parts, calling the hordes of the Shining Slave Makers to war. In due course they returned, bringing information that they were coming. Their colonies also had been attacked. Later the warriors of the allied tribes began to put in an appearance.

It was a gathering of legions. The paths in the forests about resounded with their halloos. With the arrival of the first cohorts of these friendly colonies, there was a minor encounter with an irritant host of the Sanguineæ foraging hereabout, who were driven back and destroyed. Later there were many minor encounters and deaths before the hosts were fully assembled, but the end was not yet. All knew that. The Sanguineæ had fled, but not in cowardice. They would return.

The one problem with this vast host, now that it was assembled, was food. Eventually they expected to discover this in the sacked homes of the Sanguineæ, but temporarily other provision must be made. The entire region had to be scoured. Colonies of Fuscæ and Schauffusi living in nearby territory were attacked and destroyed. Their storehouses were ransacked and the contents distributed. Every form of life was attacked and still there was not enough.

Both McEwen and Ermi, now inseparable, joined in one of these raids. It was upon a colony of Fuscæ, who had their home in a neighboring forest. The company went singing on their way until within a short distance of the colony, when they became silent.

"Let us not lose track of one another," said McEwen.

"No," said Ermi, "but they are nothing. We will take all they possess without a struggle. See them running."

As he said this, he motioned in the direction of several Fuscæ that were fleeing toward their portals in terror. The Lucidi set up a shout, and darted after, plunging into the open gates, striking and slaying as they went. In a few minutes those first in came out again

37

carrying their booty. Others were singly engaged in fiercest battle with large groups of the weaker Fuscæ. Only a few of the latter were inclined to fight. They seemed for the most part dazed by their misfortunes. Numbers hung from the topmost blades of the towering sword-trees, and the broad, floor-like leaves of the massive weeds, about their caves where they had taken refuge, holding in their jaws baby larvæ and cocoons rescued from the invaders, with which they had hurriedly fled to these nearest elevated objects.

Singly, McEwen pursued a dozen, and reveled in the sport of killing them. He tumbled them with rushes of his body, crushed them with his mandibles, and poisoned them with his formic sting.

"Do you need help?" called Ermi once, who was always near and shouting.

"Yes," called McEwen scornfully, "bring me more of them."

Soon the deadly work was over and the two comrades, gathering a mass of food, joined the returning band, singing as they went

"To-morrow," said Ermi, as they went along, "we will meet the Sanguineæ. It is agreed. The leaders are conferring now."

McEwen did not learn where these latter were, but somehow he was pleased. An insane lust of combat was now upon him.

"They will not be four to two this time," he laughed exultingly.

"No, and we will not be barricading against them, either," laughed Ermi, the lust of war simmering in his veins.

As they came near their camp, however, they found a large number of the assembled companies already in motion. Thousands upon thousands of those who had arrived were already assembled in one group or another and were prepared for action. There were cries and sounds of fighting, and long lines of Lucidi hurrying hither and thither.

"What's the matter?" asked Ermi excitedly.

"The Sanguineæ," was the answer. "They are returning."

Instantly McEwen became sober. Ermi turned to him affectionately.

"Now," he said solemnly, "courage. We're in for it."

A tremendous hubbub followed. Already vast legions of the Lucidi were bearing away to the east. McEwen and Ermi, not being able to find their own, fell in with a strange company.

"Order!" shouted a voice in their ears. "Fall in line. We are called."

The twain mechanically obeyed, and dropped behind a regular line. Soon they were winding along with other long lines of warriors through the tall sword trees, and in a little while reached a huge, smooth, open plain where already the actual fighting had begun.

Thousands were here, apparently hundreds of thousands. There was little order, and scarcely any was needed apparently, since all contacts were individual or between small groups. It all depended now on numbers, and the results of the contests between individuals, or at the most, these small groups. Ermi, McEwen, and several other Lucidi were about to seize upon one Sanguinea, who was approaching them, when an amazing rush of the latter broke them, and McEwen found himself separated from Ermi with a red demon snapping at his throat. Dazed by the shock and clamor, he almost fell a prey to this first charge. A moment later, however, his courage and daring returned. With a furious bound, he recovered himself and forced himself upon his adversary, snapping his jaws in his neck.

"Take that!" he said to the tumbling carcass.

He had no sooner ended one foe, however, than another clutched him. They were on every hand, hard, merciless fighters like himself and Ermi who rushed and tore and sawed with amazing force. McEwen faced his newest adversary swiftly. While the latter was seeking for McEwen's head and antennæ with his mandibles, the former with a quick snap seized his foe by the neck. Turning up his abdomen, he ejected formic acid into the throat of the other. That finished him.

Meanwhile the battle continued on every hand with the same mad vehemence. Already the dead clogged the ground. Here, single combatants struggled—there, whole lines moved and swayed in deadly combat. Ever and anon new lines were formed, and strange hosts of friends or enemies came up, falling upon the combatants of both sides with murderous enthusiasm. McEwen, in a strange daze and lust of death, seemed to think nothing of it. He was alone now— lost in a tossing sea of war, and terror seemed to have forsaken him. It was wonderful, he thought, mysterious—

As enemy after enemy assailed him, he fought them as he best knew, an old method to him, apparently, and as they died, he wished them to die—broken, poisoned, sawed in two. He began to count and exult in the numbers he had slain. It was at last as though he were dreaming, and all around was a vain, dark, surging mass of enemies.

Finally, four of the Sanguineæ seized upon him in a group, and he went down before them, almost helpless. Swiftly they tore at his head and body, endeavoring to dispose of him quickly. One seized a leg, another an antenna. A third jumped and sawed at his neck. Still he did not care. It was all war, and he would struggle to the last shred of his strength, eagerly, enthusiastically. At last he seemed to lose consciousness.

When he opened his eyes again, Ermi was beside him.

"Well?" said Ermi.

"Well?" answered McEwen.

"You were about done for, then."

"Was I?" he answered. "How are things going?"

"I cannot tell yet," said Ermi. "All I know is that you were faring badly when I came up. Two of them were dead, but the other two were killing you."

"You should have left me to them," said McEwen, noticing now for the first time Ermi's wounds. "It does not matter so much— one Lucidi more or less—what of it? But you have been injured."

"I—oh, nothing. You are the one to complain. I fear you are badly injured."

"Oh, I," returned McEwen heavily, feeling at last the weight of death upon him, "I am done for. I cannot live. I felt myself dying some time ago."

He closed his eyes and trembled. In another moment—

* * * * *

McEwen opened his eyes. Strangely enough he was looking out upon jingling carriages and loitering passersby in the great city park. It was all so strange, by comparison with that which he had so recently seen, the tall buildings in the distance, instead of the sword trees, the trees, the flowers. He jumped to his feet in astonishment, then sank back again in equal amaze, a passerby eyeing him curiously the while.

"I have been asleep," he said in a troubled way. "I have been dreaming. And what a dream!"

He shut his eyes again, wishing, for some strange reason— charm, sympathy, strangeness—to regain the lost scene. An odd longing filled his heart, a sense of comradeship lost, of some friend he knew missing. When he opened his eyes again he seemed to realize something more of what had been happening, but it was fading, fading.

At his feet lay the plain and the ants with whom he had recently been—or so he thought. Yes, there, only a few feet away in the parched grass, was an arid spot, over-run with insects. He gazed upon it, in amazement, searching for the details of a lost world. Now, as he saw, coming closer, a giant battle was in progress, such a one, for instance, as that in which he had been engaged in his dream. The ground was strewn with dead ants. Thousands upon thousands were sawing and striking at each other quite in the

40

manner in which he had dreamed. What was this?—a revelation of the spirit and significance of a lesser life or of his own—or what? And what was life if the strange passions, moods and necessities which conditioned him here could condition those there on so minute a plane?

"Why, I was there," he said dazedly and a little dreamfully, "a little while ago. I died there—or as well as died there—in my dream. At least I woke out of it into this or sank from that into this."

Stooping closer he could see where lines were drawn, how in places the forces raged in confusion, and the field was cluttered with the dead. At one moment an odd mad enthusiasm such as he had experienced in his dream-world lay hold of him, and he looked for the advantage of the Shining Slave Makers—the blacks—as he thought of the two warring hosts as against the reds. But finding it not, the mood passed, and he stood gazing, lost in wonder. What a strange world! he thought. What worlds within worlds, all apparently full of necessity, contention, binding emotions and unities—and all with sorrow, their sorrow—a vague, sad something out of far-off things which had been there, and was here in this strong bright city day, had been there and would be here until this odd, strange thing called life had ended.

NIGGER JEFF

The city editor was waiting for one of his best reporters, Elmer Davies by name, a vain and rather self-sufficient youth who was inclined to be of that turn of mind which sees in life only a fixed and ordered process of rewards and punishments. If one did not do exactly right, one did not get along well. On the contrary, if one did, one did. Only the so-called evil were really punished, only the good truly rewarded—or Mr. Davies had heard this so long in his youth that he had come nearly to believe it. Presently he appeared. He was dressed in a new spring suit, a new hat and new shoes. In the lapel of his coat was a small bunch of violets. It was one o'clock of a sunny spring afternoon, and he was feeling exceedingly well and good-natured—quite fit, indeed. The world was going unusually well with him. It seemed worth singing about.

"Read that, Davies," said the city editor, handing him the clipping. "I'll tell you afterward what I want you to do."

The reporter stood by the editorial chair and read:

Pleasant Valley, Ko., April 16.

"A most dastardly crime has just been reported here. Jeff Ingalls, a negro, this morning assaulted Ada Whitaker, the nineteen-year-old daughter of Morgan Whitaker, a well-to-do farmer, whose home is four miles south of this place. A posse, headed by Sheriff Mathews, has started in pursuit. If he is caught, it is thought he will be lynched."

The reporter raised his eyes as he finished. What a terrible crime! What evil people there were in the world! No doubt such a creature ought to be lynched, and that quickly.

"You had better go out there, Davies," said the city editor. "It looks as if something might come of that. A lynching up here would be a big thing. There's never been one in this state."

Davies smiled. He was always pleased to be sent out of town. It was a mark of appreciation. The city editor rarely sent any of the other men on these big stories. What a nice ride he would have!

As he went along, however, a few minutes later he began to meditate on this. Perhaps, as the city editor had suggested, he might be compelled to witness an actual lynching. That was by no means so pleasant in itself. In his fixed code of rewards and punishments he had no particular place for lynchings, even for crimes of the nature described, especially if he had to witness the lynching. It was too horrible a kind of reward or punishment. Once, in line of duty, he had been compelled to witness a hanging, and that had made him sick—deathly so—even though carried out as a part of the due process of law of his day and place. Now, as he looked at this fine day and his excellent clothes, he was not so sure that this was a worthwhile assignment. Why should he always be selected for such things—just because he could write? There were others—lots of men on the staff. He began to hope as he went along that nothing really serious would come of it, that they would catch the man before he got there and put him in jail—or, if the worst had to be—painful thought!—that it would be all over by the time he got there. Let's see—the telegram had been filed at nine a.m. It was now one-thirty and would be three by the time he got out there, all of that. That would give them time enough, and then, if all were well, or ill, as it were, he could just gather the details of the crime and the—aftermath—and return. The mere thought of an approaching lynching troubled him greatly, and the farther he went the less he liked it.

He found the village of Pleasant Valley a very small affair indeed, just a few dozen houses nestling between green slopes of low hills, with one small business corner and a rambling array of lanes. One or two merchants of K—, the city from which he had just arrived, lived out here, but otherwise it was very rural. He took notes of the whiteness of the little houses, the shimmering beauty of the small stream one had to cross in going from the depot. At the one main corner a few men were gathered about a typical village barroom. Davies headed for this as being the most likely source of information.

In mingling with this company at first he said nothing about his being a newspaper man, being very doubtful as to its effect upon them, their freedom of speech and manner.

The whole company was apparently tense with interest in the crime which still remained unpunished, seemingly craving excitement and desirous of seeing something done about it. No such opportunity to work up wrath and vent their stored-up animal propensities had probably occurred here in years. He took this occasion to inquire into the exact details of the attack, where it had occurred, where the Whitakers lived. Then, seeing that mere talk prevailed here, he went away thinking that he had best find out for himself how the victim was. As yet she had not been described, and it was necessary to know a little something about her. Accordingly, he sought an old man who kept a stable in the village, and procured

43

a horse. No carriage was to be had. Davies was not an excellent rider, but he made a shift of it. The Whitaker home was not so very far away—about four miles out—and before long he was knocking at its front door, set back a hundred feet from the rough country road.

"I'm from the Times," he said to the tall, raw- boned woman who opened the door, with an attempt at being impressive. His position as reporter in this matter was a little dubious; he might be welcome, and he might not. Then he asked if this were Mrs. Whitaker, and how Miss Whitaker was by now.

"She's doing very well," answered the woman, who seemed decidedly stern, if repressed and nervous, a Spartan type. "Won't you come in? She's rather feverish, but the doctor says she'll probably be all right later on." She said no more.

Davies acknowledged the invitation by entering. He was very anxious to see the girl, but she was sleeping under the influence of an opiate, and he did not care to press the matter at once.

"When did this happen?" he asked.

"About eight o'clock this morning," said the woman.

"She started to go over to our next door neighbor here, Mr. Edmonds, and this negro met her. We didn't know anything about it until she came crying through the gate and dropped down in here."

"Were you the first one to meet her?" asked Davies.

"Yes, I was the only one," said Mrs. Whitaker. "The men had all gone to the fields."

Davies listened to more of the details, the type and history of the man, and then rose to go. Before doing so he was allowed to have a look at the girl, who was still sleeping. She was young and rather pretty. In the yard he met a country man who was just coming to get home news. The latter imparted more information.

"They're lookin' all around south of here," he said, speaking of a crowd which was supposed to be searching. "I expect they'll make short work of him if they get him. He can't get away very well, for he's on foot, wherever he is. The sheriff's after him too, with a deputy or two, I believe. He'll be tryin' to save him an' take him over to Clayton, but I don't believe he'll be able to do it, not if the crowd catches him first."

So, thought Davies, he would probably have to witness a lynching after all. The prospect was most unhappy.

"Does any one know where this negro lived?" he asked heavily, a growing sense of his duty weighing upon him.

"Oh, right down here a little way," replied the farmer. "Jeff Ingalls was his name. We all know him around here. He worked for one and another of the farmers hereabouts, and don't appear to have had such a bad record, either, except for drinkin' a little now

44

and then. Miss Ada recognized him, all right. You follow this road to the next crossing and turn to the right. It's a little log house that sets back off the road—something like that one you see down the lane there, only it's got lots o' chips scattered about."

Davies decided to go there first, but changed his mind. It was growing late, and he thought he had better return to the village. Perhaps by now developments in connection with the sheriff or the posse were to be learned.

Accordingly, he rode back and put the horse in the hands of its owner, hoping that all had been concluded and that he might learn of it here. At the principal corner much the same company was still present, arguing, fomenting, gesticulating. They seemed parts of different companies that earlier in the day had been out searching. He wondered what they had been doing since, and then decided to ingratiate himself by telling them he had just come from the Whitakers and what he had learned there of the present condition of the girl and the movements of the sheriff.

Just then a young farmer came galloping up. He was coatless, hatless, breathless.

"They've got him!" he shouted excitedly. "They've got him!"

A chorus of "whos," "wheres" and "whens" greeted this information as the crowd gathered about the rider.

"Why, Mathews caught him up here at his own house!" exclaimed the latter, pulling out a handkerchief and wiping his face. "He must 'a' gone back there for something. Mathews's takin' him over to Clayton, so they think, but they don't project he'll ever get there. They're after him now, but Mathews says he'll shoot the first man that tries to take him away."

"Which way'd he go?" exclaimed the men in chorus, stirring as if to make an attack.

"'Cross Sellers' Lane," said the rider. "The boys think he's goin' by way of Baldwin."

"Whoopee!" yelled one of the listeners. "We'll get him away from him, all right! Are you goin', Sam?"

"You bet!" said the latter. "Wait'll I get my horse!"

"Lord!" thought Davies. "To think of being (perforce) one of a lynching party—a hired spectator!"

He delayed no longer, however, but hastened to secure his horse again. He saw that the crowd would be off in a minute to catch up with the sheriff. There would be information in that quarter, drama very likely.

"What's doin'?" inquired the liveryman as he noted Davies' excited appearance.

"They're after him," replied the latter nervously. "The sheriff's caught him. They're going now to try to take him away from him, or that's what they say. The sheriff is taking him over to Clayton, by way of Baldwin. I want to get over there if I can. Give me the horse again, and I'll give you a couple of dollars more."

The liveryman led the horse out, but not without many provisionary cautions as to the care which was to be taken of him, the damages which would ensue if it were not. He was not to be ridden beyond midnight. If one were wanted for longer than that Davies must get him elsewhere or come and get another, to all of which Davies promptly agreed. He then mounted and rode away.

When he reached the corner again several of the men who had gone for their horses were already there, ready to start. The young man who had brought the news had long since dashed off to other parts.

Davies waited to see which road this new company would take. Then through as pleasant a country as one would wish to see, up hill and down dale, with charming vistas breaking upon the gaze at every turn, he did the riding of his life. So disturbed was the reporter by the grim turn things had taken that he scarcely noted the beauty that was stretched before him, save to note that it was so. Death! Death! The proximity of involuntary and enforced death was what weighed upon him now.

In about an hour the company had come in sight of the sheriff, who, with two other men, was driving a wagon he had borrowed along a lone country road. The latter was sitting at the back, a revolver in each hand, his face toward the group, which at sight of him trailed after at a respectful distance. Excited as every one was, there was no disposition, for the time being at least, to halt the progress of the law.

"He's in that wagon," Davies heard one man say. "Don't you see they've got him in there tied and laid down?"

Davies looked.

"That's right," said another. "I see him now."

"What we ought to do," said a third, who was riding near the front, "is to take him away and hang him. That's just what he deserves, and that's what he'll get before we're through to-day."

"Yes!" called the sheriff, who seemed to have heard this. "You're not goin' to do any hangin' this day, so you just might as well go on back." He did not appear to be much troubled by the appearance of the crowd.

"Where's old man Whitaker?" asked one of the men who seemed to feel that they needed a leader. "He'd get him quick enough!"

"He's with the other crowd, down below Olney," was the reply.

46

"Somebody ought to go an' tell him."

"Clark's gone," assured another, who hoped for the worst.

Davies rode among the company a prey to mingled and singular feelings. He was very much excited and yet depressed by the character of the crowd which, in so far as he could see, was largely impelled to its jaunt by curiosity and yet also able under sufficient motivation on the part of some one—any one, really—to kill too. There was not so much daring as a desire to gain daring from others, an unconscious wish or impulse to organize the total strength or will of those present into one strength or one will, sufficient to overcome the sheriff and inflict death upon his charge. It was strange—almost intellectually incomprehensible—and yet so it was. The men were plainly afraid of the determined sheriff. They thought something ought to be done, but they did not feel like getting into trouble.

Mathews, a large solemn, sage, brown man in worn clothes and a faded brown hat, contemplated the recent addition to his trailers with apparent indifference. Seemingly he was determined to protect his man and avoid mob justice, come what may. A mob should not have him if he had to shoot, and if he shot it would be to kill. Finally, since the company thus added to did not dash upon him, he seemingly decided to scare them off. Apparently he thought he could do this, since they trailed like calves.

"Stop a minute!" he called to his driver.

The latter pulled up. So did the crowd behind. Then the sheriff stood over the prostrate body of the negro, who lay in the jolting wagon beneath him, and called back:

"Go 'way from here, you people! Go on, now! I won't have you follerin' after me!"

"Give us the nigger!" yelled one in a half-bantering, half-derisive tone of voice.

"I'll give ye just two minutes to go on back out o' this road," returned the sheriff grimly, pulling out his watch and looking at it. They were about a hundred feet apart. "If you don't, I'll clear you out!"

"Give us the nigger!"

"I know you, Scott," answered Mathews, recognizing the voice. "I'll arrest every last one of ye tomorrow. Mark my word!"

The company listened in silence, the horses champing and twisting.

"We've got a right to foller," answered one of the men.

"I give ye fair warning," said the sheriff, jumping from his wagon and leveling his pistols as he approached. "When I count five I'll begin to shoot!"

47

He was a serious and stalwart figure as he approached, and the crowd fell back a little.

"Git out o' this now!" he yelled. "One—Two—"

The company turned completely and retreated, Davies among them.

"We'll foller him when he gits further on," said one of the men in explanation.

"He's got to do it," said another. "Let him git a little ways ahead."

The sheriff returned to his wagon and drove on. He seemed, however, to realize that he would not be obeyed and that safety lay in haste alone. His wagon was traveling fast. If only he could lose them or get a good start he might possibly get to Clayton and the strong county jail by morning. His followers, however, trailed him swiftly as might be, determined not to be left behind.

"He's goin' to Baldwin," said one of the company of which Davies was a member.

"Where's that?" asked Davies.

"Over west o' here, about four miles."

"Why is he going there?"

"That's where he lives. I guess he thinks if he kin git 'im over there he kin purtect 'im till he kin git more help from Clayton. I cal'late he'll try an' take 'im over yet to-night, or early in the mornin' shore."

Davies smiled at the man's English. This countryside lingo always fascinated him.

Yet the men lagged, hesitating as to what to do. They did not want to lose sight of Matthews, and yet cowardice controlled them. They did not want to get into direct altercation with the law. It wasn't their place to hang the man, although plainly they felt that he ought to be hanged, and that it would be a stirring and exciting thing if he were. Consequently they desired to watch and be on hand—to get old Whitaker and his son Jake, if they could, who were out looking elsewhere. They wanted to see what the father and brother would do.

The quandary was solved by one of the men, who suggested that they could get to Baldwin by going back to Pleasant Valley and taking the Sand River pike, and that in the meantime they might come upon Whitaker and his son en route, or leave word at his house. It was a shorter cut than this the sheriff was taking, although he would get there first now. Possibly they could beat him at least to Clayton, if he attempted to go on. The Clayton road was back via Pleasant Valley, or near it, and easily intercepted. Therefore, while one or two remained to trail the sheriff and give the alarm in case he did attempt to go on to Clayton, the rest, followed by Davies, set off at a gallop to Pleasant Valley. It was nearly dusk now when they arrived and stopped at the corner store—supper time. The fires of evening meals were marked by upcurling smoke from chimneys. Here, somehow, the zest to follow seemed to depart. Evidently the sheriff had worsted them for the night. Morg Whitaker, the father, had not been found; neither had Jake. Perhaps they had better eat. Two or three had already secretly fallen away.

They were telling the news of what had occurred so far to one of the two storekeepers who kept the place, when suddenly Jake Whitaker, the girl's brother, and several companions came riding up. They had been scouring the territory to the north of the town, and were hot and tired. Plainly they were unaware of the developments of which the crowd had been a part.

"The sheriff's got 'im!" exclaimed one of the company, with that blatancy which always accompanies the telling of great news in small rural companies. "He taken him over to Baldwin in a wagon a coupla hours ago."

"Which way did he go?" asked the son, whose hardy figure, worn, hand-me-down clothes and rakish hat showed up picturesquely as he turned here and there on his horse.

"'Cross Seller' Lane. You won't git 'em that-a-way, though, Jake. He's already over there by now. Better take the short cut."

A babble of voices now made the scene more interesting. One told how the negro had been caught, another that the sheriff was defiant, a third that men were still tracking him or over there watching, until all the chief points of the drama had been spoken if not heard.

Instantly suppers were forgotten. The whole customary order of the evening was overturned once more. The company started off on another excited jaunt, up hill and down dale, through the lovely country that lay between Baldwin and Pleasant Valley.

By now Davies was very weary of this procedure and of his saddle. He wondered when, if ever, this story was to culminate, let alone he write it. Tragic as it might prove, he could not nevertheless spend an indefinite period trailing a possibility, and yet, so great was the potentiality of the present situation, he dared not leave. By contrast with the horror impending, as he now noted, the night was so beautiful that it was all but poignant. Stars were already beginning to shine. Distant lamps twinkled like yellow eyes from the cottages in the valleys and on the hillsides. The air was fresh and tender. Some peafowls were crying afar off, and the east promised a golden moon.

Silently the assembled company trotted on—no more than a

score in all. In the dusk, and with Jake ahead, it seemed too grim a pilgrimage for joking. Young Jake, riding silently toward the front, looked as if tragedy were all he craved. His friends seemed considerately to withdraw from him, seeing that he was the aggrieved.

After an hour's riding Baldwin came into view, lying in a sheltering cup of low hills. Already its lights were twinkling softly and there was still an air of honest firesides and cheery suppers about it which appealed to Davies in his hungry state. Still, he had no thought now of anything save this pursuit.

Once in the village, the company was greeted by calls of recognition. Everybody seemed to know what they had come for. The sheriff and his charge were still there, so a dozen citizens volunteered. The local storekeepers and loungers followed the cavalcade up the street to the sheriff's house, for the riders had now fallen into a solemn walk.

"You won't get him though, boys," said one whom Davies later learned was Seavey, the village postmaster and telegraph operator, a rather youthful person of between twenty-five and thirty, as they passed his door. "He's got two deputies in there with him, or did have, and they say he's going to take him over to Clayton."

At the first street corner they were joined by the several men who had followed the sheriff.

"He tried to give us the slip," they volunteered excitedly, "but he's got the nigger in the house, there, down in the cellar. The deputies ain't with him. They've gone somewhere for help—Clayton, maybe."

"How do you know?"

"We saw 'em go out that back way. We think we did, anyhow."

A hundred feet from the sheriff's little white cottage, which backed up against a sloping field, the men parleyed. Then Jake announced that he proposed to go boldly up to the sheriff's door and demand the negro.

"If he don't turn him out I'll break in the door an' take him!" he said.

"That's right! We'll stand by you, Whitaker," commented several.

By now the throng of unmounted natives had gathered. The whole village was up and about, its one street alive and running with people. Heads appeared at doors and windows. Riders pranced up and down, hallooing. A few revolver shots were heard. Presently the mob gathered even closer to the sheriff's gate, and Jake stepped forward as leader. Instead, however, of going boldly up to the door

50

as at first it appeared he would, he stopped at the gate, calling to the sheriff.

"Hello, Mathews!"

"Eh, eh, eh!" bellowed the crowd.

The call was repeated. Still no answer. Apparently to the sheriff delay appeared to be his one best weapon.

Their coming, however, was not as unexpected as some might have thought. The figure of the sheriff was plainly to be seen close to one of the front windows. He appeared to be holding a double-barreled shotgun. The negro, as it developed later, was cowering and chattering in the darkest corner of the cellar, hearkening no doubt to the voices and firing of the revolvers outside.

Suddenly, and just as Jake was about to go forward, the front door of the house flew open, and in the glow of a single lamp inside appeared first the double-barreled end of the gun, followed immediately by the form of Mathews, who held the weapon poised ready for a quick throw to the shoulder. All except Jake fell back.

"Mr. Mathews," he called deliberately, "we want that nigger!"

"Well, you can't git 'im!" replied the sheriff. "He's not here."

"Then what you got that gun fer?" yelled a voice.

Mathews made no answer.

"Better give him up, Mathews," called another, who was safe in the crowd, "or we'll come in an' take him!"

"No you won't," said the sheriff defiantly. "I said the man wasn't here. I say it ag'in. You couldn't have him if he was, an' you can't come in my house! Now if you people don't want trouble you'd better go on away."

"He's down in the cellar!" yelled another.

"Why don't you let us see?" asked another.

Mathews waved his gun slightly.

"You'd better go away from here now," cautioned the sheriff. "I'm tellin' ye! I'll have warrants out for the lot o' ye, if ye don't mind!"

The crowd continued to simmer and stew, while Jake stood as before. He was very pale and tense, but lacked initiative.

"He won't shoot," called some one at the back of the crowd. "Why don't you go in, Jake, an' git him?"

"Sure! Rush in. That's it!" observed a second.

"He won't, eh?" replied the sheriff softly. Then he added in a lower tone, "The first man that comes inside that gate takes the consequences."

No one ventured inside the gate; many even fell back. It seemed as if the planned assault had come to nothing.

"Why not go around the back way?" called some one else.

"Try it!" replied the sheriff. "See what you find on that side! I told you you couldn't come inside. You'd better go away from here now before ye git into trouble," he repeated. "You can't come in, an' it'll only mean bloodshed."

There was more chattering and jesting while the sheriff stood on guard. He, however, said no more. Nor did he allow the banter, turmoil and lust for tragedy to disturb him. Only, he kept his eye on Jake, on whose movements the crowd seemed to hang.

Time passed, and still nothing was done. The truth was that young Jake, put to the test, was not sufficiently courageous himself, for all his daring, and felt the weakness of the crowd behind him. To all intents and purposes he was alone, for he did not inspire confidence. He finally fell back a little, observing, "I'll git 'im before mornin', all right," and now the crowd itself began to disperse, returning to its stores and homes or standing about the postoffice and the one village drugstore. Finally, Davies smiled and came away. He was sure he had the story of a defeated mob. The sheriff was to be his great hero. He proposed to interview him later. For the present, he meant to seek out Seavey, the telegraph operator, and arrange to file a message, then see if something to eat was not to be had somewhere.

After a time he found the operator and told him what he wanted—to write and file a story as he wrote it. The latter indicated a table in the little postoffice and telegraph station which he could use. He became very much interested in the reporter when he learned he was from the Times, and when Davies asked where he could get something to eat said he would run across the street and tell the proprietor of the only boarding house to fix him something which he could consume as he wrote. He appeared to be interested in how a newspaper man would go about telling a story of this kind over a wire.

"You start your story," he said, "and I'll come back and see if I can get the Times on the wire."

Davies sat down and began his account. He was intent on describing things to date, the uncertainty and turmoil, the apparent victory of the sheriff. Plainly the courage of the latter had won, and it was all so picturesque. "A foiled lynching," he began, and as he wrote the obliging postmaster, who had by now returned, picked up the pages and carefully deciphered them for himself.

"That's all right. I'll see if I can get the Times now," he commented.

"Very obliging postmaster," thought Davies as he wrote, but he had so often encountered pleasant and obliging people on his rounds that he soon dropped that thought.

The food was brought, and still Davies wrote on, munching as he did so. In a little while the Times answered an often-repeated call.

"Davies at Baldwin," ticked the postmaster, "get ready for quite a story!"

"Let 'er go!" answered the operator at the Times, who had been expecting this dispatch.

As the events of the day formulated themselves in his mind, Davies wrote and turned over page after page. Between whiles he looked out through the small window before him where afar off he could see a lonely light twinkling against a hillside. Not infrequently he stopped his work to see if anything new was happening, whether the situation was in any danger of changing, but apparently it was not. He then proposed to remain until all possibility of a tragedy, this night anyhow, was eliminated. The operator also wandered about, waiting for an accumulation of pages upon which he could work but making sure to keep up with the writer. The two became quite friendly.

Finally, his dispatch nearly finished, he asked the postmaster to caution the night editor at K— to the effect, that if anything more happened before one in the morning he would file it, but not to expect anything more as nothing might happen. The reply came that he was to remain and await developments. Then he and the postmaster sat down to talk.

About eleven o'clock, when both had about convinced themselves that all was over for this night anyhow, and the lights in the village had all but vanished, a stillness of the purest, summery-est, country-est quality having settled down, a faint beating of hoofs, which seemed to suggest the approach of a large cavalcade, could be heard out on the Sand River pike as Davies by now had come to learn it was, back or northwest of the postoffice. At the sound the postmaster got up, as did Davies, both stepping outside and listening. On it came, and as the volume increased, the former said, "Might be help for the sheriff, but I doubt it. I telegraphed Clayton six times to-day. They wouldn't come that way, though. It's the wrong road." Now, thought Davies nervously, after all there might be something to add to his story, and he had so wished that it was all over! Lynchings, as he now felt, were horrible things. He wished people wouldn't do such things—take the law, which now more than ever he respected, into their own hands. It was too brutal, cruel. That negro cowering there in the dark probably, and the sheriff all taut and tense, worrying over his charge and his duty, were not happy things to contemplate in the face of such a thing as this. It was true that the crime which had been committed was dreadful,

53

but still why couldn't people allow the law to take its course? It was so much better. The law was powerful enough to deal with cases of this kind.

"They're comin' back, all right," said the postmaster solemnly, as he and Davies stared in the direction of the sound which grew louder from moment to moment.

"It's not any help from Clayton, I'm afraid."

"By George, I think you're right!" answered the reporter, something telling him that more trouble was at hand. "Here they come!"

As he spoke there was a clattering of hoofs and crunching of saddle girths as a large company of men dashed up the road and turned into the narrow street of the village, the figure of Jake Whitaker and an older bearded man in a wide black hat riding side by side in front.

"There's Jake," said the postmaster, "and that's his father riding beside him there. The old man's a terror when he gets his dander up. Sompin's sure to happen now."

Davies realized that in his absence writing a new turn had been given to things. Evidently the son had returned to Pleasant Valley and organized a new posse or gone out to meet his father.

Instantly the place was astir again. Lights appeared in doorways and windows, and both were thrown open. People were leaning or gazing out to see what new movement was afoot. Davies noted at once that there was none of the brash enthusiasm about this company such as had characterized the previous descent. There was grimness everywhere, and he now began to feel that this was the beginning of the end. After the cavalcade had passed down the street toward the sheriff's house, which was quite dark now, he ran after it, arriving a few moments after the former which was already in part dismounted. The townspeople followed. The sheriff, as it now developed, had not relaxed any of his vigilance, however; he was not sleeping, and as the crowd reappeared the light inside reappeared.

By the light of the moon, which was almost overhead, Davies was able to make out several of his companions of the afternoon, and Jake, the son. There were many more, though, now, whom he did not know, and foremost among them this old man.

The latter was strong, iron-gray, and wore a full beard. He looked very much like a blacksmith.

"Keep your eye on the old man," advised the postmaster, who had by now come up and was standing by.

While they were still looking, the old man went boldly forward

54

to the little front porch of the house and knocked at the door. Some one lifted a curtain at the window and peeped out.

"Hello, in there!" cried the old man, knocking again.

"What do you want?" asked a voice.

"I want that nigger!"

"Well, you can't have him! I've told you people that once."

"Bring him out or I'll break down the door!" said the old man.

"If you do it's at your own risk. I know you, Whitaker, an' you know me. I'll give ye two minutes to get off that porch!"

"I want that nigger, I tell ye!"

"If ye don't git off that porch I'll fire through the door," said the voice solemnly. "One—Two—"

The old man backed cautiously away.

"Come out, Mathews!" yelled the crowd. "You've got to give him up this time. We ain't goin' back without him."

Slowly the door opened, as if the individual within were very well satisfied as to his power to handle the mob. He had done it once before this night, why not again? It revealed his tall form, armed with his shotgun. He looked around very stolidly, and then addressed the old man as one would a friend.

"Ye can't have him, Morgan," he said. "It's ag'in' the law. You know that as well as I do."

"Law or no law," said the old man, "I want that nigger!"

"I tell you I can't let you have him, Morgan. It's ag'in' the law. You know you oughtn't to be comin' around here at this time o' night actin' so."

"Well, I'll take him then," said the old man, making a move.

"Stand back!" shouted the sheriff, leveling his gun on the instant. "I'll blow ye into kingdom come, sure as hell!"

A noticeable movement on the part of the crowd ceased. The sheriff lowered his weapon as if he thought the danger were once more over.

"You-all ought to be ashamed of yerselves," he went on, his voice sinking to a gentle neighborly reproof, "tryin' to upset the law this way."

"The nigger didn't upset no law, did he?" asked one derisively.

"Well, the law's goin' to take care of the nigger now," Mathews made answer.

"Give us that scoundrel, Mathews; you'd better do it," said the old man. "It'll save a heap o' trouble."

"I'll not argue with ye, Morgan. I said ye couldn't have him, an' ye can't. If ye want bloodshed, all right. But don't blame me. I'll kill the first man that tries to make a move this way."

He shifted his gun handily and waited. The crowd stood outside his little fence murmuring.

Presently the old man retired and spoke to several others. There was more murmuring, and then he came back to the dead line.

"We don't want to cause trouble, Mathews," he began explanatively, moving his hand oratorically, "but we think you ought to see that it won't do any good to stand out. We think that—"

Davies and the postmaster were watching young Jake, whose peculiar attitude attracted their attention. The latter was standing poised at the edge of the crowd, evidently seeking to remain unobserved. His eyes were on the sheriff, who was hearkening to the old man. Suddenly, as the father talked and when the sheriff seemed for a moment mollified and unsuspecting, he made a quick run for the porch. There was an intense movement all along the line as the life and death of the deed became apparent. Quickly the sheriff drew his gun to his shoulder. Both triggers were pressed at the same time, and the gun spoke, but not before Jake was in and under him. The latter had been in sufficient time to knock the gun barrel upward and fall upon his man. Both shots blazed harmlessly over the heads of the crowd in red puffs, and then followed a general onslaught. Men leaped the fence by tens and crowded upon the little cottage. They swarmed about every side of the house and crowded upon the porch, where four men were scuffling with the sheriff. The latter soon gave up, vowing vengeance and the law. Torches were brought, and a rope. A wagon drove up and was backed into the yard. Then began the calls for the negro.

As Davies contemplated all this he could not help thinking of the negro who during all this turmoil must have been crouching in his corner in the cellar, trembling for his fate. Now indeed he must realize that his end was near. He could not have dozed or lost consciousness during the intervening hours, but must have been cowering there, wondering and praying. All the while he must have been terrified lest the sheriff might not get him away in time. Now, at the sound of horses' feet and the new murmurs of contention, how must his body quake and his teeth chatter!

"I'd hate to be that nigger," commented the postmaster grimly, "but you can't do anything with 'em. The county oughta sent help."

"It's horrible, horrible!" was all Davies could say.

He moved closer to the house, with the crowd, eager to observe every detail of the procedure. Now it was that a number of the men, as eager in their search as bloodhounds, appeared at a low cellar entryway at the side of the house carrying a rope. Others

56

followed with torches. Headed by father and son they began to descend into the dark hole. With impressive daring, Davies, who was by no means sure that he would be allowed but who was also determined if possible to see, followed.

Suddenly, in the farthest corner, he espied Ingalls. The latter in his fear and agony had worked himself into a crouching position, as if he were about to spring. His nails were apparently forced into the earth. His eyes were rolling, his mouth foaming.

"Oh, my Lawd, boss," he moaned, gazing almost as one blind, at the lights, "oh, my Lawd, boss, don't kill me! I won't do it no mo'. I didn't go to do it. I didn't mean to dis time. I was just drunk, boss. Oh, my Lawd! My Lawd!" His teeth chattered the while his mouth seemed to gape open. He was no longer sane really, but kept repeating monotonously, "Oh, my Lawd!"

"Here he is, boys! Pull him out," cried the father.

The negro now gave one yell of terror and collapsed, falling prone. He quite bounded as he did so, coming down with a dead chug on the earthen floor. Reason had forsaken him. He was by now a groveling, foaming brute. The last gleam of intelligence was that which notified him of the set eyes of his pursuers.

Davies, who by now had retreated to the grass outside before this sight, was standing but ten feet back when they began to reappear after seizing and binding him. Although shaken to the roots of his being, he still had all the cool observing powers of the trained and relentless reporter. Even now he noted the color values of the scene, the red, smoky heads of the torches, the disheveled appearance of the men, the scuffling and pulling. Then all at once he clapped his hands over his mouth, almost unconscious of what he was doing.

"Oh, my God!" he whispered, his voice losing power.

The sickening sight was that of the negro, foaming at the mouth, bloodshot as to his eyes, his hands working convulsively, being dragged up the cellar steps feet foremost. They had tied a rope about his waist and feet, and so had hauled him out, leaving his head to hang and drag. The black face was distorted beyond all human semblance.

"Oh, my God!" said Davies again, biting his fingers unconsciously.

The crowd gathered about now more closely than ever, more horror-stricken than gleeful at their own work. None apparently had either the courage or the charity to gainsay what was being done. With a kind of mechanical deftness now the negro was rudely lifted and like a sack of wheat thrown into the wagon. Father and son now mounted in front to drive and the crowd took to their horses, content to clatter, a silent cavalcade, behind. As Davies afterwards concluded, they were not so much hardened lynchers perhaps as curious spectators, the majority of them, eager for any variation— any excuse for one—to the dreary commonplaces of their existences. The task to most—all indeed—was entirely new. Wide-eyed and nerve-racked, Davies ran for his own horse and mounting followed. He was so excited he scarcely knew what he was doing.

Slowly the silent company now took its way up the Sand River pike whence it had come. The moon was still high, pouring down a wash of silvery light. As Davies rode he wondered how he was to complete his telegram, but decided that he could not. When this was over there would be no time. How long would it be before they would really hang him? And would they? The whole procedure seemed so unreal, so barbaric that he could scarcely believe it—that he was a part of it. Still they rode on.

"Are they really going to hang him?" he asked of one who rode beside him, a total stranger who seemed however not to resent his presence.

"That's what they got 'im fer," answered the stranger.

And think, he thought to himself, to-morrow night he would be resting in his own good bed back in K—!

Davies dropped behind again and into silence and tried to recover his nerves. He could scarcely realize that he, ordinarily accustomed to the routine of the city, its humdrum and at least outward social regularity, was a part of this. The night was so soft, the air so refreshing. The shadowy trees were stirring with a cool night wind. Why should any one have to die this way? Why couldn't the people of Baldwin or elsewhere have bestirred themselves on the side of the law before this, just let it take its course? Both father and son now seemed brutal, the injury to the daughter and sister not so vital as all this. Still, also, custom seemed to require death in this way for this. It was like some axiomatic, mathematic law—hard, but custom. The silent company, an articulated, mechanical and therefore terrible thing, moved on. It also was axiomatic, mathematic. After a time he drew near to the wagon and looked at the negro again.

The latter, as Davies was glad to note, seemed still out of his sense. He was breathing heavily and groaning, but probably not with any conscious pain. His eyes were fixed and staring, his face and hands bleeding as if they had been scratched or trampled upon. He was crumpled limply.

But Davies could stand it no longer now. He fell back, sick at heart, content to see no more. It seemed a ghastly, murderous thing to do. Still the company moved on and he followed, past fields lit white by the moon, under dark, silent groups of trees, through which the moonlight fell in patches, up low hills and down into valleys, until at last a little stream came into view, the same little stream, as it proved, which he had seen earlier to-day and for a bridge over which they were heading. Here it ran now, sparkling like electricity in the night. After a time the road drew closer to the water and then crossed directly over the bridge, which could be seen a little way ahead.

Up to this the company now rode and then halted. The wagon was driven up on the bridge, and father and son got out. All the riders, including Davies, dismounted, and a full score of them gathered about the wagon from which the negro was lifted, quite as one might a bag. Fortunately, as Davies now told himself, he was still unconscious, an accidental mercy. Nevertheless he decided now that he could not witness the end, and went down by the waterside slightly above the bridge. He was not, after all, the utterly relentless reporter. From where he stood, however, he could see long beams of iron projecting out over the water, where the bridge was braced, and some of the men fastening a rope to a beam, and then he could see that they were fixing the other end around the negro's neck.

Finally the curious company stood back, and he turned his face away.

"Have you anything to say?" a voice demanded.

There was no answer. The negro was probably lolling and groaning, quite as unconscious as he was before.

Then came the concerted action of a dozen men, the lifting of the black mass into the air, and then Davies saw the limp form plunge down and pull up with a creaking sound of rope. In the weak moonlight it seemed as if the body were struggling, but he could not tell. He watched, wide-mouthed and silent, and then the body ceased moving. Then after a time he heard the company making ready to depart, and finally it did so, leaving him quite indifferently to himself and his thoughts. Only the black mass swaying in the pale light over the glimmering water seemed human and alive, his sole companion.

He sat down upon the bank and gazed in silence. Now the horror was gone. The suffering was ended. He was no longer afraid. Everything was summery and beautiful. The whole cavalcade had disappeared; the moon finally sank. His horse, tethered to a sapling beyond the bridge, waited patiently. Still he sat. He might now have hurried back to the small postoffice in Baldwin and attempted to file additional details of this story, providing he could find Seavey, but it would have done no good. It was quite too late, and anyhow what did it matter? No other reporter had been present, and he could write a fuller, sadder, more colorful story on the morrow. He wondered idly what had become of Seavey? Why had he not followed? Life seemed so sad, so strange, so mysterious, so inexplicable.

As he still sat there the light of morning broke, a tender lavender and gray in the east. Then came the roseate hues of dawn, all the wondrous coloring of celestial halls, to which the waters of the stream responded. The white pebbles shone pinkily at the bottom, the grass and sedges first black now gleamed a translucent green. Still the body hung there black and limp against the sky, and now a light breeze sprang up and stirred it visibly. At last he arose, mounted his horse and made his way back to Pleasant Valley, too full of the late tragedy to be much interested in anything else. Rousing his liveryman, he adjusted his difficulties with him by telling him the whole story, assuring him of his horse's care and handing him a five-dollar bill. Then he left, to walk and think again.

Since there was no train before noon and his duty plainly called him to a portion of another day's work here, he decided to make a day of it, idling about and getting additional details as to what further might be done. Who would cut the body down? What about arresting the lynchers—the father and son, for instance? What about the sheriff now? Would he act as he threatened? If he telegraphed the main fact of the lynching his city editor would not mind, he knew, his coming late, and the day here was so beautiful. He proceeded to talk with citizens and officials, rode out to the injured girl's home, rode to Baldwin to see the sheriff. There was a singular silence and placidity in that corner. The latter assured him that he knew nearly all of those who had taken part, and proposed to swear out warrants for them, but just the same Davies noted that he took his defeat as he did his danger, philosophically. There was no real activity in that corner later. He wished to remain a popular sheriff, no doubt.

It was sundown again before he remembered that he had not discovered whether the body had been removed. Nor had he heard why the negro came back, nor exactly how he was caught. A nine o'clock evening train to the city giving him a little more time for investigation, he decided to avail himself of it. The negro's cabin was two miles out along a pine-shaded road, but so pleasant was the evening that he decided to walk. En route, the last rays of the sinking sun stretched long shadows of budding trees across his path. It was not long before he came upon the cabin, a one-story affair set well back from the road and surrounded with a few scattered trees. By now it was quite dark. The ground between the cabin and the road was open, and strewn with the chips of a woodpile. The roof was sagged, and the windows patched in places, but for all that it had the glow of a home. Through the front door, which stood open, the blaze of a wood-fire might be seen, its yellow light filling the interior with a golden glow.

Hesitating before the door, Davies finally knocked. Receiving no answer he looked in on the battered cane chairs and aged furniture with considerable interest. It was a typical negro cabin, poor beyond the need of description. After a time a door in the rear of the room opened and a little negro girl entered carrying a battered tin lamp without any chimney. She had not heard his knock and started perceptibly at the sight of his figure in the doorway. Then she raised her smoking lamp above her head in order to see better, and approached.

There was something ridiculous about her unformed figure and loose gingham dress, as he noted. Her feet and hands were so large. Her black head was strongly emphasized by little pigtails of hair done up in white twine, which stood out all over her head. Her dark skin was made apparently more so by contrast with her white teeth and the whites of her eyes.

Davies looked at her for a moment but little moved now by the oddity which ordinarily would have amused him, and asked, "Is this where Ingalls lived?"

The girl nodded her head. She was exceedingly subdued, and looked as if she might have been crying.

"Has the body been brought here?"

"Yes, suh," she answered, with a soft negro accent.

"When did they bring it?"

"Dis moanin'."

"Are you his sister?"

"Yes, suh."

"Well, can you tell me how they caught him? When did he come back, and what for?" He was feeling slightly ashamed to intrude thus.

"In de afternoon, about two."

"And what for?" repeated Davies.

"To see us," answered the girl. "To see my motha'."

"Well, did he want anything? He didn't come just to see her, did he?"

"Yes, suh," said the girl, "he come to say good-by. We doan know when dey caught him." Her voice wavered.

"Well, didn't he know he might get caught?" asked Davies sympathetically, seeing that the girl was so moved.

"Yes, suh, I think he did."

She still stood very quietly holding the poor battered lamp up, and looking down.

"Well, what did he have to say?" asked Davies.

"He didn' have nothin' much to say, suh. He said he wanted to see motha'. He was a-goin' away."

The girl seemed to regard Davies as an official of some sort, and he knew it.

"Can I have a look at the body?" he asked.

The girl did not answer, but started as if to lead the way.

"When is the funeral?" he asked.

"Tomorra'."

The girl then led him through several bare sheds of rooms strung in a row to the furthermost one of the line. This last seemed a sort of storage shed for odds and ends. It had several windows, but they were quite bare of glass and open to the moonlight save for a few wooden boards nailed across from the outside. Davies had been wondering all the while where the body was and at the lonely and forsaken air of the place. No one but this little pig-tailed girl seemed about. If they had any colored neighbors they were probably afraid to be seen here.

Now, as he stepped into this cool, dark, exposed outer room, the desolation seemed quite complete. It was very bare, a mere shed or wash-room. There was the body in the middle of the room, stretched upon an ironing board which rested on a box and a chair, and covered with a white sheet. All the corners of the room were quite dark. Only its middle was brightened by splotches of silvery light.

Davies came forward, the while the girl left him, still carrying her lamp. Evidently she thought the moon lighted up the room sufficiently, and she did not feel equal to remaining. He lifted the sheet quite boldly, for he could see well enough, and looked at the still, black form. The face was extremely distorted, even in death, and he could see where the rope had tightened. A bar of cool moonlight lay just across the face and breast He was still looking, thinking soon to restore the covering, when a sound, half sigh, half groan, reached his ears.

At it he started as if a ghost had made it. It was so eerie and unexpected in this dark place. His muscles tightened. Instantly his heart went hammering like mad. His first impression was that it must have come from the dead.

"Oo-o-ohh!" came the sound again, this time whimpering, as if some one were crying.

Instantly he turned, for now it seemed to come from a corner of the room, the extreme corner to his right, back of him. Greatly disturbed, he approached, and then as his eyes strained he seemed to catch the shadow of something, the figure of a woman, perhaps, crouching against the walls, huddled up, dark, almost indistinguishable.

"Oh, oh, oh!" the sound now repeated itself, even more plaintively than before.

Davies began to understand. He approached slowly, then more swiftly desired to withdraw, for he was in the presence of an old black mammy, doubled up and weeping. She was in the very niche of the two walls, her head sunk on her knees, her body quite still. "Oh, oh, oh!" she repeated, as he stood there near her.

Davies drew silently back. Before such grief his intrusion seemed cold and unwarranted. The guiltlessness of the mother—her love—how could one balance that against the other? The sensation of tears came to his eyes. He instantly covered the dead and withdrew.

Out in the moonlight he struck a brisk pace, but soon stopped and looked back. The whole dreary cabin, with its one golden eye, the door, seemed such a pitiful thing. The weeping mammy, alone in her corner—and he had come back to say "Good-by!" Davies swelled with feeling. The night, the tragedy, the grief, he saw it all. But also with the cruel instinct of the budding artist that he already was, he was beginning to meditate on the character of story it would make— the color, the pathos. The knowledge now that it was not always exact justice that was meted out to all and that it was not so much the business of the writer to indict as to interpret was borne in on him with distinctness by the cruel sorrow of the mother, whose blame, if any, was infinitesimal.

"I'll get it all in!" he exclaimed feelingly, if triumphantly at last. "I'll get it all in!"

THE LOST PHŒBE

They lived together in a part of the country which was not so prosperous as it had once been, about three miles from one of those small towns that, instead of increasing in population, is steadily decreasing. The territory was not very thickly settled; perhaps a house every other mile or so, with large areas of corn- and wheat-land and fallow fields that at odd seasons had been sown to timothy and clover. Their particular house was part log and part frame, the log portion being the old original home of Henry's grandfather. The new portion, of now rain-beaten, time-worn slabs, through which the wind squeaked in the chinks at times, and which several overshadowing elms and a butternut-tree made picturesque and reminiscently pathetic, but a little damp, was erected by Henry when he was twenty-one and just married.

That was forty-eight years before. The furniture inside, like the house outside, was old and mildewy and reminiscent of an earlier day. You have seen the what-not of cherry wood, perhaps, with spiral legs and fluted top. It was there. The old-fashioned four poster bed, with its ball-like protuberances and deep curving incisions, was there also, a sadly alienated descendant of an early Jacobean ancestor. The bureau of cherry was also high and wide and solidly built, but faded-looking, and with a musty odor. The rag carpet that underlay all these sturdy examples of enduring furniture was a weak, faded, lead-and-pink-colored affair woven by Phœbe Ann's own hands, when she was fifteen years younger than she was when she died. The creaky wooden loom on which it had been done now stood like a dusty, bony skeleton, along with a broken rocking-chair, a worm-eaten clothes-press—Heaven knows how old—a lime-stained bench that had once been used to keep flowers on outside the door, and other decrepit factors of household utility, in an east room that was a lean-to against this so-called main portion. All sorts of other broken-down furniture were about this place; an antiquated clothes-horse, cracked in two of its ribs; a broken mirror in an old cherry frame, which had fallen from a nail and cracked itself three days before their youngest son, Jerry, died; an extension hat-rack, which once had had porcelain knobs on the ends of its pegs; and a sewing- machine, long since outdone in its clumsy mechanism by rivals of a newer generation.

The orchard to the east of the house was full of gnarled old apple-trees, worm-eaten as to trunks and branches, and fully ornamented with green and white lichens, so that it had a sad, greenish-white, silvery effect in moonlight. The low outhouses, which had once housed chickens, a horse or two, a cow, and several pigs, were covered with patches of moss as to their roof, and the sides had been free of paint for so long that they were blackish gray as to color, and a little spongy. The picket-fence in front, with its gate squeaky and askew, and the side fences of the stake-and-rider type were in an equally run-down condition. As a matter of fact, they had aged synchronously with the persons who lived here, old Henry Reifsneider and his wife Phœbe Ann.

They had lived here, these two, ever since their marriage, forty-eight years before, and Henry had lived here before that from his childhood up. His father and mother, well along in years when he was a boy, had invited him to bring his wife here when he had first fallen in love and decided to marry; and he had done so. His father and mother were the companions of himself and his wife for ten years after they were married, when both died; and then Henry and Phœbe were left with their five children growing lustily apace. But all sorts of things had happened since then. Of the seven children, all told, that had been born to them, three had died; one girl had gone to Kansas; one boy had gone to Sioux Falls, never even to be heard of after; another boy had gone to Washington; and the last girl lived five counties away in the same State, but was so burdened with cares of her own that she rarely gave them a thought. Time and a commonplace home life that had never been attractive had weaned them thoroughly, so that, wherever they were, they gave little thought as to how it might be with their father and mother.

Old Henry Reifsneider and his wife Phœbe were a loving couple. You perhaps know how it is with simple natures that fasten themselves like lichens on the stones of circumstance and weather their days to a crumbling conclusion. The great world sounds widely, but it has no call for them. They have no soaring intellect. The orchard, the meadow, the cornfield, the pig-pen, and the chicken-lot measure the range of their human activities. When the wheat is headed it is reaped and threshed; when the corn is browned and frosted it is cut and shocked; when the timothy is in full head it is cut, and the hay-cock erected. After that comes winter, with the hauling of grain to market, the sawing and splitting of wood, the simple chores of fire-building, meal-getting, occasional repairing, and visiting. Beyond these and the changes of weather— the snows, the rains, and the fair days—there are no immediate, significant things. All the rest of life is a far-off, clamorous phantasmagoria, flickering like Northern lights in the night, and sounding as faintly as cow-bells tinkling in the distance.

Old Henry and his wife Phœbe were as fond of each other as it is possible for two old people to be who have nothing else in this life to be fond of. He was a thin old man, seventy when she died, a queer, crotchety person with coarse gray-black hair and beard, quite straggly and unkempt. He looked at you out of dull, fishy, watery eyes that had deep-brown crow's-feet at the sides. His clothes, like the clothes of many farmers, were aged and angular and baggy, standing out at the pockets, not fitting about the neck, protuberant and worn at elbow and knee. Phœbe Ann was thin and shapeless, a very umbrella of a woman, clad in shabby black, and with a black bonnet for her best wear. As time had passed, and they had only themselves to look after, their movements had become slower and slower, their activities fewer and fewer. The annual keep of pigs had been reduced from five to one grunting porker, and the single horse which Henry now retained was a sleepy animal, not over-nourished and not very clean. The chickens, of which formerly there was a large flock, had almost disappeared, owing to ferrets, foxes, and the lack of proper care, which produces disease. The former healthy garden was now a straggling memory of itself, and the vines and flower-beds that formerly ornamented the windows and dooryard had now become choking thickets. A will had been made which divided the small tax-eaten property equally among the remaining four, so that it was really of no interest to any of them. Yet these two lived together in peace and sympathy, only that now and then old Henry would become unduly cranky, complaining almost invariably that something had been neglected or mislaid which was of no importance at all.

"Phœbe, where's my corn-knife? You ain't never minded to let my things alone no more."

"Now you hush, Henry," his wife would caution him in a cracked and squeaky voice. "If you don't, I'll leave yuh. I'll git up and walk out of here some day, and then where would y' be? Y' ain't got anybody but me to look after yuh, so yuh just behave yourself. Your corn knife's on the mantel where it's allus been unless you've gone an' put it summers else."

Old Henry, who knew his wife would never leave him in any circumstances, used to speculate at times as to what he would do if she were to die. That was the one leaving that he really feared. As he climbed on the chair at night to wind the old, long-pendulumed, double-weighted clock, or went finally to the front and the back door to see that they were safely shut in, it was a comfort to know that Phœbe was there, properly ensconced on her side of the bed, and that if he stirred restlessly in the night, she would be there to ask what he wanted.

"Now, Henry, do lie still! You're as restless as a chicken."

"Well, I can't sleep, Phœbe."

"Well, yuh needn't roll so, anyhow. Yuh kin let me sleep."

This usually reduced him to a state of somnolent ease. If she wanted a pail of water, it was a grumbling pleasure for him to get it; and if she did rise first to build the fires, he saw that the wood was cut and placed within easy reach. They divided this simple world nicely between them.

As the years had gone on, however, fewer and fewer people had called. They were well-known for a distance of as much as ten square miles as old Mr. and Mrs. Reifsneider, honest, moderately Christian, but too old to be really interesting any longer. The writing of letters had become an almost impossible burden too difficult to continue or even negotiate via others, although an occasional letter still did arrive from the daughter in Pemberton County. Now and then some old friend stopped with a pie or cake or a roasted chicken or duck, or merely to see that they were well; but even these kindly minded visits were no longer frequent.

One day in the early spring of her sixty-fourth year Mrs. Reifsneider took sick, and from a low fever passed into some indefinable ailment which, because of her age, was no longer curable. Old Henry drove to Swinnerton, the neighboring town, and procured a doctor. Some friends called, and the immediate care of her was taken off his hands. Then one chill spring night she died, and old Henry, in a fog of sorrow and uncertainty, followed her body to the nearest graveyard, an unattractive space with a few pines growing in it. Although he might have gone to the daughter in Pemberton or sent for her, it was really too much trouble and he was too weary and fixed. It was suggested to him at once by one friend and another that he come to stay with them awhile, but he did not see fit. He was so old and so fixed in his notions and so accustomed to the exact surroundings he had known all his days, that he could not think of leaving. He wanted to remain near where they had put his Phœbe; and the fact that he would have to live alone did not trouble him in the least. The living children were notified and the care of him offered if he would leave, but he would not.

"I kin make a shift for myself," he continually announced to old Dr. Morrow, who had attended his wife in this case. "I kin cook a little, and, besides, it don't take much more'n coffee an' bread in the mornin's to satisfy me. I'll get along now well enough. Yuh just let me be." And after many pleadings and proffers of advice, with supplies of coffee and bacon and baked bread duly offered and accepted, he was left to himself. For a while he sat idly outside his door brooding in the spring sun. He tried to revive his interest in farming, and to keep himself busy and free from thought by looking after the fields, which of late had been much neglected. It was a gloomy thing to come in of an evening, however, or in the afternoon and find no shadow of Phœbe where everything suggested her. By degrees he put a few of her things away. At night he sat beside his lamp and read in the papers that were left him occasionally or in a Bible that he had neglected for years, but he could get little solace from these things. Mostly he held his hand over his mouth and looked at the floor as he sat and thought of what had become of her, and how soon he himself would die. He made a great business of making his coffee in the morning and frying himself a little bacon at night; but his appetite was gone. The shell in which he had been housed so long seemed vacant, and its shadows were suggestive of immedicable griefs. So he lived quite dolefully for five long months, and then a change began.

It was one night, after he had looked after the front and the back door, wound the clock, blown out the light, and gone through all the selfsame motions that he had indulged in for years, that he went to bed not so much to sleep as to think. It was a moonlight night. The green-lichen-covered orchard just outside and to be seen from his bed where he now lay was a silvery affair, sweetly spectral. The moon shone through the east windows, throwing the pattern of the panes on the wooden floor, and making the old furniture, to which he was accustomed, stand out dimly in the room. As usual he had been thinking of Phœbe and the years when they had been young together, and of the children who had gone, and the poor shift he was making of his present days. The house was coming to be in a very bad state indeed. The bed-clothes were in disorder and not clean, for he made a wretched shift of washing. It was a terror to him. The roof leaked, causing things, some of them, to remain damp for weeks at a time, but he was getting into that brooding state where he would accept anything rather than exert himself. He preferred to pace slowly to and fro or to sit and think.

By twelve o'clock of this particular night he was asleep, however, and by two had waked again. The moon by this time had shifted to a position on the western side of the house, and it now shone in through the windows of the living-room and those of the kitchen beyond. A certain combination of furniture—a chair near a table, with his coat on it, the half-open kitchen door casting a shadow, and the position of a lamp near a paper—gave him an exact representation of Phœbe leaning over the table as he had often seen her do in life. It gave him a great start. Could it be she—or her ghost? He had scarcely ever believed in spirits; and still He looked at her fixedly in the feeble half-light, his old hair tingling oddly at the roots, and then sat up. The figure did not move. He put his thin legs out of the bed and sat looking at her, wondering if this could really be Phœbe. They had talked of ghosts often in their lifetime, of apparitions and omens; but they had never agreed that such things could be. It had never been a part of his wife's creed that she could have a spirit that could return to walk the earth. Her after-world was quite a different affair, a vague heaven, no less, from which the righteous did not trouble to return. Yet here she was now, bending over the table in her black skirt and gray shawl, her pale profile outlined against the moonlight.

"Phœbe," he called, thrilling from head to toe and putting out one bony hand, "have yuh come back?"

The figure did not stir, and he arose and walked uncertainly to the door, looking at it fixedly the while. As he drew near, however, the apparition resolved itself into its primal content—his old coat over the high-backed chair, the lamp by the paper, the half-open door.

"Well," he said to himself, his mouth open, "I thought shore I saw her." And he ran his hand strangely and vaguely through his hair, the while his nervous tension relaxed. Vanished as it had, it gave him the idea that she might return.

Another night, because of this first illusion, and because his mind was now constantly on her and he was old, he looked out of the window that was nearest his bed and commanded a hen-coop and pig-pen and a part of the wagon-shed, and there, a faint mist exuding from the damp of the ground, he thought he saw her again. It was one of those little wisps of mist, one of those faint exhalations of the earth that rise in a cool night after a warm day, and flicker like small white cypresses of fog before they disappear. In life it had been a custom of hers to cross this lot from her kitchen door to the pig-pen to throw in any scrap that was left from her cooking, and here she was again. He sat up and watched it strangely, doubtfully, because of his previous experience, but inclined, because of the nervous titillation that passed over his body, to believe that spirits really were, and that Phœbe, who would be concerned because of his lonely state, must be thinking about him, and hence returning. What other way would she have? How otherwise could she express herself? It would be within the province of her charity so to do, and like her loving interest in him. He quivered and watched it eagerly; but, a faint breath of air stirring, it wound away toward the fence and disappeared.

A third night, as he was actually dreaming, some ten days later, she came to his bedside and put her hand on his head.

"Poor Henry!" she said. "It's too bad."

He roused out of his sleep, actually to see her, he thought, moving from his bed-room into the one living-room, her figure a shadowy mass of black. The weak straining of his eyes caused little points of light to flicker about the outlines of her form. He arose, greatly astonished, walked the floor in the cool room, convinced that Phœbe was coming back to him. If he only thought sufficiently, if he made it perfectly clear by his feeling that he needed her greatly, she would come back, this kindly wife, and tell him what to do. She would perhaps be with him much of the time, in the night, anyhow; and that would make him less lonely, this state more endurable.

In age and with the feeble it is not such a far cry from the subtleties of illusion to actual hallucination, and in due time this transition was made for Henry. Night after night he waited, expecting her return. Once in his weird mood he thought he saw a pale light moving about the room, and another time he thought he saw her walking in the orchard after dark. It was one morning when the details of his lonely state were virtually unendurable that he woke with the thought that she was not dead. How he had arrived at this conclusion it is hard to say. His mind had gone. In its place was a fixed illusion. He and Phœbe had had a senseless quarrel. He had reproached her for not leaving his pipe where he was accustomed to find it, and she had left. It was an aberrated fulfillment of her old jesting threat that if he did not behave himself she would leave him.

"I guess I could find yuh ag'in," he had always said. But her cackling threat had always been:

"Yuh'll not find me if I ever leave yuh. I guess I kin git some place where yuh can't find me."

This morning when he arose he did not think to build the fire in the customary way or to grind his coffee and cut his bread, as was his wont, but solely to meditate as to where he should search for her and how he should induce her to come back. Recently the one horse had been dispensed with because he found it cumbersome and beyond his needs. He took down his soft crush hat after he had dressed himself, a new glint of interest and determination in his eye, and taking his black crook cane from behind the door, where he had always placed it, started out briskly to look for her among the nearest neighbors. His old shoes clumped soundly in the dust as he walked, and his gray-black locks, now grown rather long, straggled out in a dramatic fringe or halo from under his hat. His short coat stirred busily as he walked, and his hands and face were peaked and pale.

"Why, hello, Henry! Where're yuh goin' this mornin'?" inquired Farmer Dodge, who, hauling a load of wheat to market, encountered him on the public road. He had not seen the aged farmer in months, not since his wife's death, and he wondered now, seeing him looking so spry.

"Yuh ain't seen Phœbe, have yuh?" inquired the old man, looking up quizzically.

"Phœbe who?" inquired Farmer Dodge, not for the moment connecting the name with Henry's dead wife.

"Why, my wife Phœbe, o' course. Who do yuh s'pose I mean?" He stared up with a pathetic sharpness of glance from under his shaggy, gray eyebrows.

"Wall, I'll swan, Henry, yuh ain't jokin', are yuh?" said the solid Dodge, a pursy man, with a smooth, hard, red face. "It can't be your wife yuh're talkin' about. She's dead."

"Dead! Shucks!" retorted the demented Reifsneider. "She left me early this mornin', while I was sleepin'. She allus got up to build the fire, but she's gone now. We had a little spat last night, an' I guess that's the reason. But I guess I kin find her. She's gone over to Matilda Race's; that's where she's gone."

He started briskly up the road, leaving the amazed Dodge to stare in wonder after him.

"Well, I'll be switched!" he said aloud to himself. "He's clean out'n his head. That poor old feller's been livin' down there till he's gone outen his mind. I'll have to notify the authorities." And he flicked his whip with great enthusiasm. "Geddap!" he said, and was off.

Reifsneider met no one else in this poorly populated region until he reached the whitewashed fence of Matilda Race and her husband three miles away. He had passed several other houses en route, but these not being within the range of his illusion were not considered. His wife, who had known Matilda well, must be here. He opened the picket-gate which guarded the walk, and stamped briskly up to the door.

"Why, Mr. Reifsneider," exclaimed old Matilda herself, a stout woman, looking out of the door in answer to his knock, "what brings yuh here this mornin'?"

"Is Phœbe here?" he demanded eagerly.

"Phœbe who? What Phœbe?" replied Mrs. Race, curious as to this sudden development of energy on his part.

"Why, my Phœbe, o' course. My wife Phœbe. Who do yuh s'pose? Ain't she here now?"

"Lawsy me!" exclaimed Mrs. Race, opening her mouth. "Yuh pore man! So you're clean out'n your mind now. Yuh come right in and sit down. I'll git yuh a cup o' coffee. O' course your wife ain't here; but yuh come in an' sit down. I'll find her fer yuh after a while. I know where she is."

The old farmer's eyes softened, and he entered. He was so thin and pale a specimen, pantalooned and patriarchal, that he aroused Mrs. Race's extremest sympathy as he took off his hat and laid it on his knees quite softly and mildly.

"We had a quarrel last night, an' she left me," he volunteered.

"Laws! laws!" sighed Mrs. Race, there being no one present with whom to share her astonishment as she went to her kitchen. "The pore man! Now somebody's just got to look after him. He can't be allowed to run around the country this way lookin' for his dead wife. It's turrible."

She boiled him a pot of coffee and brought in some of her new-baked bread and fresh butter. She set out some of her best jam and put a couple of eggs to boil, lying whole-heartedly the while.

"Now yuh stay right there, Uncle Henry, till Jake comes in, an' I'll send him to look for Phœbe. I think it's more'n likely she's over to Swinnerton with some o' her friends. Anyhow, we'll find out. Now yuh just drink this coffee an' eat this bread. Yuh must be tired. Yuh've had a long walk this mornin'." Her idea was to take counsel with Jake, "her man," and perhaps have him notify the authorities.

She bustled about, meditating on the uncertainties of life, while old Reifsneider thrummed on the rim of his hat with his pale fingers and later ate abstractedly of what she offered. His mind was on his wife, however, and since she was not here, or did not appear, it wandered vaguely away to a family by the name of Murray, miles away in another direction. He decided after a time that he would not wait for Jake Race to hunt his wife but would seek her for himself. He must be on, and urge her to come back.

"Well, I'll be goin'," he said, getting up and looking strangely about him. "I guess she didn't come here after all. She went over to the Murrays', I guess. I'll not wait any longer, Mis' Race. There's a lot to do over to the house to-day." And out he marched in the face of her protests taking to the dusty road again in the warm spring sun, his cane striking the earth as he went.

It was two hours later that this pale figure of a man appeared in the Murrays' doorway, dusty, perspiring, eager. He had tramped all of five miles, and it was noon. An amazed husband and wife of sixty heard his strange query, and realized also that he was mad. They begged him to stay to dinner, intending to notify the authorities later and see what could be done; but though he stayed to partake of a little something, he did not stay long, and was off again to another distant farmhouse, his idea of many things to do

72

and his need of Phœbe impelling him. So it went for that day and the next and the next, the circle of his inquiry ever widening.

The process by which a character assumes the significance of being peculiar, his antics weird, yet harmless, in such a community is often involute and pathetic. This day, as has been said, saw Reifsneider at other doors, eagerly asking his unnatural question, and leaving a trail of amazement, sympathy, and pity in his wake. Although the authorities were informed—the county sheriff, no less—it was not deemed advisable to take him into custody; for when those who knew old Henry, and had for so long, reflected on the condition of the county insane asylum, a place which, because of the poverty of the district, was of staggering aberration and sickening environment, it was decided to let him remain at large; for, strange to relate, it was found on investigation that at night he returned peaceably enough to his lonesome domicile there to discover whether his wife had returned, and to brood in loneliness until the morning. Who would lock up a thin, eager, seeking old man with iron-gray hair and an attitude of kindly, innocent inquiry, particularly when he was well known for a past of only kindly servitude and reliability? Those who had known him best rather agreed that he should be allowed to roam at large. He could do no harm. There were many who were willing to help him as to food, old clothes, the odds and ends of his daily life—at least at first. His figure after a time became not so much a common-place as an accepted curiosity, and the replies, "Why, no, Henry; I ain't see her," or "No, Henry; she ain't been here to-day," more customary.

For several years thereafter then he was an odd figure in the sun and rain, on dusty roads and muddy ones, encountered occasionally in strange and unexpected places, pursuing his endless search. Undernourishment, after a time, although the neighbors and those who knew his history gladly contributed from their store, affected his body; for he walked much and ate little. The longer he roamed the public highway in this manner, the deeper became his strange hallucination; and finding it harder and harder to return from his more and more distant pilgrimages, he finally began taking a few utensils with him from his home, making a small package of them, in order that he might not be compelled to return. In an old tin coffee-pot of large size he placed a small tin cup, a knife, fork, and spoon, some salt and pepper, and to the outside of it, by a string forced through a pierced hole, he fastened a plate, which could be released, and which was his woodland table. It was no trouble for him to secure the little food that he needed, and with a strange, almost religious dignity, he had no hesitation in asking for that much. By degrees his hair became longer and longer, his once black hat became an earthen brown, and his clothes threadbare and dusty.

For all of three years he walked, and none knew how wide were his perambulations, nor how he survived the storms and cold. They could not see him, with homely rural understanding and forethought, sheltering himself in hay-cocks, or by the sides of cattle, whose warm bodies protected him from the cold, and whose dull understandings were not opposed to his harmless presence. Overhanging rocks and trees kept him at times from the rain, and a friendly hay-loft or corn-crib was not above his humble consideration.

The involute progression of hallucination is strange. From asking at doors and being constantly rebuffed or denied, he finally came to the conclusion that although his Phœbe might not be in any of the houses at the doors of which he inquired, she might nevertheless be within the sound of his voice. And so, from patient inquiry, he began to call sad, occasional cries, that ever and anon waked the quiet landscapes and ragged hill regions, and set to echoing his thin "O-o-o Phœbe! O-o-o Phœbe!" It had a pathetic, albeit insane, ring, and many a farmer or plowboy came to know it even from afar and say, "There goes old Reifsneider."

Another thing that puzzled him greatly after a time and after many hundreds of inquiries was, when he no longer had any particular dooryard in view and no special inquiry to make, which way to go. These cross-roads, which occasionally led in four or even six directions, came after a time to puzzle him. But to solve this knotty problem, which became more and more of a puzzle, there came to his aid another hallucination. Phœbe's spirit or some power of the air or wind or nature would tell him. If he stood at the center of the parting of the ways, closed his eyes, turned thrice about, and called "O-o-o Phœbe!" twice, and then threw his cane straight before him, that would surely indicate which way to go for Phœbe, or one of these mystic powers would surely govern its direction and fall! In whichever direction it went, even though, as was not infrequently the case, it took him back along the path he had already come, or across fields, he was not so far gone in his mind but that he gave himself ample time to search before he called again. Also the hallucination seemed to persist that at some time he would surely find her. There were hours when his feet were sore, and his limbs weary, when he would stop in the heat to wipe his seamed brow, or in the cold to beat his arms. Sometimes, after throwing away his cane, and finding it indicating the direction from which he had just come, he would shake his head wearily and philosophically, as if contemplating the unbelievable or an untoward fate, and then

74

start briskly off. His strange figure came finally to be known in the farthest reaches of three or four counties. Old Reifsneider was a pathetic character. His fame was wide.

Near a little town called Watersville, in Green County, perhaps four miles from that minor center of human activity, there was a place or precipice locally known as the Red Cliff, a sheer wall of red sandstone, perhaps a hundred feet high, which raised its sharp face for half a mile or more above the fruitful cornfields and orchards that lay beneath, and which was surmounted by a thick grove of trees. The slope that slowly led up to it from the opposite side was covered by a rank growth of beech, hickory, and ash, through which threaded a number of wagon-tracks crossing at various angles. In fair weather it had become old Reifsneider's habit, so inured was he by now to the open, to make his bed in some such patch of trees as this to fry his bacon or boil his eggs at the foot of some tree before laying himself down for the night. Occasionally, so light and inconsequential was his sleep, he would walk at night. More often, the moonlight or some sudden wind stirring in the trees or a reconnoitering animal arousing him, he would sit up and think, or pursue his quest in the moonlight or the dark, a strange, unnatural, half wild, half savage-looking but utterly harmless creature, calling at lonely road crossings, staring at dark and shuttered houses, and wondering where, where Phœbe could really be.

That particular lull that comes in the systole-diastole of this earthly ball at two o'clock in the morning invariably aroused him, and though he might not go any farther he would sit up and contemplate the darkness or the stars, wondering. Sometimes in the strange processes of his mind he would fancy that he saw moving among the trees the figure of his lost wife, and then he would get up to follow, taking his utensils, always on a string, and his cane. If she seemed to evade him too easily he would run, or plead, or, suddenly losing track of the fancied figure, stand awed or disappointed, grieving for the moment over the almost insurmountable difficulties of his search.

It was in the seventh year of these hopeless peregrinations, in the dawn of a similar springtime to that in which his wife had died, that he came at last one night to the vicinity of this self-same patch that crowned the rise to the Red Cliff. His far-flung cane, used as a divining-rod at the last cross-roads, had brought him hither. He had walked many, many miles. It was after ten o'clock at night, and he was very weary. Long wandering and little eating had left him but a shadow of his former self. It was a question now not so much of physical strength but of spiritual endurance which kept him up. He had scarcely eaten this day, and now exhausted he set himself down in the dark to rest and possibly to sleep.

Curiously on this occasion a strange suggestion of the presence of his wife surrounded him. It would not be long now, he counseled with himself, although the long months had brought him nothing, until he should see her, talk to her. He fell asleep after a time, his head on his knees. At midnight the moon began to rise, and at two in the morning, his wakeful hour, was a large silver disk shining through the trees to the east. He opened his eyes when the radiance became strong, making a silver pattern at his feet and lighting the woods with strange lusters and silvery, shadowy forms. As usual, his old notion that his wife must be near occurred to him on this occasion, and he looked about him with a speculative, anticipatory eye. What was it that moved in the distant shadows along the path by which he had entered—a pale, flickering will-o'-the-wisp that bobbed gracefully among the trees and riveted his expectant gaze? Moonlight and shadows combined to give it a strange form and a stranger reality, this fluttering of bog-fire or dancing of wandering fire-flies. Was it truly his lost Phœbe? By a circuitous route it passed about him, and in his fevered state he fancied that he could see the very eyes of her, not as she was when he last saw her in the black dress and shawl but now a strangely younger Phœbe, gayer, sweeter, the one whom he had known years before as a girl. Old Reifsneider got up. He had been expecting and dreaming of this hour all these years, and now as he saw the feeble light dancing lightly before him he peered at it questioningly, one thin hand in his gray hair.

Of a sudden there came to him now for the first time in many years the full charm of her girlish figure as he had known it in boyhood, the pleasing, sympathetic smile, the brown hair, the blue sash she had once worn about her waist at a picnic, her gay, graceful movements. He walked around the base of the tree, straining with his eyes, forgetting for once his cane and utensils, and following eagerly after. On she moved before him, a will-o'-the-wisp of the spring, a little flame above her head, and it seemed as though among the small saplings of ash and beech and the thick trunks of hickory and elm that she signaled with a young, a lightsome hand.

"O Phœbe! Phœbe!" he called. "Have yuh really come? Have yuh really answered me?" And hurrying faster, he fell once, scrambling lamely to his feet, only to see the light in the distance dancing illusively on. On and on he hurried until he was fairly running, brushing his ragged arms against the trees, striking his hands and face against impeding twigs. His hat was gone, his lungs were breathless, his reason quite astray, when coming to the edge of the cliff he saw her below among a silvery bed of apple-trees now blooming in the spring.

"O Phœbe!" he called. "O Phœbe! Oh, no, don't leave me!" And feeling the lure of a world where love was young and Phœbe as this vision presented her, a delightful epitome of their quondam youth, he gave a gay cry of "Oh, wait, Phœbe!" and leaped.

Some farmer-boys, reconnoitering this region of bounty and prospect some few days afterward, found first the tin utensils tied together under the tree where he had left them, and then later at the foot of the cliff, pale, broken, but elate, a molded smile of peace and delight upon his lips, his body. His old hat was discovered lying under some low-growing saplings, the twigs of which had held it back. No one of all the simple population knew how eagerly and joyously he had found his lost mate.

THE SECOND CHOICE

SHIRLEY DEAR:

You don't want the letters. There are only six of them, anyhow, and think, they're all I have of you to cheer me on my travels. What good would they be to you—little bits of notes telling me you're sure to meet me—but me—think of me! If I send them to you, you'll tear them up, whereas if you leave them with me I can dab them with musk and ambergris and keep them in a little silver box, always beside me.

Ah, Shirley dear, you really don't know how sweet I think you are, how dear! There isn't a thing we have ever done together that isn't as clear in my mind as this great big skyscraper over the way here in Pittsburgh, and far more pleasing. In fact, my thoughts of you are the most precious and delicious things I have, Shirley.

But I'm too young to marry now. You know that, Shirley, don't you? I haven't placed myself in any way yet, and I'm so restless that I don't know whether I ever will, really. Only yesterday, old Roxbaum—that's my new employer here—came to me and wanted to know if I would like an assistant overseership on one of his coffee plantations in Java, said there would not be much money in it for a year or two, a bare living, but later there would be more—and I jumped at it. Just the thought of Java and going there did that, although I knew I could make more staying right here. Can't you see how it is with me, Shirl? I'm too restless and too young. I couldn't take care of you right, and you wouldn't like me after a while if I didn't.

But ah, Shirley sweet, I think the dearest things of you! There isn't an hour, it seems, but some little bit of you comes back— a dear, sweet bit—the night we sat on the grass in Tregore Park and counted the stars through the trees; that first evening at Sparrows Point when we missed the last train and had to walk to Langley. Remember the tree-toads, Shirl? And then that warm April Sunday in Atholby woods! Ah, Shirl, you don't want the six notes! Let me keep them. But think of me, will you, sweet, wherever you go and whatever you do? I'll always think of you, and wish that you had met a better, saner man than me, and that I really could have married you and been all you wanted me to be. By-by,

78

sweet. I may start for Java within the month. If so, and you would want them, I'll send you some cards from there—if they have any.

Your worthless,
ARTHUR

She sat and turned the letter in her hand, dumb with despair. It was the very last letter she would ever get from him. Of that she was certain. He was gone now, once and for all. She had written him only once, not making an open plea but asking him to return her letters, and then there had come this tender but evasive reply, saying nothing of a possible return but desiring to keep her letters for old times' sake—the happy hours they had spent together.

The happy hours! Oh, yes, yes, yes—the happy hours!

In her memory now, as she sat here in her home after the day's work, meditating on all that had been in the few short months since he had come and gone, was a world of color and light—a color and a light so transfiguring as to seem celestial, but now, alas, wholly dissipated. It had contained so much of all she had desired— love, romance, amusement, laughter. He had been so gay and thoughtless, or headstrong, so youthfully romantic, and with such a love of play and change and to be saying and doing anything and everything. Arthur could dance in a gay way, whistle, sing after a fashion, play. He could play cards and do tricks, and he had such a superior air, so genial and brisk, with a kind of innate courtesy in it and yet an intolerance for slowness and stodginess or anything dull or dingy, such as characterized— But here her thoughts fled from him. She refused to think of any one but Arthur.

Sitting in her little bedroom now, off the parlor on the ground floor in her home in Bethune Street, and looking out over the Kessels' yard, and beyond that—there being no fences in Bethune Street—over the "yards" or lawns of the Pollards, Bakers, Cryders, and others, she thought of how dull it must all have seemed to him, with his fine imaginative mind and experiences, his love of change and gayety, his atmosphere of something better than she had ever known. How little she had been fitted, perhaps, by beauty or temperament to overcome this—the something—dullness in her work or her home, which possibly had driven him away. For, although many had admired her to date, and she was young and pretty in her simple way and constantly receiving suggestions that her beauty was disturbing to some, still, he had not cared for her— he had gone.

And now, as she meditated, it seemed that this scene, and all

79

that it stood for—her parents, her work, her daily shuttling to and fro between the drug company for which she worked and this street and house—was typical of her life and what she was destined to endure always. Some girls were so much more fortunate. They had fine clothes, fine homes, a world of pleasure and opportunity in which to move. They did not have to scrimp and save and work to pay their own way. And yet she had always been compelled to do it, but had never complained until now—or until he came, and after. Bethune Street, with its commonplace front yards and houses nearly all alike, and this house, so like the others, room for room and porch for porch, and her parents, too, really like all the others, had seemed good enough, quite satisfactory, indeed, until then. But now, now!

Here, in their kitchen, was her mother, a thin, pale, but kindly woman, peeling potatoes and washing lettuce, and putting a bit of steak or a chop or a piece of liver in a frying-pan day after day, morning and evening, month after month, year after year. And next door was Mrs. Kessel doing the same thing. And next door Mrs. Cryder. And next door Mrs. Pollard. But, until now, she had not thought it so bad. But now—now—oh! And on all the porches or lawns all along this street were the husbands and fathers, mostly middle-aged or old men like her father, reading their papers or cutting the grass before dinner, or smoking and meditating afterward. Her father was out in front now, a stooped, forbearing, meditative soul, who had rarely anything to say—leaving it all to his wife, her mother, but who was fond of her in his dull, quiet way. He was a pattern-maker by trade, and had come into possession of this small, ordinary home via years of toil and saving, her mother helping him. They had no particular religion, as he often said, thinking reasonably human conduct a sufficient passport to heaven, but they had gone occasionally to the Methodist Church over in Nicholas Street, and she had once joined it. But of late she had not gone, weaned away by the other commonplace pleasures of her world.

And then in the midst of it, the dull drift of things, as she now saw them to be, he had come—Arthur Bristow—young, energetic, good-looking, ambitious, dreamful, and instanter, and with her never knowing quite how, the whole thing had been changed. He had appeared so swiftly—out of nothing, as it were.

Previous to him had been Barton Williams, stout, phlegmatic, good-natured, well-meaning, who was, or had been before Arthur came, asking her to marry him, and whom she allowed to half assume that she would. She had liked him in a feeble, albeit, as she thought, tender way, thinking him the kind, according to the logic of her neighborhood, who would make her a good husband, and, until

Arthur appeared on the scene, had really intended to marry him. It was not really a love-match, as she saw now, but she thought it was, which was much the same thing, perhaps. But, as she now recalled, when Arthur came, how the scales fell from her eyes! In a trice, as it were, nearly, there was a new heaven and a new earth. Arthur had arrived, and with him a sense of something different.

Mabel Gove had asked her to come over to her house in Westleigh, the adjoining suburb, for Thanksgiving eve and day, and without a thought of anything, and because Barton was busy handling a part of the work in the despatched office of the Great Eastern and could not see her, she had gone. And then, to her surprise and strange, almost ineffable delight, the moment she had seen him, he was there—Arthur, with his slim, straight figure and dark hair and eyes and clean-cut features, as clean and attractive as those of a coin. And as he had looked at her and smiled and narrated humorous bits of things that had happened to him, something had come over her—a spell—and after dinner they had all gone round to Edith Barringer's to dance, and there as she had danced with him, somehow, without any seeming boldness on his part, he had taken possession of her, as it were, drawn her close, and told her she had beautiful eyes and hair and such a delicately rounded chin, and that he thought she danced gracefully and was sweet. She had nearly fainted with delight.

"Do you like me?" he had asked in one place in the dance, and, in spite of herself, she had looked up into his eyes, and from that moment she was almost mad over him, could think of nothing else but his hair and eyes and his smile and his graceful figure.

Mabel Gove had seen it all, in spite of her determination that no one should, and on their going to bed later, back at Mabel's home, she had whispered:

"Ah, Shirley, I saw. You like Arthur, don't you?"

"I think he's very nice," Shirley recalled replying, for Mabel knew of her affair with Barton and liked him, "but I'm not crazy over him." And for this bit of treason she had sighed in her dreams nearly all night.

And the next day, true to a request and a promise made by him, Arthur had called again at Mabel's to take her and Mabel to a "movie" which was not so far away, and from there they had gone to an ice-cream parlor, and during it all, when Mabel was not looking, he had squeezed her arm and hand and kissed her neck, and she had held her breath, and her heart had seemed to stop.

"And now you're going to let me come out to your place to see you, aren't you?" he had whispered.

And she had replied, "Wednesday evening," and then written the address on a little piece of paper and given it to him.

But now it was all gone, gone!

This house, which now looked so dreary—how romantic it had seemed that first night he called—the front room with its commonplace furniture, and later in the spring, the veranda, with its vines just sprouting, and the moon in May. Oh, the moon in May, and June and July, when he was here! How she had lied to Barton to make evenings for Arthur, and occasionally to Arthur to keep him from contact with Barton. She had not even mentioned Barton to Arthur because—because—well, because Arthur was so much better, and somehow (she admitted it to herself now) she had not been sure that Arthur would care for her long, if at all, and then—well, and then, to be quite frank, Barton might be good enough. She did not exactly hate him because she had found Arthur—not at all. She still liked him in a way—he was so kind and faithful, so very dull and straightforward and thoughtful of her, which Arthur was certainly not. Before Arthur had appeared, as she well remembered, Barton had seemed to be plenty good enough—in fact, all that she desired in a pleasant, companionable way, calling for her, taking her places, bringing her flowers and candy, which Arthur rarely did, and for that, if nothing more, she could not help continuing to like him and to feel sorry for him, and, besides, as she had admitted to herself before, if Arthur left her—***** Weren't his parents better off than hers—and hadn't he a good position for such a man as he—one hundred and fifty dollars a month and the certainty of more later on? A little while before meeting Arthur, she had thought this very good, enough for two to live on at least, and she had thought some of trying it at some time or other—but now—now—

And that first night he had called—how well she remembered it—how it had transfigured the parlor next this in which she was now, filling it with something it had never had before, and the porch outside, too, for that matter, with its gaunt, leafless vine, and this street, too, even—dull, commonplace Bethune Street. There had been a flurry of snow during the afternoon while she was working at the store, and the ground was white with it. All the neighboring homes seemed to look sweeter and happier and more inviting than ever they had as she came past them, with their lights peeping from under curtains and drawn shades. She had hurried into hers and lighted the big red-shaded parlor lamp, her one artistic treasure, as she thought, and put it near the piano, between it and the window, and arranged the chairs, and then bustled to the task of making herself as pleasing as she might. For him she had gotten out her one best filmy house dress and done up her hair in the fashion she thought most becoming—and that he had not seen before—and powdered her cheeks and nose and darkened her eyelashes, as some of the girls at the store did, and put on her new gray satin slippers, and then, being so arrayed, waited nervously, unable to eat anything or to think of anything but him.

And at last, just when she had begun to think he might not be coming, he had appeared with that arch smile and a "Hello! It's here you live, is it? I was wondering. George, but you're twice as sweet as I thought you were, aren't you?" And then, in the little entryway, behind the closed door, he had held her and kissed her on the mouth a dozen times while she pretended to push against his coat and struggle and say that her parents might hear.

And, oh, the room afterward, with him in it in the red glow of the lamp, and with his pale handsome face made handsomer thereby, as she thought! He had made her sit near him and had held her hands and told her about his work and his dreams—all that he expected to do in the future—and then she had found herself wishing intensely to share just such a life—his life—anything that he might wish to do; only, she kept wondering, with a slight pain, whether he would want her to—he was so young, dreamful, ambitious, much younger and more dreamful than herself, although, in reality, he was several years older.

And then followed that glorious period from December to this late September, in which everything which was worth happening in love had happened. Oh, those wondrous days the following spring, when, with the first burst of buds and leaves, he had taken her one Sunday to Atholby, where all the great woods were, and they had hunted spring beauties in the grass, and sat on a slope and looked at the river below and watched some boys fixing up a sailboat and setting forth in it quite as she wished she and Arthur might be doing—going somewhere together—far, far away from all commonplace things and life! And then he had slipped his arm about her and kissed her cheek and neck, and tweaked her ear and smoothed her hair—and oh, there on the grass, with the spring flowers about her and a canopy of small green leaves above, the perfection of love had come—love so wonderful that the mere thought of it made her eyes brim now! And then had been days, Saturday afternoons and Sundays, at Atholby and Sparrows Point, where the great beach was, and in lovely Tregore Park, a mile or two from her home, where they could go of an evening and sit in or near the pavilion and have ice-cream and dance or watch the dancers. Oh, the stars, the winds, the summer breath of those days! Ah, me! Ah, me!

Naturally, her parents had wondered from the first about her and Arthur, and her and Barton, since Barton had already assumed a proprietary interest in her and she had seemed to like him. But then she was an only child and a pet, and used to presuming on that, and they could not think of saying anything to her. After all, she was young and pretty and was entitled to change her mind; only, only—she had had to indulge in a career of lying and subterfuge in connection with Barton, since Arthur was headstrong and wanted every evening that he chose—to call for her at the store and keep her down-town to dinner and a show.

Arthur had never been like Barton, shy, phlegmatic, obedient, waiting long and patiently for each little favor, but, instead, masterful and eager, rifling her of kisses and caresses and every delight of love, and teasing and playing with her as a cat would a mouse. She could never resist him. He demanded of her her time and her affection without let or hindrance. He was not exactly selfish or cruel, as some might have been, but gay and unthinking at times, unconsciously so, and yet loving and tender at others—nearly always so. But always he would talk of things in the future as if they really did not include her—and this troubled her greatly—of places he might go, things he might do, which, somehow, he seemed to think or assume that she could not or would not do with him. He was always going to Australia sometime, he thought, in a business way, or to South Africa, or possibly to India. He never seemed to have any fixed clear future for himself in mind.

A dreadful sense of helplessness and of impending disaster came over her at these times, of being involved in some predicament over which she had no control, and which would lead her on to some sad end. Arthur, although plainly in love, as she thought, and apparently delighted with her, might not always love her. She began, timidly at first (and always, for that matter), to ask him pretty, seeking questions about himself and her, whether their future was certain to be together, whether he really wanted her— loved her—whether he might not want to marry some one else or just her, and whether she wouldn't look nice in a pearl satin wedding-dress with a long creamy veil and satin slippers and a bouquet of bridal-wreath. She had been so slowly but surely saving to that end, even before he came, in connection with Barton; only, after he came, all thought of the import of it had been transferred to him. But now, also, she was beginning to ask herself sadly, "Would it ever be?" He was so airy, so inconsequential, so ready to say: "Yes, yes," and "Sure, sure! That's right! Yes, indeedy; you bet! Say, kiddie, but you'll look sweet!" but, somehow, it had always seemed as if this whole thing were a glorious interlude and that it could not last. Arthur was too gay and ethereal and too little settled in his own mind. His ideas of travel and living in different cities, finally

84

winding up in New York or San Francisco, but never with her exactly until she asked him, was too ominous, although he always reassured her gaily: "Of course! Of course!" But somehow she could never believe it really, and it made her intensely sad at times, horribly gloomy. So often she wanted to cry, and she could scarcely tell why.

And then, because of her intense affection for him, she had finally quarreled with Barton, or nearly that, if one could say that one ever really quarreled with him. It had been because of a certain Thursday evening a few weeks before about which she had disappointed him. In a fit of generosity, knowing that Arthur was coming Wednesday, and because Barton had stopped in at the store to see her, she had told him that he might come, having regretted it afterward, so enamored was she of Arthur. And then when Wednesday came, Arthur had changed his mind, telling her he would come Friday instead, but on Thursday evening he had stopped in at the store and asked her to go to Sparrows Point, with the result that she had no time to notify Barton. He had gone to the house and sat with her parents until ten-thirty, and then, a few days later, although she had written him offering an excuse, had called at the store to complain slightly.

"Do you think you did just right, Shirley? You might have sent word, mightn't you? Who was it—the new fellow you won't tell me about?"

Shirley flared on the instant.

"Supposing it was? What's it to you? I don't belong to you yet, do I? I told you there wasn't any one, and I wish you'd let me alone about that. I couldn't help it last Thursday—that's all—and I don't want you to be fussing with me—that's all. If you don't want to, you needn't come any more, anyhow."

"Don't say that, Shirley," pleaded Barton. "You don't mean that. I won't bother you, though, if you don't want me any more."

And because Shirley sulked, not knowing what else to do, he had gone and she had not seen him since.

And then sometime later when she had thus broken with Barton, avoiding the railway station where he worked, Arthur had failed to come at his appointed time, sending no word until the next day, when a note came to the store saying that he had been out of town for his firm over Sunday and had not been able to notify her, but that he would call Tuesday. It was an awful blow. At the time, Shirley had a vision of what was to follow. It seemed for the moment as if the whole world had suddenly been reduced to ashes, that there was nothing but black charred cinders anywhere—she felt that about all life. Yet it all came to her clearly then that this was but the beginning of just such days and just such excuses, and that soon,

soon, he would come no more. He was beginning to be tired of her and soon he would not even make excuses. She felt it, and it froze and terrified her.

And then, soon after, the indifference which she feared did follow—almost created by her own thoughts, as it were. First, it was a meeting he had to attend somewhere one Wednesday night when he was to have come for her. Then he was going out of town again, over Sunday. Then he was going away for a whole week—it was absolutely unavoidable, he said, his commercial duties were increasing—and once he had casually remarked that nothing could stand in the way where she was concerned—never! She did not think of reproaching him with this; she was too proud. If he was going, he must go. She would not be willing to say to herself that she had ever attempted to hold any man. But, just the same, she was agonized by the thought. When he was with her, he seemed tender enough; only, at times, his eyes wandered and he seemed slightly bored. Other girls, particularly pretty ones, seemed to interest him as much as she did.

And the agony of the long days when he did not come any more for a week or two at a time! The waiting, the brooding, the wondering, at the store and here in her home—in the former place making mistakes at times because she could not get her mind off him and being reminded of them, and here at her own home at nights, being so absent-minded that her parents remarked on it. She felt sure that her parents must be noticing that Arthur was not coming any more, or as much as he had—for she pretended to be going out with him, going to Mabel Gove's instead—and that Barton had deserted her too, he having been driven off by her indifference, never to come any more, perhaps, unless she sought him out.

And then it was that the thought of saving her own face by taking up with Barton once more occurred to her, of using him and his affections and faithfulness and dulness, if you will, to cover up her own dilemma. Only, this ruse was not to be tried until she had written Arthur this one letter—a pretext merely to see if there was a single ray of hope, a letter to be written in a gentle-enough way and asking for the return of the few notes she had written him. She had not seen him now in nearly a month, and the last time she had, he had said he might soon be compelled to leave her awhile—to go to Pittsburgh to work. And it was his reply to this that she now held in her hand—from Pittsburgh! It was frightful! The future without him!

But Barton would never know really what had transpired, if she went back to him. In spite of all her delicious hours with Arthur, she could call him back, she felt sure. She had never really entirely dropped him, and he knew it. He had bored her dreadfully on occasion, arriving on off days when Arthur was not about, with flowers or candy, or both, and sitting on the porch steps and talking of the railroad business and of the whereabouts and doings of some of their old friends. It was shameful, she had thought at times, to see a man so patient, so hopeful, so good-natured as Barton, deceived in this way, and by her, who was so miserable over another. Her parents must see and know, she had thought at these times, but still, what else was she to do?

"I'm a bad girl," she kept telling herself. "I'm all wrong. What right have I to offer Barton what is left?" But still, somehow, she realized that Barton, if she chose to favor him, would only be too grateful for even the leavings of others where she was concerned, and that even yet, if she but deigned to crook a finger, she could have him. He was so simple, so good-natured, so stolid and matter of fact, so different to Arthur whom (she could not help smiling at the thought of it) she was loving now about as Barton loved her—slavishly, hopelessly.

And then, as the days passed and Arthur did not write any more—just this one brief note—she at first grieved horribly, and then in a fit of numb despair attempted, bravely enough from one point of view, to adjust herself to the new situation. Why should she despair? Why die of agony where there were plenty who would still sigh for her—Barton among others? She was young, pretty, very— many told her so. She could, if she chose, achieve a vivacity which she did not feel. Why should she brook this unkindness without a thought of retaliation? Why shouldn't she enter upon a gay and heartless career, indulging in a dozen flirtations at once—dancing and killing all thoughts of Arthur in a round of frivolities? There were many who beckoned to her. She stood at her counter in the drug store on many a day and brooded over this, but at the thought of which one to begin with, she faltered. After her late love, all were so tame, for the present anyhow.

And then—and then—always there was Barton, the humble or faithful, to whom she had been so unkind and whom she had used and whom she still really liked. So often self-reproaching thoughts in connection with him crept over her. He must have known, must have seen how badly she was using him all this while, and yet he had not failed to come and come, until she had actually quarreled with him, and any one would have seen that it was literally hopeless. She could not help remembering, especially now in her pain, that he adored her. He was not calling on her now at all—by her indifference she had finally driven him away—but a word, a word— She waited for days, weeks, hoping against hope, and then—

The office of Barton's superior in the Great Eastern terminal had always made him an easy object for her blandishments, coming and going, as she frequently did, via this very station. He was in the office of the assistant train-despatcher on the ground floor, where passing to and from the local, which, at times, was quicker than a street-car, she could easily see him by peering in; only, she had carefully avoided him for nearly a year. If she chose now, and would call for a message-blank at the adjacent telegraph-window which was a part of his room, and raised her voice as she often had in the past, he could scarcely fail to hear, if he did not see her. And if he did, he would rise and come over—of that she was sure, for he never could resist her. It had been a wile of hers in the old days to do this or to make her presence felt by idling outside. After a month of brooding, she felt that she must act—her position as a deserted girl was too much. She could not stand it any longer really—the eyes of her mother, for one.

It was six-fifteen one evening when, coming out of the store in which she worked, she turned her step disconsolately homeward. Her heart was heavy, her face rather pale and drawn. She had stopped in the store's retiring-room before coming out to add to her charms as much as possible by a little powder and rouge and to smooth her hair. It would not take much to reallure her former sweetheart, she felt sure—and yet it might not be so easy after all. Suppose he had found another? But she could not believe that. It had scarcely been long enough since he had last attempted to see her, and he was really so very, very fond of her and so faithful. He was too slow and certain in his choosing—he had been so with her. Still, who knows? With this thought, she went forward in the evening, feeling for the first time the shame and pain that comes of deception, the agony of having to relinquish an ideal and the feeling of despair that comes to those who find themselves in the position of suppliants, stooping to something which in better days and better fortune they would not know. Arthur was the cause of this.

When she reached the station, the crowd that usually filled it at this hour was swarming. There were so many pairs like Arthur and herself laughing and hurrying away or so she felt. First glancing in the small mirror of a weighing scale to see if she were still of her former charm, she stopped thoughtfully at a little flower stand which stood outside, and for a few pennies purchased a tiny bunch of violets. She then went inside and stood near the window, peering first furtively to see if he were present. He was. Bent over his work, a green shade over his eyes, she could see his stolid, genial figure at a table. Stepping back a moment to ponder, she finally went forward and, in a clear voice, asked,

"May I have a blank, please?"

The infatuation of the discarded Barton was such that it brought him instantly to his feet In his stodgy, stocky way he rose, his eyes glowing with a friendly hope, his mouth wreathed in smiles, and came over. At the sight of her, pale, but pretty—paler and prettier, really, than he had ever seen her—he thrilled dumbly.

"How are you, Shirley?" he asked sweetly, as he drew near, his eyes searching her face hopefully. He had not seen her for so long that he was intensely hungry, and her paler beauty appealed to him more than ever. Why wouldn't she have him? he was asking himself. Why wouldn't his persistent love yet win her? Perhaps it might. "I haven't seen you in a month of Sundays, it seems. How are the folks?"

"They're all right, Bart," she smiled archly, "and so am I. How have you been? It has been a long time since I've seen you. I've been wondering how you were. Have you been all right? I was just going to send a message."

As he had approached, Shirley had pretended at first not to see him, a moment later to affect surprise, although she was really suppressing a heavy sigh. The sight of him, after Arthur, was not reassuring. Could she really interest herself in him any more? Could she?

"Sure, sure," he replied genially; "I'm always all right. You couldn't kill me, you know. Not going away, are you, Shirl?" he queried interestedly.

"No; I'm just telegraphing to Mabel. She promised to meet me to-morrow, and I want to be sure she will."

"You don't come past here as often as you did, Shirley," he complained tenderly. "At least, I don't seem to see you so often," he added with a smile. "It isn't anything I have done, is it?" he queried, and then, when she protested quickly, added: "What's the trouble, Shirl? Haven't been sick, have you?"

She affected all her old gaiety and ease, feeling as though she would like to cry.

"Oh, no," she returned; "I've been all right. I've been going through the other door, I suppose, or coming in and going out on the Langdon Avenue car." (This was true, because she had been wanting to avoid him.) "I've been in such a hurry, most nights, that I haven't had time to stop, Bart. You know how late the store keeps us at times."

He remembered, too, that in the old days she had made time to stop or meet him occasionally.

"Yes, I know," he said tactfully. "But you haven't been to any of our old card-parties either of late, have you? At least, I haven't seen you. I've gone to two or three, thinking you might be there."

That was another thing Arthur had done—broken up her interest in these old store and neighborhood parties and a banjo-and-mandolin club to which she had once belonged. They had all seemed so pleasing and amusing in the old days—but now— * * * * In those days Bart had been her usual companion when his work permitted.

"No," she replied evasively, but with a forced air of pleasant remembrance; "I have often thought of how much fun we had at those, though. It was a shame to drop them. You haven't seen Harry Stull or Trina Task recently, have you?" she inquired, more to be saying something than for any interest she felt.

He shook his head negatively, then added:

"Yes, I did, too; here in the waiting-room a few nights ago. They were coming down-town to a theater, I suppose."

His face fell slightly as he recalled how it had been their custom to do this, and what their one quarrel had been about. Shirley noticed it. She felt the least bit sorry for him, but much more for herself, coming back so disconsolately to all this.

"Well, you're looking as pretty as ever, Shirley," he continued, noting that she had not written the telegram and that there was something wistful in her glance. "Prettier, I think," and she smiled sadly. Every word that she tolerated from him was as so much gold to him, so much of dead ashes to her. "You wouldn't like to come down some evening this week and see 'The Mouse-Trap,' would you? We haven't been to a theater together in I don't know when." His eyes sought hers in a hopeful, doglike way.

So—she could have him again—that was the pity of it! To have what she really did not want, did not care for! At the least nod now he would come, and this very devotion made it all but worthless, and so sad. She ought to marry him now for certain, if she began in this way, and could in a month's time if she chose, but oh, oh—could she? For the moment she decided that she could not, would not. If he had only repulsed her—told her to go—ignored her—but no; it was her fate to be loved by him in this moving, pleading way, and hers not to love him as she wished to love—to be loved. Plainly, he needed some one like her, whereas she, she—. She turned a little sick, a sense of the sacrilege of gaiety at this time creeping into her voice, and exclaimed:

"No, no!" Then seeing his face change, a heavy sadness come over it, "Not this week, anyhow, I mean" ("Not so soon," she had almost said). "I have several engagements this week and I'm not feeling well. But"—seeing his face change, and the thought of her own state returning—"you might come out to the house some evening instead, and then we can go some other time."

His face brightened intensely. It was wonderful how he longed to be with her, how the least favor from her comforted and lifted him up. She could see also now, however, how little it meant to her, how little it could ever mean, even if to him it was heaven. The old relationship would have to be resumed in toto, once and for all, but did she want it that way now that she was feeling so miserable about this other affair? As she meditated, these various moods racing to and fro in her mind, Barton seemed to notice, and now it occurred to him that perhaps he had not pursued her enough—was too easily put off. She probably did like him yet. This evening, her present visit, seemed to prove it.

"Sure, sure!" he agreed. "I'd like that. I'll come out Sunday, if you say. We can go any time to the play. I'm sorry, Shirley, if you're not feeling well. I've thought of you a lot these days. I'll come out Wednesday, if you don't mind."

She smiled a wan smile. It was all so much easier than she had expected—her triumph—and so ashenlike in consequence, a flavor of dead-sea fruit and defeat about it all, that it was pathetic. How could she, after Arthur? How could he, really?

"Make it Sunday," she pleaded, naming the farthest day off, and then hurried out.

Her faithful lover gazed after her, while she suffered an intense nausea. To think—to think—it should all be coming to this! She had not used her telegraph-blank, and now had forgotten all about it. It was not the simple trickery that discouraged her, but her own future which could find no better outlet than this, could not rise above it apparently, or that she had no heart to make it rise above it. Why couldn't she interest herself in some one different to Barton? Why did she have to return to him? Why not wait and meet some other—ignore him as before? But no, no; nothing mattered now—no one—it might as well be Barton really as any one, and she would at least make him happy and at the same time solve her own problem. She went out into the train-shed and climbed into her train. Slowly, after the usual pushing and jostling of a crowd, it drew out toward Latonia, that suburban region in which her home lay. As she rode, she thought.

"What have I just done? What am I doing?" she kept asking herself as the clacking wheels on the rails fell into a rhythmic dance and the houses of the brown, dry, endless city fled past in a maze. "Severing myself decisively from the past—the happy past—for supposing, once I am married, Arthur should return and want me again—suppose! Suppose!"

91

Below at one place, under a shed, were some market-gardeners disposing of the last remnants of their day's wares—a sickly, dull life, she thought. Here was Rutgers Avenue, with its line of red street-cars, many wagons and tracks and counter-streams of automobiles—how often had she passed it morning and evening in a shuttle-like way, and how often would, unless she got married! And here, now, was the river flowing smoothly between its banks lined with coal-pockets and wharves—away, away to the huge deep sea which she and Arthur had enjoyed so much. Oh, to be in a small boat and drift out, out into the endless, restless, pathless deep! Somehow the sight of this water, to-night and every night, brought back those evenings in the open with Arthur at Sparrows Point, the long line of dancers in Eckert's Pavilion, the woods at Atholby, the park, with the dancers in the pavilion—she choked back a sob. Once Arthur had come this way with her on just such an evening as this, pressing her hand and saying how wonderful she was. Oh, Arthur! Arthur! And now Barton was to take his old place again—forever, no doubt. She could not trifle with her life longer in this foolish way, or his. What was the use? But think of it!

Yes, it must be—forever now, she told herself. She must marry. Time would be slipping by and she would become too old. It was her only future—marriage. It was the only future she had ever contemplated really, a home, children, the love of some man whom she could love as she loved Arthur. Ah, what a happy home that would have been for her! But now, now—

But there must be no turning back now, either. There was no other way. If Arthur ever came back—but fear not, he wouldn't! She had risked so much and lost—lost him. Her little venture into true love had been such a failure. Before Arthur had come all had been well enough. Barton, stout and simple and frank and direct, had in some way—how, she could scarcely realize now—offered sufficient of a future. But now, now! He had enough money, she knew, to build a cottage for the two of them. He had told her so. He would do his best always to make her happy, she was sure of that. They could live in about the state her parents were living in—or a little better, not much—and would never want. No doubt there would be children, because he craved them—several of them—and that would take up her time, long years of it—the sad, gray years! But then Arthur, whose children she would have thrilled to bear, would be no more, a mere memory—think of that!—and Barton, the dull, the commonplace, would have achieved his finest dream—and why?

Because love was a failure for her—that was why—and in her life there could be no more true love. She would never love any one again as she had Arthur. It could not be, she was sure of it. He was too fascinating, too wonderful. Always, always, wherever she might be, whoever she might marry, he would be coming back, intruding between her and any possible love, receiving any possible kiss. It would be Arthur she would be loving or kissing. She dabbed at her eyes with a tiny handkerchief, turned her face close to the window and stared out, and then as the environs of Latonia came into view, wondered (so deep is romance): What if Arthur should come back at some time—or now! Supposing he should be here at the station now, accidentally or on purpose, to welcome her, to soothe her weary heart. He had met her here before. How she would fly to him, lay her head on his shoulder, forget forever that Barton ever was, that they had ever separated for an hour. Oh, Arthur! Arthur!

But no, no; here was Latonia—here the viaduct over her train, the long business street and the cars marked "Center" and "Langdon Avenue" running back into the great city. A few blocks away in tree-shaded Bethune Street, duller and plainer than ever, was her parents' cottage and the routine of that old life which was now, she felt, more fully fastened upon her than ever before—the lawn-mowers, the lawns, the front porches all alike. Now would come the going to and fro of Barton to business as her father and she now went to business, her keeping house, cooking, washing, ironing, sewing for Barton as her mother now did these things for her father and herself. And she would not be in love really, as she wanted to be. Oh, dreadful! She could never escape it really, now that she could endure it less, scarcely for another hour. And yet she must, must, for the sake of—for the sake of—she closed her eyes and dreamed.

She walked up the street under the trees, past the houses and lawns all alike to her own, and found her father on their veranda reading the evening paper. She sighed at the sight.

"Back, daughter?" he called pleasantly.

"Yes."

"Your mother is wondering if you would like steak or liver for dinner. Better tell her."

"Oh, it doesn't matter."

She hurried into her bedroom, threw down her hat and gloves, and herself on the bed to rest silently, and groaned in her soul. To think that it had all come to this!—Never to see him any more!—To see only Barton, and marry him and live in such a street, have four or five children, forget all her youthful companionships—and all to save her face before her parents, and her future. Why must it be? Should it be, really? She choked and stifled. After a little time her mother, hearing her come in, came to the door—thin, practical, affectionate, conventional.

"What's wrong, honey? Aren't you feeling well tonight? Have you a headache? Let me feel."

Her thin cool fingers crept over her temples and hair. She suggested something to eat or a headache powder right away.

"I'm all right, mother. I'm just not feeling well now. Don't bother. I'll get up soon. Please don't."

"Would you rather have liver or steak to-night, dear?"

"Oh, anything—nothing—please don't bother—steak will do—anything"—if only she could get rid of her and be at rest!

Her mother looked at her and shook her head sympathetically, then retreated quietly, saying no more. Lying so, she thought and thought—grinding, destroying thoughts about the beauty of the past, the darkness of the future—until able to endure them no longer she got up and, looking distractedly out of the window into the yard and the house next door, stared at her future fixedly. What should she do? What should she really do? There was Mrs. Kessel in her kitchen getting her dinner as usual, just as her own mother was now, and Mr. Kessel out on the front porch in his shirt-sleeves reading the evening paper. Beyond was Mr. Pollard in his yard, cutting the grass. All along Bethune Street were such houses and such people—simple, commonplace souls all—clerks, managers, fairly successful craftsmen, like her father and Barton, excellent in their way but not like Arthur the beloved, the lost—and here was she, perforce, or by decision of necessity, soon to be one of them, in some such street as this no doubt, forever and—. For the moment it choked and stifled her.

She decided that she would not. No, no, no! There must be some other way—many ways. She did not have to do this unless she really wished to—would not—only—. Then going to the mirror she looked at her face and smoothed her hair.

"But what's the use?" she asked of herself wearily and resignedly after a time. "Why should I cry? Why shouldn't I marry Barton? I don't amount to anything, anyhow. Arthur wouldn't have me. I wanted him, and I am compelled to take some one else—or no one—what difference does it really make who? My dreams are too high, that's all. I wanted Arthur, and he wouldn't have me. I don't want Barton, and he crawls at my feet. I'm a failure, that's what's the matter with me."

And then, turning up her sleeves and removing a fichu which stood out too prominently from her breast, she went into the kitchen and, looking about for an apron, observed:

"Can't I help? Where's the tablecloth?" and finding it among napkins and silverware in a drawer in the adjoining room, proceeded to set the table.

A STORY OF STORIES

Take a smoky Western city. Call it Omaha or Kansas City or Denver, only let the Mississippi flow past it. Put in it two rival morning papers—two, and only two—the Star and the News, the staffs of which are rather keen to outwit each other. On the staff of the News, slightly the better of the two newspapers, put Mr. David Kolinsky, alias (yes, alias) David, or "Red" Collins (a little shift of nomenclature due to the facts that, first: he was a South Russian Jew who looked exactly like a red-headed Irishman—that is a peculiarity of South Russian Jews, I believe—and secondly: that it was more distingué, as it were, to be Irish in Omaha or Denver or Kansas City than it was to be a South Russian Jew). Give him a slithery, self-confident, race-track or tout manner. Put on him "loud" or showy clothes, a diamond ring, a ruby pin in his tie, a yellowish-green Fedora hat, yellow shoes, freckles, a sneering contemptuous "tough" smile, and you have Mr. "Red" Collins as Mr.—

But wait.

On the Star, slightly the lesser of these two great dailies that matutinally thrashed the city to a foam of interest, place Mr. Augustus Binns, no less, young (not over twenty-two), tall, college-y, rather graceful as young college men go, literary of course, highly ambitious, with gold eye-glasses, a wrist watch, a cane—in short, one of those ambitious young gentlemen of this rather un-happy go un-lucky scribbling world who has distinct ideals, to say nothing of dreams, as to what the newspaper and literary professions combined should bring him, and who, in addition, inherently despised all creatures of the "Red" Collins, or racetrack, gambler, amateur detective, police and political, type. Well may you ask, what was Mr. Collins, with his peculiar characteristics, doing on a paper of the importance and distinction of the News. A long story, my dears. Newspapers are peculiar institutions.

For this same paper not long since had harbored the truly elegant presence of Mr. Binns himself, and so excellent a writer and news gatherer was he that on more than one occasion he had been set to revise or rewrite the tales which Mr. "Red" Collins, who was then but tentatively connected with the paper as a "tipster," brought in. This in itself was a crime against art and literature, as Mr. Binns saw it, for, when you come right down to it, and in the strict meaning of the word, Mr. Collins was not a writer at all, could not write, in fact, could only "bring in" his stories, and most interesting

95

ones they were, nearly all of them, whereas about the paper at all times were men who could—Mr. Binns, for instance. It insulted if not outraged Mr. Binns's sense of the fitness of things, for the News to hire such a person and let him flaunt the title of "reporter" or "representative," for he admired the News very much and was glad to be of it. But Collins! "Red" Collins!

The latter was one of those "hard life," but by no means hard luck, Jews who by reason of indomitable ambition and will had raised himself out of practically frightful conditions. He had never even seen a bath-tub until he was fifteen or sixteen. By turns he had been a bootblack, newsboy, race-track tout, stable boy, helper around a saloon, and what not. Of late years, and now, because he was reaching a true wisdom (he was between twenty-five and six), he had developed a sort of taste for gambling as well as politics of a low order, and was in addition a police hanger-on. He was really a sort of pariah in his way, only the sporting and political editors found him useful. They tolerated him, and paid him well for his tips because, forsooth, his tips were always good.

Batsford, the capable city editor of the News, a round, forceful, gross person who was more allied to Collins than to Binns in spirit, although he was like neither, was Binns's first superior in the newspaper world. He did not like Binns because, for one thing, of his wrist watch, secondly, his large gold glasses—much larger than they need have been—and thirdly, because of his cane, which he carried with considerable of an air. The truth is, Binns was Eastern and the city editor was Western, and besides, Binns had been more or less thrust upon him by his managing editor as a favor to some one else. But Binns could write, never doubt it, and proved it. He was a vigorous reporter with a fine feeling for words and, above all, a power to visualize and emotionalize whatever he saw, a thing which was of the utmost importance in this rather loose Western emotional atmosphere. He could handle any story which came to him with ease and distinction, and seemed usually to get all or nearly all the facts.

On the other hand, Collins, for all his garishness, and one might almost say, brutality of spirit, was what Batsford would have called a practical man. He knew life. He was by no means as artistic as Binns, but still—Batsford liked to know what was going on politically and criminally, and Collins could always tell him, whereas Binns never could. Also, by making Binns rewrite Collins's stories, he knew he could offend him horribly. The two were like oil and water, Mussulman and Christian.

When Batsford first told Collins to relate the facts of a certain tale to Binns and let him work it out, the former strolled over to the collegian, his lip curled up at one corner, his eye cynically fixed on him, and said, "The Chief says to give youse this dope and let youse work it out"

Youse!

Oh, for a large, bright broad ax!

Binns, however, always your stickler for duty and order, bent on him an equally cynical and yet enigmatic eye, hitched up his trousers slightly, adjusted his wrist watch and glasses, and began to take down the details of the story, worming them out of his rival with a delicacy and savoir faire worthy of a better cause.

Not long after, however, it was brought to the horrified ears of Mr. Binns that Mr. Collins had said he was a "stiff" and a "cheap ink-slinger," a la-de-da no less, that writers, one and all, college and otherwise, didn't count for much, anyhow, that they were all starving to death, and that they "grew on trees"—a phrase which particularly enraged Mr. Binns, for he interpreted it to mean that they were as numerous as the sands of the sea, as plentiful as mud.

By Allah! That such dogs should be allowed to take the beards of great writers into their hands thus!

Nevertheless and in spite of all this, the fortunes of Mr. Collins went forward apace, and that chiefly, as Mr. Binns frequently groaned, at his expense. Collins would come in, and after a long series of "I sez to him-s" and "He sez to me-s," which Mr. Binns (per the orders of Mr. Batsford) translated into the King's best Britannica, he having in the meanwhile to neglect some excellent tale of his own, would go forth again, free to point the next day to a column or column-and-a-half or a half-column story, and declare proudly, "My story."

Think of it! That swine!

There is an end to all things, however, even life and crime. In due time, as per a series of accidents and the groundless ill-will of Mr. Batsford, Mr. Binns was perforce, in self-respect, compelled to transfer his energies to the Star, a paper he had previously contemned as being not so good, but where he was now made very welcome because of his ability. Then, to his astonishment and disgust, one day while covering a police station known as the South Ninth, from which emanated many amazing police tales, whom should he encounter but "Red" Collins, no less, now a full-fledged reporter on the News, if you please, and "doing police." He had a grand and even contemptuous manner, barely deigning to notice Binns. Binns raged.

But he noticed at once that Collins was far more en rapport with the various sergeants and the captain, as well as all that was going on in this station, than ever he had dreamed of being. It was

"Hello, Red," here and "Hi, sport," there, while Collins replied with various "Caps" and "Charlies." He gave himself all the airs of a newspaper man proper, swaggering about and talking of this, that, and the other story which he had written, some of them having been done by Binns himself. And what was more, Collins was soon closeted intimately with the captain in his room, strolling in and out of that sanctum as if it were his private demesne, and somehow giving Binns the impression of being in touch with realms and deeds of which he had never heard, and never would. It made Binns doubly apprehensive lest in these secret intimacies tales and mysteries should be unfolded which should have their first light in the pages of the News, and so leave him to be laughed at as one who could not get the news. In consequence, he watched the News more closely than ever for any evidence of such treachery on the part of the police, while at the same time he redoubled his interest in any such items as came to his attention. By reason of this, as well as by his greater skill in writing and his undeniable imagination, on more than one occasion he gave Mr. Collins a good drubbing, chancing to make good stories out of things which Mr. Collins had evidently dismissed as worthless. Au contraire, now and then a case appeared in the columns of the News with details which he had not been able to obtain, and concerning which the police had insisted that they knew nothing. It was thus that Mr. Collins secured his revenge—and very good revenge too, it was at times.

But Mr. Binns managed to hold his own, as, for instance, late one August afternoon when a negro girl in one of those crowded alleys which made up an interesting and even amazing portion of O— was cut almost to shreds by an ex-lover who, following her from river-city to river-city and town to town, had finally come up with her here and had taken his revenge.

It was a glistering tale this. It appeared (but only after the greatest industry on the part of Mr. Binns) that some seven or eight months before [the O— papers curiously were always interested in a tale of this kind] this same girl and the negro who had cut her had been living together as man and wife in Cairo, Illinois, and that later the lover (a coal passer or stevedore, working now on one boat and now on another plying the Mississippi between New Orleans and O—), who was plainly wildly fond of her, became suspicious and finally satisfying himself that his mistress, who was a real beauty after her kind, was faithless to him, set a trap to catch her. Returning suddenly one day when she imagined him to be away for a week or two of labor, and bursting in upon her, he found her with another man. Death would have been her portion as well as that of her lover had it not been for the interference of friends, which had permitted the pair to escape.

Lacerated by the double offenses of betrayal and desertion, he now set out to follow her, as the cutting on this occasion proved. Returning to his task as stevedore and working his way thus from one river-city to another, he arrived by turns in Memphis, Vicksburg, Natchez and New Orleans, in each case making it a point to disguise himself as a peddler selling trinkets and charms, and in this capacity walking the crowded negro sections of all these cities calling his wares. Ambling up one of these stuffy, stifling alleys, finally, in O— which bordered on this same police station and where so many negroes lived, he encountered this late August afternoon his quondam but now faithless love. In answer to his cry of "Rings! Pins! Buckles! Trinkets!" his false love, apparently not recognizing his voice, put her head out of a doorway. On the instant the damage was done. Dropping his tray, he was upon her in a flash with his razor, cris-crossing and slashing her until she was marred beyond recognition. With fiendish cruelty he cut her cheeks, lips, arms, legs, back, and sides, so much so that when Binns arrived at the City Hospital where she had been taken, he found her unconscious and her life despaired of. On the other hand, the lover had made good his escape, as had her paramour.

Curiously, this story captured the fancy of Mr. Binns as it did that of his city editor later, completely. It was such a thing as he could do, and do well. With almost deft literary art he turned it into a rather striking black tragedy. Into it, after convincing his rather fussy city editor that it was worth the telling, he had crowded a bit of the flavor of the hot waterfronts of Cairo, Memphis, Natchez, and New Orleans, the sing-song sleepiness of the stevedores at their lazy labors, the idle, dreamy character of the slow-moving boats, this rickety alley, with its semi-barbaric curtain-hung shacks and its swarming, idle, crooning, shuffling negro life. Even an old negro refrain appropriate to a trinket peddler, and the low, bold negro life two such truants might enjoy, were pictured. An old negro mammy with a yellow-dotted kerchief over her head who kept talking of "disha Gawge" and "disha Sam" and "disha Marquatta" (the girl), had moved him to a poetic frenzy. Naturally it made a colorful tale, and his city editor felt called upon to compliment him on it.

But in the News, owing possibly to Collins's inability to grasp the full significance, the romance, of such a story as this, it received but a scant stick—a low dive cutting affray. His was not the type of mind that could see the color here, but once seen he could realize wherein he had been beaten, and it infuriated him.

"You think you're a helluva feller, dontcha?" he snarled the next day on sight, his lip a-curl with scorn and rage. "You think you've pulled off sompin swell. Say, I've been up against you wordy boys before, and I can work all around you. All you guys can do is get a few facts and then pad 'em up. You never get the real stuff, never," and he even snapped his fingers under the nose of the surprised Mr. Binns. "Wait'll we get a real case some time, you and me, and then I'll show you sompin. Wait and see."

"My good fellow," Mr. Binns was about to begin, but the cold, hard, revengeful glare in the eyes of Mr. Collins quite took his breath away. Then and there Mr. Collins put a strange haunting fear of himself into Mr. Binns's mind. There was something so savage about him, so like that of an angry hornet or snake that it left him all but speechless. "Is that so?" he managed to say after a time. "You think you will, do you? That's easy enough to' say, now that you're beaten, but I guess I'll be right there when the time comes."

"Aw, go to hell!" growled Collins savagely, and he walked off, leaving Mr. Binns smiling pleasantly, albeit vacantly, and at the same time wondering just what it was Mr. Collins was going to do to him, and when.

The sequel to this was somewhat more interesting.

As Mr. Binns came in one morning fresh from his bath and breakfast, his new city editor called him into his office. Mr. Waxby, in contrast with Mr. Batsford, was a small, waspish, and yet affable and capable man whom Binns could not say he admired as a man or a gentleman, but who, he was sure, was a much better city editor than Batsford, and who appreciated him, Binns, as Batsford never had, i.e., at his true worth. Batsford had annoyed him with such a dog as Collins, whereas Waxby had almost coddled him. And what a nose for news!

Mr. Waxby eyed him rather solemnly and enigmatically on this occasion, and then observed: "Do you remember, Binns, that big M.P. train robbery that took place out here near Dolesville about six months ago?"

"Yes, sir."

"And do you remember that the Governor of this state and his military staff, all in uniform, as well as a half dozen other big-wigs, were on board, and that they all reported that there had been seven lusty bandits, all heavily armed, some of whom went through the train and robbed the passengers while others compelled the engineer and fireman to get down, uncouple the engine, and then blow open the express car door and safe for them and carry out the money, about twenty or thirty thousand dollars all told?"

Binns remembered it well. He had been on the News at the time, and the full-page spread had attracted his keenest attention. It was illustrative, as he thought, of the character of this region—raw and still daring. It smacked so much of the lawlessness of the forties, when pack-train and stage-coach robberies were the rule and not the exception. It had caused his hair to tingle at the roots at times so real was it. Never had he been so close, as it were, to anything so dramatic.

"Yes, sir, I remember it very well," he replied.

"And do you remember how the newspapers laughed over the fact that the Governor and his military staff had crawled into their berths and didn't come out again until the train had started?"

"Yes, sir."

"Well now, Binns, just read this," and here Mr. Waxby handed him a telegram, the while his eyes gleamed with a keen humorous light, and Mr. Binns read:

"Medicine Flats, M. K.

"Lem Rollins arrested here to-day confesses to single-handed robbery of M. P. express west of Dolesville February 2d last. Money recovered. Rollins being brought to O— via C. T. & A. this p. m. Should arrive six-thirty."

"Apparently," cackled Mr. Waxby, "there was nothing to that seven-bandit story at all, Binns. There weren't any seven robbers, but just one, and they've caught him, and he's confessed," and here he burst into more laughter.

"No, Binns," went on Waxby, "if this is really true, it is a wonderful story. You don't often find one man holding up a whole train anywhere and getting away with twenty or thirty thousand dollars. It's amazing. I've decided that we won't wait for him to arrive, but that you're to go out and meet him. According to this time-table you can take a local that leaves here at two-fifteen and get to Pacific fifteen minutes ahead of the express on which he is coming in, and you've just about time to make it. That will give you all of an hour and a half in which to interview him. It's just possible that the News and the other papers won't get wind of this in time to send a man. Think of the opportunity it gives you to study him! No seven robbers, remember, but just one! And the Governor and his whole staff on board! Make him tell what he thinks of the Governor and his staff. Make him talk. Ha! ha! You'll have him all to yourself. Think of that! And they crawled into their berths! Ha! Ha! Gee whiz, you've got the chance of a lifetime!"

Mr. Binns stared at the telegram. He recalled the detailed descriptions of the actions of the seven robbers, how some of them

101

had prowled up and down outside the train, while others went through it rifling the passengers, and still others, forward, overawed the engineer and fireman, broke open and robbed the express car safe in the face of an armed messenger as well as mailman and trainmen, and how they had then decamped into the dark. How could one man have done it? It couldn't be true!

Nevertheless he arose, duly impressed. It would be no easy task to get just the right touch, but he felt that he might. If only the train weren't over-run with other reporters! He stuffed some notepaper into his pocket and bustled down to the Union Station—if Mr. Binns could be said to bustle. Here he encountered his first hitch.

On inquiring for a ticket to Pacific, the slightly disturbing response of "Which road?" was made.

"Are there two?" asked Mr. Binns.

"Yes—M.P. and C.T. & A."

"They both go to Pacific, do they?"

"Yes."

"Which train leaves first?"

"C.T. & A. It's waiting now."

Mr. Binns hesitated, but there was no time to lose. It didn't make any difference, so long as he connected with the incoming express, as the time-table showed that this did. He paid for his ticket and got aboard, but now an irritating thought came to him. Supposing other reporters from either the News or one of the three afternoon papers were aboard, especially the News! If there were not he would have this fine task all to himself, and what a beat! But if there were others? He walked forward to the smoker, which was the next car in front, and there, to his intense disgust and nervous dissatisfaction, he spied, of all people, the one man he would least have expected to find on an assignment of this kind, the one man he least wanted to see—Mr. Collins, no less, red-headed, serene, determined, a cigar between his teeth, crouched low in his seat smoking and reading a paper as calmly as though he were not bent upon the most important task of the year.

"Pshaw!" exclaimed Mr. Binns irritably and even bitterly.

He returned to his seat nervous and ill composed, all the more so because he now recalled Collins's venomous threat, "Wait'll we get a real case some time, you and me." The low creature! Why, he couldn't even write a decent sentence. Why should he fear him so? But just the same he did fear him—why, he could scarcely say. Collins was so raw, savage, brutal, in his mood and plans.

But why, in heaven's name, he now asked himself as he meditated in his seat as to ways and means, should a man like

Batsford send a man like Collins, who couldn't even write, to interpret a story and a character of this kind? How could he hope to dig out the odd psychology of this very queer case? Plainly he was too crude, too unintellectual to get it straight. Nevertheless, here he was, and now, plainly, he would have this awful creature to contend with. And Collins was so bitter toward him. He would leave no trick unturned to beat him! These country detectives and sheriff and railroad men, whoever they were or wherever they came from, would be sure, on the instant, to make friends with Collins, as they always did, and do their best to serve him. They seemed to like that sort of man, worse luck. They might even, at Collins's instigation, refuse to let him interview the bandit at all! If so, then what? But Collins would get something somehow, you might be sure, secret details which they might not relate to him. It made him nervous. Even if he got a chance he would have to interview this wonderful bandit in front of this awful creature, this one man whom he most despised, and who would deprive him of most of the benefit of all his questions by writing as though he had thought of and asked all of them himself. Think of it!

The dreary local sped on, and as it drew nearer and nearer to Pacific, Binns became more and more nervous. For him the whole charm of this beautiful September landscape through which he was speeding now was all spoiled. When the train finally drew up at Pacific he jumped down, all alive with the determination not to be outdone in any way, and yet nervous and worried to a degree. Let Collins do his worst, he thought. He would show him. Still—just then he saw the latter jumping down. At the same time, Collins spied him, and on the instant his face clouded over. He seemed fairly to bristle with an angry animal rage, and he glared as though he would like to kill Binns, at the same time looking around to see who else might get off. "My enemy!" was written all over him. Seeing no one, he ran up to the station-agent and apparently asked when the train from the West was due. Binns decided at once not to trail, but instead sought information from his own conductor, who assured him that the East-bound express would probably be on time five minutes later, and would certainly stop here.

"We take the siding here," he said. "You'll hear the whistle in a few minutes."

"It always stops here, does it?" asked Binns anxiously.

"Always."

As they talked, Collins came back to the platform's edge and stood looking up the track. At the same time this train pulled out, and a few minutes later the whistle of the express was heard. Now for a real contest, thought Binns. Somewhere in one of those cars would be this astounding bandit surrounded by detectives, and his duty, in spite of the indignity of it, would be to clamber aboard and get there first, explain who he was, ingratiate himself into the good graces of the captors and the prisoner, and begin his questioning, vanquishing Collins as best he might—perhaps by the ease with which he should take charge. In a few moments the express was rolling into the station, and then Binns saw his enemy leap aboard and, with that iron effrontery and savageness which always irritated Binns so much, race through the forward cars to find the prisoner. Binns was about to essay the rear cars, but just then the conductor, a portly, genial-looking soul, stepped down beside him.

"Is Lem Rollins, the train robber they are bringing in from Bald Knob, on here?" he inquired. "I'm from the Star, and I've been sent out to interview him."

"You're on the wrong road, brother," smiled the conductor. "He's not on this train. Those detective fellows have fooled you newspaper men, I'm afraid. They're bringing him in over the M.P., as I understand it. They took him across from Bald Knob to Wahaba and caught the train there—but I'll tell you," and here he took out a large open-face silver watch and consulted it, "you might be able to catch him yet if you run for it. It's only across the field there. You see that little yellow station over there? Well, that's the depot. It's due now, but sometimes it's a little late. You'll have to run for it, though. You haven't a minute to spare."

Binns was all aquiver on the instant. Suppose, in spite of Collins's zeal and savagery, he should outwit him yet by catching this other train while he was searching this one! All the gameness of his youth and profession rose up in him. Without stopping to thank his informer, he leaped like a hare along the little path which cut diagonally across this lone field and which was evidently well worn by human feet. As he ran he wondered whether the genial conductor could possibly have lied to him to throw him off the track, and also if his enemy, seeing him running, had discovered his error by now and was following, granting that the conductor had told him the truth. He looked back occasionally, taking off his coat and glasses as he ran, and even throwing away his cane. Apparently Collins was still searching the other train. And now Binns at the same time, looking eagerly forward toward the other station, saw a semaphore arm which stood at right angles to the station lower itself for a clear track for some train. At the same time he also spied a mail-bag hanging out on a take-post arm, indicating that whatever this train was and whichever way it might be going, it was not going to stop here. He turned, still uncertain as to whether he had made a mistake in not searching the other train. Supposing the conductor had deliberately fooled him! Suppose Collins had made some preliminary arrangements of which he knew nothing? Suppose he had! Supposing the burglar were really on there, and even now Collins was busy with the opening questions of his interview, while he was here, behind! Oh Lord, what a beat! And he would have no reasonable explanation to offer except that he had been outwitted. What would happen to him? He slowed up in his running, chill beads of sweat bursting out on his face as he did so, but then, looking backward, he saw the train begin to move and from it, as if shot out of a gun, the significant form of Collins leap down and begin to run along this same path. Then, by George, the robber was not on it, after all! The conductor had told him the truth! Ha! Collins would now attempt to make this other train. He had been told that the bandit was coming in on this. Binns could see him speeding along the path at top speed, his hat off, his hands waving nervously about. But by now Binns had reached the station a good three minutes ahead of his rival.

Desperately he ran into it, a tiny thing, sticking his eager perspiring face in at the open office window, and calling to the stout, truculent little occupant of it:

"When is the East-bound M.P. express due here?"

"Now," replied the agent surlily.

"Does it stop?"

"No, it don't stop."

"Can it be stopped?"

"No, it cannot!"

"You mean to say you have no right to stop it?"

"I mean I won't stop it."

As they spoke there came the ominous shriek of the express's whistle tearing on toward them. For the moment he was almost willing that Collins should join him if only he could make the train and gain this interview. He must have it. Waxby expected him to get it. Think of what a beat he would have if he won—what Waxby would think if he failed!

"Would five dollars stop it?" he asked desperately, diving into his pocket.

"No."

"Will ten?"

"It might," the agent replied crustily, and rose to his feet.

"Stop it," urged Binns feverishly, handing over the bill.

The agent took it, and grabbing a tablet of yellow order blanks which lay before him, scribbled something on the face of one and ran outside, holding it up at arm's length as he did so. At the same time he called to Binns:

"Run on down the track! Run after it. She won't stop here—she can't. She'll go a thousand feet before she can slow up. Get on down there, and after you're on I'll let 'er go."

He waved the yellow paper desperately, while Binns, all tense with excitement and desire, began running as fast as he could in the direction indicated. Now, if he were lucky, he would make it, and Collins would be left behind—think of it! He could get them to go ahead, maybe, before Collins could get aboard. Oh, my! As he ran and thought, he heard the grinding wheels of the express rushing up behind him. In a thought, as it were, it was alongside and past, its wheels shrieking and emitting sparks. True enough, it was stopping! He would be able to get on! Oh, glory! And maybe Collins wouldn't be able to! Wouldn't that be wonderful? It was far ahead of him now, but almost stock-still, and he was running like mad. As he ran he could hear the final gritty screech of the wheels against the brakes as the train came to a full stop farther on, and then coming up and climbing aboard, breathless and gasping painfully, he looked back, only to see that his rival had taken a diagonal course across the common, and was now not more than a hundred feet behind. He would make the train if he kept this up. It could scarcely be started quickly enough to leave him behind, even if Binns paid for it. Instead of setting himself to the stern task of keeping Mr. Collins off the train, however, as assuredly Mr. Collins would have done—with his fists or his feet, if necessary, or his money—Mr. Binns now hesitated, uncertain what to do. On the rear platform with him was a brakeman newly stepped forth and, coming out of the door, the conductor.

"Let her go!" he cried to the conductor. "Let her go! It's all right! Go on!"

"Don't that other fellow want to get on?" asked the latter curiously.

"No, no, no!" Binns exclaimed irritably and yet pleading. "Don't let him on! He hasn't any right on here. I arranged to stop this train. I'm from the Star. I'll pay you if you don't let him on. It's the train robber I want. Go ahead," but even as he spoke Mr. Collins came up, panting and wet, but with a leer of triumph and joy over his rival's discomfiture written all over his face as he pulled himself up the steps.

"You thought you'd leave me behind, didn't you?" he sneered as he pushed his way upward. "Well, I fooled you this time, didn't I?"

Now was the crucial moment of Mr. Binns's career had his courage been equal to it, but it was not. He had the opportunity to do the one thing which might have wrested victory from defeat—

106

that is, push Mr. Collins off and keep him off. The train was beginning to move. But instead of employing this raw force which Mr. Collins would assuredly have employed, he hesitated and debated, unable in his super-refinement to make up his mind, while Mr. Collins, not to be daunted or parleyed with, dashed into the car in search of the robber. In the sudden immensity of his discomfiture, Binns now followed him with scarcely a thought for the moment, only to see Collins bustling up to the bandit in the third car ahead who, handcuffed to a country sheriff and surrounded by several detectives, was staring idly at the passengers.

"Gee, sport," the latter was saying as Mr. Binns sat down, patting the burglar familiarly on the knee and fixing him with that basilisk gaze of his which was intended to soothe and flatter the victim, "that was a great trick you pulled off. The paper'll be crazy to find out how you did it. My paper, the News, wants a whole page of it. It wants your picture, too. Say, you didn't really do it all alone, did you? Well, that's what I call swell work, eh, Cap?" and now he turned his ingratiating leer on the country sheriff and the detectives. In a moment or two more he was telling them all what an intimate friend he was of "Billy" Desmond, the chief of detectives of O— and Mr. So-and-So, the chief of police, as well as various other dignitaries of that world.

Plainly, admitted Binns to himself, he was beaten now, as much so as this burglar, he thought. His great opportunity was gone. What a victory this might have been, and now look at it! Disgruntled, he sat down beside his enemy, beginning to think what to ask, the while the latter, preening himself in his raw way on his success, began congratulating the prisoner on his great feat.

"The dull stuff!" thought Mr. Binns. "To think that I should have to contend with a creature like this! And these are the people he considers something! And he wants a whole page for the News! My word! He'd do well if he wrote a half-column alone."

Still, to his intense chagrin, he could not fail to see that Mr. Collins was making excellent headway, not only with the country sheriff, who was a big bland creature, but the detectives and even the burglar himself. The latter was a most unpromising specimen for so unique a deed—short, broad-shouldered, heavy- limbed, with a squarish, inexpressive, even dull-looking face, blue-gray eyes, dark brown hair, big, lumpy, rough hands, and a tanned and seamed skin. He wore the cheap, nondescript clothes of a laborer, a blue "hickory" shirt, blackish-gray trousers, brownish-maroon coat, and a red bandana handkerchief in lieu of a collar. On his head was a small round brown hat pulled down over his eyes after the manner of a cap. He had the still, indifferent expression of a captive bird,

107

and when Binns finally faced him and sat down, he seemed scarcely to notice either him or Collins, or if so with eyes that told nothing. Binns often wondered afterward what he really did think. At the same time he was so incensed at the mere presence of Collins that he could scarcely speak.

The latter had the average detective-politician-gambler's habit of simulating an intense interest and an enthusiasm which he did not feel, his face wreathing itself in a cheery smile, the while his eyes followed one like those of a hawk, attempting all the while to discover whether his assumed enthusiasm or friendship was being accepted at its face value or not. The only time Binns seemed to obtain the least grip on this situation, or to impress himself on the minds of the detectives and prisoner, was when it came to those finer shades of questioning which concerned just why, for what ulterior reasons, the burglar had attempted this deed alone. But even here, Binns noticed that his confrère was all ears, and making copious notes.

But always, to Binns's astonishment and chagrin, the prisoner as well as his captors paid more attention to Collins than they did to himself. They turned to him as to a lamp, and seemed to be really immensely more impressed with him than with himself, although the principal lines of questioning fell to him. After a time he became so dour and enraged that he could think of but one thing that would really have satisfied him, and that was to attack Collins physically and give him a good beating.

However, by degrees and between them, the story was finally extracted, and a fine tale it made. It appeared that up to seven or eight months preceding the robbery, possibly a year, Rollins had never thought of being a train robber but had been only a freight brakeman or yard-hand on this same road at one of its division points. Latterly he had even been promoted to be a sort of superior switchman and assistant freight handler at some station where there was considerable work of this kind. Previous to his railroad work he had been a livery stable helper in the town where he was eventually apprehended, and before that a farmhand somewhere near the same place. About a year before the crime, owing to hard times, this road had laid off a large number of men, including Rollins, and reduced the wages of all others by as much as ten per cent. Naturally a great deal of labor discontent ensued, and strikes, riots, and the like were the order of the day. Again, a certain number of train robberies which were charged and traced to discharged and dissatisfied employees now followed. The methods of successful train robbing were then and there so cleverly set forth by the average newspaper that nearly any burglar so inclined could follow them. Among other things, while working as a freight handler, Rollins had heard of the many money shipments made by express companies in their express cars, their large amounts, the manner in which they were guarded, and so on.

The road for which he worked at this time, the M.P., was, as he now learned, a very popular route for money shipments both East and West. And although express messengers (as those in charge of the car and its safe were called) were well and invariably armed owing to the many train robberies which had been occurring in the West recently, still these assaults had not been without success. Indeed, the deaths of various firemen, engineers, messengers, conductors, and even passengers, and the fact that much money had recently been stolen and never recovered, had not only encouraged the growth of banditry everywhere, but had put such an unreasoning fear into most employees connected with the roads that but few even of those especially picked guards ventured to give these marauders battle.

But just the same, the psychology which eventually resulted in this amazing single-handed attempt and its success was not so much that Rollins was a poor and discharged railroad hand unable to find any other form of employment, although that was a part of it, or that he was an amazingly cold, cruel and subtle soul, which he was not by any means, but that he was really largely unconscious of the tremendous risks he was taking. He was just mentally "thick"— well insulated, as it were. This was a fact which Binns had to bring out and which Collins noted. He had never, as it now developed, figured it out from the point of danger, being more or less lobster-like in his nervous organism, but solely from the point of view of success. In sum, in his idleness, having wandered back to his native region where he had first started out as a livery hand, he had now fallen in love with a young girl there, and then realizing, for the first time perhaps, that he was rather hard pressed for cash and unable to make her such presents as he desired, he had begun to think seriously of some method of raising money. Even this had not resulted in anything until latterly, another ex-railroad hand who had been laid off by this same company arrived and proposed, in connection with a third man whom he knew, to rob a train. At this time Rollins had rejected this scheme as not feasible, not wishing to connect himself with others in any such crime. Later, however, his own condition becoming more pressing, he had begun to think of train robbing as a means of setting himself up in life, only, as he reasoned, it must be alone.

Why alone? queried Binns.

That was the point all were so anxious to discover—why alone, with all the odds against him?

Well, he couldn't say exactly. He had just "kind o' sort o' thort," as he expressed it, that he might frighten them into letting him alone! Other bandits (so few as three in one case of which he had read) had held up large trains. Why not one? Revolver shots fired about a train easily frightened all passengers as well as all trainmen, so the other robbers had told him, and anyhow it was a life to death job either way, and it would be better for him, he thought, if he worked it out alone instead of with others. Often, he said, other men "squealed," or they had girls who told on them. He knew that Binns looked at him, intensely interested and all but moved by the sheer courage, or "gall," or "grit," imbedded somewhere in this stocky frame

But how could he hope to overcome the engineer, fireman, baggage man, express messenger, mailmen, conductor, brakeman and passengers, to say nothing of the Governor and his staff? How? By the way, did he know at the time that the Governor and his staff were on board? No, he hadn't known that until afterward, and as for the others, well, he just thought he could overawe them. Collins's eyes were luminous as Rollins said this, his face radiant. Far more than Binns, he seemed to understand and even approve of the raw force of all this.

The manner in which Rollins came to fix on this particular train to rob was also told. Every Thursday and Friday, or so he had been told while he was assistant freight handler, a limited which ran West at midnight past Dolesville carried larger shipments of money than on other nights. This was due to week-end exchanges between Eastern and Western banks, although he did not know that. Having decided on the train, although not on the day, he had proceeded by degrees to secure from one distant small town and another, and at different times so as to avoid all chance of detection, first, a small handbag from which he had scraped all evidence of the maker's name: six or seven fused sticks of giant powder such as farmers use to blow up stumps; two revolvers holding six cartridges each, and some cartridges; and cord and cloth, out of which he proposed to make bundles of the money if necessary. Placing all of these in his bag, which he kept always beside him, he next visited Dolesville, a small town nearest the spot which he had fixed on in his mind as the place for his crime, and reconnoitering it and its possibilities, finally arranged all his plans to a nicety.

Just at the outskirts of this hamlet, as he now told Binns and Collins, which had been selected because of its proximity to a lone wood and marsh, stood a large water-tank at which this express as well as nearly all other trains stopped for water. Beyond it, about five miles, was the wood with its marsh, where he planned to have the train stopped. The express, as he learned, was regularly due at about one in the morning. The nearest town beyond the wood was all of five miles away, a mere hamlet like this one.

On the night in question, between eight and nine, he carried the bag, minus its revolvers and sticks of giant powder, which were now on his person, to that exact spot opposite the wood where he wished the train to stop, and left it there beside the railroad track. He then walked back the five miles to the water-tank, where he concealed himself and waited for the train. When it stopped, and just before it started again, he slipped in between the engine tender and the front baggage car, which was "blind" at both ends. The train resumed its journey, but on reaching the spot where he felt sure the bag should be, he could not make it out. The engine headlight did not seem to reveal it. Fearing to lose his chance and realizing that he was at about the place where he had left it, he rose up, and climbing over the coal-box, covered the two men in the cab, and compelled them to stop the train, dismount and uncouple the engine. Then, revolver in hand, he drove them before him to the express car door where, presenting one with a fused stick of giant powder, he forced him to blow open the door; the messenger within, still refusing to open it although he would not fire, for fear of killing either the engineer or fireman. Both engineer and fireman, at his command, then entered the car and blew open the money safe, throwing out the packages of bills and coin at his word, the while Rollins, realizing the danger of either trainmen or passengers coming forward, had been firing a few shots backward toward the rear coaches so as to overawe the passengers, and at the same time kept calling to purely imaginary companions to keep watch there. It was these shots and calls that had presumably sent the Governor and his staff scurrying to their berths. They also put the fear of death into the minds of the engineer and fireman and messenger, who imagined that he had many confrères on the other side of the express car but for some reason, because he was the leader, no doubt, preferred to act alone.

"Don't kill anybody, boys, unless you have to," is what Rollins said he called, or "That's all right, Frank. Stay over there. Watch that side. I'll take care of these." Then he would fire a few more shots, and so all were deluded.

Once the express car door and safe had been blown open and the money handed out, he had now compelled the engineer and fireman to come down, recouple the engine, and pull away. Only after the train had safely disappeared in the distance did he venture to gather up the various packages, only since he had lost his bag and had no light, he had to fumble about and make a bag of his coat for them. With this over his shoulder, he eventually staggered off into the wood and marsh, concealing it under muck and stones, and then making for safety himself.

But, as it turned out, two slight errors, one of forgetfulness and one of eyesight, caused him to finally lose the fruit of his victory. The loss of the bag, in which he had first placed and then forgotten an initialed handkerchief belonging to his love, eventually brought about his capture. It is true that he had gone back to look for the bag, without, however, remembering that the handkerchief was in it, but fearing capture if he lingered too long, had made off after a time without it. Later a posse of detectives and citizens arriving and finding the bag with the initialed handkerchief inside, they were eventually able to trace him. For, experts meditating on the crime, decided that owing to the hard times and the laying-off of employees, some of the latter might have had a hand in it, and so, in due time, the whereabouts and movements of each and every one of them was gone into, resulting in the discovery finally that this particular ex-helper had returned rather recently to his semi-native town and had there been going with a certain girl, and that even now he was about to marry her. Also, it was said that he was possessed of unusual means, for him. Next, it was discovered that her initials corresponded to those on the handkerchief. Presto, Mr. Rollins was arrested, a search made of his room, and nearly all of the money recovered. Then, being "caught with the goods," he confessed, and here on this day was he being hurried to O— to be jailed and sentenced, while Mr. Binns and Mr. Collins, like harpies, hovered over him, anxious to make literary capital of his error. The only thing that consoled Mr. Binns, now that this story was finally told, was that although he had failed to make it impossible for Collins to get it, when it came to the writing of it he would be able to outdo him, making a better and more connected narrative. Still, even here he was a little dubious. During this interview Collins had been making endless notes, putting down each least shade of Binns's questioning, and with the aid of one or several of the best men of the News would probably be able to work it out. Then what would be left?

But as they were nearing O— a new situation intruded itself which soon threatened on the face of it to rob Binns of nearly, if not quite, all his advantage. And this related, primarily, to the matter of a picture. It was most essential that one should be made, either here or in the city, only neither Waxby nor himself, nor the city editor of the News apparently, had thought to include an artist on this

112

expedition. Now the importance of this became more and more apparent, and Collins, with that keen sense he had for making tremendous capital of seeming by-products, suggested, after first remarking that he "guessed" they would have to send to police headquarters afterward and have one made:

"How would it do, old man, if we took him up to the News office after we get in, and let your friends Hill and Weaver make a picture of him?" (These two were intimates of Binns in the art department, as Collins happened to know.) "Then both of us could get one right away. I'd say take him to the Star, only the News is so much nearer" (which was true), "and we have that new flash-light machine, you know" (which was also true, the Star being but poorly equipped in this respect). He added a friendly aside to the effect that of course this depended on whether the prisoner and officers in charge were willing.

"No, no, no!" replied Binns irritably and suspiciously. "No, I won't do that. You mean you want to get him into the News office first. Not at all. I'll never stand for that. Hill and Weaver are my friends, but I won't do it. If you want to bring him down to the Star, that's different. I'll agree to that. Our art department can make pictures just as good as yours, and you can have one."

For a moment Collins's face fell, but he soon returned to the attack. From his manner one would have judged that he was actually desirous of doing Binns a favor.

"But why not the News?" he insisted pleasantly. "Those two boys are your friends. They wouldn't do anything to hurt you. Think of the difference in the distance, the time we'll save. We want to save time, don't we? Here it is nearly six-thirty, and by the time we get back to the office it'll be half-past seven or eight. It's all right for you, because you can write faster, but look at me. I'd just as lief go down there as not, but what's the difference? Besides the News has got a better plant, and you know it. Either Hill or Weaver'll make a fine picture, and they'll give you one. Ain't that all right?"

At once he sensed what it was that Collins wanted. What he really understood was that if Collins could get this great train robber into the office of the News first, it would take away so much of the sheer necessity he would be put to of repeating all he had heard and seen en route. For once there, other staff members would be able to take the criminal in hand and with the aid of what Collins had to report, extract such a tale as even Binns himself could not better. In addition, it would be such a triumph of reporting—to go out and bring your subject in!

"No, it's not," replied Binns truculently, "and I won't do it. It's all right about Hill and Weaver. I know they'll give me a picture if the paper will let them, but I know the paper won't let them, and besides, you're not doing it for that reason. I know what you want. You want to be able to claim in the morning that you brought this man to the News first. I know you."

For a moment Collins appeared to be quieted by this, and half seemed to abandon the project. He took it up again after a few moments, however, seemingly in the most conciliatory spirit in the world, only now he kept boring Binns with his eyes, a thing which he had never attempted before.

"Aw, come on," he repeated genially, looking Binns squarely in the eyes. "What's the use being small about this? You know you've got the best of the story anyhow. And you're goin' to get a picture too, the same as us. If you don't, then we'll have to go clear to your office or send a man down to the jail. Think of the time it'll take. What's the use of that? One picture's as good as another. And you can't take any good pictures down there to-night, anyhow, and you know it."

As he talked he held Binns's eyes with his own, and all at once the latter began to feel a curious wave of warmth, ease and uncertainty or confusion creep over him in connection with all this. What was so wrong with this proposition, anyhow, he began to ask himself, even while inwardly something was telling him that it was all wrong and that he was making a great mistake. For the first time in his life, and especially in connection with so trying a situation, he began to feel an odd sense of ease and comfort, or as if surrounded by a cloud of something that was comfortable and soothing. This scheme of Collins's was not so bad after all, he thought. What was wrong with it? Hill and Weaver were his friends. They would make a good picture and give him one. Everything Collins was saying seemed true enough, only, only— For the first time since knowing him, and in spite of all his opposition of this afternoon and before, Binns found himself not hating his rival as violently as he had in the past, but feeling as though he weren't such an utterly bad sort after all. Curiously, though, he still didn't believe a word that Collins said, but—

"To the News, sure," he found himself saying in a dumb, half-numb or sensuously warm way. "That wouldn't be so bad. It's nearer. What's wrong with that? Hill or Weaver will make a good picture seven or eight inches long, and then I can take it along," only at the same time he was thinking to himself, "I shouldn't really do this. I shouldn't think it. He'll claim the credit of having brought this man to the News office. He's a big bluff, and I hate him. I'll be making a big mistake. The Star or nothing—that's what I should say. Let him come down to the Star."

114

In the meantime they were entering O—, the station of which now appeared. By now, somehow, Collins had not only convinced the officers, but the prisoner himself. Binns could even see the rural love of show and parade a-gleam in their eyes, their respect for the News, the larger paper, as opposed to the Star. The Star might be all right, but plainly the News was the great place in the sight of these rurals for such an exhibition as this. What a pity, he thought, that he had ever left the News!

As he arose with the others to leave the train he said dully, "No, I won't come in on this. It's all right if you want to bring him down to the Star, or you can take him to police headquarters. But I'm not going to let you do this. You hear now, don't you?"

But outside, Collins laying hold of his arm in an amazingly genial fashion, seemed to come nearer to him humanly than he had ever dreamed was possible before.

"You come up with me to the News now," Collins kept saying, "and then I'll go down with you to the Star, see? We'll just let Hill or Weaver take one picture, and then we'll go down to your place—you see?"

Although Mr. Binns did not see, he went. For the time, nothing seemed important. If Collins had stayed by him he could possibly have prevented his writing any story at all. Even as Binns dreamed, Collins hailed a carriage, and the six of them crowded into it and were forthwith whirled away to the door of the News where, once they had reached it and Collins, the detectives, and the bandit began hurrying across the sidewalk to that familiar door which once had meant so much to him, Binns suddenly awoke. What was it— the door? Or the temporary distraction of Collins? At any rate, he awoke now and made a frantic effort to retrieve himself.

"Wait!" he called. "Say, hold on! Stop! I won't do this at all. I don't agree to this!" but now it was too late. In a trice the prisoner, officers, Collins and even himself were up the two or three low steps of the main entrance and into the hall, and then seeing the hopelessness of it he paused as they entered the elevator and was left to meditate on the inexplicability of the thing that had been done to him.

What was it? How had this low brute succeeded in doing this to him? By the Lord, he had succeeded in hypnotizing him, or something very much like it. What had become, then, of his superior brain, his intellectual force, in the face of this gross savage desire on the part of Collins to win? It was unbelievable. Collins had beaten him, and that in a field and at a task at which he deemed himself unusually superior.

"Great heavens!" he suddenly exclaimed to himself. "That's

what he's done, he's beaten me at my own game! He's taken the prisoner, whom I really had in my own hands at one time, into the office of our great rival, and now in the morning it will all be in the paper! And I allowed him to do it! And I had him beaten, too! Why didn't I kick him off the train? Why didn't I bribe the conductor to help me? I could have. I was afraid of him, that's what it is. And to-morrow there'll be a long editorial in the News telling how this fellow was brought first to the News and photographed, and they'll have his picture to prove it. Oh, Lord, what shall I do? How am I to get out of this?"

Disconsolate and weary, he groaned and swore for blocks as he made his way toward the office of the Star. How to break it to Waxby! How to explain! The exact truth meant disgrace, possibly dismissal. He couldn't tell really, as he had hoped he might, how he had all but prevented Collins from obtaining any interview. Waxby would have sniffed at his weakness in a crisis, put him down as a failure.

Reaching the office, he told another kind of story which was but a half truth. What he could and did say was that the police, being temperamentally en rapport with Collins, had worked with him and against the Star; that in spite of anything he could do, these rural officers and detectives had preferred to follow Collins rather than himself, that the superior position of the News had lured them, and that against his final and fierce protest they had eventually gone in there, since the News was on the natural route to the jail, and the Star was not.

Now it was Waxby's turn to rage, and he did—not at Binns, but at the low dogs of police who were always favoring the News at the expense of the Star. They had done it in the past, as he well knew, when he was city editor of the News. Then it had pleased him—but now—

"I'll fix them!" he squeaked shrilly. "I'll make them sweat. No more favors from me, by—," and rushing a photographer to the jail he had various pictures made, excellent ones, for that matter—only, what was the good? The fact that the News had the honor of making the first picture of this celebrity under its own roof, its own vine and fig-tree, was galling. As a matter of fact, Waxby by now was blaming himself for not having sent an artist along.

But to Binns the sad part was that Collins had him beaten, and that in the face of his self-boasted superiority. In spite of the fact that he might slave over the text, as he did, giving it, because of his despair and chagrin, all his best touches, still, the next morning, there on the front page of the News, was a large picture of the bandit seated in the sanctum sanctorum of the News, entirely surrounded

116

by reporters and editors, and with a portion of the figure, although not the head, of the publisher himself in the background. And over it all in extra large type was the caption:

"LOAN TRAIN ROBBER VISITS OFFICE OF NEWS TO PAY HIS RESPECTS" while underneath, in italics, was a full account of how willingly he had visited the News because of its immense commercial, moral and other forms of superiority.

Was Binns beaten?

Well, rather!

And did he feel it?

He suffered tortures, not only for days, but for weeks and months, absolute tortures. The very thought of Collins made him want to rise and slay him.

"To think," he said over and over to himself, "that a low dog like Collins on whom I wouldn't wipe my feet intellectually, as it were, could do this to me! He hypnotized me, by George! He did! He can! Maybe he could do it again! I wonder if he knows? Am I really the lesser and this scum the greater? Do writers grow on trees?"!

Sad thought.

And some weeks later, meeting his old enemy one day on the street, he had the immense dissatisfaction of seeing the light of triumph and contempt in his eyes. The latter was so bold now, and getting along so well as a reporter, or "newspaper man," that he had the hardihood to leer, sniff and exclaim:

"These swell reporters! These high-priced ink-slingers! Say, who got the best of the train robber story, huh?"

And Binns replied—

But never mind what Binns replied. It wouldn't be fit to read, and no publisher would print it anyhow.

OLD ROGAUM AND HIS THERESA

In all Bleecker Street was no more comfortable doorway than that of the butcher Rogaum, even if the first floor was given over to meat market purposes. It was to one side of the main entrance, which gave ingress to the butcher shop, and from it led up a flight of steps, at least five feet wide, to the living rooms above. A little portico stood out in front of it, railed on either side, and within was a second or final door, forming, with the outer or storm door, a little area, where Mrs. Rogaum and her children frequently sat of a summer's evening. The outer door was never locked, owing to the inconvenience it would inflict on Mr. Rogaum, who had no other way of getting upstairs. In winter, when all had gone to bed, there had been cases in which belated travelers had taken refuge there from the snow or sleet. One or two newsboys occasionally slept there, until routed out by Officer Maguire, who, seeing it half open one morning at two o'clock, took occasion to look in. He jogged the newsboys sharply with his stick, and then, when they were gone, tried the inner door, which was locked.

"You ought to keep that outer door locked, Rogaum," he observed to the phlegmatic butcher the next evening, as he was passing, "people might get in. A couple o' kids was sleepin' in there last night."

"Ach, dot iss no difference," answered Rogaum pleasantly. "I haf der inner door locked, yet. Let dem sleep. Dot iss no difference."

"Better lock it," said the officer, more to vindicate his authority than anything else. "Something will happen there yet."

The door was never locked, however, and now of a summer evening Mrs. Rogaum and the children made pleasant use of its recess, watching the rout of street cars and occasionally belated trucks go by. The children played on the sidewalk, all except the budding Theresa (eighteen just turning), who, with one companion of the neighborhood, the pretty Kenrihan girl, walked up and down the block, laughing, glancing, watching the boys. Old Mrs. Kenrihan lived in the next block, and there, sometimes, the two stopped. There, also, they most frequently pretended to be when talking with the boys in the intervening side street. Young "Connie" Almerting and George Goujon were the bright particular mashers who held the attention of the maidens in this block. These two made their acquaintance in the customary bold, boyish way, and thereafter the girls had an urgent desire to be out in the street together after eight, and to linger where the boys could see and overtake them.

Old Mrs. Rogaum never knew. She was a particularly fat, old German lady, completely dominated by her liege and portly lord, and at nine o'clock regularly, as he had long ago deemed meet and fit, she was wont to betake her way upward and so to bed. Old Rogaum himself, at that hour, closed the market and went to his chamber.

Before that all the children were called sharply, once from the doorstep below and once from the window above, only Mrs. Rogaum did it first and Rogaum last. It had come, because of a shade of lenience, not wholly apparent in the father's nature, that the older of the children needed two callings and sometimes three. Theresa, now that she had "got in" with the Kenrihan maiden, needed that many calls and even more.

She was just at that age for which mere thoughtless, sensory life holds its greatest charm. She loved to walk up and down in the as yet bright street where were voices and laughter, and occasionally moonlight streaming down. What a nuisance it was to be called at nine, anyhow. Why should one have to go in then, anyhow. What old fogies her parents were, wishing to go to bed so early. Mrs. Kenrihan was not so strict with her daughter. It made her pettish when Rogaum insisted, calling as he often did, in German, "Come you now," in a very hoarse and belligerent voice.

She came, eventually, frowning and wretched, all the moonlight calling her, all the voices of the night urging her to come back. Her innate opposition due to her urgent youth made her coming later and later, however, until now, by August of this, her eighteenth year, it was nearly ten when she entered, and Rogaum was almost invariably angry.

"I vill lock you oudt," he declared, in strongly accented English, while she tried to slip by him each time. "I vill show you. Du sollst come ven I say, yet. Hear now."

"I'll not," answered Theresa, but it was always under her breath.

Poor Mrs. Rogaum troubled at hearing the wrath in her husband's voice. It spoke of harder and fiercer times which had been with her. Still she was not powerful enough in the family councils to put in a weighty word. So Rogaum fumed unrestricted.

There were other nights, however, many of them, and now that the young sparks of the neighborhood had enlisted the girls' attention, it was a more trying time than ever. Never did a street seem more beautiful. Its shabby red walls, dusty pavements and protruding store steps and iron railings seemed bits of the ornamental paraphernalia of heaven itself. These lights, the cars, the moon, the street lamps! Theresa had a tender eye for the dashing Almerting, a young idler and loafer of the district, the son of a stationer farther up the street. What a fine fellow he was, indeed! What a handsome nose and chin! What eyes! What authority! His cigarette was always cocked at a high angle, in her presence, and his hat had the least suggestion of being set to one side. He had a shrewd way of winking one eye, taking her boldly by the arm, hailing her as, "Hey, Pretty!" and was strong and athletic and worked (when he worked) in a tobacco factory. His was a trade, indeed, nearly acquired, as he said, and his jingling pockets attested that he had money of his own. Altogether he was very captivating.

"Aw, whaddy ya want to go in for?" he used to say to her, tossing his head gayly on one side to listen and holding her by the arm, as old Rogaum called. "Tell him yuh didn't hear."

"No, I've got to go," said the girl, who was soft and plump and fair—a Rhine maiden type.

"Well, yuh don't have to go just yet. Stay another minute. George, what was that fellow's name that tried to sass us the other day?"

"Theresa!" roared old Rogaum forcefully. "If you do not now come! Ve vill see!"

"I've got to go," repeated Theresa with a faint effort at starting. "Can't you hear? Don't hold me. I haf to."

"Aw, whaddy ya want to be such a coward for? Y' don't have to go. He won't do nothin' tuh yuh. My old man was always hollerin' like that up tuh a coupla years ago. Let him holler! Say, kid, but yuh got sweet eyes! They're as blue! An' your mouth—"

"Now stop! You hear me!" Theresa would protest softly, as, swiftly, he would slip an arm about her waist and draw her to him, sometimes in a vain, sometimes in a successful effort to kiss her.

As a rule she managed to interpose an elbow between her face and his, but even then he would manage to touch an ear or a cheek or her neck—sometimes her mouth, full and warm—before she would develop sufficient energy to push him away and herself free. Then she would protest mock earnestly or sometimes run away.

"Now, I'll never speak to you any more, if that's the way you're going to do. My father don't allow me to kiss boys, anyhow," and then she would run, half ashamed, half smiling to herself as he would stare after her, or if she lingered, develop a kind of anger and even rage.

"Aw, cut it! Whaddy ya want to be so shy for? Dontcha like me? What's gettin' into yuh, anyhow? Hey?"

In the meantime George Goujon and Myrtle Kenrihan, their companions, might be sweeting and going through a similar contest, perhaps a hundred feet up the street or near at hand. The quality of old Rogaum's voice would by now have become so raucous, however, that Theresa would have lost all comfort in the scene and, becoming frightened, hurry away. Then it was often that both Almerting and Goujon as well as Myrtle Kenrihan would follow her to the corner, almost in sight of the irate old butcher.

"Let him call," young Almerting would insist, laying a final hold on her soft white fingers and causing her to quiver thereby.

"Oh, no," she would gasp nervously. "I can't."

"Well, go on, then," he would say, and with a flip of his heel would turn back, leaving Theresa to wonder whether she had alienated him forever or no. Then she would hurry to her father's door.

"Muss ich all my time spenden calling, mit you on de streeds oudt?" old Rogaum would roar wrathfully, the while his fat hand would descend on her back. "Take dot now. Vy don'd you come ven I call? In now. I vill show you. Und come you yussed vunce more at dis time—ve vill see if I am boss in my own house, aber! Komst du vun minute nach ten to-morrow und you vill see vot you vill get. I vill der door lock. Du sollst not in kommen. Mark! Oudt sollst du stayen—oudt!" and he would glare wrathfully at her retreating figure.

Sometimes Theresa would whimper, sometimes cry or sulk. She almost hated her father for his cruelty, "the big, fat, rough thing," and just because she wanted to stay out in the bright streets, too! Because he was old and stout and wanted to go to bed at ten, he thought every one else did. And outside was the dark sky with its stars, the street lamps, the cars, the tinkle and laughter of eternal life!

"Oh!" she would sigh as she undressed and crawled into her small neat bed. To think that she had to live like this all her days! At the same time old Rogaum was angry and equally determined. It was not so much that he imagined that his Theresa was in bad company as yet, but he wished to forefend against possible danger. This was not a good neighborhood by any means. The boys around here were tough. He wanted Theresa to pick some nice sober youth from among the other Germans he and his wife knew here and there—at the Lutheran Church, for instance. Otherwise she shouldn't marry. He knew she only walked from his shop to the door of the Kenrihans and back again. Had not his wife told him so? If he had thought upon what far pilgrimage her feet had already ventured, or had even seen the dashing Almerting hanging near, then had there been wrath indeed. As it was, his mind was more or less at ease.

On many, many evenings it was much the same. Sometimes

she got in on time, sometimes not, but more and more "Connie" Almerting claimed her for his "steady," and bought her ice-cream. In the range of the short block and its confining corners it was all done, lingering by the curbstone and strolling a half block either way in the side streets, until she had offended seriously at home, and the threat was repeated anew. He often tried to persuade her to go on picnics or outings of various kinds, but this, somehow, was not to be thought of at her age—at least with him. She knew her father would never endure the thought, and never even had the courage to mention it, let alone run away. Mere lingering with him at the adjacent street corners brought stronger and stronger admonishments—even more blows and the threat that she should not get in at all.

Well enough she meant to obey, but on one radiant night late in June the time fled too fast. The moon was so bright, the air so soft. The feel of far summer things was in the wind and even in this dusty street. Theresa, in a newly starched white summer dress, had been loitering up and down with Myrtle when as usual they encountered Almerting and Goujon. Now it was ten, and the regular calls were beginning.

"Aw, wait a minute," said "Connie." "Stand still. He won't lock yuh out."

"But he will, though," said Theresa. "You don't know him."

"Well, if he does, come on back to me. I'll take care of yuh. I'll be here. But he won't though. If you stayed out a little while he'd letcha in all right. That's the way my old man used to try to do me but it didn't work with me. I stayed out an' he let me in, just the same. Don'tcha let him kidja." He jingled some loose change in his pocket

Never in his life had he had a girl on his hands at any unseasonable hour, but it was nice to talk big, and there was a club to which he belonged, The Varick Street Roosters, and to which he had a key. It would be closed and empty at this hour, and she could stay there until morning, if need be or with Myrtle Kenrihan. He would take her there if she insisted. There was a sinister grin on the youth's face.

By now Theresa's affections had carried her far. This youth with his slim body, his delicate strong hands, his fine chin, straight mouth and hard dark eyes—how wonderful he seemed! He was but nineteen to her eighteen but cold, shrewd, daring. Yet how tender he seemed to her, how well worth having! Always, when he kissed her now, she trembled in the balance. There was something in the iron grasp of his fingers that went through her like fire. His glance held hers at times when she could scarcely endure it.

"I'll wait, anyhow," he insisted.

Longer and longer she lingered, but now for once no voice came.

She began to feel that something was wrong—a greater strain than if old Rogaum's voice had been filling the whole neighborhood.

"I've got to go," she said.

"Gee, but you're a coward, yuh are!" said he derisively. "What 'r yuh always so scared about? He always says he'll lock yuh out, but he never does."

"Yes, but he will," she insisted nervously. "I think he has this time. You don't know him. He's something awful when he gets real mad. Oh, Connie, I must go!" For the sixth or seventh time she moved, and once more he caught her arm and waist and tried to kiss her, but she slipped away from him.

"Ah, yuh!" he exclaimed. "I wish he would lock yuh out!"

At her own doorstep she paused momentarily, more to soften her progress than anything. The outer door was open as usual, but not the inner. She tried it, but it would not give. It was locked! For a moment she paused, cold fear racing over her body, and then knocked.

No answer.

Again she rattled the door, this time nervously, and was about to cry out.

Still no answer.

At last she heard her father's voice, hoarse and indifferent, not addressed to her at all, but to her mother.

"Let her go, now," it said savagely, from the front room where he supposed she could not hear. "I vill her a lesson teach."

"Hadn't you better let her in now, yet?" pleaded Mrs. Rogaum faintly.

"No," insisted Mr. Rogaum. "Nefer! Let her go now. If she vill alvays stay oudt, let her stay now. Ve vill see how she likes dot."

His voice was rich in wrath, and he was saving up a good beating for her into the bargain, that she knew. She would have to wait and wait and plead, and when she was thoroughly wretched and subdued he would let her in and beat her—such a beating as she had never received in all her born days.

Again the door rattled, and still she got no answer. Not even her call brought a sound.

Now, strangely, a new element, not heretofore apparent in her nature but nevertheless wholly there, was called into life, springing in action as Diana, full formed. Why should he always be so harsh? She hadn't done anything but stay out a little later than usual. He was always so anxious to keep her in and subdue her. For once the cold chill of her girlish fears left her, and she wavered angrily.

"All right," she said, some old German stubbornness springing up, "I won't knock. You don't need to let me in, then."

A suggestion of tears was in her eyes, but she backed firmly out onto the stoop and sat down, hesitating. Old Rogaum saw her, lowering down from the lattice, but said nothing. He would teach her for once what were proper hours!

At the corner, standing, Almerting also saw her. He recognized the simple white dress, and paused steadily, a strange thrill racing over him. Really they had locked her out! Gee, this was new. It was great, in a way. There she was, white, quiet, shut out, waiting at her father's doorstep.

Sitting thus, Theresa pondered a moment, her girlish rashness and anger dominating her. Her pride was hurt and she felt revengeful. They would shut her out, would they? All right, she would go out and they should look to it how they would get her back—the old curmudgeons. For the moment the home of Myrtle Kenrihan came to her as a possible refuge, but she decided that she need not go there yet. She had better wait about awhile and see—or walk and frighten them. He would beat her, would he? Well, maybe he would and maybe he wouldn't. She might come back, but still that was a thing afar off. Just now it didn't matter so much. "Connie" was still there on the corner. He loved her dearly. She felt it.

Getting up, she stepped to the now quieting sidewalk and strolled up the street. It was a rather nervous procedure, however. There were street cars still, and stores lighted and people passing, but soon these would not be, and she was locked out. The side streets were already little more than long silent walks and gleaming rows of lamps.

At the corner her youthful lover almost pounced upon her.

"Locked out, are yuh?" he asked, his eyes shining.

For the moment she was delighted to see him, for a nameless dread had already laid hold of her. Home meant so much. Up to now it had been her whole life.

"Yes," she answered feebly.

"Well, let's stroll on a little," said the boy. He had not as yet quite made up his mind what to do, but the night was young. It was so fine to have her with him—his.

At the farther corner they passed Officers Maguire and Delahanty, idly swinging their clubs and discussing politics.

"'Tis a shame," Officer Delahanty was saying, "the way things

124

are run now," but he paused to add, "Ain't that old Rogaum's girl over there with young Almerting?"

"It is," replied Maguire, looking after.

"Well, I'm thinkin' he'd better be keepin' an eye on her," said the former. "She's too young to be runnin' around with the likes o' him."

Maguire agreed. "He's a young tough," he observed. "I never liked him. He's too fresh. He works over here in Myer's tobacco factory, and belongs to The Roosters. He's up to no good, I'll warrant that."

"Teach 'em a lesson, I would," Almerting was saying to Theresa as they strolled on. "We'll walk around a while an' make 'em think yuh mean business. They won't lock yuh out any more. If they don't let yuh in when we come back I'll find yuh a place, all right."

His sharp eyes were gleaming as he looked around into her own. Already he had made up his mind that she should not go back if he could help it. He knew a better place than home for this night, anyhow—the club room of the Roosters, if nowhere else. They could stay there for a time, anyhow.

By now old Rogaum, who had seen her walking up the street alone, was marveling at her audacity, but thought she would soon come back. It was amazing that she should exhibit such temerity, but he would teach her! Such a whipping! At half-past ten, however, he stuck his head out of the open window and saw nothing of her. At eleven, the same. Then he walked the floor.

At first wrathful, then nervous, then nervous and wrathful, he finally ended all nervous, without a scintilla of wrath. His stout wife sat up in bed and began to wring her hands.

"Lie down!" he commanded. "You make me sick. I know vot I am doing!"

"Is she still at der door?" pleaded the mother.

"No," he said. "I don't tink so. She should come ven I call."

His nerves were weakening, however, and now they finally collapsed.

"She vent de stread up," he said anxiously after a time. "I vill go after."

Slipping on his coat, he went down the stairs and out into the night. It was growing late, and the stillness and gloom of midnight were nearing. Nowhere in sight was his Theresa. First one way and then another he went, looking here, there, everywhere, finally groaning.

"Ach, Gott!" he said, the sweat bursting out on his brow, "vot in Teufel's name iss dis?"

He thought he would seek a policeman, but there was none.

125

Officer Maguire had long since gone for a quiet game in one of the neighboring saloons. His partner had temporarily returned to his own beat. Still old Rogaum hunted on, worrying more and more.

Finally he bethought him to hasten home again, for she must have got back. Mrs. Rogaum, too, would be frantic if she had not. If she were not there he must go to the police. Such a night! And his Theresa— This thing could not go on.

As he turned into his own corner he almost ran, coming up to the little portico wet and panting. At a puffing step he turned, and almost fell over a white body at his feet, a prone and writhing woman.

"Ach, Gott!" he cried aloud, almost shouting in his distress and excitement. "Theresa, vot iss dis? Wilhelmina, a light now. Bring a light now, I say, for himmel's sake! Theresa hat sich umgebracht. Help!"

He had fallen to his knees and was turning over the writhing, groaning figure. By the pale light of the street, however, he could make out that it was not his Theresa, fortunately, as he had at first feared, but another and yet there was something very like her in the figure.

"Um!" said the stranger weakly. "Ah!"

The dress was gray, not white as was his Theresa's, but the body was round and plump. It cut the fiercest cords of his intensity, this thought of death to a young woman, but there was something else about the situation which made him forget his own troubles.

Mrs. Rogaum, loudly admonished, almost tumbled down the stairs. At the foot she held the light she had brought—a small glass oil-lamp—and then nearly dropped it. A fairly attractive figure, more girl than woman, rich in all the physical charms that characterize a certain type, lay near to dying. Her soft hair had fallen back over a good forehead, now quite white. Her pretty hands, well decked with rings, were clutched tightly in an agonized grip. At her neck a blue silk shirtwaist and light lace collar were torn away where she had clutched herself, and on the white flesh was a yellow stain as of one who had been burned. A strange odor reeked in the area, and in one corner was a spilled bottle.

"Ach, Gott!" exclaimed Mrs. Rogaum. "It iss a vooman! She haf herself gekilt. Run for der police! Oh, my! oh, my!"

Rogaum did not kneel for more than a moment. Somehow, this creature's fate seemed in some psychic way identified with that of his own daughter. He bounded up, and jumping out his front door, began to call lustily for the police. Officer Maguire, at his social game nearby, heard the very first cry and came running.

"What's the matter here, now?" he exclaimed, rushing up full and ready for murder, robbery, fire, or, indeed, anything in the whole roster of human calamities.

"A vooman!" said Rogaum excitedly. "She haf herself umgebracht. She iss dying. Ach, Gott! in my own doorstep, yet!"

"Vere iss der hospital?" put in Mrs. Rogaum, thinking clearly of an ambulance, but not being able to express it. "She iss gekilt, sure. Oh! Oh!" and bending over her the poor old motherly soul stroked the tightened hands, and trickled tears upon the blue shirtwaist. "Ach, vy did you do dot?" she said. "Ach, for vy?"

Officer Maguire was essentially a man of action. He jumped to the sidewalk, amid the gathering company, and beat loudly with his club upon the stone flagging. Then he ran to the nearest police phone, returning to aid in any other way he might. A milk wagon passing on its way from the Jersey ferry with a few tons of fresh milk aboard, he held it up and demanded a helping.

"Give us a quart there, will you?" he said authoritatively. "A woman's swallowed acid in here."

"Sure," said the driver, anxious to learn the cause of the excitement. "Got a glass, anybody?"

Maguire ran back and returned, bearing a measure. Mrs. Rogaum stood looking nervously on, while the stocky officer raised the golden head and poured the milk.

"Here, now, drink this," he said. "Come on. Try an' swallow it."

The girl, a blonde of the type the world too well knows, opened her eyes, and looked, groaning a little.

"Drink it," shouted the officer fiercely. "Do you want to die? Open your mouth!"

Used to a fear of the law in all her days, she obeyed now, even in death. The lips parted, the fresh milk was drained to the end, some spilling on neck and cheek.

While they were working old Rogaum came back and stood looking on, by the side of his wife. Also Officer Delahanty, having heard the peculiar wooden ring of the stick upon the stone in the night, had come up.

"Ach, ach," exclaimed Rogaum rather distractedly, "und she iss oudt yet. I could not find her. Oh, oh!"

There was a clang of a gong up the street as the racing ambulance turned rapidly in. A young hospital surgeon dismounted, and seeing the woman's condition, ordered immediate removal. Both officers and Rogaum, as well as the surgeon, helped place her in the ambulance. After a moment the lone bell, ringing wildly in the night, was all the evidence remaining that a tragedy had been here.

"Do you know how she came here?" asked Officer Delahanty, coming back to get Rogaum's testimony for the police.

"No, no," answered Rogaum wretchedly. "She vass here alretty. I vass for my daughter loog. Ach, himmel, I haf my daughter lost. She iss avay."

Mrs. Rogaum also chattered, the significance of Theresa's absence all the more painfully emphasized by this.

The officer did not at first get the import of this. He was only interested in the facts of the present case.

"You say she was here when you come? Where was you?"

"I say I vass for my daughter loog. I come here, und der vooman vass here now alretty."

"Yes. What time was this?"

"Only now yet. Yussed a half-hour."

Officer Maguire had strolled up, after chasing away a small crowd that had gathered with fierce and unholy threats. For the first time now he noticed the peculiar perturbation of the usually placid German couple.

"What about your daughter?" he asked, catching a word as to that.

Both old people raised their voices at once.

"She haf gone. She haf run avay. Ach, himmel, ve must for her loog. Quick—she could not get in. Ve had der door shut."

"Locked her out, eh?" inquired Maguire after a time, hearing much of the rest of the story.

"Yes," explained Rogaum. "It was to schkare her a liddle. She vould not come ven I called."

"Sure, that's the girl we saw walkin' with young Almerting, do ye mind? The one in the white dress," said Delahanty to Maguire.

"White dress, yah!" echoed Rogaum, and then the fact of her walking with some one came home like a blow.

"Did you hear dot?" he exclaimed even as Mrs. Rogaum did likewise. "Mein Gott, hast du das gehoert?"

He fairly jumped as he said it. His hands flew up to his stout and ruddy head.

"Whaddy ya want to let her out for nights?" asked Maguire roughly, catching the drift of the situation. "That's no time for young girls to be out, anyhow, and with these toughs around here. Sure, I saw her, nearly two hours ago."

"Ach," groaned Rogaum. "Two hours yet. Ho, ho, ho!" His voice was quite hysteric.

"Well, go on in," said Officer Delahanty. "There's no use yellin' out here. Give us a description of her an' we'll send out an alarm. You won't be able to find her walkin' around."

Her parents described her exactly. The two men turned to the nearest police box and then disappeared, leaving the old German couple in the throes of distress. A time-worn old church-clock nearby now chimed out one and then two. The notes cut like knives. Mrs. Rogaum began fearfully to cry. Rogaum walked and blustered to himself.

"It's a queer case, that," said Officer Delahanty to Maguire after having reported the matter of Theresa, but referring solely to the outcast of the doorway so recently sent away and in whose fate they were much more interested. She being a part of the commercialized vice of the city, they were curious as to the cause of her suicide. "I think I know that woman. I think I know where she came from. You do, too—Adele's, around the corner, eh? She didn't come into that doorway by herself, either. She was put there. You know how they do."

"You're right," said Maguire. "She was put there, all right, and that's just where she come from, too."

The two of them now tipped up their noses and cocked their eyes significantly.

"Let's go around," added Maguire.

They went, the significant red light over the transom at 68 telling its own story. Strolling leisurely up, they knocked. At the very first sound a painted denizen of the half-world opened the door.

"Where's Adele?" asked Maguire as the two, hats on as usual, stepped in.

"She's gone to bed."

"Tell her to come down."

They seated themselves deliberately in the gaudy mirrored parlor and waited, conversing between themselves in whispers. Presently a sleepy-looking woman of forty in a gaudy robe of heavy texture, and slippered in red, appeared.

"We're here about that suicide case you had tonight. What about it? Who was she? How'd she come to be in that doorway around the corner? Come, now," Maguire added, as the madam assumed an air of mingled injured and ignorant innocence, "you know. Can that stuff! How did she come to take poison?"

"I don't know what you're talking about," said the woman with the utmost air of innocence. "I never heard of any suicide."

"Aw, come now ," insisted Delahanty, "the girl around the corner. You know. We know you've got a pull, but we've got to know about this case, just the same. Come across now. It won't be published. What made her take the poison?"

Under the steady eyes of the officers the woman hesitated, but finally weakened.

"Why—why—her lover went back on her—that's all. She got so blue we just couldn't do anything with her. I tried to, but she wouldn't listen."

"Lover, eh?" put in Maguire as though that were the most unheard-of thing in the world. "What was his name?"

"I don't know. You never can tell that."

"What was her name—Annie?" asked Delahanty wisely, as though he knew but was merely inquiring for form's sake.

"No—Emily."

"Well, how did she come to get over there, anyhow?" inquired Maguire most pleasantly.

"George took her," she replied, referring to a man-of-all-work about the place.

Then little by little as they sat there the whole miserable story came out, miserable as all the wilfulness and error and suffering of the world.

"How old was she?"

"Oh, twenty-one."

"Well, where'd she come from?"

"Oh, here in New York. Her family locked her out one night, I think."

Something in the way the woman said this last brought old Rogaum and his daughter back to the policemen's minds. They had forgotten all about her by now, although they had turned in an alarm. Fearing to interfere too much with this well-known and politically controlled institution, the two men left, but outside they fell to talking of the other case.

"We ought to tell old Rogaum about her some time," said Maguire to Delahanty cynically. "He locked his kid out to-night."

"Yes, it might be a good thing for him to hear that," replied the other. "We'd better go round there an' see if his girl's back yet. She may be back by now," and so they returned but little disturbed by the joint miseries.

At Rogaum's door they once more knocked loudly.

"Is your daughter back again?" asked Maguire when a reply was had.

"Ach, no," replied the hysterical Mrs. Rogaum, who was quite alone now. "My husband he haf gone oudt again to loog vunce more. Oh, my! Oh, my!"

"Well, that's what you get for lockin' her out," returned Maguire loftily, the other story fresh in his mind. "That other girl downstairs here tonight was locked out too, once." He chanced to

130

have a girl-child of his own and somehow he was in the mood for pointing a moral. "You oughtn't to do anything like that. Where d'yuh expect she's goin' to if you lock her out?"

Mrs. Rogaum groaned. She explained that it was not her fault, but anyhow it was carrying coals to Newcastle to talk to her so. The advice was better for her husband.

The pair finally returned to the station to see if the call had been attended to.

"Sure," said the sergeant, "certainly. Whaddy ya think?" and he read from the blotter before him:

"'Look out for girl, Theresa Rogaum. Aged 18; height, about 5, 3; light hair, blue eyes, white cotton dress, trimmed with blue ribbon. Last seen with lad named Almerting, about 19 years of age, about 5, 9; weight 135 pounds.'"

There were other details even more pointed and conclusive. For over an hour now, supposedly, policemen from the Battery to Harlem, and far beyond, had been scanning long streets and dim shadows for a girl in a white dress with a youth of nineteen,— supposedly.

Officer Halsey, another of this region, which took in a portion of Washington Square, had seen a good many couples this pleasant summer evening since the description of Theresa and Almerting had been read to him over the telephone, but none that answered to these. Like Maguire and Delahanty, he was more or less indifferent to all such cases, but idling on a corner near the park at about three a.m., a brother officer, one Paisly by name, came up and casually mentioned the missing pair also.

"I bet I saw that couple, not over an hour ago. She was dressed in white, and looked to me as if she didn't want to be out. I didn't happen to think at the time, but now I remember. They acted sort o' funny. She did, anyhow. They went in this park down at the Fourth Street end there."

"Supposing we beat it, then," suggested Halsey, weary for something to do.

"Sure," said the other quickly, and together they began a careful search, kicking around in the moonlight under the trees. The moon was leaning moderately toward the west, and all the branches were silvered with light and dew. Among the flowers, past clumps of bushes, near the fountain, they searched, each one going his way alone. At last, the wandering Halsey paused beside a thick clump of flaming bushes, ruddy, slightly, even in the light. A murmur of voices greeted him, and something very much like the sound of a sob.

"What's that?" he said mentally, drawing near and listening.

131

"Why don't you come on now?" said the first of the voices heard. "They won't let you in any more. You're with me, ain't you? What's the use cryin'?"

No answer to this, but no sobs. She must have been crying silently.

"Come on. I can take care of yuh. We can live in Hoboken. I know a place where we can go to-night. That's all right."

There was a movement as if the speaker were patting her on the shoulder.

"What's the use cryin'? Don't you believe I love yuh?"

The officer who had stolen quietly around to get a better view now came closer. He wanted to see for himself. In the moonlight, from a comfortable distance, he could see them seated. The tall bushes were almost all about the bench. In the arms of the youth was the girl in white, held very close. Leaning over to get a better view, he saw him kiss her and hold her—hold her in such a way that she could but yield to him, whatever her slight disinclination.

It was a common affair at earlier hours, but rather interesting now. The officer was interested. He crept nearer.

"What are you two doin' here?" he suddenly inquired, rising before them, as though he had not seen.

The girl tumbled out of her compromising position, speechless and blushing violently. The young man stood up, nervous, but still defiant.

"Aw, we were just sittin' here," he replied.

"Yes? Well, say, what's your name? I think we're lookin' for you two, anyhow. Almerting?"

"That's me," said the youth.

"And yours?" he added, addressing Theresa.

"Theresa Rogaum," replied the latter brokenly, beginning to cry.

"Well, you two'll have to come along with me," he added laconically. "The Captain wants to see both of you," and he marched them solemnly away.

"What for?" young Almerting ventured to inquire after a time, blanched with fright.

"Never mind," replied the policeman irritably. "Come along, you'll find out at the station house. We want you both. That's enough."

At the other end of the park Paisly joined them, and, at the station-house, the girl was given a chair. She was all tears and melancholy with a modicum possibly of relief at being thus rescued from the world. Her companion, for all his youth, was defiant if circumspect, a natural animal defeated of its aim.

"Better go for her father," commented the sergeant, and by four in the morning old Rogaum, who had still been up and walking the floor, was rushing station-ward. From an earlier rage he had passed to an almost killing grief, but now at the thought that he might possibly see his daughter alive and well once more he was overflowing with a mingled emotion which contained rage, fear, sorrow, and a number of other things. What should he do to her if she were alive? Beat her? Kiss her? Or what? Arrived at the station, however, and seeing his fair Theresa in the hands of the police, and this young stranger lingering near, also detained, he was beside himself with fear, rage, affection.

"You! You!" he exclaimed at once, glaring at the imperturbable Almerting, when told that this was the young man who was found with his girl. Then, seized with a sudden horror, he added, turning to Theresa, "Vot haf you done? Oh, oh! You! You!" he repeated again to Almerting angrily, now that he felt that his daughter was safe. "Come not near my tochter any more! I vill preak your effery pone, du teufel, du!"

He made a move toward the incarcerated lover, but here the sergeant interfered.

"Stop that, now," he said calmly. "Take your daughter out of here and go home, or I'll lock you both up. We don't want any fighting in here. D'ye hear? Keep your daughter off the streets hereafter, then she won't get into trouble. Don't let her run around with such young toughs as this." Almerting winced. "Then there won't anything happen to her. We'll do whatever punishing's to be done."

"Aw, what's eatin' him!" commented Almerting dourly, now that he felt himself reasonably safe from a personal encounter. "What have I done? He locked her out, didn't he? I was just keepin' her company till morning."

"Yes, we know all about that," said the sergeant, "and about you, too. You shut up, or you'll go downtown to Special Sessions. I want no guff out o' you." Still he ordered the butcher angrily to be gone.

Old Rogaum heard nothing. He had his daughter. He was taking her home. She was not dead—not even morally injured in so far as he could learn. He was a compound of wondrous feelings. What to do was beyond him.

At the corner near the butcher shop they encountered the wakeful Maguire, still idling, as they passed. He was pleased to see that Rogaum had his Theresa once more. It raised him to a high, moralizing height.

133

"Don't lock her out any more," he called significantly. "That's what brought the other girl to your door, you know!"

"Vot iss dot?" said Rogaum.

"I say the other girl was locked out. That's why she committed suicide."

"Ach, I know," said the husky German under his breath, but he had no intention of locking her out. He did not know what he would do until they were in the presence of his crying wife, who fell upon Theresa, weeping. Then he decided to be reasonably lenient.

"She vass like you," said the old mother to the wandering Theresa, ignorant of the seeming lesson brought to their very door. "She vass loog like you."

"I vill not vip you now," said the old butcher solemnly, too delighted to think of punishment after having feared every horror under the sun, "aber, go not oudt any more. Keep off de streads so late. I von't haf it. Dot loafer, aber—let him yussed come here some more! I fix him!"

"No, no," said the fat mother tearfully, smoothing her daughter's hair. "She vouldn't run avay no more yet, no, no." Old Mrs. Rogaum was all mother.

"Well, you wouldn't let me in," insisted Theresa, "and I didn't have any place to go. What do you want me to do? I'm not going to stay in the house all the time."

"I fix him!" roared Rogaum, unloading all his rage now on the recreant lover freely. "Yussed let him come some more! Der penitentiary he should haf!"

"Oh, he's not so bad," Theresa told her mother, almost a heroine now that she was home and safe. "He's Mr. Almerting, the stationer's boy. They live here in the next block."

"Don't you ever bother that girl again," the sergeant was saying to young Almerting as he turned him loose an hour later. "If you do, we'll get you, and you won't get off under six months. Y' hear me, do you?"

"Aw, I don't want 'er," replied the boy truculently and cynically. "Let him have his old daughter. What'd he want to lock 'er out for? They'd better not lock 'er out again though, that's all I say. I don't want 'er."

"Beat it!" replied the sergeant, and away he went.

WILL YOU WALK INTO MY PARLOR?

It was a sweltering noon in July. Gregory, after several months of meditation on the warning given him by his political friend, during which time nothing to substantiate it had occurred, was making ready to return to the seaside hotel to which his present prosperity entitled him. It was a great affair, the Triton, about sixty minutes from his office, facing the sea and amid the pines and sands of the Island. His wife, 'the girl,' as he conventionally referred to her, had been compelled, in spite of the plot which had been revealed or suggested, owing to the ailing state of their child, to go up to the mountains to her mother for advice and comfort. Owing to the imminence of the fall campaign, however, he could not possibly leave. Weekdays and Sundays, and occasionally nights, he was busy ferreting out and substantiating one fact and another in regard to the mismanagement of the city, which was to be used as ammunition a little later on. The mayor and his "ring," as it was called, was to be ousted at all costs. He, Gregory, was certain to be rewarded if that came to pass. In spite of that he was eminently sincere as to the value and even the necessity of what he was doing. The city was being grossly mismanaged. What greater labor than to worm out the details and expose them to the gaze of an abused and irritated citizenship?

But the enemy itself was not helpless. A gentleman in the publishing business of whom he had never even heard called to offer him a position in the Middle West which would take him out of the city for four or five years at the least, and pay him six or seven thousand dollars a year. On his failure to be interested some of his mail began to disappear, and it seemed to him as though divers strange characters were taking a peculiar and undue interest in his movements. Lastly, one of the politicians connected with his own party called to see him at his office.

"You see, Gregory, it's this way," he said after a short preamble, "you have got a line as to what's going on in connection with that South Penyank land transfer. The mayor is in on that, but he is absolutely determined that the public is not going to find it out, and so is his partner, Tilney—not until after the election, anyhow. They are prepared to use some pretty rough methods, so look out for yourself. You're fond of your wife, are you? Well, keep her close beside you, and the kid. Don't let them get you away from her, even for a moment, where you shouldn't be. You saw what happened to Crothers two or three years ago, didn't you? He was about to expose that Yellow Point Ferry deal, but of course no one knew anything about that—and then, zip!—all at once he was arrested on an old charge of desertion, an old debt that he had failed to pay was produced and his furniture seized, and his wife was induced to leave him. Don't let them catch you in the same way. If you have any debts bring them to us and let us see what we can do about them. And if you are interested in any other woman, break it off, send her away, get rid of her."

Gregory viewed him with an irritated, half-pitying smile.

"There isn't any other woman," he said simply. Think of his being faithless to "the girl" and the kid—the blue-eyed, pink-toed kid!

"Don't think I'm trying to pry into your affairs," went on the politician. "I'm just telling you. If you need any further advice or help, come to me. But whatever you do, look out for yourself," and with that he put on his high silk hat and departed.

Gregory stood in the center of his office after his visitor had gone, and gazed intently at the floor. Certainly, from what he had discovered so far, he could readily believe that the mayor would do just what his friend had said. And as for the mayor's friend, the real estate plunger, it was plain from his whispered history that no tricks or brutalities were beneath him. Another politician had once said in describing him that he would not stop short of murder, but that one would never catch him red-handed or in any other way, and certainly that appeared to be true. He was wealthier, more powerful, than he had ever been, much more so than the mayor.

Since he and his wife had come to this seaside hotel several things had occurred which caused him to think that something might happen, although there was no evidence as yet that his suspicions were well-founded. An unctuous, over-dressed, bejeweled, semi-sporty widow of forty had arrived, a business woman, she indicated herself to be, conducting a highly successful theatrical agency in the great city, and consequently weltering in what one of Gregory's friends was wont to describe as "the sinews of war." She abounded in brown and wine-colored silks, brown slippers and stockings, a wealth of suspiciously lustrous auburn hair. Her car, for she had one, was of respectable reputation. Her skill and willingness to risk at whist of good report. She was, in the parlance of the hotel clerks and idlers of the Triton veranda, a cheerful and liberal spender. Even while Mrs. Gregory was at Triton Hall, Mrs. Skelton had arrived, making herself comfortable in two rooms and bath on the sea front, and finding familiar friends in the manager and several stalwart idlers who appeared to be brokers and real estate dealers, and who took a respectable interest in golf, tennis, and the Triton Grill. She was unctuous, hearty, optimistic, and neither Gregory nor his wife could help liking her a little. But before leaving, his wife had casually wondered whether Mrs. Skelton would be one to engage in such a plot. Her friendliness, while possible of any interpretation, was still general enough to be free of suspicion. She might be looking for just such a situation as this, though—to find Gregory alone.

"Do be careful, dear," his wife cautioned. "If you become too doubtful, leave and go to another place. At least that will compel them to provide another set of people." And off she went, fairly serene in her faith in her husband's ability to manage the matter.

Thus, much against his will, at first, Gregory found himself alone. He began to wonder if he should leave, or weather it out, as he expressed it to himself. Why should he be driven from the one comfortable hotel on this nearest beach, and that when he most needed it, away from a region where he was regularly encountering most of his political friends, particularly at week-ends? For so near a place it had many advantages: a delightful golf course, several tennis courts, food and rooms reasonably well above complaint, and a refreshing and delightful view of the sea over a broad lawn. Besides it was absolutely necessary for him to be in the near-by city the greater portion of every single working day. His peculiar and pressing investigation demanded it and a comfortable place to rest and recuperate at night was also imperative.

"It's beautiful here," he said to himself finally, "and here is where I stick. I haven't a car, and where is there any other place as convenient? Besides, if they're going to follow me, they're going to follow me."

In consequence, he traveled meditatively back and forth between this place and the city, thinking of what might happen. Becoming a little doubtful, he decided to call on Frank Blount and talk it over with him. Blount was an old newspaper man who had first turned lawyer and then broker. Seemingly clientless the major portion of the time, he still prospered mightily. A lorn bachelor, he had three clubs, several hotels, and a dozen country homes to visit, to say nothing of a high power car. Just now he was held unduly close to his work, and so was frequenting this coast. He liked golf and tennis, and, incidentally, Gregory, whom he wished to see prosper though he could not quite direct him in the proper way. Reaching the city one morning, Gregory betook him to Blount's office, and there laid the whole case before him.

"Now, that's the way it is," he concluded, staring at the pink cheeks and partially bald head of his friend, "and I would like to know what you would do if you were in my place."

Blount gazed thoughtfully out through the high towers of the city to the blue sky beyond, while he drummed with his fingers on the glass top of his desk.

"Well," he replied, after a time, scratching his cheekbone thoughtfully, "I'd stick it out if I were you. If there is to be a woman, and she is attractive, you might have some fun out of it without getting yourself in any trouble. It looks like a sporty summer proposition to me. Of course, you'll have to be on your guard. I'd take out a permit to carry a revolver if I were you. They'll hear of it if they're up to anything, and it won't cheer them any. In the next place, you ought to make out a day-to-day statement of your exact movements, and swear to it before a notary. If they hear of that it won't cheer them any either, and it may make them try to think up something really original.

"Besides," he went on, "I haven't so very much to do evenings and week-ends, and if you want me to I'll just be around most of the time in case of trouble. If we're together they can't turn much of anything without one of us knowing something about it, and then, too, you'll have an eye-witness." He was wondering whether the lady might not be interesting to him also. "I'm over at Sunset Point, just beyond you there, and if you want me I'll come over every evening and see how you're making out. If any trick is turned, I'd like to see how it is done," and he smiled in a winsome, helpful manner.

"That's just the thing," echoed Gregory thoughtfully. "I don't want any trick turned. I can't afford it. If anything should happen to me just now I'd never get on my feet again politically, and then there's the wife and kid, and I'm sick of the newspaper business," and he stared out of the window.

"Well, don't be worrying about it," Blount insisted soothingly. "Just be on your guard, and if you have to stay in town late any night, let me know and I'll come and pick you up. Or, if I can't do that, stay in town yourself. Go to one of the big hotels, where you'll feel thoroughly safe."

For several days Gregory, to avoid being a nuisance, returned to the hotel early. Also he secured a permit, and weighted his hip pocket with an unwieldy weapon which he resented, but which he nevertheless kept under his pillow at night. His uncertainty worked on his imagination to such an extent that he began to note suspicious moves on the part of nearly everybody. Any new character about the hotel annoyed him. He felt certain that there was a group of people connected with Mrs. Skelton who were watching him, though he could not prove it, even to himself.

"This is ridiculous," he finally told himself. "I'm acting like a five-year-old in the dark. Who's going to hurt me?" And he wrote

138

laughing letters to his wife about it, and tried to resume his old-time nonchalance.

It wasn't quite possible, however, for not long after that something happened which disturbed him greatly. At least he persuaded himself to that effect, for that was a characteristic of these incidents—their openness to another interpretation than the one he might fix on. In spite of Blount's advice, one night about nine he decided to return to Triton Hall, and that without calling his friend to his aid.

"What's the use?" he asked himself. "He'll be thinking I'm the biggest coward ever, and after all, nothing has happened yet, and I doubt whether they'd go that far, anyhow." He consoled himself with the idea that perhaps humanity was better than he thought.

But just the same, as he left the train at Triton and saw it glimmering away over the meadows eastward, he felt a little uncertain as to his wisdom in this matter. Triton Station was a lonely one at nearly all times save in the morning and around seven at night, and to-night it seemed especially so. Only he alighted from the train. Most people went to and fro in their cars by another road. Why should he not have done as Blount had suggested, he now asked himself as he surveyed the flat country about;—called him to his aid, or stayed in the city? After all, hiring a car would not have been much better either, as Blount had pointed out, giving a possible lurking enemy a much sought point of attack. No, he should have stayed in town or returned with Blount in his car, and telling himself this, he struck out along the lonely, albeit short, stretch of road which led to the hotel and which was lighted by only a half dozen small incandescent globes strung at a considerable distance apart.

En route, and as he was saying to himself that it was a blessed thing that it was only a few hundred yards and that he was well-armed and fairly well constructed physically for a contest, a car swerved about a bend in the road a short distance ahead and stopped. Two men got out and, in the shadow back of the lights, which were less flaring than was usual, began to examine a wheel. It seemed odd to him on the instant that its headlights were so dim. Why should they be so dim at this time of night and why should this strange car stop just here at this lonely bend just as he was approaching it? Also why should he feel so queer about it or them, for at once his flesh began to creep and his hair to tingle. As he neared the car he moved to give it as wide a berth as the road would permit. But now one of the men left the wheel and approached him. Instantly, with almost an involuntary urge, he brought the revolver out of his hip pocket and stuffed it in his coat pocket. At the same time he stopped and called to the stranger:

"Stay right where you are, Mister. I'm armed, and I don't want you to come near me. If you do I'll shoot. I don't know who you are, or whether you're a friend or not, but I don't want you to move. Now, if there's anything you want, ask it from where you are."

The stranger stopped where he stood, seemingly surprised.

"I was going to ask you for a match," he said, "and the way to Trager's Point."

"Well, I haven't a match," returned Gregory savagely, "and Trager's Point is out that way. There's the hotel...if you're coming from there, why didn't you ask for directions there, and for matches, too?" He paused, while the man in the shadow seemed to examine him curiously.

"Oh, all right," he returned indifferently. "I don't want anything you don't want to give," but instead of returning to the car, he stood where he was, following Gregory with his eyes.

Gregory's skin seemed to rise on the back of his neck like the fur of a cat. He fairly tingled as he drew his revolver from his pocket and waved it ominously before him.

"Now, I'm going to walk around you two," he called, "and I want you to stand right where you are. I have you covered, and at the first move I'll shoot. You won't have any trouble out of me if you're not looking for it, but don't move," and he began orienting his own position so as to keep them directly in range of his eyes and weapon.

"Don't move!" he kept calling until he was well up the road, and then suddenly, while the men, possibly in astonishment, were still looking at him, turned and ran as fast as he could, reaching the hotel steps breathless and wet.

"That's the last lone trip for me," he said solemnly to himself.

When he spoke to Blount about it the latter seemed inclined to pooh-pooh his fears. Why should any one want to choose any such open place to kill or waylay another? There might have been other passengers on the train. A stray auto might be coming along there at any time. The men might have wanted a match, and not have been coming from the hotel at all. There was another road there which did not turn in at the hotel.

Still Gregory was inclined to believe that harm had been intended him—he could scarcely say why to himself—just plain intuition, he contended.

And then a day or two later—all the more significant now because of this other incident—Mrs. Skelton seemed to become more and more thoughtful as to his comfort and well-being. She took her meals at one of the tables commanding a view of the sea, and with (most frequently) one or the other, or both, broker friends as companions, to say nothing of occasional outside friends. But usually there was a fourth empty chair, and Gregory was soon invited to occupy that, and whenever Blount was present, a fifth was added. At first he hesitated, but urged on by Blount, who was amused by her, he accepted. Blount insisted that she was a comic character. She was so dressy, sporty, unctuous, good-natured—the very best kind of a seaside companion.

"Why, man, she's interesting," the latter insisted one night as they were taking a ride after dinner. "Quite a sporty 'fair and forty,' that. I like her. I really do. She's probably a crook, but she plays bridge well, and she's good at golf. Does she try to get anything out of you?"

"Not a thing, that I can see," replied Gregory. "She seems to be simple enough. She's only been here about three weeks."

"Well, we'd better see what we can find out about her. I have a hunch that she's in on this, but I can't be sure. It looks as though she might be one of Tilney's stool pigeons. But let's play the game and see how it comes out. I'll be nice to her for your sake, and you do the same for mine."

Under the warming influence of this companionship, things seemed to develop fairly rapidly. It was only a day or two later, and after Gregory had seated himself at Mrs. Skelton's table, that she announced with a great air of secrecy and as though it were hidden and rather important information, that a friend of hers, a very clever Western girl of some position and money, one Imogene Carle of Cincinnati, no less, a daughter of the very wealthy Brayton Carle's of that city, was coming to this place to stay for a little while. Mrs. Skelton, it appeared, had known her parents in that city fifteen years before. Imogene was her owny ownest pet. She was now visiting the Wilson Fletchers at Gray's Cove, on the Sound, but Mrs. Skelton had prevailed upon her parents to let her visit her here for a while. She was only twenty, and from now on she, Mrs. Skelton, was to be a really, truly chaperone. Didn't they sympathize with her? And if they were all very nice—and with this a sweeping glance included them all—they might help entertain her. Wouldn't that be fine? She was a darling of a girl, clever, magnetic, a good dancer, a pianist—in short, various and sundry things almost too good to be true. But, above all other things, she was really very beautiful, with a wealth of brown hair, brown eyes, a perfect skin, and the like. Neither Blount nor Gregory offered the other a single look during this recital, but later on, meeting on the great veranda which faced the sea, Blount said to him, "Well, what do you think?"

141

"Yes, I suppose it's the one. Well, she tells it well. It's interesting to think that she is to be so perfect, isn't it?" he laughed.

A few days later the fair visitor put in an appearance, and she was all that Mrs. Skelton had promised, and more. She was beautiful. Gregory saw her for the first time as he entered the large dining room at seven. She was, as Mrs. Skelton had described her, young, certainly not more than twenty-one at most. Her eyes were a light gray-brown, and her hair and skin and hands were full of light. She seemed simple and unpretentious, laughing, gay, not altogether fine or perfect, but fairly intelligent, and good to look at—very. She was at Mrs. Skelton's table, the brokers paying her marked attention, and, at sight, Blount liked her, too.

"Say," he began, "some beauty, eh? I'll have to save you from yourself, I fancy. I'll tell you how we'll work it. You save me, and I'll save you. The old lady certainly knows how to select 'em, apparently, and so does Tilney. Well now, my boy, look out!" and he approached with the air of one who was anxious to be a poor stricken victim himself.

Gregory had to laugh. However much he might be on his guard, he was interested, and as if to heighten this she paid more attention to Mrs. Skelton and her two friends than she did to Gregory or Blount. She was, or pretended to be absolutely sincere, and ignorant of her possible role as a siren, and they in turn pretended to accept her at her own valuation, only Blount announced after dinner very gaily that she might siren him all she blanked pleased. He was ready. By degrees, however, even during this first and second evening, Gregory began to feel that he was the one. He caught her looking at him slyly or shyly, or both, and he insisted to himself stubbornly and even vainly enough that he was her intended victim. When he suggested as much to Blount the other merely laughed.

"Don't be so vain," he said. "You may not be. I wish I were in your place. I'll see if I can't help take her attention from you," and he paid as much attention to her as any one.

However, Gregory's mind was not to be disabused. He watched her narrowly, while she on her part chattered gaily of many things—her life the winter before in Cincinnati, the bathing at Beachampton where she had recently been, a yachting trip she had been promised, tennis, golf. She was an expert at tennis, as she later proved, putting Gregory in a heavy perspiration whenever he played with her, and keeping him on the jump. He tried to decide for himself at this time whether she was making any advances, but could not detect any. She was very equitable in the distribution of her favors, and whenever the dancing began in the East room took as her first choice one of the brokers, and then Blount.

The former, as did Mrs. Skelton and the brokers, had machines, and by her and them, in spite of the almost ever-present Blount, Gregory was invited to be one of a party in one or the other of their cars whenever they were going anywhere of an afternoon or evening. He was suspicious of them, however, and refused their invitations except when Blount was on the scene and invited, when he was willing enough to accept. Then there were whist, pinochle, or poker games in the hotel occasionally, and in these Gregory as well as Blount, when he was there, were wont to join, being persistently invited. Gregory did not dance, and Imogene ragged him as to this. Why didn't he learn? It was wonderful! She would teach him! As she passed amid the maze of dancers at times he could not help thinking how graceful she was, how full of life and animal spirits. Blount saw this and teased him, at the same time finding her very companionable and interesting himself. Gregory could not help thinking what a fascinating, what an amazing thing, really, it was (providing it were true) that so dark a personality as Tilney could secure such an attractive girl to do his vile work. Think of it, only twenty-one, beautiful, able to further herself in many ways no doubt, and yet here she was under suspicion of him, a trickster possibly. What could be the compulsion, the reward?

"My boy, you don't know these people," Blount was always telling him. "They're the limit. In politics you can get people to do anything—anything. It isn't like the rest of life or business, it's just politics, that's all. It seems a cynical thing to say, but it's true. Look at your own investigations! What do they show?"

"I know, but a girl like that now—" replied Gregory solemnly.

But after all, as he insisted to Blount, they did not know that there was anything to all this. She might and she might not be a siren. It might be possible that both of them were grossly misjudging her and other absolutely innocent people.

So far, all that they had been able to find out concerning Mrs. Skelton was that she was, as she represented herself to be, the successful owner and manager of a theatrical agency. She might have known the better days and connections which she boasted. Gregory felt at times as though his brain were whirling, like a man confronted by enemies in the dark, fumbling and uncertain, but he and Blount both agreed that the best thing was to stay here and see it through, come what might. It was a good game even as it stood, interesting, very. It showed, as Blount pointed out to him, a depth to this political mess which he was attempting to expose which previously even he had not suspected.

"Stick by," the other insisted sport-lovingly. "You don't know what may come of this. It may provide you the very club you're looking for. Win her over to your side if you can. Why not? She might really fall for you. Then see what comes of it. You can't be led into any especial trap with your eyes open."

Gregory agreed to all this after a time. Besides, this very attractive girl was beginning to appeal to him in a very subtle way. He had never known a woman like this before—never even seen one. It was a very new and attractive game, of sorts. He began to spruce up and attempt to appear a little gallant himself. A daily report of his movements was being filed each morning, though. Every night he returned with Blount in his car, or on an early train. There was scarcely a chance for a compromising situation, and still there might be—who knows?

On other evenings, after the fashion of seaside hotel life, Gregory and Imogene grew a little more familiar. Gregory learned that she played and sang, and, listening to her, that she was of a warm and even sensuous disposition. She was much more sophisticated than she had seemed at first, as he could now see, fixing her lips in an odd inviting pout at times and looking alluringly at one and another, himself included. Both Blount and himself, once the novelty of the supposed secret attack had worn off, ventured to jest with her about it, or rather to hint vaguely as to her mission.

"Well, how goes the great game to-night?" Blount once asked her during her second or third week, coming up to where she and Gregory were sitting amid the throng on the general veranda, and eyeing her in a sophisticated or smilingly cynical way.

"What game?" She looked up in seemingly complete innocence.

"Oh, snaring the appointed victim. Isn't that what all attractive young women do?"

"Are you referring to me?" she inquired with considerable hauteur and an air of injured innocence. "I'd have you know that I don't have to snare any one, and particularly not a married man." Her teeth gleamed maliciously.

Both Gregory and Blount were watching her closely.

"Oh, of course not. Not a married man, to be sure. And I wasn't referring to you exactly—just life, you know, the game."

"Yes, I know," she replied sweetly. "I'm jesting, too." Both Gregory and Blount laughed.

"Well, she got away with it without the tremor of an eyelash, didn't she?" Blount afterward observed, and Gregory had to agree that she had.

Again, it was Gregory who attempted a reference of this kind.

144

She had come out after a short instrumental interpretation at the piano, where, it seemed to him, she had been posing in a graceful statuesque way—for whose benefit? He knew that she knew he could see her from where he sat.

"It's pretty hard work, without much reward," he suggested seemingly idly.

"What is? I don't quite understand," and she looked at him questioningly.

"No?" he smiled in a light laughing manner. "Well, that's a cryptic way I have. I say things like that. Just a light hint at a dark plot, possibly. You mustn't mind me. You wouldn't understand unless you know what I know."

"Well, what is it you know, then, that I don't?" she inquired.

"Nothing definite yet. Just an idea. Don't mind me."

"Really, you are very odd, both you and Mr. Blount. You are always saying such odd things and then adding that you don't mean anything. And what's cryptic?"

Gregory, still laughing at her, explained.

"Do you know, you're exceedingly interesting to me as a type. I'm watching you all the while."

"Yes?" she commented, with a lifting of the eyebrows and a slight distention of the eyes. "That's interesting. Have you made up your mind as to what type I am?"

"No, not quite yet. But if you're the type I think you are, you're very clever. I'll have to hand you the palm on that score."

"Really, you puzzle me," she said seriously. "Truly, you do. I don't understand you at all. What is it you are talking about? If it's anything that has any sense in it I wish you'd say it out plain, and if not I wish you wouldn't say it at all."

Gregory stared. There was an odd ring of defiance in her voice.

"Please don't be angry, will you?" he said, slightly disconcerted. "I'm just teasing, not talking sense."

She arose and walked off, while he strolled up and down the veranda looking for Blount. When he found him, he narrated his experience.

"Well, it's just possible that we are mistaken. You never can tell. Give her a little more rope. Something's sure to develop soon."

And thereafter it seemed as if Mrs. Skelton and some others might be helping her in some subtle way about something, the end or aim of which he could not be quite sure. He was in no way disposed to flatter himself, and yet it seemed at times as if he were the object of almost invisible machinations. In spite of what had

145

gone before, she still addressed him in a friendly way, and seemed not to wish to avoid him, but rather to be in his vicinity at all times.

A smug, dressy, crafty Jew of almost minute dimensions arrived on the scene and took quarters somewhere in the building, coming and going and seeming never to know Mrs. Skelton or her friends, and yet one day, idling across some sand dunes which skirted an adjacent inlet, he saw them, Imogene and the antlike Jew, walking along together. He was so astounded that he stopped in amazement. His first thought was to draw a little nearer and to make very sure, but realizing, as they walked slowly in his direction, that he could not be mistaken, he beat a hasty retreat. That evening Blount was taken in on the mystery, and at dinner time, seeing the Hebrew enter and seat himself in state at a distant table, he asked casually, "A newcomer, isn't he?"

Mrs. Skelton, Imogene, and the one broker present, surveyed the stranger with curious but unacquainted indifference.

"Haven't the slightest idea," answered the broker.

"Never saw him before. Cloaks and suits, I'll lay a thousand."

"He looks as though he might be rich, whoever he is," innocently commented Imogene.

"I think he came Thursday. He doesn't seem to be any one in particular, that's sure," added Mrs. Skelton distantly, and the subject was dropped.

Gregory was tempted to accuse the young woman and her friends then and there of falsehood, but he decided to wait and study her. This was certainly becoming interesting. If they could lie like that, then something was surely in the air. So she was a trickster, after all, and she was so charming. His interest in her and Mrs. Skelton and their friends grew apace.

And then came the matter of the mysterious blue racer, or "trailer," as Gregory afterward came to call it, a great hulking brute of a car, beautifully, even showily, made, and with an engine that talked like no other. There was a metallic ring about it which seemed to carry a long way through the clear air and over the sands which adjoined the sea. It was the possession, so he learned later through Mrs. Skelton, of one of four fortunate youths who were summering at the next hotel west, about a mile away. The owner, one Castleman by name, the son and heir to a very wealthy family, was a friend of hers whom she had first met in a commercial way in the city. They came over after Imogene's arrival, she explained, to help entertain, and they invariably came in this car. Castleman and his friends, smart, showy youths all, played tennis and bridge, and knew all the latest shows and dances and drinks. They were very gay looking, at least three of them, and were inclined to make much of

Imogene, though, as Mrs. Skelton cautiously confided to Gregory after a time, she did not propose to allow it. Imogene's parents might not like it. On the other hand, Gregory and Blount, being sober men both and of excellent discretion, were much more welcome!

Almost every day thereafter Mrs. Skelton would go for a ride in her own car or that of Castleman, taking Gregory if he would, and Imogene for companions. Blount, however, as he explicitly made clear at the very beginning, was opposed to this.

"Don't ever be alone with her, I tell you, or just in the company of her and her friends anywhere except on this veranda. They're after you, and they're not finding it easy, and they're beginning to work hard. They'll give themselves away in some way pretty soon, just as sure as you're sitting there. They want to cut me out, but don't let them do it—or if you do, get some one in my place. You don't know where they'll take you. That's the way people are framed. Take me, or get them to use my machine and you take some other man. Then you can regulate the conditions partially, anyhow."

Gregory insisted that he had no desire to make any other arrangements, and so, thereafter, whenever an invitation was extended to him, Blount was always somehow included, although, as he could see, they did not like it. Not that Imogene seemed to mind, but Mrs. Skelton always complained, "Must we wait for him?" or "Isn't it possible, ever, to go anywhere without him?"

Gregory explained how it was. Blount was an old and dear friend of his. They were practically spending the summer together. Blount had nothing to do just now. . . . They seemed to take it all in the best part, and thereafter Blount was always ready, and even willing to suggest that they come along with him in his car.

But the more these accidental prearrangements occurred, the more innocently perverse was Mrs. Skelton in proposing occasional trips of her own. There was an interesting walk through the pines and across the dunes to a neighboring hotel which had a delightful pavilion, and this she was always willing to essay with just Gregory. Only, whenever he agreed to this, and they were about to set out, Imogene would always appear and would have to be included. Then Mrs. Skelton would remember that she had forgotten her parasol or purse or handkerchief, and would return for it, leaving Imogene and Gregory to stroll on together. But Gregory would always wait until Mrs. Skelton returned. He was not to be entrapped like this.

By now he and Imogene, in spite of this atmosphere of suspicion and uncertainty, had become very friendly. She liked him, he could see that. She looked at him with a slight widening of the eyes and a faint distention of the nostrils at times, which spelled—

what? And when seated with him in the car, or anywhere else, she drew near him in a gently inclusive and sympathetic and coaxing way. She had been trying to teach him to dance of late, and scolding him in almost endearing phrases such as "Now, you bad boy," or "Oh, butterfingers!" (when once he had dropped something), or "Big, clumsy one—how big and strong you really are. I can scarcely guide you."

And to him, in spite of all her dark chicane, she was really beautiful, and so graceful! What a complexion, he said to himself on more than one occasion. How light and silken her hair! And her eyes, hard and gray-brown, and yet soft, too—to him. Her nose was so small and straight, and her lip line so wavily cut, like an Englishwoman's, full and drooping in the center of the upper lip. And she looked at him so when they were alone! It was disturbing.

But as to the Blue Trailer on these careening nights. Chancing one night to be invited by Mrs. Skelton for a twenty-five-mile run to Bayside, Blount accompanying them, they had not gone ten miles, it seemed to him, when the hum of a peculiarly and powerfully built motor came to him. It was like a distant bee buzzing, or a hornet caught under a glass. There was something fierce about it, savage. On the instant he recalled it now, recognized it as the great blue machine belonging to young Castleman. Why should he be always hearing it, he asked, when they were out? And then quite thoughtlessly he observed to Imogene:

"That sounds like Castleman's car, doesn't it?"

"It does, doesn't it?" she innocently replied. "I wonder if it could be."

Nothing caused him to think any more about it just then, but another time when he was passing along a distant road he heard its motor nearby on another road, and then it passed them. Again, it brought its customary group to the same inn in which he and Blount and Imogene and Mrs. Skelton were.

Suddenly it came to him just what it meant. The last time he had heard it, and every time before that, he now remembered, its sound had been followed by its appearance at some roadside inn or hotel whenever he Imogene and Blount happened to be in the same party; and it always brought with it this selfsame group of young men ("joy riders," they called themselves), accidentally happening in on them, as they said. And now he remembered (and this fact was corroborated by the watchful Blount) that if the car had not been heard, and they had not appeared, either Mrs. Skelton or Imogene invariably sought the ladies' retiring room once they had reached their destination, if they had one, when later the car would be heard tearing along in the distance and the "joy riders" would arrive. But what for? How to compromise him exactly, if at all?

One night after Mrs. Skelton had left them in one of these inns, but before the joy riders had arrived, Gregory was sitting at the edge of a balcony overlooking a silent grove of pines when suddenly it seemed to him that he heard it coming in the distance, this great rumbling brute, baying afar off, like a bloodhound on the scent. There was something so eerie, uncanny about it or about the night, which made it so. And then a few moments later it appeared, and the four cronies strolled in, smart and summery in their appearance, seemingly surprised to find them all there. Gregory felt a bit cold and chill at the subtlety of it all. How horrible it was, trailing a man in this way! How tremendous the depths of politics, how important the control of all the great seething cities' millions, to these men—Tilney and his friends,—if they could find it important to plot against one lone investigating man like this! Their crimes! Their financial robberies! How well he knew some of them— and how near he was to being able to prove some of them and drive them out, away from the public treasury and the emoluments and honors of office!

That was why he was so important to them now—he a self-established newspaperman with a self-established investigating bureau. Actually, it was villainous, so dark and crafty. What were they planning, these two smiling women at his side and these four smart rounders, with their pink cheeks and affable manners? What could they want of him really? How would it all end?

As Mrs. Skelton, Imogene, Blount and himself were preparing to return, and Castleman and his friends were entering their own car, a third party hitherto unknown to Blount or Gregory appeared and engaged the two women in conversation, finally persuading them to return with them in their car. Mrs. Skelton thereupon apologized and explained that they were old friends whom she had not seen for a long time, and that they would all meet at the hotel later for a game of bridge. Blount and Gregory, left thus to themselves, decided to take a short cut to a nearby turnpike so as to beat them home. The move interested them, although they could not explain it at the time. It was while they were following this road, however, through a section heavily shaded with trees, that they were suddenly confronted by the blazing lights of another machine descending upon them at full speed from the opposite direction, and even though Blount by the most amazing dexterity managed to throw his car into the adjacent fence and wood, still it came so close and was traveling at such terrific speed that it clipped their left rear wheel as he did so.

"Castleman's car!" Blount said softly after it had passed. "I saw him. They missed us by an inch!"

"What do you think of that!" exclaimed Gregory cynically. "I wonder if they'll come back to see the result of their work?"

Even as they were talking, however, they heard the big car returning.

"Say, this looks serious! I don't like the looks of it!" whispered Blount. "That car would have torn us to bits and never been scratched. And here they are now. Better look out for them. It's just as well that we're armed. You have your gun, haven't you?"

The other group approached most brazenly.

"Hello! Any trouble?" they called from a distance. "So sorry," and then as though they had just discovered it, "—well, if it isn't Gregory and Blount! Well, well, fellows, so sorry! It was an accident, I assure you. Our steering gear is out of order."

Gregory and Blount had previously agreed to stand their ground, and if any further treachery were intended it was to be frustrated with bullets. The situation was partially saved or cleared up by the arrival of a third car containing a party of four middle-aged men who, seeing them in the wood and the other car standing by, stopped to investigate. It was Gregory's presence of mind which kept them there.

"Do you mind staying by, Mister, until that other car leaves?" he whispered to one of the newcomers who was helping to extricate Blount's machine. "I think they purposely tried to wreck us, but I'm not sure; anyway, we don't want to be left alone with them."

Finding themselves thus replaced and the others determined to stay, Castleman and his followers were most apologetic and helpful. They had forgotten something back at the inn, they explained, and were returning for it. As they had reached this particular spot and had seen the light of Blount's car, they had tried to stop, but something had gone wrong with the steering gear. They had tried to turn, but couldn't, and had almost wrecked their own car. Was there any damage? They would gladly pay. Blount assured them there was not, the while he and Gregory accepted their apologies in seeming good part, insisting, however, that they needed no help. After they had gone Blount and Gregory, with the strangers as guards, made their way to the hotel, only to find it dark and deserted.

What an amazing thing it all was, Gregory said to himself over and over, the great metropolis threaded with plots like this for spoil—cold blooded murder attempted, and that by a young girl and these young men scarcely in their middle twenties, and yet there was no way to fix it on them. Here he was, fairly convinced that on

150

two occasions murder had been planned or attempted, and still he could prove nothing, not a word, did not even dare to accuse any one! And Imogene, this girl of beauty and gayety, pretending an affection for him—and he half believing it—and at the same time convinced that she was in on the plot in some way. Had he lost his senses?

He was for getting out now posthaste, feeling as he did that he was dealing with a band of murderers who were plotting his death by "accident" in case they failed to discredit him by some trick or plot, but Blount was of another mind. He could not feel that this was a good time to quit After all, everything had been in their favor so far. In addition, Blount had come to the conclusion that the girl was a very weak tool of these other people, not a clever plotter herself. He argued this, he said, from certain things which he had been able thus far to find out about her. She had once been, he said, the private secretary or personal assistant to a well known banker whose institution had been connected with the Tilney interests in Penyank, and whose career had ended in his indictment and flight. Perhaps there had been some papers which she had signed as the ostensible secretary or treasurer, which might make her the victim of Tilney or of some of his political friends. Besides, by now he was willing to help raise money to carry Gregory's work on in case he needed any. The city should be protected from such people. But Blount considered Imogene a little soft or easy, and thought that Gregory could influence her help him if he tried.

"Stick it out," he insisted. "Stick it out. It looks pretty serious, I know, but you want to remember that you won't be any better off anywhere else, and here we at least know what we're up against. They know by now that we're getting on to them. They must. They're getting anxious, that's all, and the time is getting short. You might send for your wife, but that wouldn't help any. Besides, if you play your cards right with this girl you might get her to come over to your side. In spite of what she's doing, I think she likes you." Gregory snorted. "Or you might make her like you, and then you could get the whole scheme out of her. See how she looks at you all the time! And don't forget that every day you string this thing along without letting them bring it to a disastrous finish, the nearer you are to the election. If this goes on much longer without their accomplishing anything, Tilney won't have a chance to frame up anything new before the election will be upon him, and then it will be too late. Don't you see?"

On the strength of this, Gregory agreed to linger a little while longer, but he felt that it was telling on his nerves. He was becoming irritable and savage, and the more he thought about it the worse he felt. To think of having to be pleasant to people who were murderers at heart and trying to destroy you!

The next morning, however, he saw Imogene at breakfast, fresh and pleasant, and with that look of friendly interest in her eyes which more and more of late she seemed to wear and in spite of himself he was drawn to her, although he did his best to conceal it.

"Why didn't you come back last night to play cards with us?" she asked. "We waited and waited for you."

"Oh, haven't you heard about the latest 'accident'?" he asked, with a peculiar emphasis on the word, and looking at her with a cynical mocking light in his eyes.

"No. What accident?" She seemed thoroughly unaware that anything had happened.

"You didn't know, of course, that Castleman's car almost ran us down after you left us last night?"

"No!" she exclaimed with genuine surprise. "Where?"

"Well, just after you left us, in the wood beyond Bellepoint. It was so fortunate of you two to have left just when you did." And he smiled and explained briefly and with some cynical comments as to the steering gear that wouldn't work.

As he did so, he examined her sharply and she looked at him with what he thought might be pain or fear or horror in her glance. Certainly it was not a look disguising a sympathetic interest in the plans of her friends or employers, if they were such. Her astonishment was so obviously sincere, confusing, revealing, in a way that it all but won him. He could not make himself believe that she had had a hand in that anyhow. It must be as Blount said, that she was more of a tool herself than anything else. She probably couldn't help herself very well or didn't know the lengths to which her pretended "friends" were prepared to go. Her eyes seemed troubled, sad. She seemed weaker, more futile, than at any time since he had known her, and this, while it did not add particularly to his respect, softened his personal animosity. He felt that under the circumstances he might come to like her. He also thought that she might be made to like him enough to help him. He had the emotional mastery of her, he thought, and that was something. He had described the incident with all the vividness of detail that he could, showing how he and Blount had escaped death by a hair's breadth. She seemed a little sick, and shortly after left the table. Gregory had taken good care to make it plain that the strangers in the other car had been informed as to the exact details of the case, and had offered their services as witnesses in case they were wanted.

"But we don't propose to do anything about it," he said genially, "not now, anyhow," and it was that she seemed to become a little sick or faint, and left him.

Whether owing to this conversation or the accident itself, or to circumstances concerning which he knew nothing, there now seemed to come a temporary lull in the activities of this group. The Blue Trailer disappeared as an active daily fact in their lives. Mrs. Skelton was called to the city on business for a few days, as well as Mr. Diamondberg, the "cloak and suit man," as Blount always called him, who in all the time he had been there had never publicly joined them. Mrs. Skelton came back later as cheerful and optimistic as ever, but in the meanwhile there had been an approach on the part of Imogene toward himself which seemed to promise a new order of things. She was freer, more natural and more genial than she had been hitherto. She was with him more, smiling, playful, and yet concerned, he thought. Because of their conversation the morning after the accident, he felt easier in her presence, more confidential, as though he might be able to talk to her about all this soon and get her to help him.

They had two hours together on the second afternoon of the absence of the others which brought them within sight of each other's point of view. It began after lunch, because Gregory had some reports to examine and was staying here to do it. She came over and stood beside him.

"What are you doing?" she asked.

"Oh, I'm looking up some facts," he replied enigmatically, smiling up at her. "Sit down."

They fell into conversation first about a tennis match which was being held here, and then about his work, which he described in part after observing that she knew all about it, or ought to.

"Why do you always talk to me that way about everything in connection with you?" she asked after a moment's pause. "You have such a queer way of speaking, as though I knew something I ought not to know about your affairs."

"Well, you do, don't you?" he questioned grimly, staring at her.

"Now, there it is again! What do you mean by that?"

"Do you really need to have me explain to you?" he went on in a hard cynical manner. "As though you didn't know! I don't suppose you ever heard of the Union Bank of Penyank, for instance? Or Mr. Swayne, its president? Or Mr. Riley, or Mr. Mears, the cashier?"

At the mention of these, as at the mention of the automobile accident, there was something which seemed to click like a camera shutter in her eyes, only this time there was no sign of pain, none even of confusion. She seemed, except for a faint trace of color, to be fairly calm and poised. She opened her mouth slightly, but more in an attempted smile of tolerance than anything else.

"The Union Bank? Mr. Swayne? Mr. Tilney? What are you talking about?" she persisted. "Who is Mr. Swayne, and where is the Union Bank?"

"Really, now, Miss Carle," he said with a kind of dogmatic fury, "if you want me to have any regard of any kind for you in the future, quit lying about this. You know well enough what I mean. You know who Mr. Swayne is, all right, and why he left Eastridge. You also know Mr. Diamondberg, although I heard you say you didn't, and that right after I had seen you walking with him out here on the dunes three weeks ago. You don't remember that, I suppose?" this as she fluttered slightly.

She stared, completely shaken out of her composure, and a real flush spread over her cheeks and neck. For the moment her expression hardened the least bit, then gave way to one of mingled weakness and confusion. She looked more or less guilty and genuinely distrait.

"Why, Mr. Gregory," she pleaded weakly, "how you talk! Positively, I haven't the slightest idea of what you mean, and I wish you wouldn't be so rough. I don't think you know what you're talking about, or if you do you certainly don't know anything about me. You must have me mixed up with some one else, or with something that I don't know anything about." She moved as if to leave.

"Now listen to me a minute," he said sharply, "and don't be so ready to leave. You know who I am, and just what I'm doing. I'm running an investigation bureau on my own account with which I mean to break up the present city political ring, and I have a lot of evidence which might cause Mr. Tilney and the mayor and some others a lot of trouble this fall, and they know it, and that's why you're out here. Mr. Tilney is connected with the mayor, and he used to be a bosom friend of your friend, Jack Swayne. And Diamondberg and Mrs. Skelton are in his employ right now, and so are you. You think I don't know that Castleman and his friends were working with you and Mrs. Skelton, and Diamondberg and these 'brokers' also, and that Castleman tried to run into us the other night and kill me, and that I'm being watched here all the time and spied on, but I am, and I know it, and I'm not in the dark as to anything—not one thing—not even you," and he leered at her angrily.

"Now wait a moment," he went on quickly as she opened her mouth and started to say something. "You don't look to me to be so

154

crafty and devilish as all this seems, or I wouldn't be talking to you at all, and your manner all along has been so different—you've appeared so friendly and sympathetic, that I've thought at times that maybe you didn't know exactly what was going on. Now, however, I see that you do. Your manner the other morning at breakfast made me think that possibly you were not so bad as you seemed. But now I see that you've been lying to me all along about all this, just as I thought, only I must say that up to now I haven't been willing to believe it. This isn't the first time an attempt has been made to get people in this way, though. It's an old political trick, only you're trying to work it once more, and I don't propose that you shall work it on me if I can help it. Plainly, you people wouldn't hesitate to kill me, any more than Tilney hesitated to ruin Crothers three years ago, or than he would hesitate to ruin me or any other man or woman who got in his path, but he hasn't got me yet, and he's not going to, and you can tell him that for me. He's a crook. He controls a bunch of crooks—the mayor and all the people working with him—and if you're in with them, as I know you are, and know what you're doing, you're a crook too."

"Oh, oh, oh! Don't!" she exclaimed. "Please don't! This is too terrible! To think that you should talk to me in this way!" but she made no attempt to leave.

"Now I want to tell you something more, Miss Carle—if that's your real name—" Gregory went on as she was putting her hands to her temples and exclaiming, and she winced again. "As I said before, you don't look to me to be as bad as you seem, and for that reason I'm talking to you now. But just see how it is: Here I am, a young man just starting out in the world really, and here you are trying to ruin me. I was living here with my wife and my little two-year-old baby peacefully enough until she had to go to the mountains because our little boy was taken sick, and then you and Mrs. Skelton and Diamondberg and Castleman and the 'brokers' and all the rest of the crowd that are and have been around here watching and spying, came and began to cause me trouble. Now I'm not helpless. And you needn't think I wasn't warned before you came, because I was. There are just as many influential men on my side of the fence right now as there are on Tilney's—will be—and he isn't going to get away with this thing as easily as he thinks. But just think of your part in all this! Why should you want to ruin me or help these people? What have I ever done to you? I can understand Tilney's wanting to do it. He thinks that I have facts which will injure him, and I have, and that because I haven't made any public statement the evidence is still in my hands, and that if I am put out of the way or discredited the whole thing will blow over and nothing will

155

happen to him—but it won't. Not now any more. It can't. This thing will go on just the same, whether I am here or not. But that isn't the point either. I was told two months ago that you would come, not by Mrs. Skelton, but by friends of mine, and that an attempt would be made on my life," and at that she opened her eyes wide and sat there apparently amazed, "and here you are on schedule time and doing just as you were told, and apparently you aren't the least bit ashamed to do it. But don't you think it's a pretty shabby game for you to play?" He stared at her wearily and she at him, but now for the moment she said nothing, just sat there.

"That big blue machine that was to have killed me the other night," he went on, stretching matters a little in so far as his own knowledge was concerned, "was all arranged for long before you came down here. I haven't the slightest idea why you work for Tilney, but I know now that that's what you're doing, and I'm sick of you and the whole thing. You're just a plain little crook, that's all, and I'm through with you and this whole thing, and I don't want you to talk to me any more. What's more, I'm not going to leave this hotel, either, and you can take that news to Tilney if you want to, or Mrs. Skelton or whoever else is managing things here for him. I've kept a day-to-day record of everything that's happened so far, and I have witnesses, and if anything more happens to me here I'm going to the newspapers and expose the whole thing. If you had any sense of decency left you wouldn't be in on anything like this, but you haven't—you're just a shabby little trickster, and that lets you out, and that's all I have to say."

He stood up and made as if to walk off, while Miss Carle sat there, seemingly dazed, then jumped up and called after him:

"Mr. Gregory! Please! Please! Mr. Gregory, I want to tell you something!"

He stopped and turned. She came hurriedly up to him.

"Don't go," she pleaded, "not just yet. Wait a minute. Please come back. I want to talk to you." And though he looked at her rather determinedly, he followed her.

"Well?" he asked.

"You don't understand how it is," she pleaded, with a look of real concern in her eyes. "And I can't tell you either, just now, but I will some time if you will let me. But I like you, and I really don't want to do you any harm. Really, I don't. I don't know anything about these automobile things you're telling about—truly I don't. They're all terrible and horrible to me, and if they are trying to do anything like that, I don't know it, and I won't have anything more to do with it—really I won't. Oh, it's terrible!" and she clenched her hands. "I do know Mr. Diamondberg now, I admit that, but I didn't

156

before I came down here, and Mr. Swayne and Mr. Tilney. I did come here to see if I could get you interested in me, but they didn't tell me just why. They told me—Mrs. Skelton did—that you, or some people whom you represented, were trying to get evidence against some friends of theirs—Mr. Tilney's, I believe—who were absolutely innocent, that you weren't happy with your wife, and that if some one, any one, were able to make you fall in love with her or just become very good friends, she might be able to persuade you not to do it, you see. There wasn't any plan, so far as I know, to injure you bodily in any way. They didn't tell me that they wanted to injure you physically—really they didn't. That's all news to me, and dreadful. All they said was that they wanted to get some one to get you to stop—make it worth your while in a money way, if I could. I didn't think there was anything so very wrong in that, seeing all they have done for me in the past—Mr. Tilney, Mrs. Skelton and some others. But after I saw you a little while I—" she paused and looked at him, then away, "I didn't think you were that kind of a man, you see, and so—well, it's different now. I don't want to do anything to hurt you. Really I don't. I couldn't—now."

"So you admit now that you do know Mr. Tilney," he commented sourly, but not without a sense of triumph behind it all.

"I just told you that," she said.

She stopped, and Gregory stared at her suspiciously. That she liked him was plain, and in a sense it was different from that of a mere passing flirtation, and as for himself—well, he couldn't help liking her in a genial way. He was free to admit that to himself, in spite of her trickery, and that she was attractive, and as yet she personally had not done anything to him, certainly nothing that he could prove. She seemed even now so young, although so sophisticated and wise, and much about her face, its smoothness, the delicate tracery of hair about her forehead, the drooping pout of the upper lip, sharpened his interest and caused him to meditate.

"Well?" he inquired after a time.

"Oh, I wish you wouldn't turn on me so and leave me," she pleaded. "I haven't done anything to you, have I? Not yet, anyhow."

"That's just the point—not yet. There's the whole story in a nutshell."

"Yes, but I promise you faithfully that I won't, that I don't intend to. Really I don't. You won't believe me, but that's true. And I won't, I give you my word,—truly. Why won't you still be friends with me? I can't tell you any more about myself now than I have—not now—but I will some time, and I wish you would still be friends with me. I promise not to do anything to cause you trouble. I haven't really, have I? Have I?"

157

"How should I know?" he answered testily and roughly, the while believing that this was a deliberate attempt on her part to interest him in spite of himself, to get him not to leave yet. "It seems to me you've done enough, being with these people. You've led me into going about with them, for one thing. I would never have gone with them on most of these trips except for you. Isn't that enough? What more do you want? And why can't you tell me now," he demanded, feeling in a way the authority of a victor, "who these people are and all about them? I'd like to know. It might be a help to me, if you really wanted to do something for me. What are their plans, their game?"

"I don't know. I can't tell you any more than I have, truly I can't. If I find out, maybe I will some time. I promise to. But not now. I can't, now. Can't you trust me that much? Can't you see that I like you, when I tell you so much? I haven't any plan to injure you personally, truly I haven't. I'm obliged to these people in one way and another, but nothing that would make me go that far. Won't you believe me?" She opened her eyes very wide in injury. There was something new in her expression, a luring, coaxing something.

"I haven't any one who is really close to me any more," she went on, "not anybody I like. I suppose it's all my own fault, but—" her voice became very sweet.

In spite of his precautions and the knowledge that his wife was the best and most suitable companion for him in the world, and that he was permanently fixed through his affection for his child and the helpful, hopeful mother of it, nevertheless he was moved by some peculiarity of this girl's temperament. What power had Tilney over her, that he could use her in this way? Think of it—a beautiful girl like this!

"What about Mrs. Skelton?" he demanded. "Who is she, anyhow? And these three gardeners around here? What is it they want?" (There were three gardeners of the grounds who whenever he and Imogene had been alone together anywhere managed somehow to be working near the scene—an arrival which caused him always instanter to depart.) "And Diamondberg?"

She insisted that in so far as the gardeners were concerned she knew absolutely nothing about them. If they were employed by Mrs. Skelton or any one, it was without her knowledge. As for Diamondberg, she explained that she had only met him since she had come here, but that she really did not like him. For some reason Mrs. Skelton had asked her to appear not to know him. Mrs. Skelton, she persisted, had known her years before in Cincinnati, as she had said, but more recently in the city. She had helped her to get various positions, twice on the stage. Once she had worked for Mr.

Swayne, yes, for a year, but only as a clerk. She had never known anything about him or his plans or schemes, never. When Gregory wanted to know how it was that he was to be trapped by her, if at all, she insisted that she did not believe that he was to be trapped. It was all to have been as she said.

Gregory could not quite make out whether she was telling him the exact truth, but it was near enough, and it seemed to him that she could not be wholly lying. She seemed too frank and wishful. There was something sensuously affectionate in her point of view and her manner. He would know everything in the future, she insisted, if he wanted to, but only not now—please not now. Then she asked about his wife, where she was, when she was coming back.

"Do you love her very much?" she finally asked naively.

"Certainly I love her. Why do you ask? I've a two-year-old boy that I'm crazy about."

She looked at him thoughtfully, a little puzzled or uncertain, he thought.

They agreed to be friends after a fashion before they were through. He confessed that he liked her, but still that he did not trust her—not yet. They were to go on as before, but only on condition that nothing further happened to him which could be traced to her. She frankly told him that she could not control the actions of the others. They were their own masters, and, after a fashion, hers, but in so far as she could she would protect him. She did not believe that they intended to try much longer. In so far as she was concerned, he might go away if he chose. She could see him anywhere, if he would. She was not sure if that would make any difference in their plans or not. Anyhow, she would not follow him if he did go unless he wished it, but she would prefer that he did. Perhaps nothing more would happen here. If she heard of anything she would tell him, or try to, in time. But she could not say more than that now. After a while, maybe, as soon as she could get out of here . . . there were certain things over which she had no control. She was very enigmatic and secretive, and he took it to mean that she was involved in some difficult situation and could not easily extricate herself.

"I wouldn't take too much stock in her, at that," Blount reflected when Gregory had told him about it. "Just keep your eyes open, that's all. Don't have anything to do with her in a compromising way. She may be lying to you again. Once a crook, always a crook." Such was his philosophy.

Mrs. Skelton returned on the third day after his long conversation with Imogene, and in spite of the fact that they had seemed to come closer together than ever before, to have established a friendly semi-defensive pact, still he sensed treachery. He could not make out what it was. She seemed to be friendly, simple, gay, direct, even wooing—and yet—what? He thought at one time that she might be the unconscious psychologic victim of Mrs. Skelton or of some one else; at other times, an absolutely unprincipled political philanderer. While pretending to be "on the level," as he phrased it, with him, she was crossing his path in such odd ways, making him uncertain as to whether, in spite of all she had said and was saying, she was still engaged in trying to compromise him. The whole thing began to take on the fascination of a game with the unconquerable lure of sex at the bottom of it—steeled as he was against compromising himself in any way.

Thus once, after a late card game, when he stepped out on a small veranda or balcony which graced the end of the hall nearest which his room was situated, and which commanded a splendid view of the sea, he found her just outside his door, alone, diaphanously attired, and very sympathetic and genial. Now that they were friends and had had this talk, there was something in her manner which always seemed to invite him on to a closer life with her without danger to himself, as she seemed to say. She would shield him against all, at her own expense. At the same time he was far—very far—from yielding. More than once he had insisted that he did not want to have anything to do with her in an affectional way, and yet here she was on this occasion, and although there might or there might not have been anything very alarming in that, he argued with himself afterward, yet since he had told her, this could be made to look as though she were trying to overpersuade him, to take him off his guard. Any guest of the hotel might have done as much (her room was somewhere near there), but Rule One, as laid down by Blount, and as hitherto practised by him, was never, under any circumstances which might be misinterpreted, to be alone with her. And besides, when he withdrew, as, he did at once, excusing himself lightly and laughingly, he saw two men turning in at a cross corridor just beyond, and one, seeing him turn back, said to the other, "It must be on the other side, Jim." Well, there might not have been anything very significant in that, either. Any two men might accidentally turn into a hall on an end balcony of which a maiden was sitting in very diaphanous array, but still—

It was the same whenever he walked along the outer or sea wall at night, listening to the thunder of the water against the rapp which sustained the walk, and meditating on the night and the beauty of the hotel and the shabbiness of politics. Imogene was always about him when she might be with safety, as he saw it, but

160

never under such circumstances as could be made to seem that they were alone together. Bullen, one of the two brokers, who seemed not a bad sort after his kind, came out there one night with Mrs. Skelton and Imogene, and seeing Gregory, engaged him in conversation and then left Imogene to his care. Gregory, hating to appear asininely suspicious under such circumstances, was genuinely troubled as to what to do in such cases as these. Always now he was drawn to her, painfully so, and yet— He had told her more than once that he did not wish to be alone with her in this way, and yet here she was, and she was always insisting that she did not wish him to be with her if he objected to it, and yet look at this! Her excuse always was that she could not help it, that it was purely accidental or planned by them without her knowledge. She could not avoid all accidents. When he demanded to know why she did not leave, clear out of all of this, she explained that without great injury to herself and Mrs. Skelton she could not, and that besides he was safer with her there.

"What is this?" he asked on this occasion. "Another plan?" Feeling her stop and pull back a little, he felt ashamed of himself. "Well, you know what I've been telling you all along," he added gruffly.

"Please don't be so suspicious, Ed. Why do you always act so? Can't I even walk out here? I couldn't avoid this to-night, truly I couldn't. Don't you suppose I have to play a part too—for a time, anyhow? What do you expect me to do—leave at once? I can't, I tell you. Won't you believe me? Won't you have a little faith in me?"

"Well, come on," he returned crossly, as much irritated with himself as any one. "Give me your arm. Give a dog a bad name, you know," and he walked her courteously but firmly in the direction of the principal veranda, trying to be nice to her at the same time.

"I tell you, Imogene, I can't and I won't do this. You must find ways of avoiding these things. If not, I'm not going to have anything to do with you at all. You say you want me to be friends with you, if no more. Very well. But how are we going to do it?" and after more arguments of this kind they parted with considerable feeling, but not altogether antagonistic, at that.

Yet by reason of all this finally, and very much to his personal dissatisfaction, he found himself limited as to his walks and lounging places almost as much as if he had been in prison. There was a little pergola at one end of the lawn with benches and flowering vines which had taken his fancy when he first came, and which he had been accustomed to frequent as a splendid place to walk and smoke, but not any more. He was too certain of being picked up there, or of being joined by Mrs. Skelton and Imogene, only to be left with Imogene, with possibly the three gardeners or a broker as witnesses. He could not help thinking how ridiculous it all was.

He even took Imogene, he and Blount, in Blount's car, and Mrs. Skelton with them or not, as the case might be—it was all well enough so long as Blount was along—to one place or another in the immediate vicinity—never far, and always the two of them armed and ready for any emergency or fray, as they said. It seemed a risky thing to do, still they felt a little emboldened by their success so far, and besides, Imogene was decidedly attractive to both of them. Now that she had confessed her affection for Gregory she was most alluring with him, and genial to Blount, teasing and petting him and calling him the watchdog. Blount was always crowing over how well he and Gregory were managing the affair. More than once he had pointed out, even in her presence, that there was an element of sport or fascinating drama in it, that she "couldn't fool them," all of which was helping mightily to pass the time, even though his own and Gregory's life, or at least their reputation, might be at stake.

"Go on, go on, is my advice," Blount kept saying now that he was being amused. "Let her fall in love with you. Make her testify on your behalf. Get a confession in black and white, if you can. It would be a great thing in the campaign, if you were compelled to use it." He was a most practical and political soul, for all his geniality.

Gregory could not quite see himself doing that, however. He was too fond of her. She was never quite so yielding, so close to him, as now. When he and Blount were out with her, now, the two of them ventured to rag her as to her part in all this, asking her whether the other car were handy, whether the gardeners had been properly lined up, and as to who was behind this tree or that house. "There'd be no use in going if everything wasn't just right," they said. She took it all in good part, even laughing and mocking them.

"Better look out! Here comes a spy now," she would sometimes exclaim at sight of a huckster driving a wagon or a farm-hand pushing a wheelbarrow.

To both Blount and Gregory it was becoming a farce, and yet between themselves they agreed that it had its charm. They were probably tiring her backers and they would all quit soon. They hoped so, anyhow.

But then one night, just as they had concluded that there might not be so very much to this plot after all, that it was about all over, and Mrs. Gregory was writing that she would soon be able to return, the unexpected happened. They were returning from one of those shorter outings which had succeeded the longer ones of an earlier day, Blount and Gregory and Imogene, and true to his idea of avoiding any routine procedure which might be seized upon by the enemy as something to expect and therefore to be used, Blount passed the main entrance and drove instead around to a side path which led to a sunk-in porch flanked on either side by high box hedges and sheltered furry pines. True also to their agreed plan of never being separated on occasions like this, they both walked to the door with Imogene, Blount locking his car so that it could not be moved during his absence. On the steps of this side porch they chaffered a little, bantering Imogene about another safe night, and how hard it was on the gardeners to keep them up so late and moving about in the dark in this fashion, when Imogene said she was tired and would have to go. She laughed at them for their brashness.

"You two think you're very smart, don't you?" she smiled a little wearily. "It would serve you right if something did happen to both of you one of these days—you know so much."

"Is that so?" chuckled Blount. "Well, don't hold any midnight conferences as to this. You'll lose your beauty sleep if you do."

To which Gregory added, "Yes, with all this hard work ahead of you every day, Imogene, I should think you'd have to be careful."

"Oh, hush, and go on," she laughed, moving toward the door.

But they had not gone more than a hundred and fifty feet down the shadowy side path before she came running after them, quite out of breath.

"Oh dear!" she called sweetly as she neared them, and they having heard her footsteps had turned. "I'm so sorry to trouble you, but some one has locked that side door, and I can't open it or make them hear. Won't one of you come and help me?" Then, as the two of them turned, "That's right. I forgot. You always work in pairs, don't you?"

Blount chortled. Gregory smiled also. They couldn't help it. It was so ridiculous at times—on occasions like this, for instance.

"Well, you see how it is," Gregory teased, "the door may be very tightly closed, and it might take the two of us to get it open."

Seeing that Blount was really coming, he changed his mind. "I guess I can get it open for her. Don't bother this time. I'll have to be going in, anyhow," he added. The thought came to him that he would like to be with Imogene a little while—just a few moments.

Blount left them after a cautioning look and a cheery good night. In all the time they had been together they had not done this, but this time it seemed all right. Gregory had never felt quite so close to Imogene as he did this evening. She had seemed so warm, laughing, gay. The night had been sultry, but mellow. They had tittered and jested over such trifling things, and now he felt that he

163

would like to be with her a while longer. She had become more or less a part of his life, or seemingly so, such a genial companion. He took her arm and tucked it under his own.

"It was nice over there at the Berkeley," he commented, thinking of an inn they had just left. "Beautiful grounds—and that music! It was delightful, wasn't it?" They had been dancing together.

"Oh, dear," she sighed, "the summer will soon be over, and then I'll have to be going back, I suppose. I wish it would never end. I wish I could stay here forever, just like this, if you were here." She stopped and looked at the treetops, taking a full breath and stretching out her arms. "And do look at those fire-flies," she added, "aren't they wonderful?" She hung back, watching the flashing fire-flies under the trees.

"Why not sit down here a little while?" he proposed as they neared the steps. "It isn't late yet."

"Do you really mean it?" she asked warmly.

"You see, I'm beginning to be so foolish as to want to trust you. Isn't that idiotic? Yes, I'm even going to risk fifteen minutes with you."

"I wish you two would quit your teasing, just once," she pleaded. "I wish you would learn to trust me and leave Blount behind just once in a while, seeing that I've told you so often that I mean to do nothing to hurt you without telling you beforehand."

Gregory looked at her, pleased. He was moved, a little sorry for her, and a little sorrier for himself.

In spite of himself, his wife and baby, as he now saw, he had come along a path he should not have, and with one whom he could not conscientiously respect or revere. There was no future for them together, as he well knew, now or at any other time. Still he lingered.

"Well, here we are," he said, "alone at last. Now you can do your worst, and I have no one to protect me."

"It would serve you right if I did, Mr. Smarty. But if I had suggested that we sit down for a minute you would have believed that the wood was full of spies. It's too funny for words, the way you carry on. But you'll have to let me go upstairs to change my shoes, just the same. They've been hurting me dreadfully, and I can't stand them another minute. If you want to, you can come up to the other balcony, or I'll come back here. I won't be a minute. Do you mind?"

"Not at all," he assented, thinking that the other balcony would not be as open as this, much too private for him and her. "Certainly not. Run along. But I'd rather you came back here. I want to smoke, anyhow," and he drew out his cigar and was about to make himself comfortable when she came back.

"But you'll have to get this door open for me," she said. "I forgot about that."

"Oh, yes, that's right."

He approached it, looking first for the large key which always hung on one side at this hour of the night, but not seeing it, looked at the lock. The key was in it.

"I was trying before. I put it there," she explained.

He laid hold of it, and to his surprise it came open without any effort whatsoever, a thing which caused him to turn and look at her.

"I thought you said it wouldn't open," he said.

"Well, it wouldn't before. I don't know what makes it work now, but it wouldn't then. Perhaps some one has come out this way since. Anyhow, I'll run up and be down right away." She hurried up the broad flight of stairs which ascended leisurely from this entrance.

Gregory returned to his chair, amused but not conscious of anything odd or out of the way about the matter. It might well have been as she said. Doors were contrary at times, or some one might have come down and pushed it open. Why always keep doubting? Perhaps she really was in love with him, as she seemed to indicate, or mightily infatuated, and would not permit any one to injure him through her. It would seem so, really. After all, he kept saying to himself, she was different now to what he had originally thought, and what she had originally been, caught in a tangle of her own emotions and compelled by him to do differently from what she had previously planned. If he were not married as happily as he was, might not something come of this? He wondered.

The black-green wall of the trees just beyond where he was sitting, the yellow light filtering from the one bowl lamp which ornamented the ceiling, the fireflies and the sawing katydids, all soothed and entertained him. He was beginning to think that politics was not such a bad business after all, his end of it at least, or being pursued even. His work thus far had yielded him a fair salary, furnishing as it had excellent copy for some of the newspapers and political organizations—the best was being reserved for the last— and was leading him into more interesting ways than the old newspaper days had, and the future, outside of what had happened in the last few weeks, looked promising enough. Soon he would be able to deal the current administration a body blow. This might raise him to a high position locally. He had not been so easily frustrated as they had hoped, and this very attractive girl had fallen in love with him.

For a while he stared down the black-green path up which they had come, and then fixed his eyes in lazy contemplation on one of the groups of stars showing above the treetops. Suddenly—or was it suddenly?—more a whisper or an idea—he seemed to become aware of something that sounded, as he listened more keenly, like a light footfall in the garden beyond the hedge. It was so very light, a mere tickle of the grass or stirring of a twig. He pricked up his ears and on the instant strained every muscle and braced himself, not that he imagined anything very dreadful was going to happen, but— were they up to their old tricks again? Was this the wonderful gardeners again? Would they never stop? Removing the cigar from his mouth and stilling the rocker in which he had been slowly moving to and fro, he decided not to stir, not even to move his hands, so well concealed was he from the bushes on either side by the arrangement of the posts, one of which was to the left of him. In this position he might see and not be seen. Did they know he was there? How had they found out? Were they always watching yet? Was she a part of it? He decided to get up and leave, but a moment later thought it better to linger just a little, to wait and see. If he left and she came back and did not find him there—could it be that there was some new trick on foot?

While he was thus swiftly meditating, he was using his ears to their utmost. Certainly there was a light footfall approaching along the other side of the hedge to the left, two in fact, for no sooner was one seemingly still, near at hand, than another was heard coming from the same direction, as light and delicate as that of a cat—spies, trappers, murderers, even, as he well knew. It was so amazing, this prowling and stalking, so desperate and cruel, that it made him a little sick. Perhaps, after all, he had better have kept Blount with him—not have lingered in this fashion. He was about to leave, a nervous thrill chasing up and down his spine, when he heard what he took to be Imogene's step on the stair. Then she was coming back, after all, as she had said. She was not a part of this as he had feared—or was she? Who could tell? But it would be foolish to leave now. She would see that he was wholly suspicious again, and that stage had somehow seemed to be passing between them. She had promised on more than one occasion to protect him against these others, let alone herself. Anyhow he could speak of these newcomers and then leave. He would let her know that they were hanging about as usual, always ready to take advantage of his good nature.

But now, her step having reached the bottom of the stair and ceased, she did not come out. Instead, a light that was beside the door, but out at this hour, was turned on, and glancing back he could see her shadow, or thought he could, on the wall opposite, to

166

the right. She was doing something—what? There was a mirror below the light. She might be giving her hair a last pat. She had probably arrayed herself slightly differently for him to see. He waited. Still she did not come. Then swiftly, a sense of something treacherous came over him, a creeping sensation of being victimized and defeated. He felt, over his taut nerves, this thrilling fear which seemed to almost convey the words: Move! Hurry! Run! He could not sit still a moment longer, but, as if under a great compulsion, leaped to his feet and sprang to the door just as he thought he heard additional movements and even whispers in the dark outside. What was it? Who? Now he would see!

Inside he looked for her, and there she was, but how different! When she had gone upstairs she had been arrayed in a light summery dress, very smart and out-door-ish, but here she was clothed in a soft clinging housedress such as one would never wear outside the hotel. And instead of being adjusted with her customary care, it was decidedly awry, as though she might have been in some disturbing and unhappy contest. The collar was slightly torn and pulled open, a sleeve ripped at the shoulder and wrist, the hang of the skirt over the hips awry, and the skirt itself torn, a ragged slit over the knee. Her face had been powdered to a dead white, or she herself was overcome with fear and distress, and the hair above it was disarranged, as though it had been shaken or pulled to one side. Her whole appearance was that of one who had been assailed in some evil manner and who had come out of the contest disarranged as to her clothes and shaken as to her nerves.

Brief as his glance was, Gregory was amazed at the transformation. He was so taken aback that he could not say anything, but just what it all meant came to him in an intuitive flash. To fly was his one thought, to get out of the vicinity of this, not to be seen or taken near it. With one bound he was away and up the easy stair three at a time, not pausing to so much as look back at her, meeting her first wide half-frightened stare with one of astonishment, anger and fear. Nor did he pause until he had reached his own door, through which he fairly jumped, locking himself in as he did so. Once inside, he stood there white and shaking, waiting for any sound which might follow, any pursuit, but hearing none, going to his mirror and mocking at himself for being such a fool as to be so easily outwitted, taken in, after all his caution and sophisticated talk. Lord! he sighed. Lord!

And after all her protests and promises, this very evening, too, he thought. What a revelation of the unreliability and treachery of human nature! So she had been lying to him all the time, leading him on in the face of his almost boastful precautions and suspicions,

167

and to-night, almost at the close of the season, had all but succeeded in trapping him! Then Tilney was not so easily to be fooled, after all. He commanded greater loyalty and cunning in his employees than he had ever dreamed. But what could he say to her, now that he knew what she really was, if ever he saw her again? She would just laugh at him, think him a fool, even though he had managed to escape. Would he ever want to see her again? Never, he thought. But to think that any one so young, so smooth, so seemingly affectionate, could be so ruthless, so devilishly clever and cruel! She was much more astute than either he or Blount had given her credit for.

After moving the bureau and chairs in front of the door, he called up Blount and sat waiting for him to come.

Actually, as he saw it now, she had meant to stage a seeming assault in which he would have been accused as the criminal and if they had sufficient witnesses he might have had a hard time proving otherwise. After all, he had been going about with her a great deal, he and Blount, and after he had told himself that he would not

Her witnesses were there, close upon him, in the dark. Even though he might be able to prove his previous good character, still, considering the suspicious fact that he had trifled with her and this treacherous situation so long, would a jury or the public believe him? A moment or two more, and she would have screamed out that he was attacking her, and the whole hotel would have been aroused. Her secret friends would have rushed forward and beaten him. Who knows?—they might even have killed him! And their excuse would have been that they were justified. Unquestionably she and her friends would have produced a cloud of witnesses. But she hadn't screamed—there was a curious point as to that, even though she had had ample time (and she had had) and it was expected of her and intended that she should! Why hadn't she? What had prevented her? A strange, disturbing exculpating thought began to take root in his mind, but on the instant also he did his best to crush it.

"No, no! I have had enough now," he said to himself. "She did intend to compromise me and that is all there is to it. And in what a fashion. Horrible. No, this is the end. I will get out now to-morrow, that is one thing certain, go to my wife in the mountains, or bring her home." Meanwhile, he sat there trembling, revolver in hand, wiping the sweat from his face, for he did not know but that even yet they might follow him here and attempt the charge of assault anyhow. Would they—could they? Just then some one knocked on his door, and Gregory, after demanding to know who it was, opened it to Blount. He quickly told him of his evening's experience.

"Well," said Blount, heavily and yet amusedly, "she certainly is the limit. That was a clever ruse, say what you will, a wonder. And the coolness of her! Why, she joked with us about it! I thought you were taking a chance, but not a great one. I was coming around to thinking she might be all right, and now think of this! I agree with you that it is time for you to leave. I don't think you'll ever get her over to your side. She's too crafty."

The next morning Gregory was up early and on the veranda smoking and meditating as to his exact course. He would go now, of course, and probably never see this girl with her fiend's heart again. What a revelation! To think that there were such clever, ruthless, beautiful sirens about in the same world with such women as his wife! Contrast them—his wife, faithful, self-sacrificing, patient, her one object the welfare of those whom she truly loved, and then put on the other side of the scale this girl—tricky, shameless, an actress, one without scruples or morals, her sole object in life, apparently, to advance herself in any way that she might, and that at the expense of everybody and everything!

He wanted to leave without seeing her, but in spite of himself he sat on, telling himself that it would do no harm to have just one last talk with her in order to clear up whether she had really intended to scream or no—whether she was as evil as he really thought now, confront her with her enormous treachery and denounce her for the villainess she was. What new lie would she have on her tongue now, he wondered? Would she be able to face him at all? Would she explain? Could she? He would like to take one more look at her, or see if she would try to avoid him completely. This morning she must be meditating on how unfortunately she had failed, missed out, and only last night she had taken his hand and smoothed it and whispered that she was not so bad, so mean, as he thought her to be, and that some day he would find it out. And now see!

He waited a considerable time, and then sent up word that he wanted to see her. He did not want to see this thing closed in this fashion with no chance to at least berate her, to see what new lie she would tell. After a while she came down, pale and seemingly exhausted, a weary look about her eyes as though she had not slept. To his astonishment she came over quite simply to where he was sitting, and when he stood up at her approach as if to ward her off, stood before him, seemingly weaker and more hopeless than ever. What an excellent actress, he thought! He had never seen her so downcast, so completely overcome, so wilted.

"Well," he began as she stood there, "what new lie have you fixed up to tell me this morning?"

169

"No lie," she replied softly.

"What! Not a single lie? Anyhow, you'll begin by shamming contrition, won't you? You're doing that already. Your friends made you do it, of course, didn't they? Tilney was right there—and Mrs. Skelton! They were all waiting for you when you went up, and told you just what to do and how it had to be done, wasn't that it? And you had to do it, too, didn't you?" he sneered cynically.

"I told you I didn't have anything to say," she answered. "I didn't do anything—I mean I didn't intend to—except to signal you to run, but when you burst in on me that way—" He waved an impatient hand. "Oh, all right," she went on sadly. "I can't help it if you won't believe me. But it's true just the same. Everything you think, all except that automobile plot, and this is true, but I'm not asking you to believe me any more. I can't help it if you won't. It's too late. But I had to go through my part anyhow. Please don't look at me that way, Ed—not so hard. You don't know how really weak I am, or what it is that makes me do these things. But I didn't want to do anything to hurt you last night, not when I left you. And I didn't. I hadn't the slightest intention, really I hadn't. Oh, well, sneer if you want to! I couldn't help myself, though, just the same—believe it or not. Nothing was farther from my mind when I came in, only—oh, what a state my life has come to, anyhow!" she suddenly exclaimed. "You don't know. Your life's not a mess, like mine. People have never had you in any position where they could make you do things. That's just the trouble—men never know women really." ("I should say not!" he interpolated.) "But I have had to do so many things I didn't want to do—but I'm not pleading with you, Ed, really I'm not. I know it's all over between us and no use, only I wish I could make you believe that as bad as I am I've never wanted to be as bad to you as I've seemed. Really, I haven't. Oh, honestly—"

"Oh, cut that stuff, please!" he said viciously. "I'm sick of it. It wasn't to hear anything like that that I sent for you. The reason I asked you to come down here was merely to see how far you would face it out, whether you would have the nerve to come, really, that was all—oh, just to see whether you would have a new lie to spring, and I see you have. You're a wonder, you are! But I'd like to ask you just one favor: Won't you please let me alone in the future? I'm tired, and I can't stand it any longer. I'm going away now. This fellow Tilney you are working for is very clever, but it's all over. It really is. You'll never get another chance at me if I know myself." He started to walk off.

"Ed! Ed!" she called. "Please—just a minute—don't go yet, Ed," she begged. "There's something I want to say to you first. I know all you say is true. There's nothing you can say that I haven't

170

said to myself a thousand times. But you don't understand what my life has been like, what I've suffered, how I've been pushed around, and I can't tell you now, either—not now. Our family wasn't ever in society, as Mrs. Skelton pretended—you knew that, of course, though—and I haven't been much of anything except a slave, and I've had a hard time, too, terrible," and she began dabbing her eyes. "I know I'm no good. Last night proved it to me, that's a fact. But I hadn't meant to do you any harm even when I came alone that way—really I didn't. I pretended to be willing, that was all. Hear me out, Ed, anyhow. Please don't go yet. I thought I could signal you to run without them seeing me—really I did. When I first left you the door was locked, and I came back for that sole reason. I suppose they did something to it so I couldn't open it. There were others up there; they made me go back—I can't tell you how or why or who— but they were all about me—they always are. They're determined to get you, Ed, in one way or another, even if I don't help them, and I'm telling you you'd better look out for yourself. Please do. Go away from here. Don't have anything more to do with me. Don't have anything more to do with any of these people. I can't help myself, honestly I can't. I didn't want to, but—oh—" she wrung her hands and sat down wearily, "you don't know how I'm placed with them, what it is—"

"Yes? Well, I'm tired of that stuff," Gregory now added grimly and unbelievingly. "I suppose they told you to run back and tell me this so as to win my sympathy again? Oh, you little liar! You make me sick. What a sneak and a crook you really are!"

"Ed! Ed!" she now sobbed. "Please! Please! Won't you understand how it is? They have watched every entrance every time we've gone out since I came here. It doesn't make any difference which door you come through. They have men at every end. I didn't know anything about it until I went upstairs. Really, I didn't. Oh, I wish I could get out of all this! I'm so sick of it all. I told you that I'm fond of you, and I am. Oh, I'm almost crazy! I wish sometimes that I could die, I'm so sick of everything. My life's a shabby mess, and now you'll hate me all the time," and she rocked to and fro in a kind of misery, and cried silently as she did so.

Gregory stared at her, amazed but unbelieving.

"Yes," he insisted, "I know. The same old stuff, but I don't believe it. You're lying now, just as you have been all along. You think by crying and pretending to feel sad that you might get another chance to trick me, but you won't. I'm out of this to-day, once and for all, and I'm through with you. There's no use in my appealing to the police under this administration, or I'd do that. But I want to tell you this. If you follow me any longer, or any of this bunch around here, I'm going to the newspapers. There'll be some way of getting this before the courts somewhere, and I'll try it. And if you really were on the level and wanted to do anything, there's a way, all right, but you wouldn't do it if you had a chance, never, not in a million years. I know you wouldn't."

"Oh, Ed! Ed! You don't know me, or how I feel, or what I'll do," she whimpered. "You haven't given me a chance. Why don't you suggest something, if you don't believe me, and see?"

"Well, I can do that easily enough," he replied sternly. "I can call that bluff here and now. Write me out a confession of all that's been going on here. Let me hear you dictate it to a stenographer, and then come with me to a notary public or the district attorney, and swear to it. Now we'll see just how much there is to this talk about caring for me," and he watched her closely, the while she looked at him, her eyes drying and her sobs ceasing. She seemed to pause emotionally and stare at the floor in a speculative, ruminative mood. "Yes? Well, that's different, isn't it? I see how it is now. You didn't think I'd have just the thing to call your bluff with, did you? And just as I thought, you won't do it. Well, I'm onto you now, so good day. I have your measure at last. Good-by!" and he started off.

"Ed!" she called, jumping up suddenly and starting after him. "Ed! Wait—don't go! I'll do what you say. I'll do anything you want. You don't believe I will, but I will. I'm sick of this life, I really am. I don't care what they do to me now afterwards, but just the same I'll come. Please don't be so hard on me, Ed. Can't you see—can't you see—Ed—how I feel about you? I'm crazy about you, I really am. I'm not all bad, Ed, really I'm not—can't you see that? Only—only—" and by now he had come back and was looking at her in an incredulous way. "I wish you cared for me a little, Ed. Do you, Ed, just a little? Can't you, if I do this?"

He looked at her with mingled astonishment, doubt, contempt, pity, and even affection, after its kind. Would she really do it? And if she did what could he offer her in the way of that affection which she craved? Nothing, he knew that. She could never extricate herself from this awful group by which she was surrounded, her past, the memory of the things she had tried to do to him, and he—he was married. He was happy with his wife really, and could make no return. There was his career, his future, his present position. But that past of hers—what was it? How could it be that people could control another person in this way she claimed, especially scoundrels like these, and why wouldn't she tell him about it? What had she done that was so terrible as to give them this power? Even if he did care for her what chance would he have, presuming her faithfulness itself, to either confront or escape the

172

horde of secret enemies that was besetting him and her just now? They would be discovered and paraded forth at their worst, all the details. That would make it impossible for him to come forth personally and make the charge which would constitute him champion of the people. No, no, no! But why, considering all her efforts against him, should she come to his rescue now, or by doing so expect him to do anything for her by way of return? He smiled at her dourly, a little sadly.

"Yes. Well, Imogene, I can't talk to you about that now, not for the present, anyhow. You're either one of the greatest actresses and crooks that ever lived, or you're a little light in the upper story. At any rate, I should think that you might see that you could scarcely expect me to like you, let alone to love you, all things considered, and particularly since this other thing has not been straightened out. You may be lying right now, for all I know—acting, as usual. But even so—let's first see what you do about this other, and then talk."

He looked at her, then away over the sea to where some boats were coming towards them.

"Oh, Ed," she said sadly, observing his distracted gaze, "you'll never know how much I do care for you, although you know I must care a lot for you, to do this. It's the very worst thing I can do for me—the end, maybe, for me. But I wish you would try and like me a little, even if it were only for a little while."

"Well, Imogene, let's not talk about that now," he replied skeptically. "Not until we've attended to this other, anyhow. Certainly you owe me that much. You don't know what my life's been, either—one long up-hill fight. But you'd better come along with me just as you are, if you're coming. Don't go upstairs to get any hat—or to change your shoes. I'll get a car here and you can come with me just as you are."

She looked at him simply, directly, beatenly.

"All right, Ed, but I wish I knew how this is going to end. I can't come back here after this, you know, if they find it out. I know I owe this to you, but, oh dear, I'm such a fool! Women always are where love is concerned, and I told myself I'd never let myself get in love any more, and now look at me!"

They went off to the city together, to his office, to a notary, to the district attorney's office—a great triumph. She confessed all, or nearly so, how she had formerly been employed by Mr. Swayne; how she had met Mr. Tilney there; how, later, after Swayne had fled, Tilney had employed her in various capacities, secretary, amanuensis, how she had come to look upon him as her protector; where and how she had met Mrs. Skelton, and how the latter, at Mr. Tilney's request (she was not sure, only it was an order, she said) had engaged—commanded, rather—her to do this work, though what the compulsion was she refused to say, reserving it for a later date. She was afraid, she said.

Once he had this document in his possession, Gregory was overjoyed, and still he was doubtful of her. She asked him what now, what more, and he requested her to leave him at once and to remain away for a time until he had time to think and decide what else he wished to do. There could be nothing between them, not even friendship, he reassured her, unless he was fully convinced at some time or other that no harm could come to him—his wife, his campaign, or anything else. Time was to be the great factor.

And yet two weeks later, due to a telephone message from her to his office for just one word, a few minutes, anywhere that he would suggest, they met again, this time merely for a moment, as he told himself and her. It was foolish, he shouldn't do it, but still— At this interview, somehow, Imogene managed to establish a claim on his emotions which it was not easy to overcome. It was in one of the small side booths in the rather out-of-the-way Grill Parzan Restaurant in the great financial district. Protesting that it was only because she wished to see him just once more that she had done this, she had come here, she said, after having dropped instantly and completely out of the life at Triton Hall, not returning even for her wardrobe, as he understood it, and hiding away in an unpretentious quarter of the city until she could make up her mind what to do. She seemed, and said she was, much alone, distrait. She did not know what was to become of her now, what might befall her. Still, she was not so unhappy if only he would not think badly of her any more. He had to smile at her seemingly pathetic faith in what love might do for her. To think that love should turn a woman about like this! It was fascinating, and so sad. He was fond of her in a platonic way, he now told himself, quite sincerely so. Her interest in him was pleasing, even moving, "But what is it you expect of me?" he kept saying over and over. "You know we can't go on with this. There's 'the girl' and the kid. I won't do anything to harm them, and besides, the campaign is just beginning. Even this is ridiculously foolish of me. I'm taking my career in my hands. This lunch will have to be the last, I tell you."

"Well, Ed," she agreed wistfully, looking at him at the very close of the meal, "you have made up your mind, haven't you? Then you're not going to see me any more? You seem so distant, now that we're back in town. Do you feel so badly toward me, Ed? Am I really so bad?"

"Well, Imogene, you see for yourself how it is, don't you?" he went on. "It can't be. You are more or less identified with that old crowd, even though you don't want to be. They know things about you, you say, and they certainly wouldn't be slow to use them if they had any reason for so doing. Of course they don't know anything yet about this confession, unless you've told them, and I don't propose that they shall so long as I don't have to use it. As for me, I have to think of my wife and kid, and I don't want to do anything to hurt them. If ever Emily found this out it would break her all up, and I don't want to do that. She's been too square, and we've gone through too much together. I've thought it all over, and I'm convinced that what I'm going to do is for the best. We have to separate, and I came here to-day to tell you that I can't see you any more. It can't be, Imogene, can't you see that?"

"Not even for a little while?"

"Not even for a day. It just can't be. I'm fond of you, and you've been a brick to pull me out of this, but don't you see that it can't be? Don't you really see how it is?"

She looked at him, then at the table for a moment, and then out over the buildings of the great city.

"Oh, Ed," she reflected sadly, "I've been such a fool. I don't mean about the confession—I'm glad I did that—but just in regard to everything I've done. But you're right, Ed. I've felt all along that it would have to end this way, even the morning I agreed to make the confession. But I've been making myself hope against hope, just because from the very first day I saw you out there I thought I wouldn't be able to hold out against you, and now you see I haven't. Well, all right, Ed. Let's say good-bye. Love's a sad old thing, isn't it?" and she began to put on her things.

He helped her, wondering over the strange whirl of circumstances which had brought them together and was now spinning them apart.

"I wish I could do something more for you, Imogene, I really do," he said. "I wish I could say something that would make it a little easier for you—for us both—but what would be the use? It wouldn't really, now would it?"

"No," she replied brokenly.

He took her to the elevator and down to the sidewalk, and there they stopped for a moment.

"Well, Imogene," he began, and paused. "It's not just the way I'd like it to be, but—well—" he extended his hand "—here's luck and good-by, then."

He turned to go.

She looked up at him pleadingly.

"Ed," she said, "Ed—wait! Aren't you—don't you want to?" she put up her lips, her eyes seemingly misty with emotion.

175

He came back and putting his arm about her, drew her upturned lips to his. As he did so she clung to him, seeming to vent a world of feeling in this their first and last kiss, and then turned and left him, never stopping to look back, and being quickly lost in the immense mass which was swirling by. As he turned to go though he observed two separate moving-picture men with cameras taking the scene from different angles. He could scarcely believe his senses. As he gazed they stopped their work, clapped their tripods together and made for a waiting car. Before he could really collect his thoughts they were gone—and then—

"As I live!" he exclaimed. "She did do this to me after all, or did she? And after all my feeling for her!—and all her protestations! The little crook! And now they have that picture of me kissing her! Stung, by George! and by the same girl, or by them, and after all the other things I've avoided! That's intended to make that confession worthless! She did that because she's changed her mind about me! Or, she never did care for me." Grim, reducing thought!) "Did she—could she—know—do a thing like that?" he wondered. "Is it she and Tilney, or just Tilney alone, who has been following me all this time?" He turned solemnly and helplessly away.

Now after all his career was in danger. His wife had returned and all was seemingly well, but if he proceeded with his exposures as he must, then what? This picture would be produced! He would be disgraced! Or nearly so. Then what? He might charge fraud, a concocted picture, produce the confession. But could he? Her arms had been about his neck! He had put his about her! Two different camera men had taken them from different angles! Could he explain that? Could he find Imogene again? Was it wise? Would she testify in his behalf? If so what good would it do? Would any one, in politics at least, believe a morally victimized man? He doubted it. The laughter! The jesting! The contempt! No one except his wife, and she could not help him here.

Sick at heart and defeated he trudged on now clearly convinced that because of this one silly act of kindness all his work of months had been undone and that now, never, so shy were the opposing political forces, might he ever hope to enter the promised land of his better future—not here, at least—that future to which he had looked forward with so much hope—neither he nor his wife, nor child.

"Fool! Fool!" he exclaimed to himself heavily and then—"fool! fool!" Why had he been so ridiculously sympathetic and gullible? Why so unduly interested? but finding no answer and no clear way of escape save in denial and counter charges he made his way slowly on toward that now dreary office where so long he had worked, but where now, because of this he might possibly not be able to work, at least with any great profit to himself.

"Tilney! Imogene! The Triton!" he thought—what clever scoundrels those two were—or Tilney anyhow—he could not be sure of Imogene, even now, and so thinking, he left the great crowd at his own door, that crowd, witless, vast, which Tilney and the mayor and all the politicians were daily and hourly using—the same crowd which he had wished to help and against whom, as well as himself, this little plot had been hatched, and so easily and finally so successfully worked.

THE CRUISE OF THE "IDLEWILD"

It would be difficult to say just how the trouble aboard the Idlewild began, or how we managed to sail without things going to smash every fifteen minutes; but these same constitute the business of this narrative. It was at Spike, and the weather was blistering hot. Some of us, one in particular, were mortal tired of the life we were leading. It was a dingy old shop inside, loaded with machines and blacksmithing apparatus and all the paraphernalia that go to make up the little depots and furniture that railways use, and the labor of making them was intrusted to about a hundred men all told—carpenters, millwrights, woodturners, tinsmiths, painters, blacksmiths, an engineer, and a yard foreman handling a score of "guineas," all of whom were too dull to interest the three or four wits who congregated in the engine room.

Old John, the engineer, was one of these—a big, roly-poly sort of fellow, five foot eleven, if he was an inch, with layers of flesh showing through his thin shirt and tight trousers, and his face and neck constantly standing in beads of sweat. Then there was the smith, a small, wiry man of thirty-five, with arms like a Titan and a face that was expressive of a goodly humor, whether it was very brilliant or not—the village smith, as we used to call him. Then there was Ike, little Ike, the blacksmith's helper, who was about as queer a little cabin boy as ever did service on an ocean-going steamer or in a blacksmith's shop—a small misshapen, dirty-faced lad, whose coat was three, and his trousers four, times too large for him—hand-me-downs from some mysterious source; immensely larger members of his family, I presume. He had a battered face, such as you sometimes see given to satyrs humorously represented in bronze, and his ears were excessively large. He had a big mouthful of dirty yellow teeth, two or three missing in front. His eyes were small and his hands large, but a sweeter soul never crept into a smaller or more misshapen body. Poor little Ike. To think how near he came to being driven from his job by our tomfoolishness!

I should say here that the Idlewild was not a boat at all, but an idea. She evolved out of our position on Long's Point, where the Harlem joins the Hudson, and where stood the shop in which we all worked, water to the south of us, water to the west of us, water to the north of us, and the railroad behind us landward, just like the four—or was it the six? hundred—at Balaklava. Anyhow, we got our idea from the shop and the water all around, and we said, after much chaffering about one thing and another, that we were aboard the Idlewild, and that the men were the crew, and that the engineer was the captain, and I was the mate, just as if everything were ship-shape, and this were a really and truly ocean-going vessel.

As I have said before. I do not know exactly how the idea started, except that it did. Old John was always admiring the beautiful yachts that passed up and down the roadstead of the Hudson outside, and this may have had something to do with it. Anyhow, he would stand in the doorway of his engine room and watch everything in the shape of a craft that went up and down the stream. He didn't know much about boats, but he loved to comment on their charms, just the same.

"That there now must be Morgan's yacht," he used to say of a fine black-bodied craft that had a piano-body finish to it, an' "That there's the Waterfowl, Governor Morton's yacht. Wouldn' ja think, now, them fellers'd feel comfortable a-settin' back there on the poop deck an' smokin' them dollar cigars on a day like this? Aw, haw!"

It would usually be blistering hot and the water a flashing blue when he became excited over the yacht question.

"Right-o," I once commented enviously.

"Aw, haw! Them's the boys as knows how to live. I wouldn' like nothin' better on a day like this than to set out there in one o' them easy chairs an' do up about a pound o' tobacco. Come now, wouldn't that be the ideal life for your Uncle Dudley?"

"It truly would," I replied sadly but with an inherent desire to tease, "only I don't think my Uncle Dudley is doing so very badly under the circumstances. I notice he isn't losing any flesh."

"Well, I dunno. I'm a little stout, I'll admit. Still, them conditions would be more congenial-like. I ain't as active as I used to be. A nice yacht an' some good old fifty-cent cigars an' a cool breeze'd just about do for me."

"You're too modest, John. You want too little. You ought to ask for something more suited to your Lucullian instincts. What do you say to a house in Fifth Avenue, a country place at Newport, and the friendship of a few dukes and earls?"

"Well, I'm not backward," he replied. "If them things was to come my way I guess I could live up to 'em. Aw, haw!"

"Truly, truly, John, you're quite right, but you might throw in a few shovelfuls of shavings just to show that there are no hard feelings between you and the company while you're waiting for all this. I notice your steam is getting low, eh? What?"

"Hang the steam! If the road was decent they'd give a man coal to burn. It takes a hundred tons of shavin's a day to keep this blinged old cormorant goin'. Think of me havin' to stand here all day an' shovelin' in shavin's! Seems to me all I do here is shovel. I'm an engineer, not a fireman. They ought to gimme a man for that, by rights."

"Quite so! Quite so! We'll see about that later—only, for the present, the shavings for yours. Back to the shovel, John!" The tone was heavily bantering.

"Well, the steam was gettin' a little low," John would cheerfully acknowledge, once he was able to resume his position in the doorway. It was these painful interruptions which piqued him so.

Out of such chaffering and bickering as this it was that the spirit of the Idlewild finally took its rise. It came up from the sea of thought, I presume.

"What's the matter with us having a boat of our own, John?" I said to him one day. "Here we are, out here on the bounding main, or mighty near it. This is as good as any craft, this old shop. Ease the thing around and hoist the Jolly Roger, and I'll sail you up to White Plains. What's the matter with calling her the Idlewild? The men will furnish the idle, and the bosses will furnish the wild, eh? How's that for an appropriate title?"

"Haw! Haw!" exclaimed stout John. "Bully! We'll fix 'er up to-day. You be the captain an' I'll be the mate an'—"

"Far be it from me, John," I replied humbly and generously, seeing that he had the one point of vantage in this whole institution which would serve admirably as a captain's cabin—with his consent, of course. It was more or less like a captain's cabin on a tug-boat, at that, picturesque and with a sea view, as it were. "You be the captain and I'll be the mate. Far be it from me to infringe on a good old sea dog's rights. You're the captain, all right, and this is a plenty good enough cabin. I'm content to be mate. Open up steam, Cap, and we'll run the boat up and down the yard a few times. Look out the window and see how she blows. It's ho! for a life on the bounding main, and a jolly old crew are we!"

"Right-o, my hearty!" he now agreed, slapping me on the back at the same time that he reached for the steamcock and let off a few preliminary blasts of steam—by way of showing that we were moving, as it were. The idea that we were aboard a real yacht and about to cruise forth actually seized upon my fancy in a most erratic and delightsome way. It did on John's, too. Plainly we needed some such idyllic dream. Outside was the blue water of the river. Far up and down were many craft sailing like ourselves, I said.

Inside of fifteen minutes we had appointed the smith, bos'n, and little Ike, the smith's helper, the bos'n's mate. And we had said that the carpenters and turners and millwrights were the crew and that the "guineas" were the scullions. Mentally, we turned the engineroom into the captain's cabin, and here now was nothing but "Heave ho-s" and "How does she blow thar, Bill-s?" and "Shiver my timbers-s" and "Blast my top-lights-s" for days to come. We "heaved ho" at seven o'clock in the morning when the engine started, "lay to and dropped anchor" at noon when the engine stopped, "hoisted and set sail" again at one, for heaven knows what port, and "sighted Spike" and "put hard to port" at six. Sometimes during the day when it was hot and we were very tired we took ideal runs to Coney and Manhattan Beach and Newport, where the best of breezes are, in imagination, anyhow, and we found it equally easy to sail to all points of the compass in all sorts of weather. Many was the time we visited Paris and London and Rome and Constantinople, all in the same hour, regardless, and our calls upon the nobility of these places were always a matter of light comment. At night we always managed to promptly haul up at Spike, which was another subject of constant congratulation between the captain and the mate. For if we had missed our trains and gotten home late!— Regardless of the fact that we were seafaring men, we wanted our day to end promptly, I noticed.

During the days which followed we elaborated our idea, and the Idlewild became more of a reality than is to be easily understood by those who have not indulged in a similar fancy. We looked upon the shop as a trusty ship with a wheel at the stern, where the millwright, an Irishman by the name of Cullen, ran the giant plane, and an anchor at the prow, where the engine-room was. And there was a light in the captain's eye at times which, to me at least, betokened a real belief. It is so easy to enter upon a fancy, especially when it is pleasing. He would stand in the doorway of his small, hot engine-room, or lean out of the window which commanded the beautiful sweep of water so close to our door, and at times I verily believe he thought we were under way, so great is the power of self-hypnotism. The river was so blue and smooth these summer days, the passing boats so numerous. We could see the waters race to and fro as the tides changed. It was such a relief from the dull wearisome grind of shoveling in shavings and carrying out ashes or loading cars, as I was occasionally compelled to do—for my health, in my own case, I should explain. I am sure that, as an ordinary fifteen-cent-an-hour-shaving-carrier, I valued my title of mate as much as I ever valued anything, and the smith, "the village smith," was smilingly proud to be hailed as "Bos'n." Little Ike being of an order of mind that fancied the world ended somewhere abruptly in the Rocky Mountains, and that you really could shoot buffaloes after you left Buffalo, New York, did not grasp the meaning of it all at once, but at last it dawned upon him. When he got the idea that we really considered this a ship and that he was the bos'n's mate with the privilege of lowering the boats in case of a wreck or other disaster, he was beside himself.

"Hully chee!" he exclaimed, "me a bos'n's mate! Dat's de real t'ing, ain't it! Heave ho, dere!" And he fell back on the captain's locker and kicked his heels in the air.

"You want to remember, though, Ike," I said, once in an evil moment—what small things regulate the good and evil fortunes of all things!—"that this is the captain's cabin and bos'n's mates are not much shucks on a vessel such as the Idlewild. If you want to retain your position you want to be respectful, and above all, obedient. For instance, if the captain should choose to have you act as stoker for a few minutes now and then, it would be your place to rejoice at the request. You get that, do you?"

"Not on yer life," replied Ike irritably, who understood well enough that this meant more work.

"That's right, though," chimed in big John, pleased beyond measure at this latest development. "I'm captain here now, an' you don't want to forget that. No back lip from any bos'n's mate. What the mate says goes. The shovel for yours, bos'n, on orders from the captain. Now jist to show that the boat's in runnin' order you can chuck in a few shovelfuls right now."

"Na! I will not!"

"Come, Ike," I said, "no insubordination. You can't go back on the captain like that. We have the irons for recalcitrants," and I eyed a pile of old rusty chains lying outside the door. "We might have to truss him up, Cap, and lay him down below," and to prove the significance of my thought I picked up one end of a chain and rattled it solemnly. The captain half choked with fat laughter.

"That's right. Git the shovel there, Ike."

Ike looked as if he doubted the regularity of this, as if life on the briny deep might not be all that it was cracked up to be, but for the sake of regularity and in order not to be reduced to the shameful condition of a scullion, or worse, "irons," which was the only alternative offered, he complied. After he had thrown in eight scoopfuls we both agreed that this was true order and that the organization and dignity of the Idlewild might well be looked upon now as established.

Things went from good to better. We persuaded Joe, who was the millwright's assistant, back at the "wheel," that his dignity would be greatly enhanced in this matter if he were to accept the position of day watch, particularly since his labors in that capacity would accord with his bounden duties as a hireling of the road; for, if he were stationed in the rear (front room, actually) anyhow, and compelled, owing to the need of receiving and taking away various planks and boards as they came out of the planes and molding machines, to walk to and fro, it would be an easy matter to notice any suspicious lights on the horizon forward and to come aft at once, or at least at such times as the boss was not looking, or when he came to heat his coffee or get a drink, and report.

Amiable Joe! I can see him yet, tall, ungainly, stoop-shouldered, a slight cast in one eye, his head bobbing like a duck's as he walked—a most agreeable and pathetic person. His dreams were so simple, his wants so few. He lived with his sister somewhere in Eleventh Avenue downtown in a tenement, and carried home bundles of firewood to her at night all this great distance, to help out. He received (not earned—he did much more than that) seventeen and a half cents an hour, and dreamed of what? I could never quite make out. Marriage? A little cheap flat somewhere? Life is so pathetic at times.

"Light on the starboard bow," or "Light on the port bow," were the chosen phrases which we told him he was in duty bound to use, adding always "Sir," as respectful subordinates should. Also we insisted on his instantly making known to us at such times as we twain happened to be in the engine-room together, all bell buoys, whistle buoys, lighthouses, passing vessels and most of all the monthly pay car as it rounded the curve half a mile up the track about the fifteenth of every month. The matter of reporting the approach of the pay car was absolutely without exception. If he failed to do that we would be compelled, sad as it might be and excellent as his other services had been, to put him in irons. Here we showed him the irons also.

Joe cheerfully accepted. For days thereafter he would come back regularly when the need of heating his coffee or securing a drink necessitated, and lifting a straight forefinger to his forehead, would report, "Light on the port bow, Sir. I think it's in the steel works jist up the track here," or "Light on the starboard, Sir. It's the fast mail, maybe, for Chicago, jist passin' Kingsbridge."

"No thinks, Joseph," I used to reprimand. "You are not supposed to give your thinks. If the captain wishes to know what it is, he will ask. Back to the molding machine for yours, Joseph."

Joseph, shock-headed, with dusty hair, weak eyes and a weaker smile, would retire, and then we would look at each other, the captain and I, and grin, and he would exclaim:

"Pretty fair discipline, mate."

"Oh, I think we've got 'em going, Captain."

"Nothin' like order, mate."

"You're right, Cap."

"I don't suppose the mate'd ever condescend to take orders like that, eh, mate?"

"Well, hardly, Cap."

"Still, you don't want to forget that I'm captain, mate."

"And you don't want to forget that I'm mate, Captain."

Thus we would badger one another until one of the scullion crew arrived, when without loss of dignity on either side we could easily turn our attention to him.

And these scullions! What a dull crew! Gnarled, often non-English-speaking foreigners against or in front of whom we could jest to our hearts' content. They could not even guess the amazing things we were ordering them to do on penalty of this, that, and the other.

Things went from better to best. We reached the place where the fact of the shop's being a ship, and the engineer the captain, and I the mate, and the smith the bos'n, ad infinitum, came to be a matter of general knowledge, and we were admired and congratulated and laughed with until nearly all the workers of the shop, with some trifling and unimportant exceptions, the foreman for one, began to share our illusion—carpenters, cabinet-makers, joiners, all. The one exception, as I say, was the foreman, only he was a host in himself, a mean, ill-dispositioned creature, of course, who looked upon all such ideas as fol-de-rol, and in a way subversive of order and good work. He was red-headed, big-handed, big-footed, dull. He had no imagination beyond lumber and furniture, no poetry in his soul. But the crew, the hundred-headed crew, accepted it as a relief. They liked to think they were not really working, but out upon a blue and dancing sea, and came back one by one, the carpenters, the tinsmiths, the millwrights, one and all, with cheerful grins to do us honor.

"So you're the captain, eh?" lazy old Jack, the partner of car-loading Carder, asked of the engineer, and John looked his full dignity at once.

"That I am, Jack," he replied, "only able seamen ain't supposed to ask too many familiar questions. Are they, mate?"

"Well, I should say not," I replied, arriving with a basket of shavings. "Able seamen should always salute the captain before addressing him, anyhow, and never fail to say Sir. Still, our crew is new. It's not very able and the seamen end of it is a little on the fritz, I'm thinking. But, all things considered, we can afford to overlook a few errors until we get everything well in hand. Eh, Captain?"

"Right, mate," returned the captain genially. "You're always right—nearly."

Before I could start an argument on this score, one of the able seamen, one who was thus discourteously commented on, observed, "I don't know about that. Seems to me the mate of this here ship ain't any too much shucks, or the captain either."

The captain and I were a little dismayed by this. What to do with an able seaman who was too strong and too dull to take the whole thing in the proper spirit? It threatened smooth sailing! This particular person was old Stephen Bowers, the carpenter from the second floor who never to us seemed to have quite the right lightness of spirit to make a go of all this. He was too likely to turn rough but well-meant humor into a personal affront to himself.

"Well, Captain, there you are," I said cautiously, with a desire to maintain order and yet peace. "Mutiny, you see."

"It does look that way, don't it?" big John replied, eyeing the newcomer with a quizzical expression, half humorous, half severe. "What'll we do, mate, under such circumstances?"

"Lower a boat, Captain, and set him adrift," I suggested, "or put him on bread and water, along with the foreman and the superintendent. They're the two worst disturbers aboard the boat. We can't have these insubordinates breaking up our discipline."

This last, deftly calculated to flatter, was taken in good part, and bridged over the difficulty for the time being. Nothing was taken so much in good part or seemed to soothe the feelings of the rebellious as to include them with their superiors in an order of punishment which on the very first day of the cruise it had been decided was necessary to lay upon all the guiding officers of the plant. We could not hope to control them, so ostensibly we placed them in irons, or lowered them in boats, classifying them as mutineers and the foreman's office as the lock-up. It went well.

"Oh no, oh no, I don't want to be put in that class," old Bowers replied, the flattering unction having smoothed his ruffled soul. "I'm not so bad as all that."

"Very well, then," I replied briskly. "What do you think, Captain?"

The latter looked at me and smiled.

"Do you think we kin let him go this wunst?" he inquired of me.

"Sure, sure," I replied. "If he's certain he doesn't want to join the superintendent and the foreman."

Old Bowers went away smiling, seemingly convinced that we were going to run the boat in shipshape fashion, and before long most of the good-natured members of the crew consented to have themselves called able seamen.

For nearly a month thereafter, during all the finest summer weather, there existed the most charming life aboard this ideal

185

vessel. We used the shop and all its details for the idlest purposes of our fancy. Hammers became belaying pins, the machines of the shop ship's ballast, the logs in the yard floating debris. When the yard became too cluttered, as it did once, we pretended we were in Sargasso and had to cut our way out—a process that took quite a few days. We were about all day commenting on the weather in nautical phrases, sighting strange vessels, reporting disorders or mutiny on the part of the officers in irons, or the men, or announcing the various "bells," lighthouses, etc.

In an evil hour, however, we lit upon the wretched habit of pitching upon little Ike, the butt of a thousand quips. Being incapable of grasping the true edge of our humor, he was the one soul who was yet genial enough to take it and not complain. We called upon him to shovel ashes, to split the wood, to run aft, that was, to the back gate, and see how the water stood. More than once he was threatened with those same "irons" previously mentioned, and on one occasion we actually dragged in a length, pretending to bind him with it and fasten him to the anvil (with the bos'n's consent, of course), which resulted in a hearty struggle, almost a row. We told him we would put him in an old desk crate we had, a prison, no less, and once or twice, in a spirit of deviltry, John tried to carry out his threat, nailing him in, much against his will. Finally we went to the length of attempting to physically enforce our commands when he did not obey, which of course ended in disaster.

It was this way. Ike was in the habit of sweeping up his room—the smith's shop—at three o'clock in the afternoon, which was really not reasonable considering that there were three hours of work ahead of all of us, and that he was inclined to resent having his fine floor mussed up thereafter. On the other hand I had to carry shavings through there all this time, and it was a sore temptation to drop a few now and then just for the devil's sake. After due consultation with the captain, I once requested him to order that the bos'n's mate leave the floor untouched until half past four, at least, which was early enough. The bos'n's mate replied with the very cheering news that the captain could "go to the devil." He wasn't going to kill himself for anybody, and besides, the foreman had once told him he might do this if he chose, heaven only knows why. What did the captain think that he (the bos'n's mate) was, anyhow?

Here at last was a stiff problem. Mutiny! Mutiny! Mutiny! What was to be done? Plainly this was inconveniencing the mate and besides, it was mutiny. And in addition it so lacerated our sense of dignity and order that we decided it could not be. Only, how to arrange it. We had been putting so much upon the bos'n's mate of late that he was becoming a little rebellious, and justly so, I think.

186

He was always doing a dozen things he need not have done. Still, unless we could command him, the whole official management of this craft would go by the board, or so we thought. Finally we decided to act, but how? Direct orders, somehow, were somewhat difficult to enforce. After due meditation we took the bos'n, a most approving officer and one who loved to tease Ike (largely because he wanted to feel superior himself, I think), into our confidence and one late afternoon just after Ike had, figuratively speaking, swabbed up the deck, the latter sent him to some other part of the shop, or vessel, rather, while we strewed shavings over his newly cleaned floor with a shameless and lavish hand. It was intensely delicious, causing gales of laughter at the time—but—. Ike came back and cleaned this up—not without a growl, however. He did not take it in the cheerful spirit in which we hoped he would. In fact he was very morose about it, calling us names and threatening to go to the foreman [in the lock-up] if we did it again. However, in spite of all, and largely because of the humorous spectacle he in his rage presented we did it not once, but three or four times and that after he had most laboriously cleaned his room. A last assault one afternoon, however, resulted in a dash on his part to the foreman's office.

"I'm not goin' to stand it," he is declared to have said by one who was by at the time when he appeared in front of that official. "They're strewin' up my floor with shavin's two an' three times every day after I've cleaned it up for the day. I'll quit first."

The foreman, that raw, non-humorous person previously described, who evidently sympathized with Ike and who, in addition, from various sources, had long since learned what was going on, came down in a trice. He had decided to stop this nonsense.

"I want you fellows to cut that out now," he declared vigorously on seeing us. "It's all right, but it won't do. Don't rub it in. Let him alone. I've heard of this ship stuff. It's all damn nonsense."

The captain and mate gazed at each other in sad solemnity. Could it be that Ike had turned traitor? This was anarchy. He had not only complained of us but of the ship.—the Idlewild! What snakiness of soul! We retired to a corner of our now storm-tossed vessel and consulted in whispers. What would we do? Would we let her sink or try to save her? Perhaps it was advisable for the present to cease pushing the joke too far in that quarter, anyhow. Ike might cause the whole ship to be destroyed.

Nevertheless, even yet there were ways and ways of keeping her afloat and punishing an insubordinate even when no official authority existed. Ike had loved the engineroom, or rather, the captain's office, above all other parts of the vessel because it was so comfortable. Here between tedious moments of pounding iron for the smith or blowing the bellows or polishing various tools that had been sharpened, he could retire on occasion, when the boss was not about and the work not pressing (it was the very next room to his) and gaze from the captain's door or window out on the blue waters of the Hudson where lay the yachts, and up the same stream where stood the majestic palisades. At noon or a little before he could bring his cold coffee, sealed in a tin can, to the captain's engine and warm it. Again, the captain's comfortable locker held his coat and hat, the captain's wash bowl—a large wooden tub to one side of the engine into which comforting warm water could be drawn—served as an ideal means of washing up. Since the bos'n's mate had become friendly with the captain, he too had all these privileges. But now, in view of his insubordination, all this was changed. Why should a rebellious bos'n's mate be allowed to obtain favors of the captain? More in jest than in earnest one day it was announced that unless the bos'n's mate would forego his angry opposition to a less early scrubbed deck—

"Well, mate," the captain observed to the latter in the presence of the bos'n's mate, with a lusty wink and a leer, "you know how it goes with these here insubordinates, don't you? No more hot coffee at noon time, unless there's more order here. No more cleanin' up in the captain's tub. No more settin' in the captain's window takin' in the cool mornin' breeze, as well as them yachts. What say? Eh? We know what to do with these here now insubordinates, don't we, mate, eh?" This last with a very huge wink.

"You're right, Captain. Very right," the mate replied. "You're on the right track now. No more favors—unless— Order must be maintained, you know."

"Oh, all right," replied little Ike now, fully in earnest and thinking we were. "If I can't, I can't. Jist the same I don't pick up no shavin's after four," and off he strolled.

Think of it, final and complete mutiny, and there was nothing more really to be done.

All we could do now was to watch him as he idled by himself at odd free moments down by the waterside in an odd corner of the point, a lonely figure, his trousers and coat too large, his hands and feet too big, his yellow teeth protruding. No one of the other workingmen ever seemed to be very enthusiastic over Ike, he was so small, so queer; no one, really, but the captain and the mate, and now they had deserted him.

188

It was tough.

Yet still another ill descended on us before we came to the final loss, let us say, of the good craft Idlewild. In another evil hour the captain and the mate themselves fell upon the question of priority, a matter which, so long as they had had Ike to trifle with, had never troubled them. Now as mate and the originator of this sea-going enterprise, I began to question the authority of the captain himself occasionally, and to insist on sharing as my undeniable privilege all the dignities and emoluments of the office—to wit: the best seat in the window where the wind blew, the morning paper when the boss was not about, the right to stand in the doorway, use the locker, etc. The captain objected, solely on the ground of priority, mind you, and still we fell a-quarreling. The mate in a stormy, unhappy hour was reduced by the captain to the position of mere scullion, and ordered, upon pain of personal assault, to vacate the captain's cabin. The mate reduced the captain to the position of stoker and stood in the doorway in great glee while the latter, perforce, owing to the exigencies of his position, was compelled to stoke whether he wanted to or no. It could not be avoided. The engine had to be kept going. In addition, the mate had brought many morning papers, an occasional cigar for the captain, etc. There was much rancor and discord and finally the whole affair, ship, captain, mate and all, was declared by the mate to be a creation of his brain, a phantom, no less, and that by his mere act of ignoring it the whole ship—officers, men, masts, boats, sails—could be extinguished, scuttled, sent down without a ripple to that limbo of seafaring men, the redoubtable Davy Jones's locker.

The captain was not inclined to believe this at first. On the contrary, like a good skipper, he attempted to sail the craft alone. Only, unlike the mate, he lacked the curious faculty of turning jest and fancy into seeming fact. There was a something missing which made the whole thing seem unreal. Like two rival generals, we now called upon a single army to follow us individually, but the crew, seeing that there was war in the cabin, stood off in doubt and, I fancy, indifference. It was not important enough in their hardworking lives to go to the length of risking the personal ill-will of either of us, and so for want of agreement, the ship finally disappeared.

Yes, she went down. The Idlewild was gone, and with her, all her fine seas, winds, distant cities, fogs, storms.

For a time indeed, we went charily by each other.

Still it behooved us, seeing how, in spite of ourselves, we had to work in the same room and there was no way of getting rid of each other's obnoxious presence, to find a common ground on which we could work and talk. There had never been any real bitterness between us—just jest, you know, but serious jest, a kind of silent sorrow for many fine things gone. Yet still that had been enough to keep everything out of order. Now from time to time each of us thought of restoring the old life in some form, however weak it might be. Without some form of humor the shop was a bore to the mate and the captain, anyhow. Finally the captain sobering to his old state, and the routine work becoming dreadfully monotonous, both mate and captain began to think of some way in which they, at least, could agree.

"Remember the Idlewild, Henry?" asked the ex-captain one day genially, long after time and fair weather had glossed over the wretched memory of previous quarrels and dissensions.

"That I do, John," I replied pleasantly.

"Great old boat she was, wasn't she, Henry?"

"She was, John."

"An' the bos'n's mate, he wasn't such a bad old scout, was he, Henry, even if he wouldn't quit sweepin' up the shavin's?"

"He certainly wasn't, John. He was a fine little fellow. Remember the chains, John?"

"Haw! Haw!" echoed that worthy, and then, "Do you think the old Idlewild could ever be found where she's lyin' down there on the bottom, mate?"

"Well, she might, Captain, only she'd hardly be the same old boat that she was now that she's been down there so long, would she—all these dissensions and so on? Wouldn't it be easier to build a new one—don't you think?"

"I don't know but what you're right, mate. What'd we call her if we did?"

"Well, how about the Harmony, Captain? That sounds rather appropriate, doesn't it?"

"The Harmony, mate? You're right—the Harmony. Shall we? Put 'er there!"

"Put her there," replied the mate with a will. "We'll organize a new crew right away, Captain—eh, don't you think?"

"Right! Wait, we'll call the bos'n an' see what he says."

Just then the bos'n appeared, smiling goodnaturedly.

"Well, what's up?" he inquired, noting our unusually cheerful faces, I presume. "You ain't made it up, have you, you two?" he exclaimed.

"That's what we have, bos'n, an' what's more, we're thinkin' of raisin' the old Idlewild an' renamin' her the Harmony, or, rather, buildin' a new one. What say?" It was the captain talking.

190

"Well, I'm mighty glad to hear it, only I don't think you can have your old bos'n's mate any longer, boys. He's gonna quit."

"Gonna quit!" we both exclaimed at once, and sadly, and John added seriously and looking really distressed, "What's the trouble there? Who's been doin' anything to him now?" We both felt guilty because of our part in his pains.

"Well, Ike kind o' feels that the shop's been rubbin' it into him of late for some reason," observed the bos'n heavily. "I don't know why. He thinks you two have been tryin' to freeze him out, I guess. Says he can't do anything any more, that everybody makes fun of him and shuts him out."

We stared at each other in wise illumination, the new captain and the new mate. After all, we were plainly the cause of poor little Ike's depression, and we were the ones who could restore him to favor if we chose. It was the captain's cabin he sighed for—his old pleasant prerogatives.

"Oh, we can't lose Ike, Captain," I said. "What good would the Harmony be without him? We sorely can't let anything like that happen, can we? Not now, anyhow."

"You're right, mate," he replied. "There never was a better bos'n's mate, never. The Harmony's got to have 'im. Let's talk reason to him, if we can."

In company then we three went to him, this time not to torment or chastise, but to coax and plead with him not to forsake the shop, or the ship, now that everything was going to be as before—only better—and—

Well, we did.

MARRIED

In connection with their social adjustment, one to the other, during the few months they had been together, there had occurred a number of things which made clearer to Duer and Marjorie the problematic relationship which existed between them, though it must be confessed it was clearer chiefly to him. The one thing which had been troubling Duer was not whether he would fit agreeably into her social dreams—he knew he would, so great was her love for him—but whether she would fit herself into his. Of all his former friends, he could think of only a few who would be interested in Marjorie, or she in them. She cared nothing for the studio life, except as it concerned him, and he knew no other.

Because of his volatile, enthusiastic temperament, it was easy to see, now that she was with him constantly, that he could easily be led into one relationship and another which concerned her not at all. He was for running here, there, and everywhere, just as he had before marriage, and it was very hard for him to see that Marjorie should always be with him. As a matter of fact, it occurred to him as strange that she should want to be. She would not be interested in all the people he knew, he thought. Now that he was living with her and observing her more closely, he was quite sure that most of the people he had known in the past, even in an indifferent way, would not appeal to her at all.

Take Cassandra Draper, for instance, or Neva Badger, or Edna Bainbridge, with her budding theatrical talent, or Cornelia Skiff, or Volida Blackstone—any of these women of the musical art-studio world with their radical ideas, their indifference to appearances, their semisecret immorality. And yet any of these women would be glad to see him socially, unaccompanied by his wife, and he would be glad to see them. He liked them. Most of them had not seen Marjorie, but, if they had, he fancied that they would feel about her much as he did—that is, that she did not like them, really did not fit with their world. She could not understand their point of view, he saw that. She was for one life, one love. All this excitement about entertainment, their gathering in this studio and that, this meeting of radicals and models and budding theatrical stars which she had heard him and others talking about—she suspected of it no good results. It was too feverish, too far removed from the commonplace of living to which she had been accustomed. She had been raised on a farm where, if she was not actually a farmer's daughter, she had witnessed what a real struggle for existence meant.

Out in Iowa, in the neighborhood of Avondale, there were no artists, no models, no budding actresses, no incipient playwrights, such as Marjorie found here about her. There, people worked, and worked hard. Her father was engaged at this minute in breaking the soil of his fields for the spring planting—an old man with a white beard, an honest, kindly eye, a broad, kindly charity, a sense of duty. Her mother was bending daily over a cook-stove, preparing meals, washing dishes, sewing clothes, mending socks, doing the thousand and one chores which fall to the lot of every good housewife and mother. Her sister Cecily, for all her gaiety and beauty, was helping her mother, teaching school, going to church, and taking the commonplace facts of mid-Western life in a simple, good-natured, unambitious way. And there was none of that toplofty sense of superiority which marked the manner of these Eastern upstarts.

Duer had suggested that they give a tea, and decided that they should invite Charlotte Russell and Mildred Ayres, who were both still conventionally moral in their liberalism; Francis Hatton, a young sculptor, and Miss Ollie Stearns, the latter because she had a charming contralto voice and could help them entertain. Marjorie was willing to invite both Miss Russell and Miss Ayres, not because she really wanted to know either of them but because she did not wish to appear arbitrary and especially contrary. In her estimation, Duer liked these people too much. They were friends of too long standing. She reluctantly wrote them to come, and because they liked Duer and because they wished to see the kind of wife he had, they came.

There was no real friendship to be established between Marjorie and Miss Ayres, however, for their outlook on life was radically different, though Miss Ayres was as conservative as Marjorie in her attitude, and as set in her convictions. But the latter had decided, partly because Duer had neglected her, partly because Marjorie was the victor in this contest, that he had made a mistake; she was convinced that Marjorie had not sufficient artistic apprehension, sufficient breadth of outlook, to make a good wife for him. She was charming enough to look at, of course, she had discovered that in her first visit; but there was really not enough in her socially, she was not sufficiently trained in the ways of the world, not sufficiently wise and interesting to make him an ideal companion. In addition she insisted on thinking this vigorously and, smile as she might and be as gracious as she might, it showed in her manner. Marjorie noticed it. Duer did, too. He did not dare intimate to either what he thought, but he felt that there would be no peace. It worried him, for he liked Mildred very much; but, alas! Marjorie had no good to say of her.

As for Charlotte Russell, he was grateful to her for the pleasant manner in which she steered between Scylla and Charybdis. She saw at once what Marjorie's trouble was, and did her best to allay suspicions by treating Duer formally in her presence. It was "Mr. Wilde" here and "Mr. Wilde" there, with most of her remarks addressed to Marjorie; but she did not find it easy sailing, after all. Marjorie was suspicious. There was none of the old freedom any more which had existed between Charlotte and Duer. He saw, by Marjorie's manner, the moment he became the least exuberant and free that it would not do. That evening he said, forgetting himself:

"Hey, Charlotte, you skate! Come over here. I want to show you something."

He forgot all about it afterward, but Marjorie reminded him.

"Honey," she began, when she was in his arms before the fire, and he was least expecting it, "what makes you be so free with people when they call here? You're not the kind of man that can really afford to be free with any one. Don't you know you can't? You're too big; you're too great. You just belittle yourself when you do it, and it makes them think that they are your equal when they are not."

"Who has been acting free now?" he asked sourly, on the instant, and yet with a certain make-believe of manner, dreading the storm of feeling, the atmosphere of censure and control which this remark forboded.

"Why, you have!" she persisted correctively, and yet apparently mildly and innocently. "You always do. You don't exercise enough dignity, dearie. It isn't that you haven't it naturally—you just don't exercise it. I know how it is; you forget."

Duer stirred with opposition at this, for she was striking him on his tenderest spot—his pride. It was true that he did lack dignity at times. He knew it. Because of his affection for the beautiful or interesting things—women, men, dramatic situations, songs, anything—he sometimes became very gay and free, talking loudly, using slang expressions, laughing boisterously. It was a failing with him, he knew. He carried it to excess at times. His friends, his most intimate ones in the musical profession had noted it before this. In his own heart he regretted these things afterward, but he couldn't help them, apparently. He liked excitement, freedom, gaiety— naturalness, as he called it—it helped him in his musical work, but it hurt him tremendously if he thought that any one else noticed it as out of the ordinary. He was exceedingly sensitive, and this developing line of criticism of Marjorie's was something new to him. He had never noticed anything of that in her before marriage.

194

Up to the time of the ceremony, and for a little while afterward, it had appeared to him as if he were lord and master. She had always seemed so dependent on him, so anxious that he should take her. Why, her very life had been in his hands, as it were, or so he had thought! And now—he tried to think back over the evening and see what it was he had done or said, but he couldn't remember anything. Everything seemed innocent enough. He couldn't recall a single thing, and yet—

"I don't know what you're talking about," he replied sourly, withdrawing into himself. "I haven't noticed that I lack dignity so much. I have a right to be cheerful, haven't I? You seem to be finding a lot that's wrong with me."

"Now please don't get angry, Duer," she persisted, anxious to apply the corrective measure of her criticism, but willing, at the same time, to use the quickness of his sympathy for her obvious weakness and apparent helplessness to shield herself from him. "I can't ever tell you anything if you're going to be angry. You don't lack dignity generally, honey-bun! You only forget at times. Don't you know how it is?"

She was cuddling up to him, her voice quavering, her hand stroking his cheek, in a curious effort to combine affection and punishment at the same time. Duer felt nothing but wrath, resentment, discouragement, failure.

"No, I don't," he replied crossly. "What did I do? I don't recall doing anything that was so very much out of the way."

"It wasn't that it was so very much, honey; it was just the way you did it. You forget, I know. But it doesn't look right. It belittles you."

"What did I do?" he insisted impatiently.

"Why, it wasn't anything so very much. It was just when you had the pictures of those new sculptures which Mr. Hatton lent you, and you were showing them to Miss Russell. Don't you remember what you said—how you called her over to you?"

"No," he answered, having by now completely forgotten. He was thinking that accidentally he might have slipped his arm about Charlotte, or that he might have said something out of the way jestingly about the pictures; but Marjorie could not have heard. He was so careful these days, anyway.

"Why, you said: 'Hey, Charlotte, you skate! Come over here.' Now, what a thing to say to a girl! Don't you see how ugly it sounds, how vulgar? She can't enjoy that sort of remark, particularly in my presence, do you think? She must know that I can't like it, that I'd rather you wouldn't talk that way, particularly here. And if she were the right sort of girl she wouldn't want you to talk to her at all that way. Don't you know she wouldn't? She couldn't. Now, really, no good woman would, would she?"

Duer flushed angrily. Good heaven! Were such innocent, simple things as this to be made the subject of comment and criticism! Was his life, because of his sudden, infatuated marriage, to be pulled down to a level he had never previously even contemplated? Why—why— This catechising, so new to his life, so different to anything he had ever endured in his youth or since, was certain to irritate him greatly, to be a constant thorn in his flesh. It cut him to the core. He got up, putting Marjorie away from him, for they were sitting in a big chair before the fire, and walked to the window.

"I don't see that at all," he said stubbornly. "I don't see anything in that remark to raise a row about. Why, for goodness' sake! I have known Charlotte Russell—for years and years, it seems, although it has only been a little while at that. She's like a sister to me. I like her. She doesn't mind what I say. I'd stake my life she never thought anything about it. No one would who likes me as well as she does. Why do you pitch on that to make a fuss about, for heaven's sake?"

"Please don't swear, Duer," exclaimed Marjorie anxiously, using this expression for criticising him further. "It isn't nice in you, and it doesn't sound right toward me. I'm your wife. It doesn't make any difference how long you've known her; I don't think it's nice to talk to her in that way, particularly in my presence. You say you've known her so well and you like her so much. Very well. But don't you think you ought to consider me a little, now that I'm your wife? Don't you think that you oughtn't to want to do anything like that any more, even if you have known her so well—don't you think? You're married now, and it doesn't look right to others, whatever you think of me. It can't look right to her, if she's as nice as you say she is."

Duer listened to this semipleading, semichastising harangue with disturbed, opposed, and irritated ears. Certainly, there was some truth in what she said; but wasn't it an awfully small thing to raise a row about?

Why should she quarrel with him for that? Couldn't he ever be lightsome in his form of address any more? It was true that it did sound a little rough, now that he thought of it. Perhaps it wasn't exactly the thing to say in her presence, but Charlotte didn't mind. They had known each other much too long. She hadn't noticed it one way or the other; and here was Marjorie charging him with being vulgar and inconsiderate, and Charlotte with being not the right sort of girl, and practically vulgar, also, on account of it. It was too much. It was too narrow, too conventional. He wasn't going to tolerate anything like that permanently.

He was about to say something mean in reply, make some cutting commentary, when Marjorie came over to him. She saw that she had lashed him and Charlotte and his generally easy attitude pretty thoroughly, and that he was becoming angry. Perhaps, because of his sensitiveness, he would avoid this sort of thing in the future. Anyhow, now that she had lived with him four months, she was beginning to understand him better, to see the quality of his moods, the strength of his passions, the nature of his weaknesses, how quickly he responded to the blandishments of pretended sorrow, joy, affection, or distress. She thought she could reform him at her leisure. She saw that he looked upon her in his superior way as a little girl—largely because of the size of her body. He seemed to think that, because she was little, she must be weak, whereas she knew that she had the use and the advantage of a wisdom, a tactfulness and a subtlety of which he did not even dream. Compared to her, he was not nearly as wise as he thought, at least in matters relating to the affections. Hence, any appeal to his sympathies, his strength, almost invariably produced a reaction from any antagonistic mood in which she might have placed him. She saw him now as a mother might see a great, overgrown, sulking boy, needing only to be coaxed to be brought out of a very unsatisfactory condition, and she decided to bring him out of it. For a short period in her life she had taught children in school, and knew the incipient moods of the race very well.

"Now, Duer," she coaxed, "you're not really going to be angry with me, are you? You're not going to be 'mad to me'?" (imitating childish language).

"Oh, don't bother, Marjorie," he replied distantly. "It's all right. No; I'm not angry. Only let's not talk about it any more."

"You are angry, though, Duer," she wheedled, slipping her arm around him. "Please don't be mad to me. I'm sorry now. I talk too much. I get mad. I know I oughtn't. Please don't be mad at me, honey-bun. I'll get over this after a while. I'll do better. Please, I will. Please don't be mad, will you?"

He could not stand this coaxing very long. Just as he thought, he did look upon her as a child, and this pathetic baby-talk was irresistible. He smiled grimly after a while. She was so little. He ought to endure her idiosyncrasies of temperament. Besides, he had never treated her right. He had not been faithful to his engagement-vows. If she only knew how bad he really was!

Marjorie slipped her arm through his and stood leaning against him. She loved this tall, slender distinguished-looking youth, and she wanted to take care of him. She thought that she was doing this now, when she called attention to his faults. Some day, by her persistent efforts maybe, he would overcome these silly, disagreeable, offensive traits. He would overcome being undignified; he would see that he needed to show her more consideration than he now seemed to think he did. He would learn that he was married. He would become a quiet, reserved, forceful man, weary of the silly women who were buzzing round him solely because he was a musician and talented and good-looking, and then he would be truly great. She knew what they wanted, these nasty women—they would like to have him for themselves. Well, they wouldn't get him. And they needn't think they would. She had him. He had married her. And she was going to keep him. They could just buzz all they pleased, but they wouldn't get him. So there!

There had been other spats following this—one relating to Duer not having told his friends of his marriage for some little time afterward, an oversight which in his easy going bohemian brain augured no deep planted seed of disloyalty, but just a careless, indifferent way of doing things, whereas in hers it flowered as one of the most unpardonable things imaginable! Imagine any one in the Middle West doing anything like that—any one with a sound, sane conception of the responsibilities and duties of marriage, its inviolable character! For Marjorie, having come to this estate by means of a hardly won victory, was anxious lest any germ of inattentiveness, lack of consideration, alien interest, or affection flourish and become a raging disease which would imperil or destroy the conditions on which her happiness was based. After every encounter with Miss Ayres, for instance, whom she suspected of being one of his former flames, a girl who might have become his wife, there were fresh charges to be made. She didn't invite Marjorie to sit down sufficiently quickly when she called at her studio, was one complaint; she didn't offer her a cup of tea at the hour she called another afternoon, though it was quite time for it. She didn't invite her to sing or play on another occasion, though there were others there who were invited.

"I gave her one good shot, though," said Marjorie, one day, to Duer, in narrating her troubles. "She's always talking about her artistic friends. I as good as asked her why she didn't marry, if she is so much sought after."

Duer did not understand the mental sword-thrusts involved in these feminine bickerings. He was likely to be deceived by the airy geniality which sometimes accompanied the bitterest feeling. He could stand by listening to a conversation between Marjorie and Miss Ayres, or Marjorie and any one else whom she did not like, and miss all the subtle stabs and cutting insinuations which were exchanged, and of which Marjorie was so thoroughly capable. He did not blame her for fighting for herself if she thought she was being injured, but he did object to her creating fresh occasions, and this, he saw, she was quite capable of doing. She was constantly looking for new opportunities to fight with Mildred Ayres and Miss Russell or any one else whom she thought he truly liked, whereas with those in whom he could not possibly be interested she was genial (and even affectionate) enough. But Duer also thought that Mildred might be better engaged than in creating fresh difficulties. Truly, he had thought better of her. It seemed a sad commentary on the nature of friendship between men and women, and he was sorry.

But, nevertheless, Marjorie found a few people whom she felt to be of her own kind. M. Bland, who had sponsored Duer's first piano recital a few months before, invited Duer and Marjorie to a—for them—quite sumptuous dinner at the Plaza, where they met Sydney Borg, the musical critic of an evening paper; Melville Ogden Morris, curator of the Museum of Fine Arts, and his wife; Joseph Newcorn, one of the wealthy sponsors of the opera and its geniuses, and Mrs. Newcorn. Neither Duer nor Marjorie had ever seen a private dining-room set in so scintillating a manner. It fairly glittered with Sèvres and Venetian tinted glass. The wine-goblets were seven in number, set in an ascending row. The order of food was complete from Russian caviare to dessert, black coffee, nuts, liqueurs, and cigars.

The conversation wandered its intense intellectual way from American musicians and singers, European painters and sculptors, discoveries of ancient pottery in the isles of the Ægean, to the manufacture of fine glass on Long Island, the character of certain collectors and collections of paintings in America, and the present state of the Fine Arts Museum. Duer listened eagerly, for, as yet, he was a little uncertain himself of his position in the art world. He did not quite know how to take these fine and able personages who seemed so powerful in the world's affairs. Joseph Newcorn, as M. Bland calmly indicated to him, must be worth in the neighborhood of fifteen million dollars. He thought nothing, so he said, of paying ten, fifteen, twenty, thirty thousand dollars for a picture if it appealed to him. Mr. Morris was a graduate of Harvard, formerly curator of a Western museum, the leader of one of the excavating expeditions to Melos in the Grecian Archipelago. Sydney Borg was a student of musical history, who appeared to have a wide knowledge of art tendencies here and abroad, but who, nevertheless, wrote musical criticisms for a living. He was a little man of Norse extraction on his father's side, but, as he laughingly admitted, born and raised in McKeesport, Pennsylvania. He liked Duer for his simple acknowledgment of the fact that he came from a small town in the Middle West, and a drug business out in Illinois.

"It's curious how our nation brings able men from the ranks," he said to Duer. "It's one of the great, joyous, hopeful facts about this country."

"Yes," said Duer; "that's why I like it so much."

Duer thought, as he dined here, how strange America was, with its mixture of races, its unexpected sources of talent, its tremendous wealth and confidence. His own beginning, so very humble at first, so very promising now—one of the most talked of pianists of his day—was in its way an illustration of its resources in so far as talent was concerned. Mr. Newcorn, who had once been a tailor, so he was told, and his wife was another case in point. They were such solid, unemotional, practical-looking people, and yet he could see that this solid looking man whom some musicians might possibly have sneered at for his self-complacency and curiously accented English, was as wise and sane and keen and kindly as any one present, perhaps more so, and as wise in matters musical. The only difference between him and the average American was that he was exceptionally practical and not given to nervous enthusiasm. Marjorie liked him, too.

It was at this particular dinner that the thought occurred to Marjorie that the real merit of the art and musical world was not so much in the noisy studio palaver which she heard at so many places frequented by Duer, in times past at least—Charlotte Russell's, Mildred Ayres's and elsewhere—but in the solid commercial achievements of such men as Joseph Newcorn, Georges Bland, Melville Ogden Morris, and Sydney Borg. She liked the laconic "Yes, yes," of Mr. Newcorn, when anything was said that suited him particularly well, and his "I haf seen dat bardicular berformance" with which he interrupted several times when Grand Opera and its stars were up for consideration. She was thinking if only a man like that would take an interest in Duer, how much better it would be for him than all the enthusiasm of these silly noisy studio personalities. She was glad to see also that, intellectually, Duer could hold his own with any and all of these people. He was as much at ease here with Mr. Morris, talking about Greek excavations, as he was with Mr. Borg, discussing American musical conditions. She could not make out much what it was all about, but, of course, it must be very important if these men discussed it. Duer was not sure as yet whether any one knew much more about life than he did. He suspected not, but it might be that some of these eminent curators, art critics, bankers, and managers like M. Bland, had a much wider insight into practical affairs. Practical affairs—he thought. If he only knew something about money! Somehow, though, his mind could not grasp how money was made. It seemed so easy for some people, but for him a grim, dark mystery.

After this dinner it was that Marjorie began to feel that Duer ought to be especially careful with whom he associated. She had talked with Mrs. Newcorn and Mrs. Morris, and found them simple, natural people like herself. They were not puffed up with vanity and self-esteem, as were those other men and women to whom Duer had thus far introduced her. As compared to Charlotte Russell and Mildred Ayres or her own mother and sisters and her Western friends, they were more like the latter. Mrs. Newcorn, wealthy as she was, spoke of her two sons and three daughters as any good-natured, solicitous mother would. One of her sons was at Harvard, the other at Yale. She asked Marjorie to come and see her some time, and gave her her address. Mrs. Morris was more cultured apparently, more given to books and art; but even she was interested in what, to Marjorie, were the more important or, at least, more necessary things, the things on which all art and culture primarily based themselves—the commonplace and necessary details of the home. Cooking, housekeeping, shopping, sewing, were not beneath her consideration, as indeed they were not below Mrs. Newcorn's. The former spoke of having to go and look for a new spring bonnet in the morning, and how difficult it was to find the time. Once when the men were getting especially excited about European and American artistic standards, Marjorie asked:

"Are you very much interested in art, Mrs. Morris?"

"Not so very much, to tell you the truth, Mrs. Wilde. Oh, I like some pictures, and I hear most of the important recitals each season, but, as I often tell my husband, when you have one baby two years old and another of five and another of seven, it takes considerable time to attend to the art of raising them. I let him do the art for the family, and I take care of the home."

This was sincere consolation for Marjorie. Up to this time she appeared to be in danger of being swamped by this artistic storm which she had encountered. Her arts of cooking, sewing, housekeeping, appeared as nothing in this vast palaver about music, painting, sculpture, books and the like. She knew nothing, as she had most painfully discovered recently, of Strauss, Dvořák, Debussy, almost as little of Cézanne, Goguin, Matisse, Van Gogh, Rodin, Ibsen, Shaw and Maeterlinck, with whom the studios were apparently greatly concerned. And when people talked of singers, musicians, artists, sculptors, and playwrights, often she was compelled to keep silent, whereas Duer could stand with his elbow on some mantel or piano and discuss by the half hour or hour individuals of whom she had never heard—Verlaine, Tchaikowsky, Tolstoy, Turgenieff, Tagore, Dostoyevsky, Whistler, Velasquez—anybody and everybody who appeared to interest the studio element. It was positively frightening.

A phase of this truth was that because of his desire to talk, his pleasure in meeting people, his joy in hearing of new things, his sense of the dramatic, Duer could catch quickly and retain vigorously anything which related to social, artistic, or intellectual development. He had no idea of what a full-orbed, radiant, receptive thing his mind was. He only knew that life, things, intellect—anything and everything—gave him joy when he was privileged to look into them, whereas Marjorie was not so keenly minded artistically, and he gave as freely as he received. In this whirl of discussion, this lofty transcendentalism, Marjorie was all but lost; but she clung tenaciously to the hope that, somehow, affection, regard for the material needs of her husband, the care of his clothes, the preparation of his meals, the serving of him quite as would a faithful slave, would bind him to her. At once and quickly, she hated and feared these artistically arrayed, artistically minded, vampirish-looking maidens and women who appeared from this quarter and that to talk to Duer, all of whom apparently had known him quite well in the past—since he had come to New York. When she would see him standing or leaning somewhere, intent on the rendering of a song, the narration of some dramatic incident, the description of some book or picture, or personage, by this or that delicately chiseled Lorelei of the art or music or dramatic world, her heart contracted ominously and a nameless dread seized her. Somehow, these creatures, however intent they might be on their work, or however indifferent actually to the artistic charms of her husband, seemed to be intent on taking him from her. She saw how easily and naturally he smiled, how very much at home he seemed to be in their company, how surely he gravitated to the type of girl who was beautifully and artistically dressed, who had ravishing eyes, fascinating hair, a sylphlike figure, and vivacity of manner—or how naturally they gravitated to him. In the rush of conversation and the exchange of greetings he was apt to forget her, to stroll about by himself engaging in conversation first with one and then another, while she stood or sat somewhere gazing nervously or regretfully on, unable to hold her own in the cross-fire of conversation, unable to retain the interest of most of the selfish, lovesick, sensation-seeking girls and men.

They always began talking about the opera, or the play, or the latest sensation in society, or some new singer or dancer or poet, and Marjorie, being new to this atmosphere and knowing so little of it, was compelled to confess that she did not know. It chagrined, dazed, and frightened her for a time. She longed to be able to grasp quickly and learn what this was all about. She wondered where she had been living—how—to have missed all this. Why, goodness gracious, these things were enough to wreck her married life! Duer would think so poorly of her—how could he help it? She watched these girls and women talking to him, and by turns, while imitating them as best she could, became envious, fearful, regretful, angry; charging, first, herself with unfitness; next, Duer with neglect; next, these people with insincerity, immorality, vanity; and lastly, the whole world and life with a conspiracy to cheat her out of what was rightfully her own. Why wouldn't these people be nice to her? Why didn't they give of their time and patience to make her comfortable and at home—as freely, say, as they did to him? Wasn't she his wife, now? Why did Duer neglect her? Why did they hang on his words in their eager, seductive, alluring way? She hated them and, at moments, she hated him, only to be struck by a terrifying wave of remorse and fear a moment later. What if he should grow tired of her? What if his love should change? He had seemed so enamored of her only a little while before they were married, so taken by what he called her naturalness, grace, simplicity and emotional pull.

On one of these occasions, or rather after it, when they had returned from an evening at Francis Hatton's at which she felt that she had been neglected, she threw herself disconsolately into Duer's arms and exclaimed:

"What's the matter with me, Duer? Why am I so dull—so uninteresting—so worthless?"

The sound of her voice was pathetic, helpless, vibrant with the quality of an unuttered sob, a quality which had appealed to him intensely long before they were married, and now he stirred nervously.

"Why, what's the matter with you now, Margie?" he asked sympathetically, sure that a new storm of some sort was coming. "What's come over you? There's nothing the matter with you. Why do you ask? Who's been saying there is?"

"Oh, nothing, nothing—nobody! Everybody! Everything!" exclaimed Marjorie dramatically, and bursting into tears. "I see how it is. I see what is the matter with me. Oh! Oh! It's because I don't know anything, I suppose. It's because I'm not fit to associate with you. It's because I haven't had the training that some people have had. It's because I'm dull! Oh! Oh!" and a torrent of heart-breaking sobs which shook her frame from head to toe followed the outburst and declamation.

Duer, always moved by her innate emotional force and charm, whatever other lack he had reason to bewail, gazed before him in startled sympathy, astonishment, pain, wonder, for he was seeing very clearly and keenly in these echoing sounds what the trouble was. She was feeling neglected, outclassed, unconsidered, helpless; and because it was more or less true it was frightening and wounding her. She was, for the first time no doubt, beginning to feel the tragedy of life, its uncertainty, its pathos and injury, as he so often had. Hitherto her home, her relatives and friends had more or less protected her from that, for she had come from a happy home, but now she was out and away from all that and had only him. Of course she had been neglected. He remembered that now. It was partly his fault, partly the fault of surrounding conditions. But what could he do about it? What say? People had conditions fixed for them in this world by their own ability. Perhaps he should not have married her at all, but how should he comfort her in this crisis? How say something that would ease her soul?

"Why, Margie," he said seriously, "you know that's not true! You know you're not dull. Your manners and your taste and your style are as good as those of anybody. Who has hinted that they aren't? What has come over you? Who has been saying anything to you? Have I done anything? If so, I'm sorry!" He had a guilty consciousness of misrepresenting himself and his point of view even while saying this, but kindness, generosity, affection, her legal right to his affection, as he now thought, demanded it.

"No! No!" she exclaimed brokenly and without ceasing her tears. "It isn't you. It isn't anybody. It's me—just me! That's what's the matter with me. I'm dull; I'm not stylish; I'm not attractive. I don't know anything about music or books or people or anything. I sit and listen, but I don't know what to say. People talk to you—they hang on your words—but they haven't anything to say to me. They can't talk to me, and I can't talk to them. It's because I don't know anything—because I haven't anything to say! Oh dear! Oh dear!" and she beat her thin, artistic little hands on the shoulders of his coat.

Duer could not endure this storm without an upwelling of pity for her. He cuddled her close in his arms, extremely sad that she should be compelled to suffer so. What should he do? What could he do? He could see how it was. She was hurt; she was neglected. He neglected her when among others. These smart women whom he knew and liked to talk with neglected her. They couldn't see in her what he could. Wasn't life pathetic? They didn't know how sweet she was, how faithful, how glad she was to work for him. That really didn't make any difference in the art world, he knew, but still it almost seemed as if it ought to. There one must be clever, he knew that—everybody knew it. And Marjorie was not clever—at least, not in their way. She couldn't play or sing or paint or talk brilliantly, as they could. She did not really know what the world of music, art, and literature was doing. She was only good, faithful, excellent as a housewife, a fine mender of clothes, a careful buyer, saving, considerate, dependable, but—

As he thought of this and then of this upwelling depth of emotion of hers, a thing quite moving to him always, he realized, or thought he did, that no woman that he had ever known had anything quite like this. He had known many women intimately. He had associated with Charlotte and Mildred and Neva Badger and Volida Blackstone, and quite a number of interesting, attractive young women whom he had met here and there since, but outside of the stage—that art of Sarah Bernhardt and Clara Morris and some of the more talented English actresses of these later days—he persuaded himself that he had never seen any one quite like Marjorie. This powerful upwelling of emotion which she was now exhibiting and which was so distinctive of her, was not to be found elsewhere, he thought. He had felt it keenly the first days he had visited her at her father's home in Avondale. Oh, those days with her in Avondale! How wonderful they were! Those delicious nights! Flowers, moonlight, odors, came back—the green fields, the open sky. Yes; she was powerful emotionally. She was compounded of many and all of these things.

It was true she knew nothing of art, nothing of music—the great, new music—nothing of books in the eclectic sense, but she had real, sweet, deep, sad, stirring emotion, the most appealing thing he knew. It might not be as great as that exhibited by some of the masters of the stage, or the great composers—he was not quite sure, so critical is life—but nevertheless it was effective, dramatic, powerful. Where did she get it? No really common soul could have it. Here must be something of the loneliness of the prairies, the sad patience of the rocks and fields, the lonesomeness of the hush of the countryside at night, the aimless, monotonous, pathetic chirping of the crickets. Her father following down a furrow in the twilight behind straining, toil-worn horses; her brothers binding wheat in the July sun; the sadness of furrow scents and field fragrances in the twilight—there was something of all these things in her sobs.

It appealed to him, as it might well have to any artist. In his way Duer understood this, felt it keenly.

"Why, Margie," he insisted, "you mustn't talk like that! You're better than you say you are. You say you don't know anything about books or art or music. Why, that isn't all. There are things, many things, which are deeper than those things. Emotion is a great thing in itself, dearest, if you only knew. You have that. Sarah Bernhardt had it; Clara Morris had it, but who else? In 'La Dame aux Camelias,' 'Sapho,' 'Carmen,' 'Mademoiselle de Maupin,' it is written about, but it is never commonplace. It's great. I'd rather have your deep upwelling of emotion than all those cheap pictures, songs, and talk put together. For, sweet, don't you know"—and he cuddled her more closely—"great art is based on great emotion. There is really no great art without it. I know that best of all, being a musician. You may not have the power to express yourself in music or books or pictures—you play charmingly enough for me—but you have the thing on which these things are based; you have the power to feel them. Don't worry over yourself, dear. I see that, and I know what you are, whether any one else does or not. Don't worry over me. I have to be nice to these people. I like them in their way, but I love you. I married you—isn't that proof enough? What more do you want? Don't you understand, little Margie? Don't you see? Now aren't you going to cheer up and be happy? You have me. Ain't I enough, sweetie? Can't you be happy with just me? What more do you want? Just tell me."

"Nothing more, honey-bun!" she went on sobbing and cuddling close; "nothing more, if I can have you. Just you! That's all I want—you, you, you!"

She hugged him tight. Duer sighed secretly. He really did not believe all he said, but what of it? What else could he do, say, he asked himself? He was married to her. In his way, he loved her—or at least sympathized with her intensely.

"And am I emotionally great?" she cuddled and cooed, after she had held him tight for a few moments. "Doesn't it make any difference whether I know anything much about music or books or art? I do know something, don't I, honey? I'm not wholly ignorant, am I?"

"No, no, sweetie; how you talk!"

"And will you always love me whether I know anything or not, honey-bun?" she went on. "And won't it make any difference whether I can just cook and sew and do the marketing and keep house for you? And will you like me because I'm just pretty and not smart? I am a little pretty, ain't I, dear?"

"You're lovely," whispered Duer soothingly. "You're beautiful. Listen to me, sweet. I want to tell you something. Stop crying now, and dry your eyes, and I'll tell you something nice. Do you remember how we stood, one night, at the end of your father's field there near the barn-gate and saw him coming down the path, singing to himself, driving that team of big gray horses, his big straw hat on the back of his head and his sleeves rolled up above his elbows?"

"Yes," said Marjorie.

"Do you remember how the air smelled of roses and honeysuckle and cut hay—and oh, all those lovely scents of evening that we have out there in the country?"

"Yes," replied Marjorie interestedly.

"And do you remember how lovely I said the cowbells sounded tinkling in the pasture where the little river ran?"

"Yes."

"And the fireflies beginning to flash in the trees?"

"Yes."

"And that sad, deep red in the West, where the sun had gone down?"

"Yes, I remember," said Marjorie, crushing her cheek to his neck.

"Now listen to me, honey: That water running over the bright stones in that little river; the grass spreading out, soft and green, over the slope; the cow-bells tinkling; the smoke curling up from your mother's chimney; your father looking like a patriarch out of Bible days coming home—all the soft sounds, all the sweet odors, all the carolling of birds—where do you suppose all that is now?"

"I don't know," replied Marjorie, anticipating something complimentary.

"It's here," he replied easily, drawing her close and petting her. "It's done up in one little body here in my arms. Your voice, your hair, your eyes, your pretty body, your emotional moods— where do you suppose they come from? Nature has a chemistry all her own. She's like a druggist sometimes, compounding things. She takes a little of the beauty of the sunset, of the sky, of the fields, of the water, of the flowers, of dreams and aspirations and simplicity and patience, and she makes a girl. And some parents somewhere have her, and then they name her 'Marjorie' and then they raise her nicely and innocently, and then a bold, bad man like Duer comes along and takes her, and then she cries because she thinks he doesn't see anything in her. Now, isn't that funny?"

"O-oh!" exclaimed Marjorie, melted by the fire of his feeling for beauty, the quaintness and sweetness of his diction, the subtlety of his compliment, the manner in which he coaxed her patiently out of herself.

"Oh, I love you, Duer dear! I love you, love you, love you! Oh, you're wonderful! You won't ever stop loving me, will you, dearest? You'll always be true to me, won't you, Duer? You'll never leave me, will you? I'll always be your little Margie, won't I? Oh, dear, I'm so happy!" and she hugged him closer and closer.

"No, no," and "Yes, yes," assured Duer, as the occasion demanded, as he stared patiently into the fire. This was not real passion to him, not real love in any sense, or at least he did not feel that it was. He was too skeptical of himself, his life and love, however much he might sympathize with and be drawn to her. He was questioning himself at this very time as to what it was that caused him to talk so. Was it sympathy, love of beauty, power of poetic expression, delicacy of sentiment?—certainly nothing more. Wasn't it this that was already causing him to be hailed as a great musician? He believed so. Could he honestly say that he loved Marjorie? No, he was sure that he couldn't, now that he had her and realized her defects, as well as his own—his own principally. No; he liked her, sympathized with her, felt sorry for her. That ability of his to paint a picture in notes and musical phrases, to extract the last ringing delicacy out of the keys of a piano, was at the bottom of this last description. To Marjorie, for the moment, it might seem real enough, but he—he was thinking of the truth of the picture she had painted of herself. It was all so—every word she said. She was not really suited to these people. She did not understand them; she never would. He would always be soothing and coaxing, and she would always be crying and worrying.

WHEN THE OLD CENTURY WAS NEW

When William Walton, of Colonial prestige, left his father's house, St George's Square, New York, in the spring of 1801, it was to spend a day of social activity, which, in the light of his ordinary commercial duties, might be termed idleness. There were, among other things, a luncheon at the Livingstone Kortright's, a stroll with one Mlle. Cruger to the Lispenard Meadows, and a visit in the evening to the only recently inaugurated Apollo Theater, where were organized the first permanent company of players ever transported to America. Under the circumstances, he had no time for counting-house duties, and had accordingly decided to make a day of it, putting the whole matter of commerce over until such time as he could labor uninterrupted, which was to-morrow.

As he came out of the door over which was a diamond-pane lunette for a transom, he was a striking example of the new order of things which had come with the Declaration of Independence and the victory of the colonies over the British. Long trousers of light twilled cloth encased his legs, and were fastened under his shoes by straps. A flower-ornamented pink waistcoat and light blue dress coat of broadcloth, shared with brass buttons, yellow gloves, and an exceedingly narrow-brimmed silk hat, in giving his appearance that touch of completeness which the fashion of the day demanded. In the face of those of the older order, who still maintained the custom of wearing knee breeches and solemn, black waistcoats, he was a little apt to appear the exaggerated dandy; but, nevertheless, it was good form. My Madame Kortright would expect it at any luncheon of hers, and the common people knew it to be the all-desirable whenever wealth permitted.

In lower Pearl Street, below Wall, which direction he took to reach the Bowling Green and the waterfront, he encountered a number of the fashionable, so far as the commercial world was concerned, who were anything but idle like himself.

"Why, Master Walton, are you neglecting business so early in the morning?" inquired Robert Goelet, whose iron-mongering business was then the most important in the city.

"For this day only," returned Walton, smiling agreeably at the thought of a pleasant day to come. "Several engagements make it unavoidable."

"You are going to the Collect, then, possibly?" returned Goelet, looking in the direction of the old water reservoir, where all of the city's drinking supply was stored.

"No," said the other, "I had not thought of it. What is there?"

"Some one, I understand, who has a boat he wishes to try. It is said to go without sail. I should think one with as many ships upon the water as you have would have heard of any such invention as that."

"Ah, yes," answered young Walton, "I have heard of men who are going to sail in the air, also. I will believe that a vessel can go without sail when I see it."

"Well," said the other, "I do not know. These inventors are strange adventurers, at best, but there might be no harm in looking at it. I think I shall go myself later."

"Oh, I should also like to see it," said the other, "providing I have time. When is it to sail, do you know?"

"About eleven," answered Goelet. "The Post tells of it."

"Many thanks for the information," returned the other, and, with a few commonplaces as to ships expected and the news from France, they betook their separate ways.

In one of the many fine yards which spread before the old mansions below Wall Street, he beheld John Adams, the newly-elected President of the States, busy among his flowers. The elder statesman bowed gravely to the younger gentleman and returned to his work.

"A fine gentleman," thought the latter, "and well worthy to be the chief of this good government."

As he neared the Bowling Green, he observed that there was no one of the many residents about taking advantage of the pleasant sunlight to enjoy an hour at that favorite pastime, and so continued his way to the Astor docks adjoining the Whitehall slip, where never yet had the commercial New Yorker, interested in the matter of shipping, failed to find a crowd. Messrs. John Jacob Astor and William Van Rensalaer were already upon the ground, as he could see at a distance, the distinct high hat of the one and the portly figure of the other standing out in clear relief against the green waters of the bay. Elder Johannis Coop was there, he of the vast ship chandlery business, and Opdyke Stewart, importer of the finest stuffs woven in Holland. Old Jacob Cruger and Mortimer Morris, the lean Van Tassel and Julius van Brunt, merchants all and famous men of the city, chatted, smiled, and laughed together as they discussed the probabilities of trade and the arrival of the Silver Spray and the Laughing Mary, both in the service between New York and Liverpool. Almost every worthy present was armed with his spy-glass, as the three-foot telescopes were then called, and now and then one would take a look down the bay and through the distant narrows to see if any sign of a familiar sail were present.

"And how is Master Walton?" asked the elder Astor, recognizing the scion of the one exceedingly wealthy family of the community.

"Very well, thank you," returned the other, surveying the company, whose knee breeches and black coats presented a striking contrast to his modern trousers and fancy jacket.

"These modern fashions," exclaimed Cruger, the elder, coming forward, "make us old fellows seem entirely out of date. They are a wretched contrivance to hide the legs. If I were a young woman I would have no man whose form I could not judge by his clothes."

"And if I were a young man," put in the jovial John Jacob, "I would put on no clothes which a young woman did not approve of."

"Ah, well," said the other, smiling, "these fashions are strange contrivances. Not ten years since a man would have been drummed out of New York had he appeared in such finery as this, and now, by heaven, it is we old fellows who are like to be shown the door for dressing as our fathers taught us."

"Not so bad as that, surely," said Walton. "Full dress commands the old style yet at evening. This is but daylight custom. But how about the Bowling Green; is no one to play there this morning?"

"Not when two ships like the Silver Spray and the Laughing Mary are like to show their noses at any moment," observed Cruger stoutly. "I have fifty barrels of good India ale on the Silver Spray. Astor, here, has most of the hold of the Laughing Mary filled with his dress goods. No bowling when stocks must be unpacked quickly."

"It is a weary watch, this, for these dogged vessels," added Astor reflectively. "There is no good counting wind or wave. The Spaniard, too, is not dead yet, worse luck to him."

"I saw that about the Polly," said young Walton interestedly. "Perhaps the government will wake up now to our situation. The Spaniard can wipe our vessels off the seas and hide behind the piracy idea. We need more war vessels and that quickly, I think."

"And I, too," said Astor. "But we are like to have them now. Only to-day Congress voted to buy more land across the East River there," and he waved his spy-glass in the direction of the green outlines of Long Island.

"And that reminds me," said Walton, pulling out his timepiece by the fob attached to it; "I but now met Goelet, who says there is to be a boat tried at the Collect which goes without sail. It is to be run by steam."

"Ha!" exclaimed Cruger, have no time for such nonsense."

"I heard of it," remarked Astor. "Possibly there is something to it. There could be no harm in going to see."

"I am going," said Walton, "and by-the-bye, it is high time I was on my way."

"And if you have no objection I go with you," said Astor, who was seriously interested to know if there was anything to this idea or not. Others hearing this joined them.

Having thus secured companionship, young Walton proceeded up the Whitehall slip to the Bowling Green, whence, with his friends, he now turned into the Broadway, and so out past the fine residences and occasional stores of that new thoroughfare to the old White residence, where later was to be White Street, and thence eastward, across the open common, to the Collect, where is now the Tombs. Quite a formidable company of sightseers had gathered, the aristocracy, gentry, and common rabble forming in separate groups. A very plain and homely looking individual of the older school, clad in swallowtail and knee breeches, was there with a contrivance large enough to sustain his own weight in the water, which he was endeavoring with a wrench, a hammer, and an oil can to put in final shape for the very important experiment of traveling without sail. Naturally he had the undivided and even pushing and prying attention of all present.

While the citizens thus gazed, awaiting in comfortable idleness for something of the marvelous to happen, there came a clattering sound along the east road toward the city, where suddenly appeared the outlines of Van Huicken's water wagon, a great hogshead on wheels, which, by its rumbling haste, suggested fire. Close after followed the Almerich, another vehicle of the same kind, which secured its name from its owner. Both drivers hailed the crowd while yet a distance off with shouts of "Fire!" and then from distant Fulton Street were heard the sounds of a bell tolling out the same intelligence.

Everybody now wavered uncertainly between the possibility of witnessing a marvelous invention and the certainty of seeing a splendid conflagration, with the result that certainty triumphed. Instantly upon learning the nature of the fire, both commonry and gentry departed, leaving Astor and Walton, with their associates, gazing at the tinkering wonder-worker alone.

"That must be near the President's house," observed Walton, who was looking toward the city. "It may spread."

"This fellow will get nothing out of his machine to-day, I fear," returned Astor, moved by the thought of a dangerous and yet interesting fire as he gazed rather unfavorably upon the quiet

212

inventor, who had not remained unaware of this public defection. "Let us go back."

With somewhat more of eagerness than was conformable with their general stately bearing, this rather important local company now took up the trail of the water wagons and returned.

In William Street, just off the Old Boston Road and near the newly-named Liberty Street, were many signs of public excitement. The fine residence of the Athorps, recently leased by the French minister, had taken fire, and was rapidly burning. Although nine of the fourteen water-pumps of the city were upon the scene of action, and eight men were toiling at each handle, little progress was making. Bucket brigades were also in operation, the volunteer citizens drawing upon every well in the neighborhood for blocks about; but to small result. The flames gained apace. Men ran looking for Goiter's water conveyance, which had not yet been pressed into action, and Huicken's Broadway sprinkler, which, however, had already been sent to the Collect for more water. There was a deal of clatter and confusion, coupled with the absolute certainty of destruction, for no pumping could throw the water beyond the second story. More than once the tank supply, as rattled forward from the Collect and the East River, was totally suspended, while the flames gained new ground. This latter was due to the badness of the roads and the inadequacy of the help at the supply end, where, since all thought to gaze upon the fire, none were remaining to help the lone Huicken or the energetic Goiter.

When this last company of volunteer fire fighters arrived, with their buckets and other contrivances for fighting a blaze, the flames had gained such headway that there was little to be done. Walton wasted half an hour discussing fire protection, and then bethought himself of his luncheon engagement.

"I must be out of this," he said to Astor, as they stood gazing upon the flames and the surging throng. "I am late as it is."

The genial forefather scarcely heard him at all. So interested was he that his own luncheon mattered not at all. Quietly Walton withdrew then, and getting back into Boston Road and the Broadway, betook himself toward the Bowling Green and Madame Kortright's.

That lady's mansion was to the west of the old playground, looking out over lawn and lane to some space of water to be seen in the East River and a boat or two at anchor in the bay. As he tapped upon the broad door with its brazen knocker, a liveried servant opened to him, bowing profoundly in greeting.

"Will Master Walton give me his hat and gloves?"

"Ah, Master Walton," remarked the hostess, who now entered

smiling. "I had almost doubted your punctuality, though you have good reason. Whose house is it burning?"

"Count Rennay's," answered Walton, mentioning the French representative to our government.

"I have sent a servant to discover it for me, but he has not yet returned. It must have fascinated him also. We must sit to lunch at once, sir."

As the hostess said this, she turned about in her great hoops, now but recently, like long trousers, come into fashion, and led the way. Her hair was done in the curls of the post-revolution period, three at each side, about the ears, and a tall chignon that was almost a curl in itself. With stately grace she led the way to the dining chamber and bowed him to his place. Eulalia, a daughter, and Sophia, a friend, entered almost at the same moment with them through another door.

At the head of the long, oaken table there were already standing the two black table servants of this dignified household, splendid imported Africans, trained in Virginia. My lady's table was a-gleam with much of the richest plate and old Holland china in the city. An immense silver candelabra graced the center, and at every corner were separate graven gold sticks making a splendid show.

"I have the greatest terror of fire anywhere in our city," began the hostess, even as young Walton was bowing. "We have so little protection. I have urged upon our selectmen the necessity of providing something better than we have—a water tower or something of the sort but so far nothing has come of it."

"You were at the fire, Master Walton?" inquired the handsome Eulalie archly.

"I came that way with several friends from the Collect," he answered.

"Why the Collect?" asked the hostess, who was now seated with the two blacks towering above her.

"There is a man there who has a boat which is to go without sail, as I understand it, providing his idea is correct. It is to go by steam, I believe, only he did not succeed in making it so do to-day, at least not while I was there. It may have gone, though. I could not wait to see."

"Oh marvelous," exclaimed Eulalie, putting up a pair of pretty hands, "and really is it a boat that will travel so?"

"I cannot vouch for that," returned the youth gravely. "It was not going when we visited it. The fire and my engagement took the entire audience of the inventor away," and he smiled.

"I shall have no faith in any such trap as that until I see it," observed Madame Kortright. "Fancy being on the water and no sail to waft you. Mercy!"

"I fancy it will be some time before men will venture afar on any such craft," returned the youth; "but it is a bit curious."

"Dangerous, I should say," suggested Mistress Sophia.

"No," said Walton, "not that, I think. My father has often told me that Master Franklin predicted to him that men should harness the lightning before many years. That is even more strange than this."

"That may all be true," said Madame Kortright, but it has not come to pass yet. It will never be in our time, I fear. But did you hear of the case of jewels at Maton's?"

"Has he imported something new?" inquired Eulalie smartly.

"The last ship brought a case of gems for him, I hear," continued the hostess. "That should be of interest to you, Master Walton."

The youth flushed slightly at the implication involved. His attentions to Mistress Beppie Cruger were becoming a subject of pleasing social comment.

"So it is," he said gaily, as he recovered his composure. "I shall look in upon Maton this very afternoon."

"And I should like to see what is new in France," said the ruddy Sophia seriously. "I have not an earring or a pin in my collection that is not as old as the hills—"

"Nor any the less valuable, I venture," answered Walton, with an impressive air.

"I would give them for new ones, believe me," returned the girl quaintly.

Upon this gossiping company the two blacks waited with almost noiseless accuracy, one serving at each side in answer to silent looks and nods from the hostess. Walton watched them out of the corner of his eye, gossiping the while. In his new home, he thought, whenever the fair lady consented, there should be two such lackeys gracing her more tender beauty. He could not help thinking how much more effective they would appear behind her than his present hostess, who, however, was attractive enough. It made him restless to depart, for certainly this afternoon he should definitely, if he could, learn his fate. The jewels would be one excuse. He would take her to look at the jewels before the evening called them to the theater, and then he would see.

Once he was free of the entertainment provided, he hurried away into Wall Street, the spire of Trinity already beginning to cast a short eastward shadow. About the building occupied as the new National Capitol a few dignitaries from the colonies were to be seen.

215

The new mixture of stores among the residences was beginning to make lovely Wall Street less conservative. A bank had opened just below the Capitol, its entrance reaching out to the very sidewalk and hedging in the view of the gardens beyond. Soon, if the city kept on growing, all the fine old gardens would have to go.

He pondered, as he walked, until he came to a certain gateway below William Street, where he entered. From a window looking out upon a small balcony above a face disappeared, and now he was greeted by another pompous servant at the door.

"My compliments," he said, "to Mistress Cruger, if she pleases, and I am waiting."

The servant bowed and retired. In a few moments more there fluttered down into the large reception room from above the loveliest embodiment of the new order of finery that he had ever seen. Such daintiness in curls and laces, such lightness in silken flounces displayed upon spreading hoops, he felt to be without equal. With a graceful courtesy she received his almost ponderous bow.

"Mother gives you her greeting, and she cannot come with us to-day," she said. "She has a very severe headache."

"I am very sorry to hear that," he replied sympathetically, "but you will come? The weather has favored us, and I fancy the meadows will be beautiful to see."

"Oh, yes, I will come," she returned smiling. "It is not quite three, however," she added. "You are early."

"I know," he answered, "but we may talk until then. Besides there is something I wish you to see before theater time—no, I will tell you of it later. Henry will be on time."

They seated themselves very respectfully distant and took up the morning's commonplaces. Had he heard of the fire and where the French minister was now being entertained? Cards had but this morning come from the Jacob Van Dams for a reception at their new house in Broome Street. The Goelets were to build farther out in Pearl Street

"I think it is a shame," she said, "the way they are deserting us in this street. We shall have to go also very shortly, and I like Wall Street."

"When your turn comes perhaps you will not mind it so much," he returned, thinking of the proposal he hoped to find the courage to make. "Broome Street is certainly pleasing after the new style."

She thought of all the fine residences being erected in that new residence section, and for some, to him, inexplicable reason,

216

smiled. Outside, through the vine-festooned window, she could see a broad, open barouche turning.

"Here is the carriage," she said.

As they came out of the quiet chamber into the open sunlight, part of their stilted reserve vanished. Once in the carriage beside him, she smiled happily. As they rolled into William Street and up the Old Boston Road into the green shaded Bowery, she laughed for the very joy of laughing.

"It is good to feel spring again," she said, "the cold days are so many."

As they traveled, an occasional citizen before his doorway, or pleasure seeker upon horseback, greeted them. The distinguished Aaron Burr was here prancing gaily countryward. Old Peter Stuyvesant's mansion was kept as rich in flowers as when he had been alive to care for it.

"Are not the fields beautiful about here?" he observed, after they had passed the region of the Collect.

"Lovely," she returned. "I never see them but I think of dancing, they are so soft."

"Let us get out and walk upon them, anyhow," he answered. "Henry can wait for us at the turn yonder."

He was pointing to a far point, where, through a dump of trees, the winding footpath, leading out from here, joined Broadway, now a lane through the woods and fields.

Gaily she acquiesced, and he helped her down. When the servant was out of hearing, he reached for a dandelion, and pressing his lips to it said, "Here is a token."

"Of what?" she said shyly.

"What should it be?" he asked wistfully.

"Spring, probably."

"And nothing else?"

"Youth," she answered, laughing.

"And nothing else?" he questioned, drawing close with a tenderness in his voice.

"How should I know?" she said, laughing and casting it down, because of her fear of the usual significance of the situation.

"You mustn't throw it away," he said stooping. "Keep it. I'll tell you what it means. I—I—"

"See the wild roses!" she exclaimed, suddenly increasing her pace. "I should rather have some of those for a token, if you please."

He relaxed his tension, and hastened for that which she desired. When he returned to hand them to her, she was laughing at something.

"Ah, you laugh," he said sadly. "I think I know why."

217

"It is because of the day," she answered.

Somehow he could make no progress with his declaration until it was too late. Already they were near the carriage, and south along the road a quarter of a mile was the Lispenard country house. Her relatives, the Lispenards, were there as owners. He scarcely had time for what he wished to say.

"Shall we stop there?" he asked in a subdued murmur, as in driving again they neared the long piazza where guests were seated enjoying the prospect of the meadows beyond. "It is four now, and the play begins at six. There are some new jewels from France at Maton's, which I thought you might like to see before then."

"Jewels from France! Oh, yes, I should like to see those. Let us go there," she answered. "But I must have time to dress, too, you know."

To the guests then, bowing as they passed, they returned a smiling nod, and meeting others in carriages and chairs, extended this same courtesy as they went along. Walton brooded in a mock-dreary manner, but finding that it availed nothing thought to tempt her considerateness with jewels.

"What trinkets are these you have from France of which I hear?" he inquired of Maton as they entered that sturdy jeweler's shop in Maiden Lane.

"On the very last packet," explained the latter, spreading the best of his importations upon a black velvet cloth before them. "You will not see the like of these six diamonds in New York again for many years, I warrant you. Look at this."

He held up an exquisitely wrought ring of French workmanship, in which a fine stone was gleaming, and smiled upon it approvingly.

"Look," he said, "it is very large. It is cut by Toussard. Did you ever see such workmanship?" He turned it over and over, and then held it lovingly up. "The band itself is so small," he added, "that I believe it would fit the lady's finger—let us see."

Coquettishly she put out her hand, and then seeing that it marvelously slipped on and fitted, opened her eyes wide.

"Now, is not that beautiful!" exclaimed the jeweler. "What a gem! The finest of any that I have imported yet, and it fits as though it had been ordered for her." He cast a persuasive smile upon Walton whose interest in the fair Beppie he well knew. The latter pretended not the slightest understanding.

"It is well cut," she said.

"And the loveliest you have ever worn," added Walton hopefully.

218

By her side, in front of the counter and between their bodies, he was endeavoring to take her free hand.

"Let it stay," he said gently, when he had secured it, and was signalling the significance of the ring to her fingers.

"Oh," she said, smiling as if she were only jesting, "you are too daring. I might!"

"Do," he answered.

"Such a ring!" said the jeweler.

"I will then," said she.

"Then, Master Maton," said Walton, "you need only send the bill to me," and he laughed as he pushed the remaining display away.

As they came out, after having vaguely picked over the others, the young lover was all elation. Upon the narrow side-path a servant wheeling a trunk to the Liverpool dock upon a barrow brushed him rudely, but he did not notice. Only a newsboy crying out the Gazette, the blast of the bugle of the incoming stage coach from Boston, the dust of the side-path, where the helper of the Apollo was sweeping the lobby preparatory to the performance of the night, attracted and pleased him. He helped his fiancée gaily into the carriage and half bounded with joy to the seat beside her, where he smiled and smiled.

"I may not wear it, though," said his betrothed, now that the remarkable episode was over, and she held up a dainty finger; "because, as you know, you have not spoken to my father as yet."

"Keep it, nevertheless," he answered. "I will speak to him fast enough."

"I give you good-day, Master Walton," said the distinguished Jefferson as they passed from William into Wall Street, near where that statesman made temporary stopping-place when in the city.

"Master Jefferson, William," cried his fiancée softly, using for the first time his given name. "Master Jefferson has bid you good-day."

"Good evening!" cried Walton, all deference in a moment because of the error which his excitement had occasioned, "good evening to you, sir!" and he bowed, and bowed very gracefully again.

"How can I be so mindful, though, of all these formalities," he said explanatorily as he turned once more to his fair intended, "when I have you? It is not to be expected."

"But necessary, just the same," she said. "And if you are to begin thus quickly neglecting your duties, what am I to think?"

For answer he took her hand. Elatedly then they made their way to the old homestead again, and there being compelled to leave her while she dressed for the theater, he made his way toward the broad and tree-shaded Bowery, where was the only true and idyllic walk for a lover. The older houses nearest the city, redolent in their Dutch architecture of an older and even quainter period; the wide paths and broad doorways, rich in both vines and flowers; the rapidly decreasing evidences of population as one's steps led northward—all combined to soothe and set dreaming the poetic mind. Here young Walton, as so many before him, strolled and hummed, thinking of all that life and the young city held for him. Now, indeed, was his fortune truly made. Love was his, the lovely Beppie, no less. Here then he decided to build that mansion of his own—far out, indeed, above Broome Street, but in this self-same thoroughfare where all was so suggestive of flowers and romance. He had no inkling, as he pondered, of what a century might bring forth. The crush and stress and wretchedness fast treading upon this path of loveliness he could not see.

THE END